Changing Skies

God is good all the time!

Donna Coulson

donna coulson

To Mary Jane Parkison Cozzens

You've been my muse for a long time. You've provided me with a wealth of information, not just about Ed and Ella Parkison, your grandparents, but about Encampment in the early days and life in general. I'm so thankful you are also my friend.

1
Encampment, Wyoming
Tuesday morning, June 5, 1917

Claire frowned a little as she looked in the mirror. She didn't mind the tiny wrinkles that populated the corners of her eyes. *Those laugh lines speak about my blessings,* she told herself. But the three grey hairs she'd found were another story. This morning, as the sun rose on her thirty-ninth birthday, Claire spent a little extra time hunting down the grey. She zeroed in on one more and plucked it out before shrugging and reaching for her brush.

A few minutes later, she twisted her long, mostly brown hair into a comfortable knot on the back of her head and secured it with pins. Then she smoothed her skirt and stepped into the hall on the way to the kitchen. She'd barely finished tying her apron on when Greg padded in with tousled hair and sleepy eyes. "Mornin' Mama," he said as he plopped onto the bench beside the trestle table. Claire smiled at the younger of her two sons. At ten, he was nearly as tall as she and possessed a gentle kindness that contrasted sharply with the rough-and-tumble personality of his older brother. Despite their stark differences, the brothers were close and devoted to one another.

"I won't have breakfast ready for about fifteen minutes. If you are awake enough, you have time to go out and feed the bunnies."

Rubbing sleep from his eyes, he nodded and glanced toward the back door. "Alright. Do you know where my boots are?"

"I think you left them on the porch last night. Didn't they have mud on them?"

"That's right, thanks."

Claire stirred oatmeal into the water she'd been heating and turned down the flame under the pot. Then she began slicing a loaf of bread she'd baked yesterday. The table was set and breakfast ready when Greg came in the back door a few minutes later, followed by two progressively taller versions of himself.

"Good morning! You two have been out early this morning."

"Morning, Mama." Michael's voice, at thirteen, was deep and resonant now most of the time. Claire accepted a quick peck on the cheek from him as he came into the kitchen. Right behind him, Daniel hung his hat on a hook beside the back door, then crossed the kitchen to enfold his wife into a warm hug.

"Good morning, and happy birthday my love." He kissed her quickly then stood back. "The boys and I have a little birthday surprise for you outside. Would you do us the favor of accompanying us to the front yard?"

"Oh, my. Yes, of course, but let me take the oatmeal off the stove so it doesn't scorch."

As the family left the back porch in a small parade towards the front yard Greg began chanting, "Cover your eyes, cover your eyes". Claire responded by covering her face with her hands, allowing Greg to lead her the rest of the way.

"Don't peek, just wait." Claire loved the excitement in Greg's voice as her three men situated her just right.

Daniel's shoulder brushed against hers as the boys both called, "Okay, you can look. Happy Birthday!"

Claire moved her hands and stared. Sitting on the front sidewalk with a crooked bow on top was a mahogany, curved glass china cabinet.

Greg was nearly vibrating with excitement. "It's just like the one you wanted from the catalog, but this one is even better because Mr. Fisher made it especially for you."

Claire felt tears welling up. Last fall, when the Sears Roebuck catalog arrived, she pored over the pages, making lists and ordering things they needed. She'd also enjoyed wishing for things she felt were frivolous or too expensive. The china cabinet fell into the latter group. "I didn't know you were even aware that it had caught my eye," she said quietly to Daniel.

Daniel kissed her forehead and shrugged. "It was actually Greg and Mike who came up with the idea. Greg saw you looking at it but I —,"

The boy interrupted, "Remember, Mama, that day when we were looking at the catalog together and you said

2

if we lived in a mansion in Denver the first thing you'd do is order that cabinet?"

Claire laughed at the memory. It had been a cold, dreary day and Greg was suffering from a cold. They'd curled up on the couch and looked through the book together. "Yes, I remember it, and I think it is wonderful that you remembered it as well!"

"Anyway," Daniel continued good-naturedly, "I was concerned both about the cost to ship that piece all the way from Sears Roebuck in Chicago and also about getting it here safely, so the boys and I took the catalog to Tom Fisher last month and asked him to build you one."

Michael spoke up this time, "Sneaking the catalog out of the house wasn't easy, and you nearly caught me. It was that afternoon you fussed at me for wearing my work jacket when Papa and Greg and I were headed downtown. You tried to get me to change into a nicer one, but I'd already hidden the catalog inside the front of my coat and I couldn't change right there where you'd see."

This time Claire laughed out loud. "You really vexed me that day. I couldn't understand why you were being so stubborn about wearing that old coat, or why you," she turned to shake her finger in mock irritation at Daniel, "why you wouldn't make him go change." The boys laughed while Claire examined the hutch, running her hand over the smooth top. "How did you talk Tom into building this? I thought he only built homes," Claire asked Daniel.

"Actually, Tom loves doing detailed work, it's just the demand for houses is greater. When we picked it up, he said he'd really enjoyed doing it for you." Daniel looked at his pocket watch. "I'm sorry to say this, but I'm supposed to be at City Hall in just a few minutes. Greg, if you hold the front door open, Mike and I will carry the hutch inside. Then I need to leave. I'll help you move furniture around in the parlor this evening to get it where you want it."

"Do you have time for oatmeal and toast?" Claire asked with a nod.

"I don't think so, but I'll have a piece of bread to take with me."

"While you move the hutch inside, I'll get it for you." Claire took a step then turned back, "This was a wonderful birthday surprise. Thank you three so much!" Claire enfolded her brood into a messy, quick hug, then climbed the stairs of the front porch and went inside.

A few minutes later, Claire sat across the table from her sons, enjoying her breakfast and relishing the moment. She thought briefly about past birthdays, some sweet and good, others hard and bitter. *Thank you, God, for this day,* she prayed with eyes open, happily taking in the large, homey kitchen surrounding her.

Daniel and Claire purchased their house and its double lot on Lomax Avenue in Grand Encampment, Wyoming in 1908 when they moved down from the high mountain village of Dillon, Wyoming. They'd lived in Dillon from 1902 until the copper mine, where Daniel served as lead mining engineer, closed. Leaving was a time of regret and outrage for the couple. They loved their home in Dillon, a small but thriving town in the rugged mountains of south east Wyoming. They enjoyed the life they'd carved for themselves there on the Continental Divide and didn't want to give it up. Shady dealings by top management of the mining company, which included overselling of stock and getting the mine heavily in debt, along with several turns of bad luck, resulted in the closing of the mine and the end of the town of Dillon. The couple had no choice other than to board up the windows of the house they'd loved, pack most of their belongings on a freight wagon, bundle up their two small sons and Claire's younger brother who lived with them, and seek a life at lower altitudes. Thankfully, Daniel was well-known and liked in the area, and with a smile and handshake, he was hired by the city of Encampment to work as an engineer on the water system.

Encampment's history was long and colorful. In 1897, when copper was discovered in the high mountains, a group of business men including George Emerson and Barney McCaffrey, incorporated the settlement. They named it The Grand Encampment and began plotting the streets and marketing land, sure that Encampment would become the "Pittsburgh of the West." In early 1900, to attract settlers and promote growth, the town offered a free home lot, measuring twenty-five feet wide by a hundred fifteen feet long, for anyone agreeing to build. Many families took advantage of the offer and also purchased the adjoining lot so that their property would be larger.

It didn't take long before the town began sprouting homes, built mostly from green wood. Green wood was cheap and plentiful, but it had a drawback. As the new lumber cured and dried, the planks making up the walls shriveled, so that homes all over Encampment had drafty cracks. The solution was to add what they called battens, another layer of wood, offset from the first, to the outside of the house. The battens sealed the drafts to make the house warm and tight against the cold winters and the Wyoming winds.

In 1908, with the Rudefeha copper mine closed down and the Encampment Smelter no longer operable, there was an urgent exodus from Encampment, Dillon, and the other small mountain towns that had sprung up to serve the copper boom. A gentleman who had helped run the smelter in Encampment offered his holdings to Daniel. The deal was concluded quickly and Daniel prepared to move his family.

In the nine years they'd made their home in Encampment, Daniel and Claire rebuilt, remodeled, and added to their house so that what appeared now looked nothing like the battened, two-room shanty they originally purchased. They survived the first winter, literally stepping on each other's toes and learning patience. When the spring of 1909 arrived, they hired Tom Fisher to build their current two-story, three-bedroom home. The original battened house, connected to the new structure at one wall, was transformed into an extra bedroom and bathroom along with a small sitting room that Claire used for sewing.

Claire looked around now at her large kitchen. She remembered the primitive way they'd lived in the mountains and once again marveled at how nice running water and indoor bathrooms were. Though she'd loved living in Dillon, life had been much harder, and looking back, she wasn't exactly sure how they'd survived the lack of comforts they now enjoyed.

"Mama," Michael pulled Claire's thoughts back into the present. "Is it still alright if Greg and I go over to help Uncle Jesse today? He promised Greg and me each a nickel if we'd help him clean out that room full of old tack."

Claire stood and began cleaning off the table. "Yes. I'm going to Mrs. Jameson's this afternoon for a meeting, so I'll walk to the livery with you after lunch, how would that be? I'll stop for a minute and visit with my brother before I go."

The boys both grinned at the prospect of making some spending money. "Before we go, though," Claire added, "I think maybe the three of us are strong enough to move the parlor furniture around a bit to get my new birthday present where I want it. That way your father won't have to do it after work tonight. If you help me with breakfast dishes, we could give it a try. What do you think?"

It didn't take long for the three workers to get kitchen chores done and find themselves in the parlor. Claire wasn't sure how to add the hutch to the mix, but after some trial and error, they stood together and viewed the room. There were two wing back chairs covered in flowered chintz, one on each side of a small cherry wood table facing a dusty rose-colored brocade divan. All the seats were near the fireplace. The hutch fit perfectly in the corner next to the front window. Beside it, they'd placed a large pot filled with a tall, angel wing plant. The room looked balanced and inviting, and Claire was pleased. "I think this is perfect." She glanced at the mantle clock and added, "That took us longer than I'd expected. Thank you for your help, it would have been a long evening for your papa. You two can run out and play. I'll get us a bite to eat in about an hour, and I'll call you when it's ready, alright?"

"I think I see Hoyt out in his back yard," Michael told Claire. "We're going to go over there, alright?"

Claire smiled. Hoyt Parkison, the oldest son of Claire's dear friend Ella, was two years older than Michael. Despite the age difference, the boys got along well. For the past couple of weeks they'd been building a fort out of old planks. "Yes, of course."

Their answer included two quick, sideways hugs and the slamming of the back door. Claire sat down in the parlor to admire her beautiful gift and consider what she wanted to put in it.

Across town, Jesse Atley, Claire's younger brother, walked out of the post office determined to appear fine even though his insides were quaking. Standing alone on the sidewalk, he looked down at the card in his hand. Jesse considered how such a small, innocuous looking card— just two and a half inches by four inches—could carry such potential for calamity on his life. The eagle embossed at the top looked fierce. Its wings were spread, a shield with stars and stripes at its chest, a sheaf of grain gripped in one talon, three arrows in the other. The card announced:

Jesse Atley of Encampment, Wyoming
submitted himself to registration and has
by me been duly registered this
5th of June, 1917

Jesse concentrated on the number just below the eagle. The registrar's flowing script made the number almost pretty, *2552.*

Just a small card of paper, he thought, *but one that most probably will change everything.* Jesse was a Class One registrant. At twenty-seven and unmarried, he was prime real estate for use in the war that President Wilson had so reluctantly declared against the Germans just two months ago on April second. Like most people in Encampment, until recently, Jesse read the papers and had a dim awareness of world issues and the fighting in Europe over the past years. When he read the newspaper descriptions of U-boat attacks and European battles, it had been with a removed nonchalance. He mirrored the general feeling in south-central Wyoming that the problems so far away, 'over there', were none of their business.

Now that the United States had entered the war, Jesse's nonchalance was replaced with unwelcome urgency. The Selective Service Act of 1917, passed by Congress less than a month ago on May 18, had guaranteed that he no longer was going to be allowed to be an observer. Today, June fifth, Jesse and all men aged twenty-one to thirty, were required to sign up for the draft lottery. Jesse glanced back down at the card in his hand.

"I hope two thousand, five hundred fifty-two is a lucky number," Jesse said quietly to himself, then he uttered a silent prayer. *God, you know how I feel about this. I hunt and fish and I enjoy shooting my rifle, but I just don't know how I can shoot at people, even if they are our enemies. God, if I'm called up—or when I'm called up—please give me courage and strength.*

Boots sounded behind him as Jesse concluded his prayer and looked up. John Peryam clapped him on the back. "Looks like we're all going to war, don't it, Jess?"

Jesse tucked his card in his back pocket and shrugged. "Looks like it."

The chance meeting lightened Jesse's mood. John, who was the same age as Jesse, along with his older brother Tom, had been close friends at school. They'd had many fun evenings at dances and socials together. Jesse had spent time at the Peryam Roadhouse with the boys as they were growing up, happy to help with haying in the summer, and enjoying skating on the frozen Encampment River in the winter. Mr. and Mrs. Peryam always made Jesse feel welcome. Jesse realized with regret that he hadn't seen them in a long time. Now that they were adults, their time together was limited to church picnics and business encounters, but the friendship remained.

"I'm not going to wait for the draft," John declared after they'd discussed the dry spring, cattle prices and the new draft horse John's dad, W.T. had recently purchased. "Tom and I both are going to Rawlins next week to enlist in the AEF. Pa says that the Germans better look out if the Peryams are part of the American Expeditionary Force."

Jesse nodded and grinned, then waited for John to continue.

"Remember when my cousin Joe was part of Bill Cody's Wild West show? When he came home for the winter in 1903 we spent a lot of time together. Ever since, I haven't been able to get his stories out of my head. I'm aching to go new places and see something else beside the dry dust of summers and the blinding blizzards that are Wyoming."

Jesse shrugged again, "Aw, Wyoming isn't that bad."

"Well, I guess not, but I'd like to find that out for myself." John put his hand on Jesse's shoulder, a serious look in his eyes. "War isn't really the way I wanted to get out of here, but we've got it to do. You remember that Pa spent time in Cheyenne as a member of the Wyoming legislature from 1907 to 1915? While he was there, he made friends with a Colonel at Fort D.A. Russell just outside Cheyenne. They've kept in contact through the years, and Colonel Parks recently suggested that a soldier might get better assignments if he enlisted before he was drafted. Pa and Tom and I talked it over and decided that's just what we are going to do."

Jesse nodded again. His palms felt sweaty as he listened to John. The idea of war seemed to be stalking him. The friends talked for a few moments longer, then John shrugged. "Even though we are leaving next week, the law says I still need to register for the draft today, so I better get in there and get my paperwork done."

"Say, send me a postcard, will you?" Jesse didn't want their friendship to be severed because of war and distance. "If you let me know where you are and how to write to you, we can keep in touch."

John's smile covered his whole face. "That's a great idea. As soon as I get an address, I'll drop you a line."

They shook hands and John disappeared inside the post office where the Wyoming draft board had a table set up for registration. Jesse adjusted his cowboy hat and headed for the livery.

An hour later, Jesse wiped the dust from his hands on the back of his pants and looked around. When he'd arrived in Encampment in 1898 he was eight years old. Daniel was working up on the Divide at the mine then, living in a bunkhouse for miners close to the mine itself. He came down to the valley as often as possible to see Claire and Jesse, who were living in a small rented house in Encampment. As Jesse grew, Claire and Daniel encouraged him to pursue activities he loved, so when he was just eleven, Jesse began working at the livery for Cody Hatch for an hour or two after school each day. He was thrilled to be with the horses no matter what he was asked to do.

The city of Dillon was established just one mile from the Rudefeha Mine up on the Continental Divide in 1902. Claire and Jesse were among the town's first residents when they moved up there to join Daniel that summer. With Cody Hatch's recommendation, Jesse began working for the Transportation Company in Dillon a few hours a day. In the beginning he tended the horses and gear. Later, he learned to handle teams and freight wagons. Jesse was proud that at seventeen he bought his own wagon and team. He began making a good living for himself hauling local freight.

Moving back down to Encampment had been a temporary setback for the young businessman. The closing of the mine, along with the completion of a long-awaited railroad spur from Wolcott to Encampment in 1908, severely impacted his income. Freight began coming on the train, cheaper and often quicker than Jesse could haul it. Business fell sharply at first, and Jesse was thankful that Daniel had taught him not to carry much debt. He persevered, working long hours and never turning down a load or job, no matter how small or difficult. Word got around that Jesse could be counted on, and his reputation in the area among ranchers and townspeople proved more valuable to his business than anything else.

Two years later, Jesse bought the livery business where he'd worked as a child, paying 'Old Man' Hatch for the whole operation. The deal included the business, the large barn that housed the livery, and a small home less than a block away. He'd made some changes, doing what he needed to do to keep up with the times. He still called his barn building the livery, but he'd expanded the operation. Now, half the barn held the four Belgian draft horses, their tack, a buckboard and the wagon he still used to haul heavy freight and to occasionally aid in haying and gathering crops. The other half, though, Jesse converted to a garage for the truck he also owned. Motor cars were gaining popularity, and Jesse grudgingly admitted that hopping in the pickup truck he'd added to his fleet to make a run to Riverside or Saratoga or out to a local ranch with a small delivery was quicker and much more economical than using the horses.

Jesse was just wiping his hands when Claire and her boys came into the barn that early June afternoon.

"Uncle Jess! Mama loved her present. You should have stayed around to see the surprise!" Greg reported.

Claire looked confused. "You were at the house this morning?"

Jesse gave his sister a one-armed hug. "Happy birthday. Yes, the hutch has been hidden here for the last week. I ran over early this morning with it in the truck. Dan and I unloaded it."

"Why didn't you stay for breakfast?"

"I had another delivery to make at the Oldham's ranch out by the Encampment River. Plus," he hesitated, "plus errands to finish here this morning. You know, no rest for the wicked and all that."

Claire noticed and understood the worried look in her brother's eyes but didn't mention it. "You are one of the least wicked people I know."

"We are here to work for you, Uncle Jesse," Michael told Jesse. "What job can we do?" The boys' excitement overtook the moment and Jesse turned toward the tack room. "Well," he began but Claire interrupted.

"I have to go to a garden club meeting, but I'm hoping you'll come for supper tonight and celebrate my birthday with us? About six?"

Jesse nodded. "I wouldn't miss it."

2
Encampment, Wyoming
Tuesday evening, June 5, 1917

For her birthday dinner Claire roasted some potatoes, sprinkling fresh parsley over them before putting them in the oven. Then she dredged chicken breasts and drumsticks in flour and paprika and fried them. The table was set with her good dishes and one of her 'Sunday tablecloths'. After her meeting, she'd been restless, thinking about war and the upcoming draft, and decided to channel her worries into making a nice meal for her family. She wanted to make the evening special, not because of her birthday but because she saw in her brother's eyes the concern he was carrying. Jesse had been so busy lately, they hadn't seen much of him, and she hoped she could make the evening relaxing for him.

Daniel came in as she finished frying the chicken. He held the oven door open for her as she put a roasting pan full of golden chicken in to keep it warm. Then he kissed his wife and pulled her into a tight embrace. They'd married on New Year's Eve in 1897. The twenty years of their marriage had been full of blessings, hard times, and surprises. Daniel knew the woman in his arms to be strong and courageous as well as soft and vulnerable, and he treasured each facet of her.

Their quiet moment didn't last long. Laughing voices drifted in through the window at about the same time the back door swung open. "Mama, we're home!"

"Good," responded Claire as Daniel released his hold on her and stepped away. "Supper is ready. Go get washed up." She took a quick glance at her boys and added, "Wash your faces, too, please." Good-natured groans came the answer from her sons.

"Does that include my face, too?" Jesse taunted her from the doorway.

"Well, usually you are the reason the boys are dirty, so probably, yes!" she retorted.

Claire reached in the ice box and pulled out a dish of pickles she'd prepared as well as a plate of butter. She glanced up and caught Jesse's eye, then noticed the bouquet of flowers in his hand. "Oh, those are so pretty!"

"I had to promise Mary Bohn at the Bohn Hotel that I'd give her a discount for shoeing her old mare in exchange for allowing me to cut some of her lilacs for you. I've been watching those bushes all week hoping they'd be blooming for your birthday."

Claire hugged Jesse and turned to find an empty canning jar to put them in. By the time Daniel, Jesse, and the boys finished washing up and were sitting at the table, the room was filled with delicious smells of chicken and lilacs and the table was filled with a feast.

"I think it is your turn to pray, Mike," Daniel prompted, and the family bowed their heads.

"Dear God, thank you for Mama and her birthday. She's the best mother a boy could have, and I thank You for her. Thank you for this food and for this day. Bless us and help us to keep our eyes on You. Amen."

Claire kept her eyes closed for a moment longer, relishing her son's heartfelt prayer, feeling the blessings they had. When she was a girl, prayers before meals had been rote, meaningless recitations. As soon as the boys were old enough to talk, she and Daniel had taught them to pray from their hearts, not from memory.

The family enjoyed a leisurely meal. The boys took turns describing their day of work at the livery. "I think we are done with the job," Michael concluded. "We threw away the old nasty pieces and hung the useable ones on hooks on the outside of the barn. I painted a sign on a piece of wood advertising that they are for sale. I hope they sell for you, Uncle Jess."

"I hope so, too. I hate throwing away anything that's still good, but since I bought the truck and sold half my horses, I just don't need that much tack."

"I miss those horses," Greg admitted, "especially Big George."

"I know you do, Buddy," Jesse answered. "I miss him, too, but he was just too old to keep on the smaller team. I saw Bill Condict the other day, and he told me that Big George has settled in at their place and that they used him just last week to pull a plow for his wife's garden. The old boy is getting a little work to make him feel useful and plenty of rest and green grass. He has a great life out there."

Satisfied that his friend was alright, Greg nodded.

The family ate and talked happily through their meal. When everyone was full and plates were empty, Daniel asked the boys to clear the table.

"I'd planned to bake a pie for dessert, but Daniel adamantly forbade me from making any kind of treat tonight, so I guess we have to go without," Claire used an exaggeratedly pouty voice, covering her smiling eyes with a forced scowl.

"Well if you remember, I suggested we go out to the Bohn Hotel or to that new place, the Copper Pot, for supper tonight so you wouldn't have to cook your own birthday dinner but you refused," Daniel teased her right back.

"I love cooking, you know that, and sitting here is so much more comfortable than going out."

"I know that's how you feel, but I couldn't have you make your own birthday dessert, so," Daniel pushed himself away from the table. He left the room, but in just a minute was back carrying a treat covered carefully with a clean dish cloth. He sat the surprise on the table then turned to get small plates and forks. "I asked Ella Parkison to bake you a birthday treat," he explained as he returned. Then, with a dramatic flourish, Daniel removed the dish cloth to reveal one of Ella's famous jelly rolls.

"Oh, heavenly!" Claire gasped. "I've never tasted anything better than the jelly rolls she makes. Thank you for enlisting her, Daniel!"

"She was more than happy to help. Though, when I stopped on the way home to pick it up from her, she said that this afternoon she nearly slipped and told you about it."

Claire laughed, "I don't remember anything she said today that would have tipped me off, but that sounds like Ella. She's usually so matter of fact, she isn't one to keep secrets or surprises."

Claire served the family thick slices of the roll and the table was quiet while they enjoyed the sweet treat.

"Boys, your gift to your Mama tonight will be to

wash the dishes and clean the kitchen on your own. Can I trust you to do a great job of it?"

"Yes, Sir!" they both answered with a mix of seriousness and cooperation. Since Claire was the only female in the house, Daniel insisted that her men help her out with cleaning the kitchen after supper. While Jesse had lived with them, Daniel and Jesse usually did the dishes. The chore evolved in a quiet time to talk over the day and any problems Jesse was having. By the time Jesse moved out, the boys were old enough for Daniel to continue the tradition, having the boys trade off nights so that he had alone time with each one.

The three adults moved into the parlor as the boys went to work. It took a few minutes before the conversation rested on Jesse and the events of his morning. He answered Claire's question with a quiet voice. "It only took a few minutes, and only a couple of men were in line ahead of me. I had to fill out a form, then the registrar did some paperwork and handed me this card." He reached into his back pocket, withdrew a worn black leather billfold, and handed the card he pulled from it to Claire.

She studied it for a minute, then handed it to Daniel. "I don't like this at all. I'm still not convinced that America should be involved in a war so far away. So now that you have registered, what happens next?"

Jesse met her eyes and answered. He was surprised that his voice sounded much more assured than he felt. "On July 20th they will have a lottery drawing in Washington, D.C. They will choose random numbers from a bin of some kind, and those numbers will tell a man when he can expect to be inducted into the military."

Daniel was still staring at the card in his hand. "Your number is right here on the top, right?" Jesse nodded. "So, let's hope that two thousand, five hundred fifty-two is the last to be chosen."

The words hung suspended in the room, echoing in each of their minds. Claire sent a prayer heavenward then searched for a way to change the subject.

"I had a fun afternoon at Lillian's."

"She's sure a nice old lady," remarked Jesse. "How is she doing?"

"I think she's feeling well for the most part," Claire answered. "But she is getting more and more thin and frail. You know, I don't know if we will ever get an actual garden club started here in Encampment, but I certainly enjoy meeting with Lillian, Ella, and a few other ladies to discuss our gardens. Today, Lillian showed us how to transplant dieffenbachia plants. She even had a cutting for each of us. We've begun considering putting on a flower show this fall."

She paused, then frowned and continued. "I heard something interesting and sad today though." Jesse and Daniel looked at her with interest. "Do you remember hearing about a horrid stage coach accident the fall after we moved here from Rapid City?"

"Do you mean the tour of mine officials and investors that upset outside of town?" Daniel didn't wait for her response before he continued. "I do remember that. I was in Encampment instead of up at the mine that day. Jim Rankin came tearing into town with the news of the accident. Crever and Benjamin Peryam, Tom and John's older brothers, were just coming into town to pick up supplies with a buckboard, so I joined them as their outrider and we headed out there. When we got to the crash site, others already had the coach off the four men who were dragged. They were loaded on a wagon first and sent to Saratoga. I don't think any of them survived. It took the rest of us a while to cut through the walls and get inside the coach. The men in there were in bad shape as well. The Peryam boys ended up with George Emerson and a couple of the visitors from Cripple Creek in their wagon. They were all hurt, but not as badly as some. The brothers rushed the injured back to town. I stayed to help them get the coach up righted and clean up the site. It was a grisly afternoon."

"I remember that even though I was small. Wasn't that "South Paw" Cunningham who was driving? I remember much later hearing him describe how he came around that curve. He had six men riding inside, and twelve men on the top and boot. That's what caused the accident, the weight overbalanced the rig on the turn and it flipped and just kept rolling down the embankment." Jesse shook his head.

Claire considered their description of the accident and frowned. "That is the accident I was thinking of, too, but now I don't think that's the one Ella meant. This one must have happened at nearly the same time, but it was a passenger stage coming from Rawlins."

Daniel rubbed the back of his neck as he tried to remember. Finally, he answered, "I think you are right, but I don't remember the details of that one."

"Well, according to Ella, this stage was carrying only four people. Along with the driver were a husband and wife and their young daughter. The driver and parents died, and the girl was injured in the crash, but survived."

"That does ring a bell. I think I do recall hearing about it," Daniel added. "It seems like maybe no one found the wreck for several hours."

"Yes, that's right. Anyway, apparently the little girl was sent away to an orphanage somewhere, but now she's grown and has returned. It sounds like once she reached eighteen, they just turned her out on her own. She has no family, but somehow she's come back here and is working at the Copper Pot."

"That is a sad tale, Claire," Daniel shook his head.

"That isn't all. Ella said that she's seen the girl, and that she's horribly disfigured. I can't imagine being young and alone and also living with a burden like that."

Jesse cleared his throat. "I hope that story has been embellished by retelling and that most of it isn't true." At that moment the boys came into the parlor from the kitchen and the subject changed.

"The kitchen is sparkling clean, Mama. Can we play Parcheesi now?"

"I'd love it," Claire smiled and stood up. "Jesse, will you and Daniel play, too?"

The sun was drifting low in the afternoon sky a week later and Jesse was working at his desk in the front corner of the livery when he heard Dawson Wiley drive the truck into the barn. Gears ground as Dawson put the transmission in reverse and backed in beside the freight wagon across from the horse stalls. Jesse winced at the sound, certain Dawson would get better at shifting in time, but concerned about the damage being done to the transmission in the meantime.

Jesse knew that to keep up with the times, he'd made a good decision to buy the 1912 Ford pickup truck that his employee was backing in. Jesse owned one of the first motorized delivery vehicles in the area. He liked the modern look of the spoked wheels, the canvas top over the two-seated driver's compartment, and the hauling bed in the back. Having a glass windshield to protect him as he drove and not having to worry about the health and feeding of a team of horses on a long drive were also added bonuses. Jesse smiled to himself with pride as he finished adding a column of numbers.

A few minutes later, Jesse watched Dawson leave the far stall and walk toward the front. His eyes were on the ground in front of him, looking thoughtful. His limp was pronounced, and Jesse knew that meant his employee was tired. Dawson stopped when he got to the post that hinted the beginning of the business' office space. He leaned against the post, looked up, and said, "Hey, Boss how's it going?"

"Not bad," Jesse replied. "I'm just finishing up all the accounts for last month."

"Are we making any money with this operation?"

Dawson had worked for Jesse for the past six years and they'd formed a close and trusted bond. Jesse shrugged good-naturedly and answered, "Well, we've paid all the bills and have enough left over to give you and me both a little pay. I don't guess we can ask for more than that."

"You got that right," came the answer.

"Hey, Dawson, I'll be done here in a few minutes. How about you and I close up and walk over to that new restaurant and grab some supper? I have a few things I'd like to talk with you about."

"Sure thing, Boss. That sounds good. I'll just feed the horses and get them settled for the night. I'll meet you back here in a few minutes."

Jesse stared into the space Dawson had just occupied and thought about the upcoming conversation. He'd been praying and thinking about having this discussion for a while, and he just didn't want to put it off any longer.

Half an hour later, Jesse was focused on what he wanted to talk about with Dawson so pointedly that he barely noticed the thick carpeting in the hotel lobby, the gilt crown molding around the high ceilings, or the posh artwork and furnishings at the Copper Pot Hotel and Restaurant. He and Dawson easily spotted the restaurant entrance across the lobby and presented themselves to a formally dressed host who seated them immediately at a small table on one side of the room. Jesse worried about their dusty work clothes until he looked around the dining room and realized that they weren't the only working men in the room.

Jesse smiled as he watched Dawson look at the dining room. Dawson didn't miss a detail. His head swiveled around even after he'd settled into his seat, taking in the grandeur. Having grown up on a small ranch just outside of Encampment along with his younger brother and two sisters, Dawson was comfortable with dirt beneath his fingernails and aching muscles at the end of the day. His parents had raised him to a stern life of understanding the value of thankfulness and callouses.

Dawson looked at the bill of fare and made his decision, then resumed his unabashed inspection of the room. Jesse put down his menu and took a moment to admire the surroundings himself.

"Some place, huh?"

Jesse agreed. "It's a bit rich for Encampment, though I suppose that as the town grows there will be more and more of a need for nice places. We've got eighteen saloons and dancehalls but only a couple restaurants for ladies and families."

Dawson nodded. Jesse continued, changing the subject. "It sounds as if your delivery to Big Creek Ranch went well. No problems?"

"Nope, truck ran fine. Turns out I delivered everything to one of the Big Creek owners, Mr. Sterrett. He seemed happy to get the supplies. I mentioned to him that we have some tack to sell. He sounded interested and said he'd have one of the hands stop by tomorrow or Thursday to take a look. He said they'd probably be able to use it all."

"Thanks for mentioning it to him, good thinking."

A waiter arrived to take their orders. When he'd left the table, Jesse cleared his throat and met Dawson's eyes. "You've worked for me almost since I bought the livery, and you already know how much I rely on you, Dawson."

This sort of talk was a rarity for both men, and the compliment made Dawson uncomfortable. He nodded and dropped his eyes.

Jesse continued. "In just a few weeks, the government is going to hold their lottery and begin drafting men to go fight Europe's war. I know that you registered, but," Jesse hesitated, took a breath and then continued, "but we both know that with that leg of yours, you aren't going to pass the physical that will allow you to serve."

The statement didn't insult Dawson. It was a fact of his life that he'd come to terms with. When he was fourteen he'd come off a horse, breaking his leg in several places. Instead of calling for a doctor, old man Wiley set his son's leg himself and they let it heal for a couple of weeks. By the time a doctor did see it, the bones had knitted together unevenly. While the breaks had eventually healed, Dawson was left with a crooked shin that caused a pronounced limp. He didn't seem to be too bothered by his plight, and found ways to do nearly everything he wanted. He never complained, though over the years Jesse came to recognize how, like today, the limp became more pronounced by the end of the day, and Dawson favored that leg a little more when winter blizzards blew in.

Dawson nodded, "I went ahead and registered, but they told me that all I need to do is get a local doctor to sign a form declaring me unfit for duty and that will be the end of it for me. I have to admit, though, knowing I won't be going makes me feel like a coward."

"We both know that's not the case at all, Dawson," Jesse continued. "Actually, the fact that you'll still be here relieves me of some worry." Jesse couldn't tell if his friend was anticipating what's coming or not. "Ever since they announced the draft, I've been certain that I'm going to be called up. I've been awake nights thinking about what to do with what I've got here. I've spent a lot of time in prayer about this, Dawson, and it is clear to me what has to happen."

Dawson tried to keep his face neutral but inside he was dreading to hear that Jesse was going to close down the company. Before his fears could grow too large, Jesse continued, "In nearly every way, you and I have become partners. I rely on you to make decisions and do what needs to be done. It only makes sense for you take over and keep things running."

Before Dawson could answer, they were interrupted as their meals arrived. The server carefully placed the plates on the table. Jesse, too caught up in what he'd just said to Dawson, didn't look up at first, but then he noted how soft and pretty the serving hands were. When she spoke in a soft, low voice to ask if either of them needed anything more, Jesse raised his glance and met a set of blue eyes. His first thought was how like the mountain sky her eyes appeared, but that impression was quickly replaced as he registered ragged, consuming scars which covered the entire right half of her face. He was shocked by the evident violence that had resulted in such damage. From just under her eye down to her jawline and all the way from the side of her nose to her earlobe, the woman's skin was a mass of angry, uneven lines and creases. He recalled the conversation at Claire's birthday, and realized that the town gossips hadn't exaggerated the young woman's injuries.

Hoping that there was nothing in his gaze other than kindness, Jesse smiled at the woman and thanked her. In a practiced move, she ducked her head low and to the right so that Jesse could only see the perfect left side of her face as she nodded and withdrew.

The two men sat in stunned silence for a few heart beats. Then, Jesse picked up his fork and remarked, "This looks delicious."

Dawson took a moment longer to recover, but took Jesse's lead and concentrated on his own meal. They ate in silence for a few minutes, listening to the hum of conversations around them and thinking their own thoughts.

For some reason he couldn't explain, Jesse wanted to allow his thoughts to remain on the woman, but he forced himself to move his mind back to Dawson and the transportation company. He slowly chewed another bite of his meal. Finally, he put his fork down and continued. "What I was saying is that I need to make some decisions about my business since I am certain to get called up and sent off to war. I've worked—. No. We've worked too hard to get established to just close it down. I don't see anyone having interest in buying it except maybe that greedy old cuss in Wolcott, and I'll be darned if I ever sell out to him. What I'd like to propose is that you and I become legal partners so that you can run things while I'm gone."

Shock was evident on Dawson's face. He hadn't expected this. Jesse waited patiently and continued eating his supper as the man across from him processed the proposal. A few minutes later, Dawson looked down at his empty plate then up at Jesse. "I'm honored, Jesse, that you'd trust me with the livery while you are away. You know I enjoy the work and that I'd do everything and anything I possibly could to run it well. But I just don't see how I could possibly buy in. You know that I committed myself to helping my ma since Pa died. For a while, Evan was helping her out also, but since the first of the year he's been working as a tie hack up the Encampment River. No one's seen or heard from him in a while. I'm Ma's only support. Jesse, I don't have any money saved up, I haven't got anything to sell or use as collateral for a loan."

"I didn't say anything about you buying in up front, Mr. Wiley. I have no need for a nest egg of your money in the bank when I'm leaving the country and might not ever come back. I just need to know that something I've worked for will continue when I'm gone."

In the silence as Dawson digested his meal and Jesse's generous offer, the woman returned. She calmly removed Jesse's plate then Dawson's, then asked if they would like apple pie or peach cobbler for dessert. This time, Jesse was more confident as he flashed her a genuine smile. He met her eyes and ordered pie. Dawson kept his own eyes on the table and quietly asked for the cobbler.

It wasn't until after his dessert had been served and eaten that Dawson responded. "Jesse, I'm sure I'm going to be hounded in my mind about how I don't deserve to be partners with you since I haven't added a financial stake, but I'm pledging to you that I'll stake this company with every ounce of toil and loyalty that I have. I'm damned proud that you'd trust me and also proud to be in business with a man like you."

Jesse grinned and offered Dawson his hand. "Shake on it, partner, and be assured that the peace of mind you've just given me is stake enough. I know you'll do your best, and that's all we need to make a go of this."

A few minutes later, the men stepped outside the restaurant. The evening was pleasantly cool after the heat of the afternoon. Jesse glanced down the street then up toward the west. Dregs of the sun's last rays silhouetted Bridger Peak with muted hues. Northward, Jesse noted a large thunderhead and wondered if a change in the weather was on its way. Without speaking, Dawson and Jesse walked together up Freeman Street toward Encampment's main business center. At the corner in front of Parkison's Mercantile, Jesse made a final suggestion. "I think we should stop in and talk to B.L. Miner in the next few days to draw up some papers so you have legal authority at the bank and anywhere else you need it."

Dawson stopped in mid stride. "Really? You are that serious about this?"

Jesse laughed at his incredulity. "Oh yeah, I'm serious. Now we need to make it legal."

A block further down Freeman, Jesse shook his new partner's hand and wished him goodnight. Then he stood and watched as Dawson hitched eastward down the sidewalk on Seventh on his way to his small apartment. Certain he'd made a good decision about sustaining the livery, Jesse set off in the opposite direction toward his home just a block and a half to the west.

When Jesse slid into bed that night, he felt calmer than he'd felt in several weeks. Knowing that his business would be in good hands was a huge relief. He whispered a quiet prayer of thanks as he settled in.

3
Encampment, Wyoming
June 1917

Sari avoided mirrors as much as possible. Each morning she made a quick sideways glance to the small mirror on her wall to make sure her hair was combed properly, then turned away. She didn't need to be reminded of her own ugliness, there were plenty of stares and whispered comments to remind her. She'd learned long ago there was nothing she could do to stave off the reaction her face caused, so she confronted each day with resigned resolve to be as kind and useful, yet as invisible, as possible.

Sari's early childhood was perfect. She had two doting parents to herself in a comfortable home filled with joy and love. Her father, who ran sheep on their land, was kind and funny. Sari and her mother spent their days together, finding adventure in everything from reading and arithmetic lessons as well as cooking, quilting and crocheting, and taking long walks to enjoy their prairie home. Their homestead was isolated and off the beaten track, but Sari never felt lonely.

Just a month after her tenth birthday, the family took a two-day trip to Rawlins. Sari and her mother enjoyed the stores and the bustle of the city streets while her father attended a Wyoming Wool Growers meeting and then met with some buyers from back east interested in both wool and meat. In her memory, the dinner they enjoyed on their last night in Rawlins was a magical celebration filled with smiles and candlelight.

The next day, the excitement of riding home on the stage turned to horror when about an hour into the journey the stage hit something hard enough to crack one of the front wheels. The rig lurched dizzily then whomped onto its side. The driver, who was sitting on top of the stage, was thrown nearly ten feet into a cascade of rocks, slamming his head into the granite outcropping, never regaining consciousness. The four-horse team, spooked at the catastrophe occurring behind them, panicked and continued to pull the now tangled and gnarled rigging. In their fear, they pulled the coach off the road and the entire unit began a sliding, terrifying trip to the bottom of a sagebrush covered hill where the horses finally lost their footing.

The only memory Sari had of the accident itself was the sensation of tumbling. She never recalled how her father was pulled out through the carriage door by a gnarled root and drug beneath the coach, or of her mother's whimpers as she bled to death trapped inside wreckage. Thankfully, she also never remembered being thrown from the coach and skidding face first through the sharp shards of granite, ending under some sagebrush on the side of the hill.

She did remember glimmers of the aftermath of the crash. The hot sun on her head. Feeling thirsty. Calling out for her mother and receiving no help. Burning pain in her face and fear as she sat watching men carry up the blanketed bundles that contained her parents' bodies.

After the accident, Sari was overwhelmed by her physical pain, her sudden aloneness, and the choices that the unfamiliar adults made for her. She stumbled through hazy days without comprehension or question.

The funeral was a blur of black clothing and unfamiliar faces. Before the pastor began speaking, she sat alone in the front pew of the church, staring at the oak boxes in front of her and listening to the murmur of voices behind her. They spoke as if she couldn't hear them. "Such tragedy. She's bound to be alone her whole life with a face like that."

She didn't understand what was happening when a day later she was taken out to the ranch. At first she thought she was going home, but instead she'd listened to the auctioneer's warbling cadence and watched as strangers carried off all her family's belongings except a few things they'd reserved for her in a small case. The next morning, she'd been taken to the train station in Wolcott and handed over to the eastbound conductor.

"Since you have no living relatives to take you in, you're on your way to an orphanage," someone told her the morning she left. "They'll take good care of you there."

As the train swayed its way from Wyoming to Missouri, Sari stared out the window, watching the flat terrain scoot by. Her face, still unhealed and painful, and her heart both hurt. She was mired in her grief and aloneness, missing her parents and afraid of what the end of the train trip would bring. She cried, but only a little. Tears stung her raw cheek and blowing her nose hurt, so instead, she concentrated on remembering her parents. To comfort herself, she reached under the collar of her dress and withdrew a key suspended from a leather string.

The day of the auction, Sari had roamed through the rooms of her home, unnoticed by the adults intent on scavenging her parents' lives. Sari rubbed her hand over her mother's dresser, now bare and unadorned, feeling the familiar smooth softness of the oak. She tried to picture the silver hairbrush and mirror that her mother had kept there. As she turned away, Sari's eye caught a glimpse of something underneath the dresser and she knelt down to investigate. It was a small key. She looked around to be sure no one was watching before she snatched it up. Later in the day, she managed to pocket a shoe lace she spied in one of the drawers in the kitchen. Soon, she'd looped the lace through the key and hidden her treasure under her shirt.

Holding that last memento of her childhood home, she stared out the window. As evening approached and the passing farmland became bathed in softer light, they passed a farm that reminded Sari of the home she'd been forced to leave.

A vivid memory surfaced. The train's rhythmic noise and motion faded as she remembered a day when she was about eight. A small orange kitten she'd loved had been killed by a coyote, and she was distraught. It was her first experience with death. Her father sat next to her on the back porch and rubbed her back as she cried over her lost pet. "It's over," she'd lamented, "He's gone and I'll never hear him mew again or be able to play with him. Oh Papa, it's so unfair."

"Yes, Sari, it is. And I know it hurts. But God gives us two gifts that make life a little more fair. He gives us our memories and He gives us hope."

"How do those things make life more fair?"

"Little Sweetie, nothing can ever take away your memory of how much fun you had with your kitty."

"He was the softest kitten I've ever touched."

"Yes, and you will always have that recollection, no one can take it away. Remembering it can always give you joy even though the kitten is gone. And, I think those memories give us hope."

"I don't understand."

"The hope God gives us, just like our belief in Him, is a choice. We can keep our eyes focused on the hardness of life, or we can choose to look forward with a kind of enthusiasm or optimism about what kind of good thing He has for us next."

Sari replayed that memory again and again, deciding to hold on to it and the wisdom her father shared with her that day and try to put it into practice.

The staff at Miss Milton's School for Orphaned Girls in Pinetree, Missouri included three teachers, a cook who was only called Cook, and Mr. Zeke who maintained the school building and ran errands. Sari clearly remembered stepping off the train, frightened and lonely, tired, and dusty from the trip, to be met by Mr. Zeke.

"I'm sure you're the little one what's coming to Miss Milton's school. I couldn't miss ya with that face." With that, he picked up Sari's small suitcase and walked away, assuming she'd follow.

She had followed, walking quickly past store fronts and into a neighborhood of nice homes with well-kept gardens. Soon, they arrived at the three-story Victorian house that would be her home for the next eight years. Wordlessly, her escort led her into a small parlor, dumped her valise unceremoniously by the door and told her, "Wait here. I'll tell the Miss you arrived." Then he was gone.

While she waited, she let her eyes wander around the lavish room. The walls were richly carved oak with bookcases on two walls. The center of the room held two Queen Anne chairs and a settee on one side and a large desk on the other. Sari dared to step closer to the books displayed on the shelves and became excited to see a few familiar titles. A warm memory rushed in of the shelves at the ranch house filled with books.

Footsteps at the door made her turn. She met eyes with a very tall woman dressed severely in a fitted black wool skirt and jacket. A stiff, white collar peeked above the rounded neckline of her jacket. The woman's face was pale and pinched. The effect was both forbidding and timeless, and Sari was reminded of an oil painting of an aristocrat from one of her father's art books.

"Oh my," were Miss Milton's first words to the girl. Then she motioned to her to come closer. Sari felt shaky as she complied, but soon stood looking up at the matron. "Your name is Sari Webber, correct?" Miss Milton pronounced her first name 'Sar-eye'.

Sari was frightened, but spoke quietly to correct her, "Yes, but my name is pronounced Sar-ee. It's like Sara only with a long e sound at the end."

"I shall try to remember. You are ten years old, correct?"

Again, Sari nodded.

"Now, girls who attend this school are required to be useful and compliant. You will be assigned a job, I think probably you'll do in the kitchen where you are out of sight. You will have classes in literature, hand writing, and arithmetic each morning. In the afternoon you will work to earn your keep here, since you come to us destitute. On Friday afternoons all the girls assemble at two o'clock for lessons in housewifery, though I sincerely doubt you will ever find yourself the mistress of your own home, no matter how poor. Keep yourself neat and clean, your bed made, and your area tidy. Do you have any questions?"

Sari knew instinctively that asking anything of this woman would be badly received so she responded by dropping her eyes and bowing her head.

"Good. Follow me." Sari picked up her valise and followed Miss Milton up a long flight of stairs and down a dark, wood paneled corridor. Miss Milton opened a door on the left and motioned for Sari to go ahead of her. It was a dormitory room holding four beds along one wall and four more mirror-imaged against the opposite wall. The rich furnishings from the parlor were absent. This floor was bare, well-worn hardwood. The beds were narrow with iron head and foot boards. Yet, it was clean and seemed to offer a homey sort of comfort. There were two windows at the end of the long room covered with yellowing lace curtains. Each bed had a small bedside table with two drawers beside it and a small wooden trunk at the foot.

"Your place is at the far end on the left. Empty your suitcase using the trunk and table. Do you have a Bible with you?"

Sari nodded.

"First lesson. Girls are to answer aloud when directly spoken to."

Sari nodded again and answered, "Yes, Ma'am."

"That's better. You have a few minutes before the girls will be released from classes to return here to prepare for lunch and the afternoon. I will leave you to get settled. Introduce yourself to the girls, and then join them downstairs."

Any hope that she might find a loving home to replace the one she'd lost was quickly forgotten. Miss Milton was always cordial to the girls, though strict and aloof. She was never warm, but treated them all, even Sari, with cool respect. The teachers, by varying degrees were the same. Lessons were precise and expectations high. The teachers were adept at conveying ideas and skills but not care and compassion. Accustomed to an abundant outpouring of love and laughter from her parents, the distance and lack of emotion from the new adults in her world left Sari empty and yearning.

The most difficult hurdle for Sari came with the sixteen girls at Miss Milton's. Eight older girls shared a room at the other end of the hall. Seven girls of about Sari's age were her roommates and constant companions in the dormitory room and in classes. All the girls were orphans, and Sari quickly realized that each girl came wanting and needing to belong and be loved. This showed in how possessive they were of friends and jealous for attention and recognition. In the company of the staff and teachers, the girls smiled and flirted with the adults, hungry for their approval for even minor accomplishments. Away from the sight of the adults however, the girls lived with constant bickering and fighting amongst themselves. They looked for new ways to compete with and defeat the others in an effort to gain Miss Milton's and the other teachers' attention and regard while diminishing their rivals.

When the girls entered the dorm room that first afternoon, as one entity they rejected Sari. It was clear to them that this new girl, with her horrid face, could offer them nothing, and she became a target for their taunts.

Sari knew immediately that she would not become a favorite of the adults at the school, either. Like their students, her teachers did not bother to hide their revulsion to her appearance.

On her first Sunday morning at the orphanage, Miss Milton led the girls, in an orderly file two by two, on a walk to church. The sanctuary was beautiful, paneled with rich, dark wood and adorned with an ornate stained glass window behind the chancel. For Sari, the beauty ended there. The liturgical service was long and unfamiliar. The clergyman raised his voice, his face filled with anger. His long sermon was filled with recrimination and stern warnings of hell and damnation. The god who reigned here was not the loving, caring Father she knew. To make matters even worse, the girls who sat on either side of her scooted as far away from her as possible, tucking their skirts under them so that she wasn't touching any part of them.

In the crush of parishioners waiting to shake the reverend's hand after the close of the service, Sari became detached from the group. When she rejoined them on the sidewalk, her seatmates were in serious conversation with Miss Milton. They glanced furtively at her then back at Miss Milton, who nodded.

Not long after their return to the orphanage, Miss Milton summoned Sari. "How did you enjoy the service this morning, Sari?" her matron asked.

Sari stood straight and tall before the woman. She tried to find something positive to say. "It's a beautiful church, Ma'am. I've never seen such pretty glass windows."

"You would do well to concentrate on the message instead of the trappings," came a quiet rebuke. "I noticed that our pew was a bit overly crowded this morning. I think that from now on I will ask that you sit with the teachers in the row behind me. You will have more room with that arrangement." Understanding the truth behind the request, Sari was embarrassed and hurt but merely dropped her eyes and answered, "Yes, Ma'am."

Thusly ostracized by adults and peers, Sari felt lost in a well of loneliness.

It took months for Sari to realize it, but their aversion to her looks was her saving. Without knowing it, the teachers made her life easier among the others by not liking her. Her roommates rapidly realized that the newcomer was not a threat. The teachers had so completely rejected her, the girls understood she wasn't competition so they didn't have a need to be openly mean. Within weeks of her arrival, since she offered neither advantage or threat, Sari settled into a routine of invisibility.

Sari knew from overheard conversations that many of the girls at Miss Milton's had been there since they were very small. Most had no memories of their parents. Sari pitied them. Many times as she lay in their quiet room waiting for sleep to overtake her, she entertained memories of her Mama and Papa. She did it intentionally so that the memories wouldn't fade, and so that she could remember what if felt like to be loved and happy. She remembered talking about God and reading the Bible with her folks. She pictured praying with her Mama to invite Jesus to come into her heart, and she relived her baptism in the creek when she was six. Sometimes when she had trouble sleeping, she could almost hear her father's deep voice reading Bible passages and then the three of them discussing what he'd read.

Stubbornly, Sari held on to her faith that Jesus was her Savior and that God loved her, though she didn't understand His choices and didn't feel His love. She held tightly to the idea that somewhere in heaven her parents were looking down, forming her own personal cloud of witnesses. That inner faith gave her courage and hope for her days and comfort at night.

Though they didn't know it, the girls at Miss Milton's taught Sari many valuable lessons. Since they rarely took note of her, she was free to watch them, and soon she recognized that anger and bitterness resulted only in hotter anger and deeper bitterness. Sari, in her cocoon of solitude among the other girls, began to cultivate in herself the traits and actions that produced the best results. She learned to keep her thoughts to herself, work hard, and be thankful and kind. Soon, while she wasn't considered anyone's friend, the girls and the staff came to appreciate her, and life at the school became manageable and comfortable.

As the years resolved themselves into routine, Sari grew from a gawky child into a slim young woman. She perfected the arts of being inconspicuous and making meringue. Aware that she would leave Miss Milton's school when she turned eighteen, after her seventeenth birthday she began thinking about her future. With Cook's blessing, she wrote a few letters to restaurants in Pinetree asking about possible positions as a cook.

One afternoon just a few weeks before her eighteenth birthday Miss Milton summoned Sari to the parlor. She was anxious but hopeful as she sat for the first time in the room on one of the Queen Ann chairs, accompanied by Miss Milton and a man introduced to her as Mr. Henry Bagley from the Rawlins Central Bank.

"I've just been telling Mr. Bagley that you have been a model student, Sari. You have excelled at your studies and devoted yourself to the hard work of the kitchen. When Cook became ill last year, you stepped in for her and took over, and I commend your resourcefulness and fervor. I have assured him that you are hardworking and diligent."

"Thank you, Miss Milton, I've been taught well here." The praise was a surprise to the girl. She'd rarely been complemented, and never by Miss Milton herself.

Sari sat straight and tall, filled with a sudden hope and anticipation. She could feel the small brass key hanging from the leather lace thump against her chest and asked, "You are here from Rawlins? Might this be concerning a deposit box my father left for me at your bank, Mr. Bagley?"

His surprise was genuine. "I have no knowledge of any deposit box, Miss Webber. We have never had such boxes at our bank. That is not why I am here."

Before he could go on, Sari responded, "But I found a letter in my mother's Bible. It's in her handwriting and it talks of a strong box containing important papers plus a necklace that was my grandmother's. I felt certain she meant the box was at the bank." She put her hand to her throat and felt the key hanging there, giving her courage.

"You must be mistaken. There are no deposit boxes at the bank, and no strong boxes were found among your parents' effects."

He cleared his throat, dismissing her question and continued with words that crushed her with a weight she didn't think she could hold. He explained to her about an unresolved debt. According to Mr. Bagley, her father died owing the bank a huge sum as mortgage on the ranch and livestock, one that had not been fully satisfied by the sale of his holdings. He went on, explaining how the debt was now hers.

Sari sat, dumbfounded. She knew what he'd just said couldn't be true, but when she tried to speak he waved her off and Miss Milton scowled. Sari stopped listening to Miss Milton and Mr. Bagley and allowed a series of vivid snapshots of memory flood her thoughts. *One special afternoon not long before the accident, her mother's laughter and the smell of vanilla permeating the kitchen as mother and daughter baked and decorated a cake together. A special supper in the oven. The round oak table set with her mother's best china atop Sari's grandmother's hand crocheted table cloth. Her father returning from a trip to Rawlins with a tight hug and a small sack of candy for Sari. Her mother and father dancing around the kitchen. The final image, the sweetest of all, a toast. Sari with a glass of milk, Mama and Papa each with cups of coffee, "To the ranch – all ours and only ours."*

"Miss Webber, are you listening?"

Sari blinked twice and let the memory fade. "Yes, well. Mr. Bagley, there must be some mistake. I clearly remember celebrating that my father paid off the mortgage on the ranch."

Mr. Bagley was instantly irate. "Miss Webber, you are young and simply do not understand. You may wish that your father had paid this debt, but he did not, I assure you. Your father's untimely death and his careless financial choices were both unfortunate, and I am sorry that you have suffered his consequences. The offer my bank is making to you is generous. You are really in no position to argue."

Feeling frightened and shy, Sari had to swallow before she could go on. "Mr. Bagley, how much did my father owe you? May I see the loan he signed?"

Bagley's slight grin made her feel small and stupid. "Miss Webber, legal documents are difficult to navigate through, especially for someone young and inexperienced as yourself. I have shown the necessary papers to Miss Milton, and you can rest assured you are being dealt with fairly and honestly."

Miss Milton nodded formally to close the topic. Mr. Bagley added, "Based on the skills you've learned here, we have arranged for you to take a position in a small town near Rawlins where you will be able to work off your debt."

He informed her where she would be accommodated, dismissing Sari with his tone before turning to face Miss Milton. "In the envelope I gave you earlier is a train ticket for the young woman to Wolcott Junction. She will then transfer trains for a connection to Encampment. If you will telegraph a confirmation of her departure to the address I've enclosed, someone will be at the station to meet her and get her settled. You have been most kind to help with these arrangements."

The memory of her father's toast remained crystal sharp in her mind. Sari wanted to argue, she wanted to scream, but there was nothing inside of her that gave her the courage to even raise her eyes. As Miss Milton and the banker planned her future, Sari's invisibility was complete.

Now, just a few weeks later, Sari stretched and turned over in her bed, looking at the dusky orange sky peeping through the small window of her room and knowing she had a few minutes before she needed to get up and start her day. She'd been in Encampment,

Wyoming for less than a week. To combat the looming hopelessness that constantly threatened to invade her thoughts, she whispered a morning prayer of thanks and took a deep breath. While her living arrangements were trying, she searched for ways to be thankful. She had the small room to herself, a retreat from the world and the eyes of others. She relished the privacy but not the austerity. She tried to concentrate on the freedom she had. After living in the constant company of others in the dormitory at Miss Milton's, her solitary room gave her welcome privacy.

Sari tried to consider Lilith and Chetley Wills, proprietors of the Copper Pot, as blessings as well. From the moment she'd heard about them, Sari feared her new bosses would be severe and hard, reminiscent of the women at Miss Milton's school or the sullen Mr. Bagley. She was relieved when she arrived in Encampment and received a cordial welcome. It was clear to Sari that they had been forewarned about her scars. Neither stared when introductions were made, though Mr. Will's eyes lingered on her face, his own a mask. Both asked about her trip and seemed truly concerned that she get settled right away. Lilith was the warmer of the two, and Sari harbored the hope that they might become friends. From the beginning, however, Chetley made her nervous. He was not openly unkind, yet there was something just under the surface that created a tension between them. Sari arrived in Encampment in the evening, so nothing more than her housing and making sure she had supper claimed her arrival. They installed her in her new lodgings with directions on how to get to the restaurant.

Early the next morning Sari sat across from the couple as they began to explain her job and responsibilities. "As I'm sure you understand from your conversation with Mr. Bagley, you will be working for us in order to pay off your debt to the bank. We agreed to this situation out of a desire to help you, and we will expect you to keep that in mind as you perform your duties. We don't want your gratitude, just an honest day's work."

Mr. Wills stared at Sari until she nodded. *I understand,* she thought, making sure her own face was a mask. *You do expect my gratitude, and probably a great measure of it, as well as my hard work.*

He continued, "Most of your pay will be sent to the bank in Rawlins. At the end of this contract, five years from now, you will be free of debt. In the meantime, you will be allotted two dollars a week for your living expenses. You will pay one dollar per week for your accommodations at the boarding house and I'll only charge you fifty cents a week, a true bargain certainly, for your meals here. The rest is yours to do with as you see fit. It's a generous offer under the circumstances, as I'm sure you will agree. Do you have any questions?"

Sari studied their faces for a heartbeat. Her stomach was knotted and she felt a little queasy. "I understand the contract." She understood that she was obligated to it whether she wanted to or not. "Will I mostly be acting as the cook for the restaurant? What will my work hours be?"

Lilith leaned forward, "Until we see how you do, I will share the cooking duties. We have a restaurant host and an able waiter to do the serving. Sometimes, though, you may be asked to aid in the dining room, but mostly you will be in the kitchen."

Wills continued, "We expect you to be at work at six each morning. We serve breakfast from six-thirty until nine. Then you will prepare the mid-day meal so that we can serve between eleven-thirty and half-past one. We will serve supper from five o'clock until seven."

"Depending on what we are cooking for supper and how efficient you are in the kitchen, you will have an hour or two during the afternoon for a rest, then you'll need to come back until we are done with supper serving and cleaning up. How does that sound?"

She didn't let herself dwell on the fourteen- or fifteen-hour days she faced for fifty cents a week. She knew there was nothing she could do about it. Trying to ignore the hopelessness of the situation, she concentrated on trying to feel encouraged. Lilith leaned forward and watched Sari intently. The close scrutiny was perhaps meant to be friendly but felt invasive to Sari. Leaning back and dropping her eyes, she nodded. "I think that sounds fine," she answered quietly.

"Oh, but we are closed for supper on Sundays, so you have that time off."

Sari was surprised.

Yes, Sari thought as she stretched again, *I have a lot to be thankful for. I have half a day off each week and I have this little room as a sanctuary. Things could be worse.*

Intentionally, Sari tried to dismiss the aloneness she felt in her new situation. Miss Milton, from the very first day, had sequestered Sari in the kitchen most of the time, keeping her out of sight of strangers. Sari suspected that she'd done this out of her own revulsion and embarrassment, not as protection. Even so, the situation had worked to shelter her from judging eyes. Here, though, Sari was a stranger and the reactions of each person she met rubbed a new and painful wound down deep. Sari often used a strategy she'd learned soon after her accident of keeping her head low with the right side of her face turned away from others. She'd also begun wearing her hair down as well, so that it could shield her face from passing glances.

The morning light streaming from the window had changed from soft shades of orange and violet to brighter, clearer light. The sun was still below the horizon, but Sari threw the covers back and began her day. The early June air was already warm during the six-block walk to the restaurant a while later, foretelling a hot day to come.

Time went quickly and smoothly, and Sari found herself with an extra half hour before the supper serving began. Sari stepped out the back door of the kitchen, blinking from the bright sun beating down out of the rich blue sky and decided to take a walk to enjoy some fresh air. She had vague memories of visiting Encampment with her parents, but remembered very little about the town. Since her return, she'd seen very little of her new home town, so she set off to explore.

Encampment in 1917 was a small town with a population of about two hundred seventy people. The streets lay in a neat grid, with numbered streets running east to west and named streets crossing them. The exception to the organization was one named street among the numbered. Named for and by George Emerson, who had paid to have the town laid out at the beginning of the copper boom, Emerson Boulevard ran east and west between 5th and 6th streets. Normally when she exited the alley behind the Copper Pot onto Emerson, Sari turned left. Then she'd walk half a block until she reached McCaffrey Avenue. A right on McCaffrey and four blocks more took her to her room, which adjoined to the Old Wyoming Rooming house.

Today, Sari turned right at the end of the alleyway. The first street she encountered, the one that ran in front of the Copper Pot, was Freeman Avenue. She stopped for a moment to look around. On one corner was a hardware store, across from that was the Baker Cafe. Beside the cafe a sign advertised "Plummer Store". A bit farther down she could see a barber pole. Sari's attention, though, was drawn to a wooden tower, perhaps thirty to forty feet tall, standing in the middle of the intersection. Suspended from the tower and continuing in both directions diagonally across the street was a thick cable. Not far from the tower itself and hanging from the cable, a large, rusty bin rested. Sari guessed that this was some sort of conveyance, and she'd wondered about it in the days she'd been in Encampment, but she'd never seen the system in operation, and she'd not had the courage to ask anyone about it.

Curious, she turned south and walked down Freeman. She passed the New Bohn Hotel, a large and impressive building, then crossed the street at the next intersection. She could see another tower a couple blocks down, so she turned right.

This must be the main commercial section of town, she thought as she passed a series of businesses. The Parkison General Merchandise Store sat on one side of the street. Across the wide, dusty road, a large brick building boasted its tenants: the North American Bank, the post office, Smizer's Store. Signs also announced a barber shop and a billiards parlor.

Sari crossed another street, the sign said Rankin Avenue, and noted the City Hall and Opera House on her right. Her focus, though, rested on another wooden tower in the middle of the street by the alley. Identical to the first with its cables and evenly spaced hanging bins, from here Sari could see that a line of towers continued out of town and up toward the mountains.

At the end of her walk, Sari returned to the kitchen feeling relaxed and energized. She tied a scarf around her hair and set to work. She was serving a plate of roast beef and vegetables when she heard Lilith swear. Shocked, Sari turned around.

"Damn it," Lilith said again quietly. "This ladle broke, and the bowl part of it is somewhere in the soup."

Lilith leaned over the pot, staring into it as if the spoon would raise to the top by itself. Her face was red and creased in a tight frown. The look on her face along with surprise of her language somehow tickled Sari, and a tiny giggle escaped. Lilith looked up, her face a study in irritation and met Sari's eyes. Then, her face softened and she added a giggle of her own. Embarrassed at her outburst, she apologized as Sari grabbed a long spoon.

"I'm sorry I laughed, you just took me by surprise." Sari said. "Try this to fish the piece out, it might work better."

When both pieces of the ladle had been retrieved and the women were satisfied that nothing foreign remained in the soup pot, Sari began again to apologize. Lilith cut her off, "No, don't be sorry. Your reaction was exactly what I needed. Thank you for rescuing me from my own bad temper."

The rest of the afternoon and evening went smoothly. That night, as Sari was climbing into bed, she thought again about the scene. She'd never heard such language from a lady before and hearing Lilith use that word shocked her, but what puzzled her more was that Lilith hadn't been overly embarrassed by the word, nor had she been angry at Sari.

4
Encampment, Wyoming
June 1917

Jesse pulled off his hat and wiped the sweat from his eyes and face with his shirttail. The last two days had been unusually hot for June, and here he stood in front of the forge. When he'd worked at the Transportation Company in Dillon, one of his jobs had been to help with horseshoeing. As the time went by, the blacksmith, skilled not only as a farrier but with many kinds of metal work, took Jesse on as an unofficial apprentice. He taught Jesse the art of shoeing horses and shared his knowledge about working with the forge. Later, after he'd purchased the livery, Jesse found an old, dusty forge and all the tools he needed in a dark corner of the barn. He started practicing on his own equipment and horses until he felt confident in his ability, then he made it known that he'd be willing to use his skill as part of his business. It was the job he liked the least but was the most thankful for because it was a constant source of good pay.

Today, Dawson was out with the truck delivering a load to one of the few open mines left while Jesse worked at the forge. He'd already shoed two horses for the Oldhams and had repaired a part for the Sweetwater Ranch's water mill.

As he wiped his face, he saw a shadow at the door of the barn. "I'll be right with you," he called, smoothing his hair and replacing his hat. He left his gloves on the work table and strode up to the door.

He didn't recognize her at first. She stood with her back to him, looking out of the livery door toward the Snowy Range and Medicine Bow Peak. The sun caught her brown hair and he saw a hint of auburn in the curls. She turned around and stepped into the shadow of the doorway as he approached and Jesse once again met her sky blue eyes.

"Good afternoon," his voice faltered, but he wasn't sure why. Later, he'd wonder if it was because of her disfigurement and decided that it was something else. "May I help you with something?"

40

She dropped her eyes and ducked her head so that her hair hung down in front. "Hello, I work at the Copper Pot and yesterday we broke this ladle. Mr. Wills suggested that you might be able to fix it."

"Oh, yes. He mentioned it this morning when I saw him at the post office. Let me see it." He stepped forward and extended his hand.

Sari looked up just enough to see him nod and grin as she handed over the two severed pieces.

"Your timing is perfect, Miss, uhm," he hesitated.

She quickly supplied the rest of his sentence. "Webber. My name is Sari Webber."

Jesse smiled again. "It's nice to meet you, I'm Jesse Atley. Well, Miss Webber, I was just finishing some metal work and the forge is hot. If you could wait for maybe fifteen minutes, I'll have this back as good as new."

"I hadn't expected such quick service. Thank you."

"No trouble. There's a bench out front if you'd like to wait, though it's probably not the cleanest spot to sit."

"I'm sure it will be fine," she answered as he turned and walked away from her. Normally, she hated running errands like this, giving others the opportunity either to avert their eyes or else to stare, revulsion—or, maybe worse, overt pity—apparent in their scowls or raised eyebrows. But this Mr. Atley didn't shy away from looking at her and his reaction was open and kind. A sudden picture appeared in her mind and she realized she'd seen this man before. When the waiter had been called away to help Mr. Wills, Sari had been asked to serve guests in the dining room last night. This man had been one of the diners. He'd reacted to her the same way then as today. Somehow, his open response made her feel confused and unsettled.

For a few minutes, Sari did sit on the bench. She'd passed Rankin's Livery, on 6th Street across from City Hall, on her walk the previous afternoon. This place, just a block south on 7th, was new to her. The street was quiet and tree-lined. The majority of the buildings surrounding the livery were homes and not businesses. Despite the quiet, sitting in front of the livery made Sari feel restless and exposed. She stood and moved back inside the door. She could see Mr. Atley pumping bellows at the far end of the long barn. From a stall between her and the forge, a large draft horse watched her with fringed, kind eyes. He nickered quietly. She walked slowly up to him, paused, then reached a tentative hand out to rub his soft jawline. He reacted by leaning in to her touch and lowering his head. She scratched his ears and rubbed his forelock obligingly. She'd had very little contact with animals in many years, but the smell of the horses and the warmth beneath her hand brought forward joyful memories, warm and welcome, of being with her father in their barn.

She glanced again at the corner of the barn, and watched as Mr. Atley laid the handle of the ladle, glowing from its time in the fire, on an anvil up against the bowl. With a few sharp raps of a small hammer, the ladle was once again in one piece. Sari watched as the farrier picked it up with a pair of tongs and plunged it into a tub of water. A few minutes later, he was standing next to her.

He gave the golden blond horse a loving pat then extended the ladle towards Sari. "That should take care of this ladle, Miss Webber. It should be good for many more servings of that delicious stew you served me yesterday."

The compliment embarrassed Sari, and she dropped her head. "Thank you very much. How much do we owe you?"

He put his hands in his pockets and answered, "How about a piece of pie the next time I come in for dinner?" She could hear the smile in his voice without looking up.

"I'm sure that's a good deal for us, Mr. Atley. Again, thank you."

Jesse watched her as she left, wondering about her shyness and feeling the remnants of her discomfort still lingering in the air. She'd no sooner disappeared around the corner when Jesse heard the sound of the truck engine. Within moments, Dawson pulled into the barn and parked.

"Hey, Partner," he greeted Jesse. "Delivery all made. They said to tell you thanks and that they are expecting a new whim to be on next Wednesday's train. Wondering if we could deliver it."

"They must be doing alright out there if they are buying a new whim to pull the ore up from the mine. The bigger mines often have units that are powered by steam. I wonder if this one will run the pulleys with a steam engine or with a set of mules."

Dawson shrugged.

"Anyway," finished Jesse, "That's going to be a heavy load to haul. We can certainly pick it up, but we'll need to use the horses and wagon, it'll be too big for the truck."

"That's what I told 'em. Hey, did I just see that ugly waitress from the Copper Pot just leaving here?"

"That's not a very nice way to talk about a person," Jesse answered.

"Well, it's true. Her face is pretty hideous."

Jesse walked away without comment. He knew that he didn't want to argue with Dawson's opinion of the girl's looks, but he felt mean and guilty just thinking it, let alone hearing something so harsh said aloud. As he straightened up his tools and tended to the bed of coals that heated the forge, he thought about her. *It isn't pity I'm feeling, exactly,* he told himself. He thought again about those crystal blue eyes and the soft, slender hands that had so kindly served him his dinner and stroked his horse's mane a few minutes ago. He continued to work, but his thoughts stayed on Miss Webber.

He recalled Claire's description of the accident. The daughter had been ten years old at the time and she was eighteen now. So young. He'd been only six, on a farm in South Dakota, when yellow fever took his Mama and his own life became a trial at the hands of his father and uncle, selfish men who were ill-equipped to raise a child. *Yes, I understand what it's like to lose a family.* Jesse thought, *Claire was gone, sent out to work, by the time Mama died, and there was no one at home who could control Pa's temper and meanness or Uncle Horace's wickedness. My older brother Marcus tried, but Papa drove him away. I'm sure I had it better than Miss Webber, though, in the end. I got to stay first with our neighbors Haddie and William Foster, kind people who tried to make me part of their family, and then I got to come to a real home with Claire and Daniel.*

Just then, a customer came in to the barn, and his thoughts went elsewhere.

At the end of the afternoon, Jesse looked around the forge and the livery, satisfied at his days' work. He wiped his hands on a rag as he stood in the wide doorway and cooled himself in the fresh air. A lone cloud, tinged with grey, obscured the sun and he felt a quick chill. The rest of the sky was deep, unsullied blue, and its depth made him think once again of Miss Webber. He recalled the contrast between the fine clarity of her eyes and the ravaged scars on her cheek. *I wonder, who is she underneath those scars?*

5
Encampment, Wyoming
July, 1917

June drifted by, ending with a hot, dry spell that
shortened tempers and covered tables with thin, gritty
dust. On the surface, life continued as normal.
Underneath, tensions grew. The newspaper was filled now
with news from Europe and details of America's growing
involvement with the war. Claire and Daniel discussed the
events after the boys went to bed at night, and Claire
became more and more worried not only about Jesse
being called up to serve, but also her older brother,
Marcus and even Daniel.

"I don't really think that will happen, Claire,"
Daniel soothed. "I know there's talk about increasing the
draft age, but I'm certain that at nearly forty-five, I'm too
old. I don't think you have to worry about Marcus, either.
Not only has he already served his country in the Spanish-
American War, he's nearly forty himself. No, I think the
only one we need to be praying for in our family is Jesse."

"Have you noticed how tense he's been lately? I
sure can't blame him," Claire answered.

"I have noticed that he doesn't smile as easily, and
he's putting in long hours at the livery. Has he told you
that he's made Dawson Wiley his partner?" asked Daniel.

"Yes, and I hope that's a good choice. He seems
like a hard worker, but he's a little rough around the
edges."

"I hope so, too. I keep telling myself to see it from
Jesse's view. Wiley's been with him a long time. Jesse told
me that Wiley was excited to accept the offer."

Daniel replayed that conversation several times in
his mind over the next several days, so a few days later, he
made a point to stop in at the livery. "Hey, anyone here?"

"In the back," came a muffled reply. Daniel found
Jesse with his head ducked under a shelf, covered in dirt
and grime.

"What are you doing back here? You look like a dust ball."

Jesse chuckled and slowly straightened his tired back. "Oh, I'm searching for a spare part for the winch and I'm certain I kicked it under here a while back. I sure can't find it, though. It'll turn up, or maybe Dawson moved it."

"I've been sent by your sister to remind you that she's asked you to supper tonight."

"I remembered. I'm going to have to stop by the house and clean up before I come over, though."

"That's good. You have time." The men passed the horse stalls and stood together by the front door. "Mostly, I just wanted to stop in and check on you. How are you holding up?"

"I'm okay, Dan. Really. Though I'll be glad when the lottery is done and we know just how long before I have to leave."

Trying to lighten the mood, Daniel nudged Jesse with his shoulder. "Well, you aren't gone yet, so let's enjoy the days God's given us. Next week is the town's Fourth of July picnic. Claire has all kinds of plans to go along with the celebration. You're planning on joining us, aren't you?"

"Of course. I wouldn't miss it." Jesse concentrated on making his voice more jovial and only partly succeeded. "After that, there's a little over two weeks before the lottery. Then we'll know for sure what the immediate future holds."

Sari walked to work on the morning of July 4th feeling light and happy. She'd awakened with a memory of a Fourth of July celebration on the ranch from when she was eight or nine. Instead of making her sad like many memories of her old life did, this one buoyed her and left her smiling. It had been a simple day, an outing to a small pond near the ranch for fishing and a picnic with her parents and a dear family friend she called Uncle Nathan. She'd taken a long walk with her mother, been complimented on the pie she'd help bake, and caught three fish that day. There was plenty of food, laughter and love that afternoon.

She entered the Copper Pot's kitchen with high hopes. Since the entire town would be at the Independence Day Celebration in the park, Lilith had decided to close the kitchen after breakfast and only offer a light meal of noodle soup and biscuits for supper. Sari had no one to share a picnic with, but she was looking forward to finding a secluded spot from which to watch the games and fun.

Breakfast was easy that morning, they'd had considerably fewer diners than usual. The kitchen and the dining room were cleaned, biscuits were baked and covered with a cloth and soup for tonight was simmering on the back of the stove. Sari dried her hands and took off her apron. She was reaching for her bonnet when Chetley Wills appeared in the doorway.

"Good afternoon, Mr. Wills. Are you getting ready to go to the celebration? It's going to be a fine afternoon." Talking with Chetley was difficult for Sari as he often had a criticism or cutting remark for her. She waited for his reply.

"Well, yes, I was just about to leave. I believe all our guests are already at the park, and most of the other employees have departed. Lilith left a few minutes ago carrying our blanket and leaving me the food basket. I don't expect anyone to come in for the next few hours, but you will need to keep an ear out on the lobby just in case a guest comes in and needs something."

Sari faltered, "But..."

"Now Miss Webber, you'll never get your debt paid back to the bank if you take days off. You know I can't in good conscience pay you for a day if you don't work. I noticed the other day that the pantry shelves are dusty. This will be a good afternoon for you to clean them, don't you think?"

Sari nodded, unable to respond, and turned away. Her disappointment had been obvious yet she tried to raise her chin and not let him know just how small his words made her feel.

When she was alone, she shed a few tears as she scrubbed the shelves and mopped the kitchen floor.

A week later as Sari was finishing the dishes, Lilith stopped in the kitchen doorway. "Sari, before you leave for your lunch rest, could you find me, please? I need to talk with you."

Sari felt nervous at Lilith's request. She nodded and answered that she'd be free as soon as the dishes were dried. The rest of the chore was accompanied by the worry she'd done something to upset her boss.

When she'd dried her hands and removed her apron, she left the kitchen to find Lilith. Sari finally located her in one of the upstairs rooms.

"There you are," Lilith said. "I was just hanging this painting I bought at Ed Smizer's store last week. I think it looks pretty in this room, don't you?"

Sari didn't exactly like the still life. Pictures of apples and candles didn't interest her, but she answered, "The colors go well in here."

"That's what I thought, too! Here," Lilith pulled a chair from the desk and motioned for Sari to sit down.

"I want to start by thanking you for your hard work. You are doing a good job in the kitchen, and we get complements every day on what we serve," her smile was genuine, but Sari was worried about what was coming next.

"While I've enjoyed being in the kitchen," Lilith continued, "Chetley has been after me to spend more time at the front desk greeting customers and being the hostess, so now that we know how capable you are as our cook, we've decided that I am going to hand over the kitchen full time to you."

Sari was pleased. She had worked hard and was thankful that her efforts were appreciated. She looked up and gave Lilith a small smile and thanked her.

"I know, though, that there's more work in that kitchen than one person can handle. So, Chetley and I have hired a local girl to join you. Now, you two need to work together. At first, you'll need to direct her and tell her what needs to be done and how to do it."

This news made Sari nervous. She had never taught anyone anything. "Thank you, Lilith, but I'm not sure I know how..."

Lilith cut her off. "Don't you worry about a thing. This girl, her name is Meredith Tucker, comes from a respected ranch just east of here. It's a large family with several hired hands and she's used to helping her mother cook for that family. We're told she's already very capable in the kitchen, so you won't have to teach her much, just tell her what needs to be done. You'll be fine. Now, I better get downstairs. Are you off for a rest?"

Rest was the last thing on Sari's mind after the news she'd just received. Actually, it was no surprise that Lilith was abandoning the kitchen. In fact, Sari had been handling things for quite some time now nearly without help. She'd been proud of her efficiency and confident that things were running smoothly. That Lilith felt she needed help and had hired someone left Sari anxious and angry.

She slept badly that night, convinced that the changes coming to the kitchen would not be for her best. All night she encountered memories of the way the girls at Miss Milton's treated her when they had to help in the kitchen or when it was Sari's turn to help with the laundry. She knew from cruel experience that girls could be mean even while they smiled, and she'd learned that the prettier the face, the deeper the danger was of being hurt.

All Sari's fears were realized the next morning when Lilith entered the kitchen a few minutes after Sari arrived. Next to her stood a smooth-cheeked blond. Large brown eyes ringed by long lashes looked from above a pert, freckled nose. The girl was a few inches taller than Lilith, who in turn was taller by several inches than Sari. She was thin, dressed in a blue gingham dress that showed the beginnings of womanly curves. Sari took an instant dislike for the girl, certain that she was the type who would speak softly and sweetly for as long as anyone else was around, but then switch to venom and deceit.

"Sari, this is Meredith. Meredith, you will need to depend on Sari to show you around and teach you how we do things around here."

Meredith extended her hand and smiled at Sari, "I'm pleased to meet you. My family and I ate here once a few weeks ago, and I thought the roast pork you made was the best I'd ever had. I'm looking forward to working with you." Her voice was breathy and nervous, but her handshake was firm and the smile seemed real. Sari didn't trust her.

"Thank you," she answered quietly. "It's nice to meet you."

"Well, I'll leave you two to get acquainted and get breakfast going. I'll check back with you both in a while." Lilith smiled encouragingly and departed.

The two stood quiet and uncomfortable for a few seconds, before Meredith broke the silence. "It really is nice to meet you. I hope we can be friends. I just moved into town and I'm so nervous, this is my first job."

Sari considered the girl for a moment, then answered, "The eggs need to be scrambled, aprons are hanging by the back door." Then she retreated to the stove and began frying bacon.

6

Encampment, Wyoming
Friday, July 20, 1917

When July twentieth arrived, it brought a sunrise of startling oranges and reds mixed with deep purple. Claire stood at her window braiding her hair and praying for the events of the day. She asked God to be merciful in the outcome of the lottery, well aware that she was praying for her brother to be chosen last just like every mom, wife, and sister in the nation. She realized that the selfishness of her love for Jesse made her pray for someone else to be put in harm's way before him, and that thought grated on her. She ended up amending her prayer, *God, thy will be done. Give us all strength and courage to be thankful for whatever the lottery brings. Grant safety and peace to all the men who have to go.*

A few blocks away, Sari was also taking in the sunrise on her walk to work. The vibrant colors to the east were offset by a bank of twisted grey on the western horizon beyond the mountains, portending the possibility of a storm. She, too, was praying, but her mind was far from the war and the upcoming lottery. Her thoughts were for peace and patience. Ever since Lilith had handed the kitchen over to Sari and added Meredith to help her, Sari's life had grown more and more trying. Meredith had shown herself to be a quick learner and gave Sari a great deal of help in the kitchen, that was certain. Even so, Sari walked on eggshells keeping the new addition to the kitchen at arm's length. She felt as if she couldn't let her guard down, she'd been hurt too often at Miss Milton's by giving in and trusting one of the 'pretty girls' and then being hurt as a result. It was a familiar situation, and maybe even more treacherous as Sari was not able to just duck her head and avoid the girl. Becoming invisible wasn't an option since it was just the two of them in the kitchen.

Sari interrupted her walk to work, stopping at a corner where she had a good view of the horizon. She stood, watching the day dawn but lost in thoughts of yesterday afternoon. Satisfied that her potato soup was perfect, she slid it to the back of the stove with the burner on low. Certain the soup would stay perfectly warm, she'd turned her attentions to dredging chicken in flour so it would be ready for frying. Meredith was preparing the green salad. They'd worked for nearly ten minutes when Sari began smelling something burning. She turned to the stove and was horrified to see that the flame under the potato soup was on high, not low, and the liquid was rapidly boiling and definitely scorched. Sari rushed over to turn off the burner just as Chetley walked into the kitchen.

"What's that smell?" he asked frowning. "Don't tell me you've ruined the soup, Miss Webber."

Sari was angry and humiliated. She moved the heavy pot to the counter, anguished that the soup was unserveable and that she'd been blamed when she was all but certain she'd turned the flame down. Could Meredith have done this to make Sari look bad? It was a possibility Sari instantly believed was true.

Chetley chided her and left the kitchen. His words stung, but not nearly as much as Meredith's back. The girl never even looked up from the cutting board.

In the new morning's light, Sari tried to shuck off yesterday's scene, but she was weary of taking the brunt of Chetley's mean remarks. The threat of more sneaky attacks by her coworker left Sari depressed. She felt like crying. Trying to gain control of her emotions, she straightened her shoulders, set her mind on the day ahead, then continued her walk to work. This morning would be an easy breakfast, she told herself. She'd baked muffins yesterday afternoon and planned to offer eggs and bacon or oatmeal. She'd ask Meredith to take charge of the oatmeal and serving, so maybe the morning would be smooth.

A third set of eyes watched the sunrise that July twentieth morning. Jesse had been up for several hours, keeping his hands busy so that he wasn't concentrating on what was coming that afternoon. He'd swept all the floors in his small house, washed the dishes and the counters and straightened the cupboards in the kitchen.

His bed was made, his clothes were folded or hung neatly. *Claire would be proud of how this place looks,* he thought with a wry smile. Now, with a cup of lukewarm coffee in his hand, he sat on his back porch and watched the first rays of sunlight break free over Medicine Bow Peak. After enjoying the colorful sunrise Jesse felt restless, so he decided to use up some of his energy at the livery where there were always tasks to do that needed a minimum of thought but lots of brawn. He had plenty to spend today.

He'd been at work about an hour when Chetley Wills stepped into the barn. "Good morning," Jesse called from the second stall. He'd just finished mucking out all the stalls and was pouring grain into the feed bins. "I'll be right there."

Wills waited patiently, leaning against the sliding barn door until Jesse approached. "Good morning. Looks like you're already hard at it."

The men shook hands. "What can I do for you, Mr. Wills?"

"Well, it isn't for me exactly. Crever Peryam stopped in very early this morning and had a cup of coffee. He was on his way to Saratoga and didn't have time to wait and talk with you, but he dropped off a small hand plow that he uses to till his wife's garden. Seems that one of the blades hit a rock and needs repairing. He asked if I'd get you to come take a look at it and fix it if you can."

"Be happy to. Where is it?"

"He dropped it off in the alley behind the Copper Pot. He didn't want it to be in anyone's way if you were out on a delivery or busy."

"Good enough. I'll be done here in just a few minutes, then I'll take the truck over and pick it up."

"I appreciate it. Peryam said to tell you he'd be back in a couple of days and he'd stop in and talk with you."

They walked together to the front sidewalk. "It's going to be another hot day, looks like," Jesse remarked.

"Yes, though I suppose all of us are going to be more focused on the news this afternoon than the heat."

Jesse nodded. "That's the truth. It has seemed all morning that the country is holding its breath, there's not even a breeze."

"I know I'll be listening to the radio broadcast of the lottery this afternoon. I have two nephews in Cheyenne who have draft numbers in this lottery. You do too, I'm thinking?"

"Yes, sir, I do."

"Well, good luck to you."

"Thank you." Jesse watched the man walk away, then returned to the shadows of the barn to finish feeding the horses.

Breakfast preparations were going well for Sari. Everything was ready on time. Meredith had greeted her cordially and gone right to work, stopping only once to ask advice about how much milk to add to the oatmeal. Sari filled two bowls with the hearty cereal and added a side order of eggs and toast to take to a table in the dining room as Meredith began washing dishes.

Chetley came in to the kitchen, stopped and stared at Sari, her hands laden with a serving tray. He turned to Meredith. "Young lady," he began. Meredith turned around at the sound of his voice. "I think a better use of your talents and pretty visage than washing dishes is serving our guests in the dining room. From now on, when one of the wait staff is unavailable to deliver food to the tables, I want you to do it."

She nodded at him and dried her hands, then quietly took the tray from Sari and moved toward the dining room. Chetley glanced back at Sari and quietly added, "Now that you have help, I'll expect you to stay in the kitchen, Miss Webber. I'm sure you understand."

Jesse backed the truck out of the livery and pulled the door closed. He turned left onto Freeman. Two blocks later, he made a right turn and parked on Emerson near the alley. He walked into the narrow alley, passing the back of Englehart Hardware and Mortuary to reach the back door of the Copper Pot.

He'd only taken a few steps past Englehart's when he spotted the rusty old hand plow near the back wall of the Copper Pot building. Right beside the plow, a woman was leaning, her head against the wall and her back to him. He knew it was Miss Webber right away from the way her hair caught the sunlight. He was immediately concerned at the defeat and despair in her posture. He slowed his steps, not wanting to intrude or frighten her, unsure of how to proceed. As he got closer, he could hear quiet sobs and see her shoulders shaking.

He coughed softly and said, "I don't mean to scare you Ma'am, but is there anything I can do to help?"

Sari stiffened and fought to wipe her eyes and gain her composure. Without turning around, she took a breath and then answered, "Thank you, but no, I'm fine. Just a silly moment. I'm alright."

Jesse didn't believe her and stepped closer. "It sure doesn't sound silly. It sounds like you might could use a friend."

The kindness in the deep voice and the sweet words threatened to undermine her attempt to stop her tears. She turned part way around, intentionally keeping the right side of her face hidden from his view. She kept her head low, but lifted her eyes to him. She recognized him and with a shrug tried to smile. "It's nothing really. Just an unkind word or two from someone. I will be fine in a minute."

Jesse studied her, "Well Miss Webber, I have an older sister and I've come to learn that when she gets to the point that tears are falling, she's been hurt more than just nothing. I can guess that you are the same way. Sometimes it helps to just talk it out."

Sari looked up again, braver more from the kindness in his voice than the words themselves. She answered, "Good morning, Mr. Atley." She knew it was an odd response, but she could think of nothing else to say.

"Good morning, Ma'am. I'm glad to meet you again, though I'm sorry you're having a hard day."

A new herd of tears trampled their way down her cheeks. She leaned her shoulder against the wall, keeping her face in profile to him and said, "Sad? No, not really. You'd think after all this time that my heart would be as calloused as—" she broke off then restarted, "I should be immune to mean comments and jeers, and most of the time I suppose I am, but there are days when it all seems too much."

As soon as the words were out of her mouth, Sari regretted them. She couldn't believe that she'd just said her thoughts aloud, and to a man she barely knew. In reactionary desperation, she turned and faced him squarely. "I am so sorry. That was unfitting and undignified. I beg your pardon and ask you please to forget as best you can what I just said." She reached into her apron pocket and quickly withdrew a handkerchief. She wiped her face with determination, took a ragged breath, and squared her shoulders. "Again, I am so sorry, I need to go." She stepped away, aiming toward the back door.

Jesse was stunned for a moment. He was still processing what she'd said, when he realized she was walking away. "Stop!" The command came out sharper and louder than he'd expected and it surprised them both. "I mean, please, wait." He fought to gain a calmness he didn't completely feel, then continued, "There's no shame in feeling bad if someone is treating you poorly, and it doesn't matter the reason. I can't walk in your shoes, I don't know what you've endured, but I know I had a measure of meanness and cruelty when I was young, and for a long while I didn't have anyone to go to for help or just to listen, and that made me feel desolate."

He stopped. She stood frozen, her back to him. He watched as she took a few moments to absorb his words. When she didn't move, he continued. "I'm offering a friendly ear, Miss Webber, because keeping hurt deep inside just eats away at you, and it doesn't heal."

He watched her shoulders rise and fall with two deep breaths, then she turned to face him once more. "Thank you, Mr. Atley. Your kindness isn't something I'm used to, and it comes to me as a precious gift. I really do need to go back to work, lunch is probably burning to a crisp. I do thank you for your kindness."

"Oh, there you are," Lilith Wills' sudden appearance in the doorway startled them both. She looked a bit cross until Sari spun around and she saw the remnants of tears below the girl's eyes. "Is everything alright?"

Jesse stepped in, "I'm sorry, Mrs. Wills, I'm afraid I detained Miss Webber to help me. Mr. Wills asked me to come pick up this plow that Mr. Peryam left, and I was having some trouble moving it out from the wall so I could get ahold of it, so I enlisted her assistance. I think I can get it from here, though, so thanks for the help!" Urgently needing to end the scene, Jesse began dragging the plow down the alleyway toward his truck. A backward glance as he rounded the corner told him that the women had returned inside. He hoped that Mrs. Wills had been satisfied enough with his explanation to let the matter rest.

For a long while after he'd delivered the plow to the barn and went about his morning's work, he thought about his meeting with Miss Webber. He railed at the cruelness she'd experienced and considered ways she could overcome the prejudices and heartlessness.

Dawson returned at about eleven thirty, reporting that his delivery went well and that he was on his way to Riverside to pick up a load of coal.

"I'll get enough to refill the hopper here at the shop and I'll stop and make sure the coal bin is full at your house. The rest I'll deliver to Mrs. Fulkerson. She stopped in and let me know she was nearly out."

"That sounds like a good plan," Jesse answered. "I'll be gone by the time you get back, so I'll see you tomorrow."

"Good enough," came the answer as Dawson got in the truck.

As the clock ticked its way closer and closer to noon, Jesse's thoughts were recaptured by the upcoming lottery. He'd arranged to listen to the proceedings at Claire's on their wireless radio, so at eleven forty-five he closed up the livery and walked the three blocks to her house on Lomax.

Claire gave Jesse a solid hug when he came in the back door. "You look a little peaked. Are you feeling alright?"

"Yup, nothing to worry about," was all he said.

"Have you eaten today? How about I make you a sandwich?"

"Thanks, but I don't think I'm too hungry just now."

Claire gave her brother a sad smile, "I have ham. I can add cheese and onions just like you like it. I think I have some lemonade, too."

"Just lemonade sounds good."

Daniel opened the kitchen door and joined them. "Claire, he's a grown man and you are still spoiling him, aren't you?" he quipped.

Claire ignored the traditional jab and asked, "He's not taking it, though. Would you like a sandwich?"

"Sure, I could use some lunch. I'll just go get the wireless turned on and tuned in."

Claire hugged her brother again. "This is all going to be fine," she said. "Tell me again, what is your number?"

"Two thousand five hundred fifty-two," came his succinct answer as the first sounds of the broadcast filled the kitchen.

"Here's your drink," Claire handed him a sweating glass then turned back to the counter. Jesse sat down next to Daniel in the parlor.

Claire quickly joined them. She handed Daniel a plate filled with a sandwich and cold baked beans, before taking her seat in a semi-circle around the radio. The reporter explained that the broadcast was coming from public hearing room two-two-six of the Senate office building in Washington D.C. He described the Department of War officials who were in charge, as well as the members of the House and Senate military committees who were there as witnesses. "Folks, this is going to take a while. We won't stay on the airwaves for the entire lottery. They are expecting to draw numbers for the rest of today and probably well into the night before having all ten thousand five hundred numbers they will need for the first round of call-ups. I'd like to describe for you the tension in this room. Each man here is carrying with him a great weight as a result of today's events.

"I'm watching now as Secretary of War Newton

Baker, former mayor of Cleveland, Ohio prepares to begin the proceedings by addressing this assembly."

Claire, Daniel and Jesse could hear rustling and movement over the wireless, and then a new voice began. "Gentlemen, this is a solemn and historic moment. We come here to determine which of ten million of our young men who have registered for national service will be selected to answer the President's call for an army of 687,100 and what the position of the others will be for service in the future. This is the first time in our history that we are to have a demonstration of selecting men from the nation for service. These men have all registered and are waiting. For them I bespeak the honor of the nation."

Claire glanced over at Jesse. His eyes were rooted to a spot on the floor. He held his Selective Service card in his hand.

The voice on the radio continued, "They are not conscripts. They are men who are chosen among their fellows in a nation-wide selection and they are on an equal footing with any other man in the Army or Navy. It has been necessary to draw ten thousand five hundred numbers to determine the order in which these men shall serve. Before we proceed with the drawing, the machinery will be explained by Provost Marshal General Crowder."

Claire adjusted her position and took an impatient breath, "Oh just get on with it," she muttered.

Crowder spoke for several minutes, explaining the draft procedures and describing how numbers had been encapsulated in gelatin encasements and then put in a large glass jar for the lottery.

Finally, they heard Secretary Baker's voice again. "I shall draw the first number and I ask that the chairmen of the Senate and House military committees, official witnesses at this historic occasion, draw the second and third respectively."

The reporter's voice intoned quietly, "At this moment, members are assisting Secretary Baker by tying a blindfold over his eyes."

The static and rustling over the radio seemed to take forever until finally Secretary Baker spoke again. "I have drawn the first number," he paused, then "the number is two hundred fifty-eight."

Another voice echoed the number as the reporter came back on, "The first number is two hundred fifty-eight. Now we are watching as Senator Chamberlain of the Senate is donning the blindfold to take his turn. Senator Chamberlain looks pale, and his hands are shaking as he is now reaching for a capsule from the glass bowl."

After a pause, Jesse listened as the number read aloud was the same number as that on his draft card. The reporter repeated the number, "Two thousand, five hundred and fifty-two."

No one in the parlor moved. The voice over the radio continued, but they didn't listen. They were frozen, unwilling to accept what had just happened. Tears filled Claire's sight. She didn't bother to wipe them away when they began journeying downward. Finally, Jesse broke free of the inertia of shock and raised his eyes. "I expect that time is going to move very fast now with my getting ready to go, but I have a few things I'd like to say to the both of you before I do go, and this feels like the best time for it."

Claire rooted around in her pocket for a handkerchief. Daniel nodded, then reached over and turned off the wireless. Jesse took a breath and then said, "Daniel, I'm plenty thankful for you and all you have done to take me in and raise me like a son. You've made me the man I am, and I don't think I've ever been thankful enough to you for that."

Daniel tried to speak but couldn't. Jesse continued. "Claire, I love you so much. You have always been my best friend and protector. I don't know where I'd be if you hadn't been willing to take me in and make me belong with you. Thank you for all your scolding and nagging and how you always demanded that I do my best."

He wiped his eyes and then started once again. "There are no guarantees in this life, so who knows what the coming months are going to bring? Being called up second doesn't really surprise me. Ever since I first heard we'd entered the war, and of the draft, I've just had this feeling, call it a premonition if you want, but it's a gut feeling that I was going to go, go soon, and," he glanced at Claire first and then Daniel, "I've had the feeling that I'm not coming back."

Claire jumped up at that and started to argue. Daniel silently put out his hand and pulled her back down. "Shhh, Claire, let him talk."

Jesse gave them both a resigned, sad grin and continued. "I love you both and the boys so much. There's never been anyone more blessed than I when it comes to having you as a family. I know the good Lord will watch out for you when I go and He'll be watching over me. Whatever does happen, all is well with my soul, so don't spend much time worrying, okay?"

At that Claire rose again. Jesse folded her into a hug and they stood there a long time, grieving and fearful, while also absorbing every ounce of love and warmth from the other.

Eventually, Jesse pulled back. He hugged Daniel, strong and fierce, then he looked around for his hat. "The paper said that reporting for physicals and then leaving for training would happen within only a couple of weeks for the first called up. The one thing Dawson isn't very skilled at for the livery is running the forge, so I'll need to finish up all the work I have before I go. I'd better get to it."

Claire found her voice, though it was wobbly, "Will you come back for supper?"

Jesse touched her cheek. "Not tonight, okay? How about tomorrow night?"

She nodded.

Working at the forge turned out to be exactly what Jesse needed. The combination of solitude, sweat, and the hard work of using his muscles to pound the hot metal, along with the mindfulness the job demanded helped him find his balance. By the time he looked around to see that every job, large or small, that required the forge was complete, his muscles were tired and he felt calm and peaceful. The sky was nearly dark and the evening quiet as he walked the half block separating the livery from his house. He bathed and shaved, then fell into bed and let sleep prevail.

7
Encampment, Wyoming
mid- July, 1917

"Uncle Jesse? Are you scared?" Mike's brown eyes looked up at Jesse from the parlor floor where he'd been reading the *Encampment Echo* newspaper.

"Yes, I'm scared your brother here is going to beat me at checkers again if I don't pay attention."

"No, you know what I mean. Are you scared to go to war?"

"Mike that's a dumbhead question," Greg answered. "Of course he's not scared. He's going to be a soldier and soldiers are brave. They don't get scared. He's going to be a hero by killing lots of Germans."

Jesse shook his head. He and Claire had quietly discussed how his leaving would affect the boys. "Greg, just because a man is a soldier, it doesn't mean he isn't scared. Courage doesn't mean you aren't scared, it means you don't give up even though you are." Greg looked disappointed. "Mike, I just don't know what to expect, and that does make me feel nervous and a little scared."

Claire called from the kitchen, "Boys, I need table setters. Dinner will be ready by the time you wash up and help me."

"Coming." Two heads popped up to answer their mother's call. Jesse picked the newspaper up, folded it and left it on the end table. He'd read it earlier today, and his head was filled with the day's news.

After supper, Jesse, and Claire sat out on the front porch while Daniel and the boys washed dishes. Jesse was tired and he'd rather have just kissed Claire goodnight and gone home, but he'd promised the boys a game of Parcheesi, so he nursed a last glass of iced tea and watched darkness inch its way from the top of Bridger Peak, down the slopes of the Sierra Madres until shadows finally touched the front yard and darkness fell.

"Did you read about the rest of the lottery, Claire?" Jesse asked.

"I did. Can you believe it took until the middle of the night to draw all the numbers?"

"It's ironic, isn't it?" Jesse added. "The last number they chose was pulled at two o'clock and it was the number two."

"That is strange," Claire agreed.

"I'm guessing that you didn't hear something even more ironic?" Jesse waited until Claire looked up and nodded. "Dawson Wiley, who we all know won't be able to pass the physical, was number two."

"Oh my," was all Claire could say. Internally, she raged at the injustice of the numbers.

Daniel joined them. Sitting down beside Claire, he remarked, "I had a look at the *Denver Post* this morning at City Hall. There was an article explaining the benefits the government is offering men who enlist or are drafted."

"I didn't see that. What did it say?" Jesse asked.

"I'll see if I can find the paper at work and get it to you. It had the pay for newly inducted men, and it also talked about a widow's benefits and other details. It sounds like a fair plan."

"Huh," Claire interjected.

"Are you ready, Uncle Jesse?" The boys arrived loudly on the porch and grabbed their uncle's hands. "We've got the board set up inside. Let's go."

Jesse followed Claire and Daniel out of the church at the end of the service the next morning. On the front lawn, Claire turned and waited for her brother to catch up. "I'm making fried chicken and gravy for dinner today," she told him. "We'd love to have you come over. I want to spend as much time as I can with you."

Jesse kissed her on the cheek and shook his head. "I want to spend time with you also, but I was thinking that maybe I'd take a short drive this afternoon. I need a little time out in the mountains before I go."

Claire knew that her brother felt closest to God in the mountains. "I understand. How about you come by again for supper on Tuesday evening after work?"

"I'll be there. No chance I'll miss it, especially if you promise a rhubarb pie."

"Deal."

The family split then, with Claire, Daniel and their brood heading home while Jesse went the other direction.

Jesse changed out of his Sunday clothes and grabbed a chunk of bread, some cheese and an apple. He snatched up his jacket and left his house a few minutes later. He'd just reached the edge of his grass when a voice called from across the street. Jesse veered in that direction and was soon shaking his neighbor's hand. "Good to see you, Royce."

"How's everything going, Jesse?"

Royce and Harriet Rogers had moved into the house across the street from Jesse over a year ago. Royce worked as a deputy for the City Marshall, George Helugs. Jesse had enjoyed dinner with them several times and admired the level-headed police work his neighbor offered the community.

"Good, under the circumstances. I leave for training in just a few days, and it seems like the list of things I need to do is never-ending."

"I understand," Royce answered. They discussed the war for a few minutes, then Royce added some personal news. "We just got word that Harriet's little sister is coming to live with us. She'll arrive the end of August. The country school she'd been going to lost its teacher, so we invited her to come here to continue at school. She's seventeen with only a year left, and it's important to her to finish."

Jesse remembered how hard it had been to continue his studies when they'd moved up to Dillon. He nodded as Royce continued with a chuckle, "You'd think, though, that a queen was coming for a visit. Harriet is frantically scrubbing and polishing the house from top to bottom, all that work for her sister!"

Royce assured Jesse they'd keep an eye on his place while he was gone, and they ended their encounter with another handshake. Soon, Jesse was on his way again. He smiled to discover that Dawson had left the gas tank in the pickup truck nearly full as he backed out of the livery and headed west towards MacFarlane Avenue, the street that would take him out of town and up into the Sierra Madres.

He let his mind idle, trying to put away the worries and pressure he'd felt since the lottery.

He was already past her by the time his mind registered who he'd seen. A quick glance behind him confirmed the solitary woman was Miss Webber, so he pulled the truck to the side and calmly got out.

He waited, leaning against the fender of the truck, for her to come up the sidewalk. "Good afternoon," he said with a smile when she was a few feet away.

She raised her eyes then dropped them again. "Good afternoon, Mr. Atley."

"Are you feeling better today?"

"Yes, thank you." He took a step towards her to hear her better as she continued. "I'm embarrassed at our last meeting. Thank you for your kindness to check on me, and also for rescuing me with Mrs. Wills."

It took Jesse a moment to recall that he'd spun a little tale about asking the woman for help. "You aren't appalled at how easily I can make up a lie?"

Sari smiled at the ground in response to the teasing in his voice. "I wouldn't consider it a lie, just a kind act."

There was a pause, Jesse suddenly felt uncomfortable. He searched for a topic. "You are off work this afternoon? The Copper Pot is closed Sunday evenings, correct?"

"Yes, I have the rest of the day off. I thought maybe I'd take a walk and enjoy the day. I understand the Encampment River is a nice place and not too far."

"Oh, it's about a mile or a bit more. The river bank is a nice place. The trees make it cooler than out here. The sandy river banks close to town are usually lined with fishermen and families having picnics on Sunday afternoon."

Sari was disappointed, she had looked forward to some solitude on her walk, not a crowd. She stood quietly, unsure of herself and wondering how to end their conversation when he spoke again, "Say, I was looking for some cooler air and some peace and quiet myself. I'm headed a little farther up into the mountains. Would you care to ride along with me?"

Sari felt fearful and confused. She wasn't afraid of the man in front of her exactly, but the idea of being alone and under the close scrutiny of his open gaze unnerved her. At the same time, something about his warmth lured her. "Well, I... I just don't think—"

"Miss Webber." There was a soft plea in his voice and she looked up. "Miss Webber, the last time we met I offered a friendly ear. Today, maybe I need one of those myself. I'd be thankful to have your company today." He realized as the words escaped that they were true, in spite of what he'd told Claire earlier.

They stood, eyes touching, for what felt like a long time. She answered softly then dropped her gaze, "I'd enjoy a drive very much."

He opened the passenger door for her and waited until she was situated before closing it and getting in on the other side. The engine sputtered to life and Jesse put the truck into gear and pulled out. There was only a smattering of houses left on the outskirts of Encampment as he turned onto MacFarlane. The road began climbing upwards into grassy, rolling foothills.

Neither of them spoke again as the town fell away below and behind them. Jesse glanced at his passenger several times as he drove. She wore a green cotton dress tied with a wide ribbon at her thin waist. Auburn hair fell in a tangle of curls down her back, but a few strands broke free from the rest and danced in the wind as they drove. She looked contented, though she wasn't smiling, and her hands rested comfortably in her lap. She watched raptly out the window, taking in the passing scenery.

The hill they climbed was steep, and the engine of the truck toiled loudly. They were nearly at the top of the rise when Jesse broke the noisy silence between them. "I'm going to stop just up here at the top of this hill. It'll give the truck a minute to cool down, and you can see the view."

Sari nodded but didn't reply.

Jesse pulled over soon after. He left the truck running, and got out. He started around to open her door, but by the time he got there, she'd opened it herself and had her feet on the ground. She walked a few steps toward the top of the hill and looked back towards Encampment. Jesse followed and the two stood side-by-side.

"This is stunning," she said.

"You've never been up here?"

She shook her head, "No, I haven't."

Jesse began pointing out landmarks. "That is Encampment, of course. It stretches out from where we started the climb all the way over to those trees way down there. If you follow that snake of trees over there, you can see the path the Encampment River takes. Keep following it way past Encampment and you can see Riverside." He pointed, making sure she'd found the spot.

After a minute, Sari pointed to a spot on the opposite side of Encampment up from Riverside. "That looks like a huge set of buildings down there, but they look funny. What is that?"

"It was the Encampment smelter. Do you know anything about the history of this area?"

Sari looked at him and shook her head, thankful that he was standing on her left so that he wasn't staring at her scars. She tried to forget her self-consciousness and listen to him as he explained.

"The mountains behind us are rich with copper and gold and other metals. Back in 1897 a man named Ed Haggarty—he's prospecting in Alaska right now— found a rich vein of copper way up high on the Continental Divide. He staked the claim, and through a complicated path, a mine was sunk to get the ore out." He turned to his left a little and pointed. "Do you see those towers that form a line over there, leading to Encampment?"

"Yes, I see them. There are several in town, by the Opera House and the Copper Pot. I've certainly wondered about them."

"Well, that was a tram system that the mining company built to carry the copper down from the mountains and to the smelter over there. The tram carried buckets of ore about sixteen miles from the mine down here."

"Wow. That's remarkable. But, I'm not sure what a smelter is, and why does it look so strange?"

"This smelter was a set of buildings where the copper ore was processed. First, they crushed the rock with big crushing machines, then they put that into furnaces that melted the copper out and separated it from everything else. Then, the copper was formed into bars and sent away. The smelter looks the way it does because it burned. All that's left are the foundations and a few walls."

"So the mine is closed?" Sari asked. Jesse nodded and she continued. "Did they close when the copper ran out?"

"Nope. There's still plenty of copper up there. No, the mine closed because the people who bought it from Haggarty and his original partners were a combination of over-hopeful and a bit devious and they got the company in debt. Then copper prices fell, the smelter burnt down, and everything fell apart."

The pair returned to the truck as Jesse continued. "My sister Claire and her husband Daniel came here so Daniel could be the engineer for the biggest mine up on the divide. It's called Rudefeha. I came to live with them just a year after Haggarty started the mine, so we've been around to watch all the changes."

"So you lived up there? It's hard to imagine towns among those peaks, the mountains look very formidable."

Jesse laughed. "That's a great word for them." He put the truck into gear and continued away from Encampment. "There were actually several towns up there. We lived in Dillon, the largest. It was about a mile from the big mine." He regaled her with several stories of living in Dillon.

"Does anyone still live in Dillon?" Sari asked.

"No," Jesse's voice was quiet and tinged with sadness, and Sari turned to look at him. "When the mine closed, everyone moved away. Daniel and I boarded up the house, we brought down some things and left most of the furniture, and just left. Daniel and Claire still own the house, and in the summers Dan usually takes the boys up there for a week or so."

"Do you ever go with them?"

"Yes, I try to. I love it up there. We went up the end of May this year for a few days. I hoped to get back up there again, but it doesn't look like I will." Jesse didn't want to pursue his thoughts in that direction, so he launched into a light-hearted description of using snowshoes and skis to get around town on a normal day in the winter. Soon, the road curved and they found themselves in pine trees and aspens.

"Do you see those run-down buildings over there?" Sari nodded at his question and Jesse continued. "That is the former town of Ellwood. It's a ghost town now that the mine is closed, but about a hundred people used to live here. Freight that needed to come up to the mine and the towns around it all came through here. In the winter, they'd use this livery station to put snowshoes on the horse's hooves so they could make it up higher."

Sari chuckled at the thought of a horse with snowshoes. "I've never heard of such a thing."

"Not every horse is willing or smart enough to walk with them. None of my horses were ever trained for them. It is impressive to watch a team using them."

"How long have you been involved in the livery business, Mr. Atley?" Sari asked.

Jesse recounted how he had worked at liveries first in Encampment then in Dillon. "I learned to be a teamster living in Dillon. I spent a lot of time watching freighters, especially one named Jack Fulkerson. Beside my brother-in-law Daniel, G-String Jack was my hero growing up. I'd watch him handle twenty mules or his beautiful team of white horses, freighting everything from dynamite to cable from the valley up to the mine. He never sat in the wagon, always on the animal closest to the wagon on the left side. That's where he got his nick name G-string. He had such steely nerves and a perfect rapport with his teams."

The awe in Jesse's voice was unmistakable. As she listened, Sari realized that this man's honest and earnest manner along with his easy banter and warm spirit had made her feel more at ease with another person than she could remember being in a long while.

The truck struggled as it crisscrossed up one side and down the other of several steep grades. Finally, Jesse steered off to a small clearing at the side of the road, braked and turned off the engine.

"This is called Lost Treasure Gulch. It's a nice little spot. Since we moved back to Encampment, I like to come here just to smell the mountains and hear the quiet. Feel free to look around."

They got out. Sari stepped away from the truck and let the tranquility of the forest engulf her. The tinkling of water called to her and she walked through the mountain flowers and grass to the bank of a creek barely two feet wide. Comfortable in the welcoming solitude, Sari let peace saturate her. She watched the water run merrily over rocks smoothed and polished by the constant flow and breathed deeply the fresh, earthy smell of the forest floor. She walked idly along the creek bank, not thinking. Soon, she came to the thick trunk of a fallen log. She delighted in an odd-shaped group of mushrooms sprouting from the underside of one branch, then moved to a portion of the trunk that was covered in dappled sunlight. She sat down and closed her eyes.

Jesse watched as his companion moved away from the truck towards the creek. Satisfied that she was enjoying her own moment, he stepped across the creek with one large stride and climbed a short rise toward an outcropping of rocks. He often day-dreamed of this spot, especially when troubles crowded him. He'd set off today with this spot in mind, hoping to refresh and secure the memory of its welcome serenity to last when he went off to war.

Michael's question from the other night echoed in his thoughts. He answered it again, honestly for himself now, *No, I'm not scared. I'm terrified. I'm afraid that I'll die on some unknown ground and be forgotten before I've ever given this world anything of value.* His thoughts turned to prayer. *God, I trust the plans You have for me. I trust Your Will. Thank you that my soul is secure with you because of the sacrifice Jesus made for me. I'm pretty confused, though, about how I'm supposed to serve You and further Your kingdom by going to the other side of the world with the intent of killing others. I guess what I need is Your leading hand to show me the way.*

Jesse sat for a few more minutes, letting his mind remain blank. After a while, his stomach growled. Thinking that his guest might be waiting for him and counting him rude for leaving her for so long, he got up and followed the creek back in the direction of the truck.

She wasn't there. Calmly, he set off slowly in the direction he'd last seen her. It didn't take long before he spotted the green of her dress through a stand of aspen trees. He didn't want to startle her, so he called to her and worked his way to where she stood.

He came up on her left side as she stood facing a thick, white barked birch tree. She stepped to keep him at her side, then said quietly, "I've just discovered these interesting carvings on many of these trees. Who put them here?"

Jesse studied the tree for a moment. Etched in the bark at about eye level were the words: Eusabio Spain 1904. "Oh, carving on these trees is a common pastime for sheepherders in the area. Lots of ranchers bring their sheep up to graze for the summer, and they hire Basques to stay up here. Often you can see sheep wagons or run across a herd being guarded by several dogs and a herder. Sheep herding is a lonely job and unless there's a bear, coyote, or mountain lion, there isn't much to do, so they carve a record that they were here. Sometimes you'll see more than one date on a tree showing the fellow was here more than one summer. The birch trees scar over and heal so that the carvings are protected until the tree dies."

As soon as the words were out of his mouth, he was horrified. His companion dropped her head, looked down, and turned away. Jesse froze, unsure how to apologize without making it worse. She'd gone several steps when he found his voice.

"Miss Webber, I'm sorry. What I said was insensitive, and I didn't think. Please forgive me."

Sari retreated inside, uncomfortable and wishing she could just disappear. She murmured something he couldn't hear and began walking toward the truck.

He watched her take two more steps. Suddenly he was irritated. He was angry at himself for ruining the moment, but also at her. He ran to catch up with her. "Just wait. This is the second time we've met and the second time you've walked away from me. How are we ever supposed to be friends if you keep leaving?"

She turned halfway around, keeping her head low and letting her hair cover most of her face. "Friend? You want to be friends?"

"Of course I do, and I didn't intend to say anything mean. I was talking about *trees* for heaven's sake. I'm sorry that my words had two edges."

Sari watched him warily, fighting an inner battle. Her first inclination was to run and hide away in a safe solitude that disincluded words that hit so close to her hurt, but at the same time, she searched his face and her own feelings and realized that he probably did not mean to ridicule her. "Mr. Atley, there are certain things I'm sensitive about, and I react quickly when I feel like I'm being judged."

He took two steps closer and put his hands, palms up, out in front of him in a gesture of surrender. "My sister Claire has never accused me of thinking before I speak. I truly am sorry, I really was only talking about the trees. Forgive me?"

She hesitated, then shrugged and smiled slightly. She didn't look up, though. "I forgive you." Her words were tentative, and both of them wondered if she meant them.

He took two more steps toward her, stopping when he was directly in front of her. She was uncomfortable, but stayed rooted to her spot. "I want to be friends. I have lots of faults, and you've just encountered one of them. I have a big mouth I don't always keep under control, and that fact embarrasses me. I have lots of other faults as well, and the longer we know each other, the more of them you will see." He paused, knowing what he wanted to say next.

With trepidation, he continued, his voice soft and gentle. "When I notice a tree like one of those back there, I consider how the marks serve as a record, a history. I don't blame the tree. I've wondered sometimes how that tree survived the cruelty of the carving, and how it can continue to reach upward, to grow and be beautiful." He watched her face then continued, "I have lots of scars of my own, to tell the truth. But mine are mostly on the inside where people can't see them. As a friend, I hope you'll accept me with all those faults, and believe me when I tell you that's what I'm offering you."

She swallowed hard, willing herself not to cry, then answered, "Those are beautiful thoughts, Mr. Atley. Acceptance is something I've not experienced since the death of my parents. It might take me a while to believe them and to put it into safe practice."

"But you'll try?"

She looked up at him and smiled then, a smile made crooked by scars, but beautiful in its own way. "Yes, I'll try."

Jesse nodded, and they turned to walk side by side back towards the truck. They were both relieved to have the scene behind them and walked together in silence for several yards.

"I didn't expect to have company for this afternoon," Jesse said at last. "but I did bring a little to eat. It isn't much, but will you share my picnic with me?"

"I am a little hungry. I hadn't intended to be gone this long either. Thank you. I'd love to join you, Mr. Atley."

They sat on the tailgate of the truck. Jesse opened the canvas bag holding his lunch. He broke the bread into two halves and handed her one of them. Then, he retrieved the knife from his pocket, opened the blade, and cut off a slice of cheese and offered it to her. They ate in silence for a minute. Then Jesse spoke up again, "Since we've agreed to be friends, I think the first thing we should do to celebrate is to begin addressing one another a little less formally. I'm Jesse."

Sari nodded and smiled tentatively. "I think that's a good idea. My name is Sari."

"Well, Sari, tell me what you think of my mountains."

Later that night, safely tucked away in her little room, Sari replayed the day again and again. She tried to find a reason to distrust Jesse. She thought about the encounters she'd had at Miss Milton's when a girl would pretend to be her friend for a while only to use her or set her up as the butt of a cruel joke. She thought about Meredith at work, confident that her workmate was of similar ilk, and intent on eventual cruelty. No matter how critically she viewed this afternoon, though, she could find no portent of something bad to come. She just couldn't recognize any guile in Mr. Atley—Jesse she corrected herself. Certainly, the idea of having a friend enticed her. Actually, she didn't expect they'd spend much time together, especially since he'd told her about being drafted and that he was leaving soon, but she went to sleep gratified at his gracious offer of friendship.

Jesse sat on his front porch for a long time before he went to bed that evening as well. He, too, replayed the afternoon, wondering why God would choose now that he was leaving to bring someone into his life like this. Jesse knew that he wasn't in love with the girl, they'd only met, but inexplicably, he felt protective of her and for the first time wondered if love might someday be possible for him. As he slipped into bed, he whispered a prayer for guidance, then he turned out the light and slept well.

Encampment, Wyoming
late July, 1917

At seven fifteen on Thursday evening, Jesse was on his way home from Claire and Daniel's. Claire had fixed a nice supper, all his favorites including rhubarb pie, but Jesse was restless. They'd asked him to stay, but he couldn't. He felt tense and irritable and knew he wasn't good company, so he'd kissed Claire's cheek and promised the boys he'd be back tomorrow night. His thoughts were like a dust devil, whirling, spewing pebbles and dirt that kept him from seeing clearly, tearing at him from all directions. He'd felt this way all day. Urgency assailed him. He walked with a quick, even stride, not really seeing his surroundings but instead going over for the hundredth time all he needed to finish in the next few days.

He was a block from home when he stopped, so caught up in himself that he didn't notice the clear stars overhead or the thick, sweet smell from the overgrown rosebush he skirted. *I don't want to go home,* he thought. *I don't know what I want.* A few minutes later he found himself on Winchell Avenue heading north towards the 'sporting district.' While Jesse wasn't much of a drinker, he decided that a beer would taste good, *And maybe it will settle my mind a little.*

The Royal Bodega was nearly empty. Relieved, Jesse said hello to A.J. Rosander, the proprietor, asked for a beer, then carried his mug to a table at one side. He settled in, sipping and trying to relax his tense shoulders and his mind.

His thoughts returned to a place they'd been often as the day progressed, an article from the newspaper. Jesse rubbed the back of his neck and recalled the details. Because his draft number was the second called, he was required to report to the induction center in Rawlins on Wednesday, August first. That deadline was nine days away. Daniel had agreed to drive him the sixty miles to Rawlins. Jesse had seen the hurt in Claire's eyes when he'd told her he didn't want her to go. "Claire," he'd whispered to her when she hugged him. "I love you, and it will be hard enough to say good-bye. I just can't do it there." He knew she'd understood then, when she nodded in silent assent.

Jesse took another drink and recalled the rest of the article's information. Inductees would be sent to camps set up across the country for training. Pay started at $30 a month. Jesse considered the sum. America valued its young men at a dollar per day to fight and die. Jesse winced at the thought and took another drink.

He was so lost in his reverie he didn't hear his visitor until the second time his name was called. Then, he looked up to see Chetley Wills standing in front of him, a glass of amber liquid in his hand.

"I said, do you want some company?" His smile was broad and Jesse decided that maybe the drink in the man's hand wasn't his first.

"Sure, sit down. Let's talk about anything but the news."

"I heard your number was among the first, I'm sorry to hear it."

"Thanks," he mumbled and took another drink. The men did talk then, about hay and livestock prices, the hot weather this July had brought with her. Jesse was on his second beer, compliments of his tablemate, when the conversation turned to the early success of the Copper Pot.

"Lilith and I have been really lucky. We didn't have a lot of money to stake ourselves to begin the Copper Pot. We'd been saving for years, but weren't sure we'd ever have enough to even start. One of the big problems was being able to afford to pay good help at first until the hotel began to turn a profit. Both of us wanted the restaurant to be something special, and good cooks just aren't cheap."

"All the meals I've eaten have been delicious. Looks like you worked that problem out."

"Yes, that worked out well for us. I could feel a little guilty about the whole affair, but I tell myself that she's better off with us than somewhere else."

Jesse met the man's eyes, "I don't understand."

"Well, you've met our cook, Miss Webber, right?"

Jesse nodded, suddenly uncomfortable.

"Well, it turns out that her daddy took a large cash

loan from the bank, and then was killed before he paid it back. The bank president was willing just to write it off as a loss, but that's no way for a bank to succeed. Their vice president has better business sense than his boss. He wouldn't let the loan drop. He came up with a plan to recoup the bank's money." Wills paused and finished his drink, then signaled toward the bar for another.

"The first thing they did was take the family ranch land and house. That got them a portion of the total loan. The board and the president were satisfied, and again wanted to write off the rest, but the VP wouldn't hear of it. He decided to go after the heir of the man's estate and get the rest of the money there. Thing was, since she was a child, they had to wait for her to become an adult before they could go after her."

"After years passed?" Jesse was having trouble believing that anyone would be so relentless toward a child.

"Yes. Apparently the bank kept track of her and now that she's eighteen, they've brought her back to Wyoming and pursued her for payment. When it was proven that she had no funds, they agreed she could work off the amount she owes."

"I don't understand how that involves you," Jesse struggled to grasp what the man was telling him partly because of the beer in his head, and partly because it all seemed so unfair and cruel.

"Well, at first they were just going to have her work at the bank in Rawlins, give her a small allowance and apply the rest to her debt, but—well. The girl is pretty unsavory to look at and no one wanted her at the bank. When they found out she was trained in the kitchen at that orphanage, they approached Lilith and me with a deal. We asked for a loan to get started and they had a cook, so they gave us the cook and are counting her work as our payment. It's a good deal for everyone."

Jesse was furious. He grit his teeth and spoke quietly, "Sounds like a great deal for you and the bank, but not for Miss Webber."

"Aw now. They used to indenture servants all the time. She'll work off her years, then she can do what she wants. She's a good cook, though, and since she's not marriageable, we are hoping maybe she'll decide to stay with us."

Jesse felt sick to his stomach. He finished his beer in one quick gulp and stood up. "I need to go," he muttered as he left an astonished Chetley Wills sitting at the table.

Full of new anger and renewed nervous energy, Jesse walked westward towards the edge of town. Everywhere was quiet now, and the stars were out. The graded road ended, and he struck off across the prairie, not caring where he headed but sure he couldn't sit still. The moon, which had cleared the Snowy Range and was making its way over the valley floor, was nearly full, giving him plenty of light for his trek.

In the first mile, he didn't think. Anger eddied through him and he let himself feel it. At first, he thought only about the bank in Rawlins and Wills and his wife – thinking of Sari as a means to an end, not a person. But as he continued, his rage grew to include war and the draft and being forced to leave his home. Unchecked, he railed at the world's injustices and selfishness.

The line of dusty boot prints grew behind him. Eventually his pace slowed and he began capturing his thoughts. Finally, he was at the top of a small butte about three miles from town, Jesse stopped. He surveyed the wide, gentle valley. It was light enough that he could see the shadowed trees lining the North Platte River down below. The starlit sky revealed the heavy black outline of the Snowy Range in the east. When he turned to the west, the black shadow that was Bridger Peak, tallest of all the peaks in the Sierra Madres, stood proudly. Though the moon was bright, the Milky Way was clearly visible. Its billions of stars created a bridge of soft lights from one mountain range to the other. The thick, sweet smell of sage brush enfolded him.

A coyote howled from the foothills and was answered by two more farther down the ridge. Jesse was tired and weary from the recent days' worry and his anxiety about what was to come. The hot rage he'd felt when he left the bar was cooled. His anger about Sari remained, but as a glowing coal deep down. He put aside everything as he took in the grandeur of the night.

Eventually, Jesse began to pray. Out there, alone on the prairie he felt close to his Creator and speaking aloud felt natural. With his eyes on the stars above, he began with praise and thanks. It wasn't hard to name his blessings. Then, he talked about his faults, asking forgiveness and strength to let go everything that hindered him from being what God intended. The night grew quiet again. Jesse was silent while he listened.

Then his voice broke the silence again, "Father, you know that I'm not afraid to die in war. You have Your hand on my soul, and it's Yours. But God, what I am afraid of is not having contributed anything to this world. I'm just not sure that I've accomplished the job You sent me to do. Standing in front of You when I get up there and finding out I didn't complete my task, now that is one thing that does scare me. Show me, please what I need to do.

"And now, now that I have to leave here, you've brought a woman into things. You made sure I was aware of what has been done to her—is being done right now—and I'm just not sure what You want me to do with this. God, I like her, but don't have strong romantic feelings for her, and I hope that it isn't because of the way she looks. I hope I'm better than that, Lord. Please let it be because I barely know her. Anyway, God please show me what You want me to do."

He let go of all words and thoughts then. He didn't know how long he stood, a solitary shadow on the prairie. He hadn't expected to hear a Voice or see a Messenger. He was satisfied with the comfort that came to him from the peace and the soft darkness.

The clock on his mantle claimed it was nearly three when he finally walked through his living room and up the stairs to his small bedroom. He kicked off his boots, slid out of his clothes, then welcomed the caress of his feather bed. He slept soundly.

Before he knew it, and certainly before anyone felt ready, Jesse stood holding Claire in a long hug on the front porch. He whispered quietly, "No tears now, okay?

I'll be in training for at least a few months, and I'll write so you can write to me. I'll not be in harm's way, so there's nothing to worry about." He felt Claire nod, but when they separated, her cheeks were wet.

The drive to Rawlins was dusty and quiet. Daniel tried to make conversation, but it was clear Jesse wasn't up for small talk, so they made the trip without many words. Main Street in front of the county building was busier than usual when they drove up. Daniel had agreed to simply drop Jesse off and return to Encampment. Neither looked forward to saying farewell, and they didn't want to prolong it. Jesse retrieved his carpetbag from the back seat and put it on the sidewalk beside him. He stood stoic, meeting Daniel's gaze without words. At a loss, Jesse offered his hand to the man who was both brother and father to him. Daniel shook his head and then embraced Jesse. "I love you, and my prayers are with you, Jess."

Jesse returned the embrace, then stepped back. He nodded, ran the back of his hand over his eyes, then picked up his bag and walked away. It was a tough parting for both men.

Daniel watched until Jesse disappeared into the building, then got back in his car and drove through his own tears back towards Claire and home.

From the moment he entered the Courthouse Building in Rawlins, raw with emotion after saying good-bye to Daniel, until he slipped into his bunk for the first time at Fort Riley, Kansas' cantonment center, Jesse weathered a constant onslaught of new experiences full of excitement and fear, blessing and foreboding.

His first stop inside the Rawlins Court House building had been at the end of a long line down one corridor to complete his physical. The doctor, one of the local general practitioners in Rawlins, listened to his heart and lungs with his cold stethoscope, checked the straightness of his back, the health of his feet, hands and mouth, and asked a few questions. He finished by signing a form stating Jesse was fit and ready for military service.

Next, Jesse was ushered down another corridor to one of the courtrooms, where a clerk checked his name off a list and asked him to sit down. Jesse surveyed the room. It held perhaps a hundred men, some familiar and some strangers, most of them dusty-looking farmers or ranchers. Jesse noted that some looked 'stricken and scared, some resigned, some excited. Each face mirrored one of the emotions he felt inside.

They hadn't waited long when a bailiff entered the room and called for all to stand. They complied quietly as a judge dressed in a black robe entered the room. He made a few remarks about the great service the men were about to embark upon then asked them to raise their right hands and take the induction oath. They repeated the oath of office. Then, with no more ceremony, the judge thanked the men and then left the room. A tall man in an Army uniform walked smartly to the front of the courtroom as the new soldiers took their seats. He waited for them to get settled, then introduced himself as Lieutenant Walters. He welcomed them to the army and lined out what they might expect in the next few weeks of training and preparation.

After the introduction, the men were directed to a series of waiting rooms to await the completion of their intake.

Jesse found a seat in one of the rooms and settled in to wait. A few minutes later, a familiar face came down the hall and perched in the chair next to him.

"Jesse Atley, I thought I saw you when I was on the steps outside. How are you?"

They shook hands as Jesse answered, "Wilbur Toothaker, good to see you. You got called up right away also, I see." Jesse had done some hauling for Wilbur's father out at their Beaver Creek Ranch. Jesse had come to know well Wilbur's mischievous grin and tendency to find adventure for himself by frequently running away to engage in some new occupation or event. His quick laugh and sense of humor made Wilber an easy friend.

"I didn't see any of your family out front, did you come from Encampment by yourself?" Wilber asked.

"No. Daniel brought me and just dropped me off."

Toothaker nodded slowly. "I understand. Mama

and Papa and my sister Alice brought me in from Walcott. They stayed brave, but leaving is hard." His voice buckled with strain. Finally, he finished his sentence. "I just stood there and watched while they disappeared when they drove away. T'weren't an easy moment." The men were silent, each fighting for his own calm. "Guess we are all invited for a banquet tonight at the Ferris Mansion," Wilber said at last.

Jesse was surprised at this news. "I hadn't heard."

"You haven't been in to get your orders yet, then?"

Jesse shook his head. "No, I just finished with the doc."

"They'll be calling you in soon, I expect, to give you your official orders. Looks like we are all going to be part of Company C of the 316th Combat Engineers. That's a fancy name for being on the front line, isn't it?" His rhetorical question fell hard between them. After a few moments, Wilbur continued, "They're sending us to Fort Lewis, Washington for training. Our train leaves tonight at 10:15, but before that the county put together a thank you banquet for us at the Ferris House."

Jesse opened his mouth to reply just as his name was called by a short, sturdy man in uniform. He turned to Toothaker, "I'll see you tonight if not sooner."

Jesse followed the uniform down the hall. They took one turn, then his guide motioned Jesse into an office of the right. Jesse was then directed to a seat across from Lieutenant Walters, who was sitting behind a desk strewn with papers and files. The officer rifled through a file for a moment, then looked up.

"You are Jesse Atley, correct?"

"Yes, Sir."

"Well, Atley, I am happy to have your file come across my desk. I've been looking for the past few days for inductees with your skills to fill a few empty billets I've been notified of."

Jesse wasn't sure how to answer. He wasn't sure he understood.

The officer studied another set of papers, then continued, "I hope you won't be too upset not to join the other Wyoming boys who are destined for the Engineer Corps of the 91st Division. There's a need in another division for men skilled with horses. Your file says you have a livery business and are a blacksmith. Is this correct?"

Again Jesse answered, "Yes, Sir."

"Good, you are being assigned, along with a few other horsemen, to a cavalry division. Your train is scheduled for seven-oh-five tomorrow morning. You will be transported to the Fort Riley, Kansas training center."

Jesse took in the information, unsure whether or not this was good news. Without looking up the officer continued, "Private Atley, based on your age and this recommendation from the mayor in Encampment," he lifted a paper and then returned it to the file, "I am making you the man in charge of your traveling group. You will carry all the paperwork and hold your group's files, tickets and meal vouchers for the trip from here to Cheyenne, on to Denver, then to Kansas. You need to keep an eye on the inductees as you travel. Be at the train station by six thirty tomorrow morning. One of my men will be there by the ticket agent's office to meet you. He will have all the files and paperwork you will need, and he will help as your group checks in at the station. See the purser at the end of the hall and show him these orders. He will hand you a voucher you can use for a room for tonight and breakfast tomorrow. You are free to go get checked in. The banquet at the Ferris House begins at seven this evening. All right then, you are dismissed."

Jesse followed his instructions. Within an hour he found himself alone in a nice, though small, hotel room near the train depot. The sadness and anxiety he'd felt saying goodbye to his family was pushed into the back of his mind as he wondered about what his future held. Jesse had read enough to know that Wilbur was right and the Engineering Divisions were destined to populate the front lines. Knowing he wasn't assigned to one was a relief, yet Jesse didn't know anything about the group to which he was assigned, and he hoped he hadn't been pulled from the frying pan in favor of the fire.

Jesse had never been to the Ferris house before. The mansion had been built by George Ferris, a Civil War veteran and one of the original stakeholders for the Rudefeha Mine. He had many interests, including mining, but the bulk of his wealth came from raising sheep in Carbon County. Ferris made a name for himself as a member of the Wyoming Constitutional Convention and later as a state legislator. Sadly, he was killed in a wagon accident while still in his prime, but his stoic and adept wife, Julia, took over as partner in the mine, continued the sheep ranching operations, and finished building the mansion she and her husband had planned.

As expected, the celebration at Ferris House was replete with music and pompous speeches by important locals. The food was good and the overall atmosphere was one of celebration and good cheer. For Jesse, the evening was bittersweet. He talked with many friends, customers, and acquaintances from the area, most of whom would be boarding the 10:15 train to Washington state. The few ladies present were dressed beautifully, and the men were jovial and happy. Spirits were generally high, yet also present at the gala was the hovering awareness that many would never come home and that life as they'd always known it, along with friendships, were ending tonight with a finality of time and war.

At nine thirty, Jesse joined the crowd, walking beside Wilbur Toothaker, in a solemn parade from the mansion to the depot. The two friends exchanged addresses at the depot, thankful that the orders they'd been given included that information, and promised to keep in touch. They shook hands and Jesse watched as Wilbur joined the flow of men onto the train.

Jesse stood back, out of the bustle, and watched as the train filled and finally pulled out of the station. Then he set out for the hotel, feeling hollow and suddenly very alone. The feeling intensified after he'd closed the door to his room. To fight the long night ahead, he sat down at the small desk and wrote Claire and Daniel a letter, describing the day, telling them about his orders, and giving them his address. He sealed the envelope and sat in the quiet. He jotted a quick postcard with his address to John Peryam who was in training in California. With each pen stroke, the walls felt as if they were moving toward him. Willing himself to be calm, he got ready for bed.

Later, wide awake in the dark, he concentrated on a place on Haggarty Creek near Dillon that he'd loved when they'd lived up there. Deliberately, he searched his memory and recreated the scene with as much detail as he could. He tried to hear the water as it splashed across the rocks and smell the cool green grass that lined the bank. Finally, he drifted to sleep.

The next morning, Jesse arrived at the depot early. The purser approached him, nodded, then handed Jesse two brown envelopes. "Atley, here are the documents you need," he explained. "The thick packet contains all the paperwork for you. You are not to open that one, you'll just hand it over when you get to Fort Riley. In this envelope," the purser indicated the smaller packet, "are your travel documents. On the top there is your itinerary. Don't miss any trains, if you do there will be trouble. You are responsible for these men. You are travelling on one ticket for sixteen men. When you board each train, identify yourself to the conductor. You will need to familiarize yourself with the men enough to point them out to the conductor so they can verify their passage. You have meal vouchers here for each of you for Cheyenne, where you have about a four-hour stopover, and a second set of vouchers for the men to have a meal in Denver. There won't be any other stops until you get to Fort Riley. An Army representative will meet you at the Fort Riley station and will take over from there."

"Um, may I ask why the lieutenant chose me? He mentioned a recommendation, but I wasn't aware of any."

The man smiled briefly. "The lieutenant is very astute at searching out men with potential. He contacted the mayors' offices in nearby cities and asked for recommendations of outstanding citizens who we should be looking out for. Encampment's mayor, I believe his name is Rankin, spoke highly of you. A second consideration was your age. Clearly, you are older than most of these men and therefore likely mature enough to take charge. Last, meeting you yesterday confirmed for the lieutenant that you would be the right choice. You impressed him. He told me it was clear "You hadn't just stepped off a plow.""

The answer resulted in a chuckle from both the purser and from Jesse. He handed the packets to Jesse and turned away, then turned back. "Young man, I'm not supposed to tell you this, but since the Army is taking on so many at one time, promotions are going to come to those who prove themselves able. Delivering your group smartly will likely draw the positive attention of the officers and higher enlisteds as soon as you get to Kansas. The faster you make rank right now, the better it will be for you." He studied Jesse to make sure his advice was understood. When Jesse nodded and offered his thanks and his hand, the man smiled again and they shook hands. "Good luck to you."

The journey went smoothly. The men were all cooperative and cordial, and by the time they arrived at the Denver station, they had become a band of companions. When they left Denver, it was apparent that there were several other groups like theirs traveling. One group came aboard the train with several of the men carrying whiskey bottles. As the miles clacked over the rails, the liquid in the bottles diminished and voices filled with bravado and spirits increased. They began to tease each other, then noticed another, smaller group of men seated in their car. It wasn't long before insults and brags were all anyone could hear. Jesse, worried that there could be trouble, quietly suggested to his group that they'd be smart to change cars. Without making it obvious, a few of them at a time sauntered to the rear car until they all had moved.

Several miles disappeared behind them when a haggard, tired-faced conductor entered their car. He looked around and nodded to Jesse. "That set of hellions in the next car has been pummeling each other for the last ten minutes. They are making quite a mess, and I swear, the Army is going to pay for the damages. I appreciate it that you got yourselves out of the fray." He said it loud enough that the whole group heard. When he'd left, Jesse heard a chorus of thanks from his companions for his foresight.

The flat Kansas countryside slipped past the train windows, unremarkable except for unrelenting miles of corn. The fields rushed by, lulling them into nothingness.

Jesse was dozing when the conductor came through to announce they'd be at the Fort Riley station in about fifteen minutes. Jesse thanked him, then looked around. His fellow travelers were all sitting in a loose group in the front of the car, no one else was nearby. "Um, Fellas," he began and fifteen faces turned to him. "Before we left Rawlins, the purser gave me some advice I want to pass on to you. He said that because of the draft and the fact that the Army is getting so many new soldiers so fast, being promoted will mostly be merit based."

"What's that mean?" asked a sleepy voice two rows back.

"It means that if you prove yourself responsible and reliable and show that you have a good head on your shoulders, then instead of staying among the bottom rungs, you are more likely to be promoted and put into positions of leadership. I don't like the idea of just being cannon fodder for the Germans, so I'm going to do all I can to show the officers and higher-ups that I'm worth more than that. I'm just passing that thought on to you."

He heard several thanks before he continued. "I'd like to make sure that when we get off this train and meet with the men who are going to be making our assignments, we show them that men from Wyoming need to be noticed. I was thinking, if we get off the train and then line up in four rows of four, looking smart and ready, then maybe we'll get their attention from the beginning."

Half an hour later, Jesse and the Wyoming inductees stood quietly in rank and file on one end of the platform while civilian passengers retrieved their belongings from the porters and left. The other groups of inductees roamed around. The loudest group simply transferred their drunken behavior to the platform. The train station was general chaos for a few minutes. Jesse spotted four men in Army uniforms standing against the station building, talking quietly among themselves. The conductor spotted them, too, and approached the men with determined steps. From where they stood, the Wyoming men couldn't hear what was being discussed, but it didn't take long for the conductor to point them out, nodding and smiling. They watched as his face turned dark and his gestures more animated as he pointed to the rowdy group.

Soon, the four uniformed men split apart. The taller of the four came directly to the formation at the platform's end. "Who is the yeoman for this group?"

Jesse stepped forward one pace. "Here, Sir. Name's Atley."

"Where are y'all from, Atley? Do you have your papers?"

"Wyoming, Sir." He handed over the packet he'd been carrying.

The man nodded to Jesse, who stepped back into line, then he addressed the entire group. "I'm Sergeant Maycomb. I'll be your training officer for the next few months. Men, I've spent the last six days picking up groups of new inductees, and you are the first to come through that look like you are ready to go to work. I thank you. Usually, I would accompany you to the cantonment center, but it just so happens that this evening it looks like we are going to have our hands full over there," he jerked his head towards the other end of the platform. The men watched where his other three companions, whose shouts were going mostly unheeded, were working to find order in the bedlam. "Anyways, there's a truck with a wagon out front that you fellas can go get on. Atley, tell the driver not to wait once all your men are aboard, tell him that we'll be marching the rest of these yahoos up to camp to get some of the mischief out of them. Ask him to take you to the Company J tent. When you get there, each of you pick a cot and get whatever bags you brought stowed away. Atley, as the platoon leader, I want you in the first cot on the right side. Stay close to your barracks tent. The latrine is out behind if you need it. I'll be along shortly."

With that, the sergeant hurried away, leaving Jesse and the Wyoming troops to follow his directions.

9
Encampment, Wyoming
mid- August, 1917

In all her seventeen years, Beatrice Reid had never been wholly comfortable on her family's remote ranch. It wasn't that she'd been an unhappy or uncooperative child, it was more of an underlying assurance in her soul that this was not the life she was intended for. Her parents, Clarence and Eileen Reid, were kind but unimaginative people, satisfied with the hard requirements of homesteading dry, sagebrush covered flatland at the base of the Sierra Madres just fifteen miles west of Encampment. That they found their satisfaction with tending their land, caring for the sheep and children they raised, and having enough food on the table was a puzzle for Bea.

Bea, for her part, was a mystery to her parents as well. She never complained or shirked her chores, but they could feel her unrest. Bea's mother didn't understand the hours her youngest could while away with her nose in a book when there were lambs to enjoy and clouds to study. Neither could she fathom Bea's constant curiosity, her never ending questions of *why* and *how*. Bea's eternal musings of *what if* disrupted Eileen's solitude and tried her patience.

When Clarence and Eileen came to the realization that Bea was not ever going to settle in to ranch life and that the sky and the prairie would never satisfy her, they shrugged their shoulders with love and resignation and looked around for something that would. The final straw came when the country school near them shut its doors. After that, it didn't take long to decide to move their youngest into town. Now, knowing that their decision was for the best, Eileen piloted their dented old truck over the ruts of the two-track road that would convey them to the highway and then into Encampment.

As she drove, Eileen thought about her children. Her first three were boys, Clancy, Russell, and Harlan. They were cut from the same cloth as their father. They were hard working men with good common sense and few words. Clancy worked in Rawlins as a guard at the penitentiary, while the other two had found wives and homesteaded ground not far away from the ranch. Their youngest boy, fifteen-year-old Chance, was already taller than his mother and happily doing a man-sized day's work on the ranch. Chance loved the ranch, and Eileen and Clarence fully expected him to stay on with them, slowly stepping in and taking over as they slowed down.

There were three girls. Her oldest, Harriet, was tenderhearted and kind. She and Beatrice had been close for a long time, so her willingness to take her youngest sister in hadn't been a surprise. Eileen mentally shook her head as her thoughts touched her youngest. She knew the move would be good for talkative, energetic Bea, and therefore Eileen felt no guilt at the relief she felt as she anticipated the quieter, calmer ranch house she'd be returning to. Eileen glanced over Bea's head at her middle daughter. Nineteen-year-old year old Addy, the family cook, sat dozing beside her sister despite the rough ride. Eileen had relinquished control of the kitchen to her middle daughter some years ago, and she dreaded next spring when Addy would marry Merle Overstreet and move away to her own ranch house out near Elk Mountain. Eileen comforted herself at the idea of being stuck in the kitchen with the fact that there would only be three family members remaining at home by the time Addy left. Cooking for Clarence, herself, and Chance wouldn't keep her inside too long each day she hoped. She harbored a hope that Chance would marry young and bring his wife to the ranch so that she could once again be unchained from the drudgery of being inside.

Bea was elated to be leaving home, excited she was on her way to becoming a 'town girl'. She didn't mind that she was scrunched between her bony, angled mother and her soft and ample sister Addy, her legs straddling the gear shift. As one of seven, she was used to being mashed between her siblings. For once, she didn't mind that the road was too rough for reading, and spent the miles watching the prairie fly by.

Bea bounced along joyfully in the middle seat. Her voice was quiet, but her thoughts flew as she watched the prairie pass the windows of the truck. They made the wide, sweeping turn that took them towards the highway and Bea sat forward in the seat. They were still on ranch property, traversing what they usually called the upper acres. Bea craned her neck to the east to see if she could catch a glimpse of the charred remains of the house that used to stand there. Memories from ten years ago flooded her mind.

The winter Bea turned seven was a hard one for the family as blizzard after blizzard howled across the prairie. Locked inside, everyone became restive. Bea's sister Harriet fought the boredom by teaching Bea to read. Using the older kids' school primers, both girls enjoyed their makeshift school. For the first time, Bea was the center of someone's attention, not just in the way. Reading wasn't a difficult task for her, and Bea caught on quickly. By the time the snow melted and spring gained a foothold across the ranch, Bea and Harriet had grown a close friendship and Bea began a romance with the written word.

Once the family was freed from the confines of the ranch house and the clan began going about their outdoor chores, life threatened to return to its old pattern. Once again, Bea found herself more and more often alone. She minded it even less than before, though, since she now had books to keep her company. Then, in May, something extraordinary happened.

The blessing had just been said and plates served when Ma and Pa began a discussion that Bea didn't understand at first.

"I just couldn't believe that there weren't more folks interested in it," Pa was saying.

Clancy, oldest of the boys, took a mouthful of potatoes then said, "They didn't advertise it much, I'm glad I saw that flyer when I was in Wolcott."

"Me, too. We got a good deal, I'll warrant that." Pa smiled.

Ma broke in then, "I expect you'll want to go over there and survey the area and check the grass land."

Pa nodded. "Yup, sound's like the old owners were running sheep on it, so fences should be in good shape. We'll have to check them to make sure, of course, before we turn any animals out on it. From the walk I took around the place after the auction I know there's a small stream running through the property. I'm thinking Harlan and I will see about adding a spreader dam to help increase the grass production in that section. I imagine it's going to take us several days. Since there's a house on the property, I was thinking of taking Harriet also. She could do the cooking, and maybe do some work at the house besides."

Harriet lifted her head and nodded enthusiastically. Ma agreed to the plan when Harriet spoke up. "Um, Pa, how about we take Bea with us? She could help me in the house and I'd keep an eye on her."

Ben hesitated. "Well, it isn't going to be just a time for play, I expect we'll all have a lot to do."

Harriet winked at Bea beside her and answered, "We'll work hard, won't we Bea-Bea?"

Bea's eyes were large and serious as she nodded in agreement.

The adventure began the next morning at sunrise. Bea started to complain when Harriet shook her awake. "Fine, I'll just leave you here then and you won't get to go with us," was all she said, but it was enough to spur Bea into action. She dressed quickly, hurried through a breakfast of toast and bacon, and was waiting beside the wagon when Pa and Harlan came out of the house.

Before that morning, Bea had only been away from the ranch house a few times. This was an adventure, then, of huge proportion. She didn't mind the bumpy roughness as they trundled over the two-track road. It was nearly noon when they came in sight of the house. "We've been riding over our new land for a while," Pa explained to Harlan. "This property is a hundred and sixty acres, and its north boundary butts up against our southern line. On our ride this morning, we haven't ever left our own land. That made it a perfect purchase for us."

Harlan looked around with a controlled scowl.

"It would have been easier to just take the county road," he commented.

Pa ignored his son's disapproval and answered, "We could of, but I wanted to check out a route inside our land instead. Plus, I don't like having the horses on the big road."

Harriet didn't want to have the two argue, so she changed the subject, "Pa, how much land in all do we own. Are we rich?"

Pa shrugged his shoulders and let out a grunt. "Rich, no. But we are lucky. Your Ma and I each set a claim to three hundred eighty acres. So how much is that?"

Harriet thought for a minute than answered. "The two together are seven hundred sixty acres."

"Right, now add a hundred sixty more, which is what this new land is."

"It equals nine hundred and twenty acres."

"Right. There's six hundred forty acres in a square mile, so we own well over a square mile of land. That gives us plenty of room to run about twice the sheep we have now."

The numbers flying over her head didn't mean much to Bea, but the house that was slowly growing closer in front of them did. Tucked into the bottom of a wide, gentle bowl, the white, two-story house sported a red door and blue shutters. A short, white picket fence around a yard in the front added to its charm. Bea stared, wondering if there could ever be a nicer place to live.

Harriet's eyes were riveted to the house as well. As they drove alongside the pickets, Harlan voiced what Harriet had been thinking, "Does Ma know this house looks like this?"

"Like what?" Ben tried to ignore the obvious appreciation in his son's question.

Harlan sighed. "Does she know that this is a really nice place? She always says that someday she's going to save enough to be able to paint the ranch house."

"Pa?" Bea spoke up. "Can we move here and live here always?"

Ben answered with smiling eyes as he stepped down from the wagon. "Well, your ma hasn't seen it yet. Let's spend a few nights here and see how it feels. We got nothing to attend to right now except fixing fences and putting in that spreader dam."

"Pa," Bea asked, "What's a spreader dam?"

"Well, it's a small dam used to divert the water from the stream. Harlan and I will dig a trench and pile rocks up in the stream bed to create it."

"Why?"

"The dam will make the water spread out along a wide swath of the floor of the vale. That will help grass to grow farther out and give the sheep more to eat." Pa turned his attention to his son and added, "Harlan, help the girls carry in our supplies. I'm going to get the horses unhitched from the wagon and saddled up. Then you and I are going to go to work checking fences. Harriet, we'll take some bread and bacon with us for lunch. While we're gone, you and Bea can get us some bed rolls laid out. I don't know if they left the cook stove here or not, so you might have to make a campfire out back to cook up dinner."

"Yes, Sir." Harriet nudged Bea with a surprised smile as they climbed the stairs to the porch. Inside, Harlan, Harriet, and Bea took a quick look around. The rooms were mostly empty. One room held a broken shelf, while the floor of another was littered with papers and several ragged, empty boxes. Harriet peeked into the kitchen and squealed. "Look at that Blue Bird stove!" A combination heating and cook stove sat, dusty and forlorn, in one corner. "That's better than any stove I've ever seen," she continued. "This is going to be fun."

Harlan sat a box with food and pots on a narrow shelf below a window. "Mind yourself when you light it. There could be nests of mice or birds in the flue, only start a little fire until you know."

"I will."

It wasn't long before the girls heard the dull thump of horses' hooves as Pa and Harlan left the yard. "Can you believe this place, Bea?"

"If this is ours, why can't we just live here?"

"I think Pa likes it here, too. Maybe we will," answered Harriet. "But, you know that he built our house all by himself when he and Ma staked their claims. We might hurt his feelings if we think this house is better."

Bea didn't understand her sister's reasoning, but didn't argue. "Can we look around some more?"

"Let's decide where we are all sleeping. We can sweep the floors and roll the beds out while we explore."

The afternoon became one of their fondest memories. Discovering the house and searching for its secrets gave them unbridled joy. The house held three bedrooms, two upstairs and one beside the kitchen downstairs. There was a dining room, a large parlor, and a bathroom on the main floor. The empty rooms echoed with their footsteps and voices, giving the impression of cavernous size. Each room provided new surprises. One of the bedrooms upstairs had cheery wallpaper sporting small yellow and white flowers set on an ivory background. Bea sat in the middle of that room in the center of a sunbeam from the afternoon sky, and wondered what it would be like to live in a house this fancy. Harriet had to call her little sister several times before Bea tore herself away from her spot and joined her sister in the kitchen.

Time flew by. The girls carried their bedrolls up to the wallpapered room and after sweeping, laid them out on the floor. Then, they carried Harlan's into the other upstairs bedroom and prepared his bed.

They decided to reserve the downstairs bedroom for Pa. "This is the last room I need to sweep," Harriet said as she leaned against the doorframe before they carried in Pa's things. Several strands of hair had escaped from the bun at the nape of her neck, and she pushed one away from her face. In a short time, Harriet finished sweeping the room and began to whisk the dust pile into the dustpan.

"Let's finish rolling out Pa's bedding, then I better go work on making a fire and start getting ready for supper, Pa and Harlan will be back soon, I suppose." Bea groaned. "If you want to go explore more, you can. Just, stay in the house, okay? We don't know how many rattle snakes are around these buildings."

Bea promised and immediately climbed the stairs toward the room with the flowered wallpaper. For a while, she pretended she was a princess from one of the primer books, living in a castle surrounded by gardens filled with yellow flowers. After a time, she tired of the game and wandered downstairs to the parlor. This room was wallpapered as well, but the print was of large swirls of white on a dusty blue background. A chair rail, about shoulder height to Bea, circled the room. The wood on the rail was painted, and though dusty, it was smooth. Bea began trailing a finger on the board, circling the room while she sang "Ring around the rosies."

On her second revolution, something sharp caught her finger. She snatched her hand away and saw a drop of blood. Instantly, she put her finger in her mouth, then began examining the chair rail for what had stabbed her.

At first, she saw nothing at all. Then she spied a break in the wood. She followed the line with her eyes and realized that here there was a straight line cut in the middle of the rail. Further inspection showed her that this wasn't a line, but instead a box-shaped cut that extended from the middle of the chair rail down about six inches into the wall paper. It was very well camouflaged in the pattern, and at first, Bea thought it was just where the builder had needed another length of board.

She stared at it a bit longer, then withdrew her finger from her mouth and pressed in the middle of the square. To her surprise, the entire square popped out of the wall, revealing a hidden drawer. Bea opened her mouth to call for Harriet, then shut it again tightly. Here was something all hers, and she decided she didn't want to share, at least not yet.

Bea had to stand on her tiptoes to see inside the drawer. At first she thought the space was empty, but then she realized that inside was something nearly the same size and shape as the drawer itself. She carefully wedged her fingers on each side, and was able to withdraw her treasure. She sat it carefully on the floor and peeked again into the drawer. Assured that it was now empty except for some remaining dust, she carefully pushed the secret drawer back into place. She stepped back and marveled how even though she knew the surprise was there, she could barely see it.

Now Bea focused her attention on the box. The wood was smooth, and as the dust slid off, a lovely wood-grained, lacquered container revealed itself. There were two rounded cylinders on one of the narrow ends, indicating hinges, and on the opposite side she found a small keyhole. Bea stood up immediately and reopened the drawer, hoping to find the key. Tip toed again, she felt every inch of the drawer, disappointed that the key wasn't there. Bea plopped back down on the floor to examine her prize. She lifted it again and tried to force it open, but it wouldn't budge. She shook it gently. There was certainly something inside, she could feel the weight shift inside as she moved it and could hear a faint rattle, but try as she might, she couldn't open it.

"Hey, Bea! Where are you?"

Bea jumped at Harriet's call, then put the box behind her, covering it with her skirt. "I'm in the parlor," she answered.

"There you are. You were so quiet I wondered if you'd fallen asleep." Harriet stopped at the entrance and leaned against the doorjamb.

"No. I'm just wishing we lived here, it's so pretty."

"Well, it would be a lot of work to build lambing sheds and holding pens close to this house like we have at the other house, and you know Ma wouldn't ever let the ewes be too far from her in the spring, but maybe if Ma sees this house, she'd think it was worth the trouble. It sure is nice."

"Lots nicer than our house," Bea added, but Harriet shushed her.

"Be careful what you say, Bea-Bea. You don't want to make Pa mad, now do you?"

Bea shook her head and Harriet continued. "The fire's started and I'm all done getting food set out. Do you want to come for a walk with me?"

Bea had been sitting very still, hoping that Harriet wouldn't spy what she was hiding. She scrambled to think of an excuse. Harriet misread her hesitation.

"It's okay if you don't want to come. I understand wanting to stay here a while longer. I sat in the kitchen for a few minutes myself, just soaking in the place." With a smile, Harriet was gone and Bea sighed with relief. She didn't know exactly why keeping the box a secret was important, but the idea of knowing and having something just to herself made her smile.

She carefully rubbed the shiny top, marveling at how smooth and soft the wood felt. She tiptoed upstairs and stowed her treasure beneath the blanket of her bedroll, then went outside to meet up with her sister.

Even though it had been years, the memory of that trip absorbed Bea as the truck rumbled along on its way to Encampment. She forced herself out of her memories when Riverside came into view. Bea mentally shrugged away the recollection of that trip and smiled internally, knowing that her secret box was safe, still unopened, under her sweaters in her suitcase. Now that Encampment was near, she focused on the present. They came across the bridge at Riverside and turned up the hill on the last climb into Encampment.

"Didn't Mr. Peryam build this bridge to be a toll bridge, Ma?" Addy asked as they started across.

"He did. He built the bridge even before the roadhouse went in. He decided that since he'd paid for building the bridge it would only be fair to charge people to use it."

Bea had never heard of charging for using a bridge. "Do we have to pay now?"

Addy shook her head and answered. "No, it isn't a toll bridge anymore. Not long after the bridge opened, a farmer from out near Walden on his way to Saratoga thought paying a dime to cross the bridge was too much and he refused. He turned around and went downstream a piece, then tried to cross. He had his wife and a little girl with him. The current of the river caught them and pulled the little girl out of her mother's arms, and she drowned. W.T. Peryam was so upset about that drowning, that he took down the toll and opened the bridge for everyone."

Bea shuttered. "That's a terrible story."

"Yes, it is," answered Addy. "It's funny how Mr. Peryam blamed himself. Most folks around here agree that if that fella hadn't been so cheap, his daughter would still be alive."

They rode in silence as the streets of Encampment grew nearer.

Within minutes Ma pulled up in front of a small house on a quiet, tree-filled street and Bea took a look at Harriet's house. Partially hidden under a large cottonwood, the small white bungalow sat shyly in the middle of the block. The lace curtained windows were framed with blue trim, and Bea was instantly enamored with her new home. As she slid off the seat, the front door opened and Harriet stepped lightly off the porch to greet her family with hugs.

Harriet had become Royce Rogers' wife just a little over a year ago. They'd lived for a time in Rawlins. Then, Royce was offered a deputy position by the marshal in Encampment. With the money they'd saved by living frugally in Rawlins, they put a down payment on this house and happily moved. Royce understood that his wife was accustomed to the noise and commotion of her large family and was sometimes overwhelmed by the quiet of their new home, especially when work kept him away long hours at a time. So, when Eileen wrote asking if they'd have room and willingness to let Beatrice come live with them, Harriet and Royce readily agreed.

Since it was the first time any of her family had visited her new home, Harriet was nervous at first. She gave her mother and sisters a tour, and began to relax at Bea's excitement when Harriet showed her the room that would be hers.

"This is mine?" Bea stood awestruck, turning slowly in a circle in the middle of the room. "It's so pretty, and it has wallpaper!"

Addy was similarly impressed with her sister's kitchen. "It isn't as big as the one at the ranch," Harriet demurred.

"That's true," answered Addy, "But there are so many cupboards, and I really admire that deep sink and long counter. It will be easy for you to roll out pie crusts with that much space."

Shrugging in self-deprecation Harriet replied, "If I ever manage to mix a pie crust that isn't crumbly that is."

Harriet served her guests lunch and then chocolate cake and coffee, and the four Reid women enjoyed a long chat as they relaxed at the table. Bea became restless when her cake was gone and excused herself to carry in her suitcase and the two small boxes she'd packed for her move.

The afternoon sun crawled across the kitchen floor, and finally Eileen stood. "Addy and I have some shopping to do, and I want to be home before it's too dark," she announced. "You've done well for yourself here, Harriet. I'm proud of you."

Harriet rarely heard those words from her mother, and she didn't even try to blink back the emotion they caused. She didn't know how to respond, the moment had taken her so by surprise.

A few minutes later Harriet and Bea stood shoulder to shoulder as they said their farewells and waved goodbye to their mother and sister. When the car turned the corner and was out of sight, Bea did a little dance and then hugged her sister. "Thank you, Harri, for letting me come here. I'll do all the chores you want, I'll do them all for that matter, just to show you how thankful I am to be here."

Harriet laughed. "I'm happy to have you here, Bea-Bea. We'll get you enrolled at school, first. Then we can work out what chores will be yours, dear girl, but you have to leave me something to do or I'll die of boredom."

Laughing, they walked up the sidewalk.

10
Encampment, Wyoming
early October, 1917

Claire finished the third row of the doily she was crocheting, laid her work in her lap and picked up her tea cup. She and Ella Parkison were enjoying one of their frequent afternoon visits. Eleven-year-old Mildred Parkison sat beside her mother, her face pinched in concentration as she worked to master the needle in her hand. Ella looked down and nodded. "Those stitches look very even, Milly, don't worry about making them smaller, you'll get better at hand quilting as you practice."

Claire leaned over for a better view. "I admire the colors you chose for your first quilting project," she told the child. "They go so nicely together, and the pinwheel has perfect corners."

Milly shrugged. "Mama had me tear this one out so many times I thought the cloth would fall apart."

"Well, it looks nice now, my darling, so don't you think that extra effort was worth it?"

"I suppose."

Claire chuckled. "Oh, Ella, did I tell you I got a letter from Jesse this week?"

"No! How's he doing?"

"Very well. After they inoculated everyone for smallpox and suffered through their quarantine, they began actual training. Did I tell you that because of the way he conducted himself as leader of his group from Rawlins to the camp, they made him the head trainee in his group and gave him the rank of private first class?"

"That's wonderful, Claire."

"He's been told that in all likelihood he will be promoted to corporal when he finishes training."

"He's always shown a great deal of leadership skill, so that doesn't surprise me."

"He says in his latest letter that many of the men in his group have been given promotions, and that several have already been transferred to other companies as a result of their leadership. The men that Wyoming sent have done well."

"They make us proud. When will he be finished with training? He should be nearly done, shouldn't he?"

"From the sound of it he'll be finished in Kansas within just a couple of weeks. He thinks that he will be able to come home for a short time before they ship him out."

"Oh, I'm so glad. Does he have his final orders, then?"

Claire took a breath. This news wasn't easy for her to think about. "Yes, he's been assigned to the Second Cavalry Regiment, and they will be leaving for France on the tenth of November."

"Oh my. France is in the thick of it, isn't it?"

"Yes, my stomach hurts every time I even think of Jesse going over there. But, he says that I shouldn't worry too much. The American Cavalry forces haven't engaged in any fighting yet, and his job is farrier to the regiment, not an actual mounted soldier. He claims he won't be getting shot at."

"That is encouraging." Ella looked up from the quilt block she was hand piecing and watched her friend's face. "You know God will watch out for him."

"I know that God is in charge, but Ella, German mothers are praying for their sons and brothers just like I pray for Jesse. He can't answer all our prayers the way we want Him to."

Three heads bent down to their handwork, and at least two prayers went up.

Two weeks and three days later, Claire, Daniel, Michael, and Gregory stood at the platform at Wolcott Junction waiting for the train. They'd arrived early, eager to have Jesse back with them. It was Greg who first spotted the wisp of black smoke in the distance that signaled the approaching train, and soon the rumble of the engine, the vibration of the tracks, and the hissing of the engine announced its arrival.

As the train pulled in, Daniel thought about another time he'd waited for a train at Wolcott to meet Jesse. The boy had been a beanpole, eight years old, scared and unsure of himself. He'd watched his mama die of Yellow Fever and his father descend into a bottle before neighbors took him in. Daniel was always thankful that he and Claire had been able to take Jesse into their family. Now, Daniel had to fight to keep his emotions down as he caught sight of the man who stepped off the train. It was more than the sharpness of his new uniform and the short cut of his hair, Daniel thought. *Everything about Jesse seems different.*

Claire was so relieved to have her brother near her that at first she didn't notice the changes in him. As they drove back to Encampment she listened to him regale the boys with stories about Kansas and his training, and she began to sense a new strength and maturity.

They were close to town when Claire began asking practical questions. "Jesse, today is Thursday the twenty-fifth. You have to leave on the first, right?"

"Yes, I'll need to catch the train the afternoon of November first so I can meet my regiment. I should be able to leave from the Encampment station instead of going all the way to Wolcott."

"That's good, but will you let me come this time?" Claire teased.

"Maybe, if you promise not to get all blubbery." Claire loved the sparkle in his teasing eyes.

"Okay, then. I'll work on that. That gives us six days not counting today and the first. How are you planning to spend that time?"

Daniel interjected, "Wow, you are sounding a little like the drill sergeant." Everyone laughed at the quip.

"Well," Jesse answered, serious now. "I need to spend some time and check in with Dawson and the livery, to see how everything is going. I'm hoping the weather holds so maybe we could take a picnic up to the mountains one day, and I have one other thing I want to look into. What are you thinking?"

"I'm thinking I want to spend as much time as possible with you in the next six days, but I'll share you also. How about this? I'll plan for a picnic with all of us on Sunday after church, and I'll fix supper tomorrow night and expect you to come. Beyond that, we will just have to see."

"Good plan. I want to spend tomorrow at the livery, and then I'll come over to your house in time for supper."

"And games of rummy, too?" This from Greg.

"Yes, I'm sure I'll have time for that. And while we are making plans, how about you and Mike and I take the draft horses and go for a trail ride one afternoon?"

The boys were still cheering when they pulled up in front of Jesse's small house.

Claire hugged her brother and told him, "I put a few groceries in your kitchen. You have a can of soup and some home-made bread if you get hungry tonight, though I know we all ate heartily when we stopped in Saratoga. There's enough bread and some ham in the ice box for breakfast. I didn't know if you'd want to eat many meals at your house, but I thought you'd need a few things."

"Thank you. You always take such good care of me."

He hugged his family again and stood at the sidewalk to watch them drive away. Smiling, he entered his house, happy to be home. He could tell that Claire had been there, cleaning and primping. The house smelled like lye soap and borax, and there wasn't a dust speck to be found.

He walked through the downstairs, grateful to be back if even for a short time. Eventually, he carried his duffle bag upstairs and dropped it at the foot of his bed. He shucked off his uniform, anticipating how nice his civilian clothes would feel. As he pulled on his work clothes, he glanced outside. The sun was still hovering above Bridger Peak. He was weary from the trip and tired from the activity and stress of the past months, but knew it was too early to go to bed. Minutes later, he grabbed his hat from a hook by the back door and set out for the livery.

There, he greeted the horses, adding feed and water to their supplies, noting that the stalls were in top shape. The truck was parked in its spot, newly washed and full of gas. Jesse was touched that, like Claire, Dawson had gone to the effort to make everything as shiny as possible. A profound sense of gratitude filled him.

When he climbed into bed a while later, he noted that his sheets smelled like mountain air. It was his last thought for the night before a deep, satisfying sleep overtook him.

Late the next afternoon, when Daniel came in the back door, he found Claire sweaty and frazzled. The heat from the kitchen and her desire to make a perfect meal had her agitated. He caught a quick hug as his wife rushed by to the oven to remove a pie. "Mmmm, that smells and looks wonderful."

"Well, it's apple, not Jesse's favorite, but it will do."

"It's my favorite. Don't I count?" Daniel asked.

Claire knew she was being teased and ignored him. "How'd your day go?"

"Pretty well. Nothing much exciting, which is a good thing, I think."

Two hours later, the family sat at the table. "You out did yourself, Claire," Jesse told her. "I am so full I can't breathe."

"I have pie," she began, and the others groaned happily in unison.

"Let's wait a while," Daniel suggested.

Michael grinned, "Hey we could play rummy while we wait."

"Well," Daniel put in, "I'll bet you'll work off dinner quicker by being active. The kitchen is calling you."

Both boys groaned and Daniel continued, "Anyway, I want to hear boring things from your uncle, like how things are at the livery, so you will be spared business talk while you work."

"Anyone need a cup of coffee or tea?" Claire asked.

Jesse nodded, "Tea sounds terrific."

"Make it two," Daniel added as they headed towards the parlor.

Clare already had the water hot, so she quickly filled her tea pot with water and tea, added three cups to a tray, and carried them into the parlor.

Jesse, his boots off and his stockinged feet up on the footstool, had just begun telling Daniel about his day.

"Dawson had the place spotless. He's landed a contract with the Plummer Saloon for a dedicated run to

Saratoga once a week that will be nicely profitable. He's been busy, that's for sure."

"That's good to hear. I talked with Nathan Jameson at the hardware store the other day. He asked about you, and then told me his contract with that hauling crew out of Riverside is up at the end of the month. He was wondering if you'd like to give him a bid on it."

"That's a big contract, big commitment. I'll go over and talk to him about it before I leave." Jesse was quiet as Claire handed him his tea.

She sat down then ventured, "I understand you need someone to run the business, but I've been worried if asking Dawson Wiley was a good idea. I know he's is a good guy. He seems honest, and he's done his best for you and the company so far, but we all know how much trouble his brother has caused around here. Jesse, I've just been wondering if Dawson is as trustworthy as you hope."

"Well, Claire, Dawson isn't at all like his brother and it seems that he's got a good head for running the livery and making a go of it. But..." Jesse answered.

"But?"

"But the business isn't just hauling and doing the work. He is having some troubles with the accounting. The good thing is, he knows it. He told me that he'd been in to see you a couple of times for advice, Dan."

"Yes, he wasn't sure how to do some entries in the ledger and I gave him some general ideas."

"He told me that, and as we talked and looked over the accounts, I found some problems and mistakes. Dawson admitted that he felt like he needed some help, but he's worried about what it will cost to hire a bookkeeper. It's been keeping him up at night."

"Can the business afford a bookkeeper?" Daniel's concern for Jesse was apparent in his voice.

"I guess we could," Jesse answered with a sigh. "Dawson made a suggestion that I think might be workable, but it puts a lot of the weight on you, Dan."

"Oh? What's his idea?"

"He suggested that you and he meet on a weekly basis. You could go over accounts with him and catch any trouble, teach him as you go, and also act as a kind of overseer of the business."

Daniel thought for a minute, then asked, "Do you think Dawson and I could manage it in just one meeting a week?"

"Actually, I do. For the first month or so, it could be that he stops in a bit more often, but he catches on fast. He just needs to be taught." Jesse hesitated, then added, "The business can pay you, I'm just not sure how much right now. With the contract Dawson just signed and if I can get the Jameson's business—"

Daniel interrupted, "No need to worry about that right now. Let's leave it this way. I will meet with Wiley and give him all the help I can as my support to you while you are gone. At the end of six months, we can talk about whether I'm still needed and if so, we can talk about pay then. For now, you can count on me, and I don't want you to worry about it."

Claire was quiet for a minute then suggested, "Daniel, you don't really have time during the day to meet with Mr. Wiley. I'd be happy to have dinner for him here each week. Then you could use the kitchen table to meet afterwards."

Jesse put his head down and took a deep breath. "Dawson would really appreciate that, I'm sure. And I can't thank you both enough. Thank you so much for the work and sacrifice you are willing to do for me and the livery. You have always rescued me, and here you are doing it again." Emotion showed on his face and in his voice.

With that, Claire stood up and placed her tea cup back on the tray. Then she bent down and kissed her brother on the forehead. "It isn't a sacrifice. It's what we do when we love someone, and we definitely love you."

Daniel nodded. "Jess, I think that it would be good for us to meet together before you leave so that I'm more informed about how you do the accounting, and it might help us all be a team."

Jesse appreciated how Claire and Daniel glossed over his sentimentality without embarrassing him. "I agree. When would be good for you?"

"Well, how about tomorrow afternoon? Since it's Saturday, I won't have to be at work and we can take our time."

"Sounds good. I'll stop by Dawson's house on my walk home tonight and get it planned."

The next afternoon found Jesse, Daniel, and Dawson with their heads bent over a large ledger book around Jesse's kitchen table.

At length, Daniel sat back, rubbing his neck. "I have to say, Jesse, that I'm highly impressed with how organized and clear this system you've devised is. I just don't see us having much trouble maintaining your accounting just the way you have it. Dawson, all you'll need to do is keep receipts of the work you do, and the money you bring in and spend. Then, we can sit down each week and enter the transactions one by one. I'll help you with paying the bills for the livery and the house and generally keeping things going."

The relief on Dawson's face was evident and he chuckled. "You don't know how many hours of sleep I've lost in the last few weeks worrying about this. I know I can satisfy our customers and make good decisions about what to haul, how to haul it, and what to charge for it. I even think that with some practice I can take care of most of the forge work we need done, but every time I open this ledger book, my belly feels like I've been kicked by a mule. I get that nervous. Ciphering has never been something I'm good at."

Daniel nodded. "We'll make a good team, then, because I haven't any idea how to run the business."

Jesse looked relieved as well. He leaned back in his chair and sipped the last of his coffee. "Now I can relax."

"Well, I should head for home. Claire will be wondering."

"I'll walk out with you," Jesse answered, "Dawson, how about you?"

"Well, my brother is in town, and I told him I'd meet him at the White Dog Saloon and have a beer with him. I'll see you Monday morning." Dawson grabbed his hat then turned to Daniel and offered his hand. "Daniel, thanks again."

"My pleasure."

They watched until Dawson turned the corner and was out of sight before Daniel spoke up, "That went well, don't you think?"

"Yes, I do think between his hard work and your help, I'll be able to leave and not worry about what I left behind."

Dawson felt Jesse and Daniel watching him as he walked down the street. He wasn't self-conscious about his uneven step, he'd made peace years ago with the deformity that caused it, and he was confident that with the support and advice Daniel so willingly offered he could do a good job running the livery while Jesse was gone. He knew he should be feeling optimistic about the future. He'd visited the doctor last week and had already mailed his medical deferment papers to the Selective Service office in Rawlins. Unlike Jesse and nearly all of his friends, he now knew for sure he wasn't facing military service and wouldn't be in the cross hairs of some German's rifle.

I have nothing at all to complain of, he told himself. Yet, the closer he got to the White Dog, the heavier his feet felt. *If I had just one wish from a genie in a bottle, I'd ask for a family like Jesse's. I wonder what new trouble Evan has found this time.*

Dawson resolved to have just one beer with his brother. *I can afford him that,* he coached himself, *but no more. And I'm not going to let him entice me or cajole me into getting involved in his newest scheme.*

The White Dog, one of sixteen saloons in Encampment, was a far cry from the rich ambiance of the Copper Pot. Cigarette smoke and the stench of warm beer assaulted Dawson as he entered. The room was small and cramped. Tables were usually sticky and the drinks were well watered. He allowed his eyes to adjust to the murky interior until he spotted Evan at a back table. Dawson stopped at the bar, waited for the bartender to draw a beer from the tap, and joined his brother. The table was littered with two empty glasses, and the drink in Evan's hand was nearly finished.

"Hey big brother, how are you?"

"Evan," Dawson nodded and sat on the opposite side of the table. "You look a little rough. Are you staying somewhere here in Encampment?"

"Naw, I got a tent set up out by the river. Been there just for a day or two. I got myself a little lady, and I was hungry for a little companionship."

"A lady? Someone from here in town?"

Evan hesitated, not wanting to give his brother details. "Yeah, she lives here," was all he said.

"Evan, if you care about her, you should be treating her with respect."

The smirk on Evan's face told Dawson he didn't agree. "I didn't say I cared much. But, well, she's a pretty thing and plenty malleable."

Dawson felt sick to his stomach. Changing the subject he asked, "You still working at the Big Creek Tie Camp?"

"Those slave drivers? No, I quit the other day. I didn't mind living out there, Mrs. Anderson is a real cook, but the bosses have no sense of humor, and they like to work the hacks to death."

"I thought you enjoyed the work,"

"Well, I don't mind spending my time at the spud peeler—that's the machine that scrapes the bark from the ties—but they wanted me to join the felling crew and that's just too hard a work. I told them I needed a raise to do that kind of labor. The old man foreman laughed at me and I took a swing at him, so we parted ways."

Dawson shook his head, "Evan, not everyone thinks you hung the moon like Pa did. A man can't expect to always call the shots."

"Pa always favored you over me, big brother, until you got stupid and came off that horse."

Dawson let the statement sit between them. It was a traditional jibe, one that had caused the brothers to come to blows more than once. After the last go 'round, Dawson decided not to rise to the taunts ever again. *The truth of the matter,* Dawson reminded himself as he slowly sipped his beer, *is that Pa wouldn't have insisted I try to ride that renegade stallion if it hadn't been for Evan's jeering. We both knew that horse was not rideable, but Pa, like Evan, couldn't ever back down from a challenge, and he wouldn't let me walk away either.*

Dawson watched his brother finish his drink and hail the bartender for another. *That makes four. Soon he'll be belligerent, I need to cut this short.*

"So, what are you going to do for work?"

"Well, I thought I'd come work for you for a while. You told me this morning when I ran into you that you'd taken over the livery while the owner is gone. I'm sure you need help."

"Um, well, there isn't anything for you to do. It's a one-man operation right now."

"C'mon, Daw, I'm your brother, I'm sure you can figure something out for me."

Dawson took a deep breath and steadied his resolve in anticipation of a blow-up. "I'm sorry, but I can't. There really is only enough work for one, and anyway, Jesse's brother is holding the purse strings, so I don't have the ability to hire anyone."

He could see his brother's temper rising and wanted nothing more than to avert a scene. "I'm sorry, Evan, I just can't help you."

"That's just like you, Dawson, always letting family down. You let Pa down by busting up your leg, and you're letting me down now." Evan stood up unsteadily and clenched his fists. Dawson stood up also, and walked away.

11
Encampment, Wyoming
Sunday, October 28, 1917

Sitting on one corner of a large quilt, Claire leaned back against a boulder in the clearing beside Lost Treasure Gulch Creek. The remains of an extravagant picnic were strewn across the rest of the bright blanket. Greg and Michael's muffled voices filtered through the forest as they explored the creek nearby. Daniel, dozing, lay beside Claire. Jesse sat nearby on the tailgate of his truck. Claire studied his smile as he gazed at the forest surrounding him.

"I can't believe the weather today. It's a gift from God, Claire, so warm and still. That sky is a perfect blue with just a few scattered clouds to the north."

"Well I've spent the better part of two days either praying about this picnic or cooking for it," she answered lightly. "We could just as easily have had a blizzard this time of year."

Jesse loved the warm sunshine on his back. He drank in the colors and sounds of the day.

"Everything is perfect today. Lunch was grand, Claire. Thank you."

"I had fun putting it together. We don't often get up in the mountains for a picnic in October."

Claire closed her eyes and tried to relax. The day was perfect and she certainly felt thankful, but the fact that in just four days she'd be saying goodbye to Jesse and he'd be off to war haunted her. The niggling fears that this was the last picnic she'd ever get with him, the last Sunday she'd ever spend with Jesse, loomed on the horizon of her mind and threatened to ruin the afternoon. Since she'd gotten out of bed this morning, she'd had to remind herself over and over to enjoy today and not worry about tomorrow. In unguarded moments she wasn't successful.

Daniel sighed and shifted his position, indicating that he was fast asleep. Claire chuckled, then cautiously got up so she wouldn't disturb him. She moved to sit beside Jesse on the tailgate.

Claire didn't say anything. She just inched closer to her brother when she sat down. She leaned into him and asked quietly, "How are you doing?"

Jesse took a breath, gaining strength from the warmth of the sun and his sister's touch. "I am good. I feel confident that I've made good arrangements about the livery, though I worry too much is falling on Daniel. I am at peace, Claire. Really." He waited a few seconds, then returned the question.

After a ragged breath, she answered, "I know you are in God's hands. We aren't supposed to be fearful, we are supposed to have faith, and I'm working on that. But honestly. I am afraid. I just don't want you to go through this. I don't want to go through this." She shrugged and tried to laugh. "I'm such a coward compared to you."

They sat without talking. Each time a breeze disturbed one of the nearby aspens, a shower of yellow and red drifted downward. Laughter and voices echoed through the trees as the boys played together in the woods. At last, Claire broke the silence, "Is there anything else that you need to do before you leave? Can I help get your house ready or anything?"

Jesse took so long to answer that she wasn't sure he would. Then, "I think there is just one thing more to do. I might need your help, I'll let you know, okay?"

Claire wanted to ask more, but just then Michael began calling through the trees, "Hey, Uncle Jesse! Greg and I found a swell hideout. Will you come see it with me?"

Jesse smiled, "I'd love to."

Every morning, Sari read from her Bible when she awoke. She enjoyed the Old Testament, and returned often to read about David, a man God loved but who was flawed and sinful at times. On Monday morning, October 29, 1917, Sari read from Second Samuel twenty-two. David was singing a praise song to God. "They continued to confront me in the day of my disaster, but the Lord was my support. He brought me out into a spacious place; he rescued me because he delighted in me."

Sari smiled. Without a doubt, God had brought her to the spacious, rolling prairie of Wyoming, and she knew He was her support. "I guess I'm still waiting on the rescue part," she whispered, then immediately felt guilty. *No,* she thought. *He has rescued me. I am an adult, I have a little room to myself, and work for my hands.* She refused to allow herself any more time for self-pity as she finished reading the chapter and began her day.

Within just a few minutes Sari closed her room's door and began the walk to work. The sky, clear and deep except for a bank of clouds far away to the west, was a dusty blue. Bright yellow and red aspen leaves contrasted against the deep sky and the rough green of the pines, making the day seem celebratory.

She let her thoughts drift to the coming day. She was trying a new recipe for chicken pot pie for the evening entre. She'd need to ask Meredith's help, something she hated to do. Meredith was still a puzzle to her. The girl often acted as if she wanted to be helpful but Sari just knew that her friendliness was a trick, just like the girls at Miss Milton's. She knew she just couldn't let her guard down even a little. Overall, they did seem to work together well, even if it was an uneasy sort of relationship that kept Sari anxious.

The kitchen was dark when Sari slipped in through the alley door. She tied on an apron and went to work. Toast, scrambled eggs and bacon were easy. She'd baked the bread yesterday, so her first task was to slice the loaves and get out the wire rack she used for toasting. Next, she pulled out the griddle and began frying bacon. She worked methodically, calm and assured. When the bacon was finished and safely stowed in the Dutch oven to stay warm, Sari looked around. The eggs would be the last preparations for breakfast. Sari had hoped Meredith would take charge of them this morning, but she hadn't arrived.

Sari finished cracking the eggs and had just begun to heat the skillet when Chetley entered the kitchen. "You have a group of guests just sitting down for breakfast. Is it ready?"

"Very nearly, I just need to cook the eggs and finish the toast. How many are there?"

"Four, and I think I saw another couple in the lobby. Where is Meredith? Have her get them coffee while they wait."

" Um. well, I haven't heard from her yet this morning."

Just then, Meredith appeared through the side door. She looked pale, her eyes red.

"Good morning," their boss growled. "You are late and guests are waiting. Make yourself presentable and get out there, I've told you before I don't want *her* waiting tables."

Sari watched Meredith lower her head, fighting tears as she tied on an apron. "Yes, Sir, I'm sorry I'm late."

"It better not become a habit or you'll be looking for a new job."

"I'm so sorry. It won't happen again." Meredith glanced at Sari. "What's on the menu?"

Sari quickly told her. Meredith smoothed her hair as she listened, then grabbed the coffee pot and hurried to greet the guests.

Chetley stomped out on her heels.

They were very busy that morning. Sari watched Meredith as the morning drew on. While out in the dining room the girl seemed to have regained her composure and Sari could hear her exchanging pleasantries and even teasing with the guests as she served them. In unguarded moments in the kitchen, however, Sari noted that her coworker remained pale, and when she thought no one was watching she seemed to melt into discouragement. Sari also noticed her hands trembling as she dried glasses and put them away. It made Sari sad, and she resolved to make an effort to show kindness to the girl.

Both Lilith and Chetley visited the kitchen several times that morning, adding to the tension that boiled in the kitchen along with the food.

Sari felt frazzled by the time lunch was cleaned up. Even so, she needed to talk with her partner.

"Meredith, I'm going to need your help getting supper ready." Sari made sure her voice was quiet and kind. "I'm trying a new recipe for chicken pot pie."

"Okay." The girl's response was guarded, tentative.

"I've got the crusts all ready. Now I need these vegetables cut up, but they all need to be uniform in size."

"Okay," Meredith repeated, reaching for a knife.

Sari stopped and put her hand on Meredith's arm. "I know you've had a hard morning. You look pale. Are you feeling alright?"

Meredith's head stayed low and she answered with a muffled, "I'm fine."

Standing shoulder to shoulder, they began paring carrots, potatoes, onions, and then celery. When they'd worked in silence for a while Sari complimented Meredith on her work. She got no response. Sari forged on, trying to make the atmosphere in the room a little less oppressive. "Something I've learned is that a good meal isn't just about filling a person's stomach. It's about having something hearty to eat that also looks pretty on the plate or in the bowl. Cutting the meat and vegetables all the same size helps the pot pie look good. When something looks pretty, people think it tastes better, too."

When again Meredith didn't answer, Sari fell into silence.

They'd been working about twenty minutes when Sari stepped back and surveyed the bowl filled with vegetables. "That looks really great! And we did it so fast. I would never have gotten this done without you. It's only going to take a minute to fill these crusts and put the pies in the oven. Thank you."

Meredith met Sari's glance. "Why are you being nice to me? Are you just lording over me that I came in late and got in trouble with Mr. Wills?"

Sari hesitated. "I wouldn't do that! I, well, I'm always nice to you."

Meredith shrugged.

"No, really. Aren't I always nice to you?"

Meredith's eyes filled with tears. "Honestly, no. You made it really clear from the beginning that you've never wanted me here and that don't want me to be your friend. I know I'm not a great cook, but I've tried so hard to please you and make you like me." She stopped to take a shuttering breath. "And this is the first time ever you've told me I did something well."

Sari was horrified at Meredith's words. She swallowed, then quietly asked, "How did I make it clear I didn't want to be friends?"

Meredith stepped backward. She didn't feel up to this conversation, but knew that now that it was started, she had to continue. "You've never smiled at me. I brought you cookies that second day, and you didn't eat them, they just sat on the counter. I've tried to make conversation with you, but you never give me more than a few words in reply. I know you blame me for the time your soup scorched, but I honestly never even went near the stove that morning. I just never do anything right enough for you."

Sari opened her mouth to respond, then closed it again.

Before she could consider how to answer Meredith, Lilith bounded into the kitchen, heading straight for Meredith. "Mr. Wills says that since you were late this morning, he won't dock your pay if you give up your afternoon break and go help out Jennie to get the floors all scrubbed. Can you start on them now?"

"Yes, Ma'am," Meredith answered with a shrug. She glanced at Sari and turned to go.

For the first time all day, Sari was alone. Meredith's words whirled through her mind as she dried her hands and untied her apron, thinking that a walk in the fresh air might help her consider what she'd just heard and ease the tension in her neck. She'd taken a step toward the back door when Lilith returned.

"Oh, Sari, I'm glad I caught you. I have an errand you need to run."

Sari turned around and nodded, resigned to give up her break.

"I got a message a few minutes ago that the pot you took to the farrier for repair is ready. They'd like you to go pick it up this afternoon."

"I haven't taken any pots in for repair," Sari answered, "There must be a mistake."

"I thought that same thing when I read the message, but here it is and very specific, asking that you come pick it up this afternoon."

"I'll just go over and straighten this out. Thank
you."

This won't take long. Afterward I can take a walk,
she decided. Knowing she'd probably be meeting many of
the townspeople on the busy street, she pulled the pins
out of the bun at the nape of her neck and gathered her
hair to the side in a ribbon. Her route to the livery took
her down Freeman to Sixth Street. She passed in front of
the E & H Building, home of the North American Copper
Company Bank, Smizer's store and the barber shop before
turning south again at the next corner.

At first when she entered the barn a few minutes
later, she didn't see anyone. The room was cool and
shadowed and it took several blinks before the inside
began to take shape.

Jesse, sitting to the side at his desk, saw her
before she saw him. He took advantage of the moment and
looked carefully at her. She wasn't tall, and her thin frame
gave her a delicate, fragile impression. Her hair was down,
gathered together to fall in soft curls over her right
shoulder and down the front. As he studied her, he
realized that by wearing it that way, she could hide the
right side of her face by simply dropping her chin.

He pulled out of his gaze when she called out.
"Hello? Hello? It's Sari Webber from the Copper Pot."

He stood up and came around the desk as he
replied, "Sari, I'm here. It's good to see you."

Sari was shocked to see Jesse. Without thinking,
she moved a bit sideways, shielding his view of her
mangled face but keeping her gaze on him. She knew it
was impossible, but he seemed taller. He wore a chambray
shirt buttoned clear to the collar and a string tie. His hair
was cropped short, his face very tan. As the words
escaped her, she knew they sounded silly. "I'd heard you
left for the Army. I didn't know you were in Encampment."

"I'm only home for a few days. It's good to see you,
Sari. How have you been?"

"I'm uh, I'm well. Thank you." She felt stiff and off
kilter. He watched her patiently with smiling brown eyes.
"Um, Lilith Wills gave me a message that there was
something for me to pick up, but I don't think I've left

118

anything for repair." They were standing at the edge of an area she could tell was Jesse's office. No one else was around.

"Well," Jesse stammered. He hesitated, then continued, "Well, I ask your forgiveness for the lie I told her. I don't have any repairs, I'm just home for a short time, and this was the first idea I had to be able to talk with you privately."

Sari paused to replay his words a second time. "You lied to get me to come see you?"

Jesse shrugged. Oddly, Sari pictured him as a little boy, shrugging just that way when caught in some mischief. "I wasn't sure when you got off work, and I didn't want to embarrass or bother you there. Please don't be offended."

"Offended?" Sari replied. She was confused and all of a sudden very worried that this was the beginning of some cruelty.

Jesse saw the concern on Sari's face and worried that the conversation wasn't starting out well at all. He searched for a way to lighten the mood and put their meeting on a more positive course. "Um, would you come sit over here with me? Please?" He motioned for her to follow him then led her toward the office area. He'd placed two chairs beside one another facing the back of the building, and as they reached them he motioned for her to sit on his right. She realized with a rush of emotion that he'd very intentionally set the scene so that she'd be comfortable.

"Are things going well at the Copper Pot?"

Her voice and body were stiff, wary. "Though today has been a trial in the kitchen, I'm well. My days are spent at the restaurant. Business has been good, so I stay quite busy."

Their attempts at conversation continued to be awkward, stilted. They labored through the weather and the change of seasons, then Sari asked about his training. Jesse seemed to relax some as he described the camp and some of the high points.

"So," asked Sari after he'd finished. "Are you leaving again soon?"

119

"Yes, the Second Cavalry Regiment, the regiment I'm assigned to, leaves for France soon and I need to meet them in New York. I leave on the train on November first. Only three days from now."

"I'll be sorry to know you are gone, and so far away," Sari said after a moment, her eyes were on the dirt floor in front of her. She felt a sadness she couldn't name.

They sat together in the silent livery for nearly a minute, until Jesse cleared his throat. Her past experiences united within to convince her that Jesse was up to nothing good, yet some small voice deep inside wanted and hoped that he was, in fact, her friend and that was the only motive behind this meeting.

"Sari, I have something to say to you, and I wanted a private place to say it, so I sent you that message."

She glanced at him. He studied her as she sat beside him, back straight and her hands in her lap. Another half a minute passed. *Whatever he wants to say, it's hard for him,* Sari thought. She began to think his plan was to renege on their agreed friendship, she could imagine nothing else.

Finally, Jesse cleared his throat again and began. "I hope you will be patient with me. I've never done this before and I want to make sure I do it well." He took a deep breath, then turned so his body was facing her. She responded by turning just enough so that she could meet his eyes.

"As I've just told you, I leave for France very soon." Sari opened her mouth to respond but Jesse held up his hand with a grin, "Wait, please don't say anything until I get through this, okay?" She nodded.

He took another deep breath and went on. "Sari, I want you to know that I have thought often in the last two months about the Sunday afternoon we took that drive together. It was a good day, and I'm thankful that you consider me your friend. I have deep respect for you."

Sari felt confused. She couldn't imagine where he was going with this.

He rubbed his eyes. "There's a lot to say and I'm not sure what to say first." He looked down at the floor then stood up. He paced a few steps then returned to his seat. His eyes stared at the dirt floor in front of him, panning over until they lit on the small hands resting in Sari's lap. Impetuously, he reached over and covered them with one of his. "Sari, I want to marry you. I want you to become my wife before I leave." The words came fast and breathlessly.

They echoed off the coarse barn walls then faded into stunned silence. One of the horses stomped and shook his head.

Sari sat motionless, unable to fathom what she'd just heard.

Jesse felt an urgency to explain and coerce her into considering it. "I know we aren't sweethearts, I know we are just barely friends. I don't expect you to, well, um, I don't expect that you love me and I'm not asking you to let me bed you, or even kiss you if you don't want me to. It's not that at all." His face flushed first red and then a little paler than before.

These were not words she'd expected to ever hear in her life, and certainly not from a man she'd spent only a few hours with and hadn't seen in months. Sari was stunned. She didn't want this to be a cruel joke. A series of breaths steadied her and gave her courage. She stared at the rough, tan hand in her lap. Its warmth sent a comfort through her she didn't understand.

After what seemed like an eternity to Jesse, Sari raised her eyes and met his. "I don't understand. You can't love me, and well, if we are honest you'll agree that I'm not the kind of person a nice, handsome man like you could ever love. I'm certainly not someone you should marry." She shook her head slightly when he started to protest and he closed his mouth. "I have no illusions about the importance of how a woman looks, Jesse. I'm sorry, and I certainly don't understand your intentions, but no, I can't marry you."

"Wait, that's what I was afraid you'd say. I knew you'd dismiss me and the idea just like this, and I need to make you change your mind. Sari, I can't explain why I know this is right, but I do. I just know that this is something I'm supposed to do, we're supposed to do. I've been thinking and praying about this since before I left in August. Time is short. I leave in three days, and I'd like to leave knowing you are my wife."

"Why? Why me? If by some strange plan we are supposed to be married, then why not wait until you return?" Before he could respond she went on. "Jesse, there are many things you don't know about me. As if it weren't enough to be obligated to someone, well, someone who looks like me, marrying me would mean connecting yourself to a financial debt I have that isn't yours to bear. If I work hard, my debt will be resolved in about five years. You will be back by then. We can wait and see what the time brings."

"Sari, what if I don't return and this is the only chance we have?"

She wanted to dismiss his fear, but they both knew she couldn't. She dropped her eyes. His hand was still there, still covering her own with his touch.

Ignoring him she asked, "Jesse, what about when you do come home? I don't understand what prompts you to want this now, but think about the future. You don't really want to come back to me. To this." She turned so that she was facing him full on. Slowly she reached up, gathered her hair and dropped it down her back so that her scarred face was completely exposed. It was an excruciating moment for her and her eyes filled with the tears of her own shame and revulsion, yet she believed that her stark ugliness would make him begin thinking rationally.

Jesse had been meeting her argument by looking straight into her eyes. Now, deliberately and slowly, he moved his eyes from hers and focused on her right cheek. Sari sucked in an untidy breath as he held his gaze on her. She'd never allowed anyone to study her disfigurement. Her heart pounded. She was afraid of the loathing he'd surely be unable to mask and she lowered her eyes.

Slowly, he raised his hand. With a gentle finger, he touched her right cheek, drawing a line across the mottled and ragged, mutilated skin. He lowered his hand to beneath her chin, lifting it to force her to look at him.

"I'm pretty sure that you've been led to believe that these scars make you unattractive. The truth is, they tell a story about lots of pain and sadness you've had to endure, and that's all. As far as ugly goes, I know several people who have perfect faces with no blemishes that are misshapen and hideous on the inside. I'd much rather look at you than them."

Sari was overwhelmed. She broke from him, stood, and walked away. Jesse watched as she paced the length of the barn. When she stopped to rub the nose of the big blond draft horse in the second stall, he slowly approached her and stood facing her from her left.

"I told you already that I came to live with my sister and her husband when I was about eight. My ma died and my pa was a mean, selfish drunk. Claire and Daniel rescued me from the life I would have had with him. I have watched them over the years. The one thing I know from them about marriage is that honesty is important. Come sit down with me again, please, and I'll finish what I wanted to say to you."

He held out his hand. She took it and they held hands as they returned to the office and resumed the chairs they'd left.

"I want you to know that one night just before I left for training, I stopped in at the bar for a drink and ran into Chetley Wills. He'd had a couple too many and his mouth got loose. He told me about the deal he has with you and the bank."

Sari's head came up sharply and she pulled her hand away from his. "That's horrid! I can't believe he'd tell others my personal business. It just isn't right!"

"I agree with you completely. I was so angry that he was talking so freely and also at what you've been subjected to. I walked nearly all night long out on the prairie when I left that bar, asking God for His revenge and justice."

Sari turned away from Jesse and her voice got so quiet he almost couldn't hear her. "Even if the news is all over town, my debt is not your concern, not anyone's but mine. You are a nice man, and you feel sorry for me. You want to rescue me, though I don't understand why. I can't accept money from you, and so I don't see how you can think marrying me would solve anything. I won't agree to this. Your desire to do something gallant is clouding your thinking."

There was resolve tinged with bitterness behind her words, and it took Jesse by surprise. "Wait, no, my thoughts are clear. This isn't pity, and I'm not being selfless. Well, not exactly."

There was hurt in his tone, and something else. Sari took a breath and then looked at him. "Go on."

"Please don't think I'm trying to be a hero. I'd like to be, I suppose, but I'm just not like that. I have about two hundred dollars to my name and as a soldier I'll be making about a dollar a day. My business has been my living, but it hasn't ever provided an extravagant one. Since I've been gone, it hasn't been doing all that well. I think, with Daniel's help, that we may have solved that problem. But. Well, ever since America became involved with this war with the Germans and I heard about the draft lottery, I've known that I was going to be called up right away." He paused and she met his eyes. "I also have this feeling that I'm not coming home." He paused again.

The only sound was the guttural call of a crow outside the window and the low, crisp rumble of one of the horses eating grain. "I'm willing to go and do my duty. It's just that I want to know that when I die, I've done something worthwhile. The only thing I'm really afraid of with the thought of war is dying without having done something important with my life. Then I met you. Marrying me makes sense for both of us. If I die and am married, then my wife would receive a monthly pension from the government for the rest of her widowhood. In addition, Congress just passed a bill that offers life insurance to any soldier. I could go to war and get killed. Then I'd just be dead, and I'd leave so little behind. But if you and I get married and I die, then you can receive the ten-thousand-dollar life insurance money plus the widow's pension and a home and business. It would make me feel as if I were doing something of value and it's a sound financial opportunity for you. I'm not being heroic because the benefits won't cost me anything, but they could help you for years to come." Jesse inwardly cringed, knowing he was telling a small lie. He'd looked into the life insurance policy plan and knew that it would cost him sixty cents a month for that policy. But he was unwilling to tell Sari that truth.

Sari couldn't think of a response. She saw his logic and heard his proposal but couldn't quite grasp it all. Finally, she stood up and took a step away. "I think I need to be alone and have some time to think your offer through. I think and hope that you are making this suggestion with kind intentions, but I'm struggling with the most important question. Why? Why me and not another woman who could benefit from your..." she stopped. She couldn't finish the sentence.

Jesse stood up. His calm voice came from behind her, and filled her with a warmth she didn't understand. "Since that day you came in here for me to fix that ladle, I've felt drawn to you. I've never been in love with a woman, and I don't know how that feels for sure. I am certain, though, that I care for you and that if we had the time, what I am feeling would grow into love. I'd like to think that you'd learn to love me back. I think God brought us together for a reason. What if that reason is this?"

One of the horses shifted in his stall, there was no other sound.

"I need to think, Jesse, and I need to get back to the restaurant. Would it be alright if we met to take a walk together this evening when I get off? I'll try to have an answer for you then."

"I'll wait for you in front of the Copper Pot."

"I can usually leave around seven or so."

"May I walk you back there now?"

Sari shook her head, more in wonder at his proposal than to say no. "I think I'd benefit more from walking alone if you don't mind."

"Alright," Jesse answered.

Sari lingered for a moment, then quietly slipped out of the livery and was gone. Jesse felt as if the air had been knocked out of him. A wave of weariness washed through him. He pulled his chair behind his desk and sat down. He knew there was paperwork he should be doing, but he couldn't think clearly. For nearly an hour, he sat, his chin resting on his fists, elbows on the desk. He didn't pray with words, merely the silent groaning of his spirit.

Sari paid scant attention to her surroundings on her walk back to the kitchen. She tried and tried to convince herself that Jesse's intentions were in some way wicked, but try as she might, she just couldn't hold on to that dire view.

"Jesse? Jesse, are you here?"

Claire's call startled him and he jerked himself back into the world. He stood up with force enough that his chair overturned. Claire was laughing as she approached him. "You must have been asleep. You should see the dazed look on your face!"

Her mirth at his reaction was infectious, and Jesse's laugh returned her greeting. "You took me by surprise," he said, rounding the end of the desk and kissing her on the cheek, "but I wasn't asleep, I was actually praying."

Her face clouded with seriousness as she answered, "I understand. I've been spending lots of time with the Lord myself." Pausing, Claire waited while Jesse righted his chair and came to stand beside her. "I was in town and just decided to stop by and see what you are doing for supper. We didn't talk about it yesterday at the picnic."

"I, well, I'm not very hungry and, um, I have to be somewhere about seven, so I don't think I can come tonight."

Smiling, Claire searched her brother's face, then commented, "You are being a bit secretive. The other day when you listed things you needed to do this week, you hinted at something but wouldn't say what, now you are being evasive and seem nervous. What's going on?"

Jesse stood for a long time without answering, then finally made a decision. "Do you have a few minutes? I need to tell you something."

"I have as much time as you need," she answered. "It's dusty in this barn. How about we go over to your house and sit on the porch?"

It was such a relief for Jesse to talk over his thoughts and plans with Claire. It didn't take long for him to finish telling his sister about meeting Sari, and their afternoon together. He didn't share about Sari's financial burden, deciding that it wasn't important for Claire to know, but he ended by telling her about the marriage proposal he'd just made. When he was finished, he leaned back and watched white strings of clouds scud across the tops of the Sierra Mountains. After a few moments of silence, he glanced sideways at Claire sitting next to him on the porch swing. Her eyes were closed. *She's praying*, Jesse realized.

Seconds later, Claire shifted so that she was leaning against her brother. "Are you expecting me to encourage you or talk you out of this?" She asked it in all seriousness. "Or do you want me to just listen and nod?"

Jesse smiled and answered, "Well, I think I want encouragement. I've had this in my mind since before I left for training, I've prayed and prayed for God's leading, and talking to Sari today just made me more determined that this is the right thing to do."

"Right for her." Claire added, her voice careful and quiet.

"Yes, it is right for her, but it's good for me also."

"Tell me more about that, because I don't see it. I'm afraid that you are giving up. You say you have a feeling and are at peace with dying on the other side of the world. But what I hear is that you are going to war and you aren't going to be careful." Jesse began to argue and she cut him off. "No, listen to me. I have heard you say several times that you don't think you are coming back. Every time you say that I feel like I've been stabbed in the stomach. If you are so sure you aren't coming home, then how can I know you aren't going to be taking wild chances and not looking out for yourself so that you do die when you don't need to?"

Jesse considered her words, then answered. "I haven't ever thought of it that way. I've only wanted to do something that matters. Claire, I don't want to be killed. I promise you I won't take risks I can avoid. I want to survive and I'm not giving up. I promise to look out for myself and do all I can to come home. Please understand. Please support me in marrying Sari. I just know it's the right thing to do."

"Jess, I do stand with you and will always support you, as long as you keep your promise to take care of yourself." Claire punched Jesse's arm and stood up. "What you can't possibly understand, though, is that if there's going to be a wedding, I have lots of work to do."

"Work? What work?" his question was only half mocking.

"Did you say you are meeting her this evening?"

Jesse nodded. "She said she'd give me an answer tonight."

"I tell you what, no matter what her answer is, come over to our house after you talk with her. If there's to be a wedding bring her over. We need to meet her, then we can have some coffee cake and tea and do some planning."

12
Encampment, Wyoming
Monday, October 29, 1917

The chilly night sky was filled with stars. Inside the house, Greg and Michael played checkers quietly on the parlor floor, their faces scrubbed and hair combed, much to their chagrin. Earlier at dinner, Claire and Daniel talked with them, telling them only that Uncle Jesse might be bringing a young lady over later to meet them.

"Boys," Daniel paused, searching for the best way to say what he knew he needed to. "Jesse's friend has some scars on her face, and I'm trusting that you will be able to be perfect gentlemen to her."

Michael nodded. "I think I know who you mean, Dad. I was with Petey and Homer a few weeks back and we passed a lady with marks on her face on the street. Homer said something mean after we passed her, and I was afraid she'd heard him. I told him to shut up."

Daniel patted Michael's shoulder. "Good for you. There's never a place for meanness, son, and it's always right to stand up for what's kind and good." He looked seriously at both boys. "I expect perfection tonight, Fellas. Got it?"

"Yes, sir!"

"Now, why don't you go find something to do. Your mom and I will clean up the kitchen together and give you the night off.

It didn't take any coaxing for them to leave the dinner table after that.

Now, an hour later, Daniel remained at the kitchen table, openly chuckling at his wife. Claire had been scurrying since she arrived home from Jesse's, straightening the house, baking a coffee cake, rummaging through trunks and drawers. Daniel watched as she retrieved a cut glass serving platter from a tall cabinet, then gently transferred a delicious smelling treat onto it.

"There," she said as she looked around. "Everything's ready, the water is hot for tea. If she doesn't like tea, I can offer her milk I suppose."

Daniel stood up and reached for Claire. "Darling, stop worrying. You are a wonderful hostess and she'll like everything you offer. Now relax. If you are nervous, you'll just make it worse for her."

He'd barely gotten the last word out when a knock on the door and Jesse's voice interrupted Daniel's embrace.

Claire jumped away and quickly removed her apron, then smoothed her hair. Daniel winked at her as he motioned for her to precede him into the parlor.

The boys answered the knock. Greg stood quietly while Michael stepped up to take Jesse's hat and ask if he could take Sari's sweater. Claire and Daniel came in as he was hanging them carefully on the hooks beside the door.

"Everyone, I want you to meet someone." Jesse took control of the group with his soft speech. "I'd like you to meet Sari Webber. Sari," he turned and looked at the girl who had been standing a bit behind him. He gently put his arm on the small of her back and brought her forward. "Sari, this is my sister Claire, my brother-in-law Daniel, and my nephews Michael and Greg." He paused with each name as they shook hands and said their individual hellos. Shyly, Greg glanced at his dad, then offered his hand and a smile.

Claire took over. "Won't you come sit down? Let me just go get a tray from the kitchen." Jesse guided Sari to the settee while the boys found their places back on the floor. Daniel began the conversation after they'd all been seated, "Sari, am I right that you are the magician who provides such amazing meals at the Copper Pot?"

Sari ducked her head. "I am the cook there, yes," she answered. "You are kind to say you enjoy what we serve."

"Enjoy it? I don't think that's a strong enough word." Daniel turned to Jesse, "Have you tasted the way she makes potatoes? I had some the other night when I was meeting with the mayor. They were cut into chunks and baked with a wonderful spice on them. What was that?"

Sari looked at Jesse then at Daniel and answered, "I added some rosemary before I put them in the oven."

Claire returned and set a large tray on the table in

front of the settee. As she busied herself with serving, she glanced at her brother and at Sari. Clearly, the girl had been crying. She sat beside Jesse, rigid, her back very straight. Sari's hand shook as she accepted the china cup and saucer Claire offered her, and she put it down on the table in front of her with care. Claire sent a silent prayer of thanks to God and Daniel for the conversation.

The group was quiet as they enjoyed the dessert. Jesse finished first and put his fork and plate on the table. "I want to make an announcement."

Claire looked up. Sari had taken only a bite or two, but carefully placed her plate next to Jesse's. *She's so nervous,* Claire thought, *too nervous to eat.*

"Well," Jesse took a breath and grinned. "I have asked Sari to marry me, and she's just agreed."

Even years later, what Sari remembered most about that evening was the unbridled and wholehearted kindness the family showed her. Before Jesse had even finished telling the group their news, Claire was up and pulling Sari into a warm hug.

"Oh congratulations! I always wanted a sister, now we will be sisters-in-law!"

Daniel shook Jesse's hand, then both boys joined in with handshakes of their own.

When the group had settled back down some, Claire began, "Have you made any plans yet? For the ceremony?"

Daniel interrupted with a smile towards his sons, "If you boys are done with your dessert, you are welcome to take your plates into the kitchen and then go play checkers."

Relief flooded Greg's eyes, "Thanks, Papa," and both boys were gone.

In answer to Claire's question, Sari shook her head, and Jesse spoke up. "We thought we could just go see Mayor Rankin at City Hall tomorrow afternoon."

Claire gasped. "Jesse, a wedding without a pastor? No, you can't! I'm sure that Pastor Abraham would be more than happy to do the ceremony at the church. Have you met him, Sari?"

"No, I work each Sunday morning so I'm not able to go to church." Sari felt ashamed, worried what Claire would think of her. Dispelling Sari's fears, Claire responded, "That's a shame. Pastor Emmett Abraham is a loving and wonderful leader for the church. I'm sure you would like him."

Jesse looked at Sari, who flashed him a frightened look then looked down. "Claire, we want this to be very quiet and simple. The mayor would do."

Claire realized how her outburst had come across and regretted it. She searched for a way to backtrack. "I am sorry, I didn't mean to speak out of turn. Sari, Jesse, I apologize."

Daniel broke the looming silence with a chuckle. "This feels a little familiar to me." He paused then continued. "Claire and I got married with only two day's planning. We were both living in South Dakota. We had courted for a while, but hadn't ever discussed marriage. When I was offered a job up here at the Ferris-Haggarty Mine, I barged in, asked her to marry me, and then carried her away in less than three days."

"I didn't know that," replied Jesse.

Daniel laughed again and added, "I think what Claire and I are trying to say is that even though time is very short, we'd love to make your wedding as memorable as we can."

Sari took a breath, then, and looked up. "Jesse's first idea was to talk to the pastor, but I told him on our walk over here that I would not like to be married in a church but I didn't explain to him why. I don't want anyone to get the wrong idea. I love the Lord, and would like very much for a minister to do our marriage, but I am very uncomfortable in large rooms. I feel, well, exposed. I suggested the justice of the peace because that would be in a small office instead."

All the while she'd been talking, Sari had been holding a linen handkerchief in her lap, wringing and twisting it. Jesse gently put his hand over hers. "I didn't understand, I'm sorry." He said it softly, as if they were alone, and Claire saw in an instant the kind of care he had to offer her.

Sari smiled shyly at him and nodded.

This time, when Claire spoke, she made sure her tone was kind and tender, "I wonder how you'd feel about asking Pastor Abraham to come here? We could move this table out to give us some more space, and have the ceremony in this room."

This time when she looked up, Sari was fighting to hold back tears. "That would be very nice. But I'd hate to have you go to any trouble."

"It won't be any trouble at all. I'd love to do it. We could make it an evening ceremony and then eat supper together."

Sari shook her head. "I will only have an hour or so available, in the middle of the afternoon, but then I will need to go back to work for the supper guests."

Claire opened her mouth to question the girl, but a warning look from Jesse stopped her. "Sari, how about a late supper after you are finished at the Copper Pot?" he suggested.

She nodded and Jesse flashed Claire a grin.

"That settles it," Claire summarized with a happy lilt, "Jesse, you are in charge of getting the pastor here tomorrow afternoon, I am in charge of making things ready here for the afternoon ceremony and then for a late wedding supper tomorrow evening. "Hmm. Daniel, what are you in charge of?"

"My darling wife, I have no illusions that you won't find something for me."

Even Sari giggled at that.

Claire laid a finger against her cheek in an exaggerated pose that was supposed to attest to deep thought, then she said, "I know, your job will be to meet Sari at the Copper Pot tomorrow afternoon and escort her here. It's bad luck for a groom to see the bride before the wedding, so you can be her official escort."

"I'd be honored," answered Daniel.

Sari could only nod.

13
Encampment, Wyoming
Tuesday, October 30, 1917

Sari finished adding the vegetables to the roasting pan and put the roast beef in the oven. Wiping her hands on her apron, she looked around. It had been a hectic day, made worse with nerves and second thoughts about the afternoon. She hadn't slept well, worrying and praying that she'd made the right decision by agreeing to marry Jesse. Meeting his family last evening had told her two things. First, that they were a generous and beautiful family and second, even though she didn't understand why, they all seemed genuine in their welcome of her.

Meredith returned to the kitchen with a dish cloth in her hand, interrupting Sari's thoughts. "All the tables are clean and ready for supper. I'm going to leave if that's alright with you."

Sari nodded, then said, "Meredith, I will try not to be, but I could be back here a bit late this afternoon. Would you mind too much coming back by four to check on the roast and start making the cornbread?"

Meredith's surprise was evident. "I don't know, I, well, is there a written recipe? Um, I've never made a large batch of cornbread before."

"I have it written right here. I've set everything out for you so that you are ready."

"I'd be happy to," was Meredith's quiet answer.

All morning Sari had wanted to continue the discussion she and Meredith had started yesterday, but with Jesse's proposal and the way her stomach roiled every time she thought about the wedding, she knew that would have to wait. Carefully, Sari tried to explain today's request, "I have something rather important to take care of this afternoon, and I might return a bit late. I really appreciate your help."

Chetley, unobserved in the doorway, stepped fully into the room. "What's this? I haven't heard anything about you not being at work as scheduled, Miss Webber. Really, what can you possibly need to do that is so important it would call for you to shirk your responsibilities?" Lilith walked in before Sari could answer and the two proprietors of the Copper Pot, along with Meredith stood waiting for an answer.

Sari had tried all day to no avail to catch Lilith in a quiet moment in order to share her news. This wasn't how she wanted the conversation to go, but there was no getting around it now. "Well, I'm to be married in an hour from now."

Lilith was taken aback. "Did you say married? To whom?"

The voice that answered came from behind her. The door to the dining room was suddenly filled as Daniel spoke up, "Good afternoon Mrs. Wills, Chetley. It's nice to see you and it looks like I'm just in time for the big announcement. Miss Sari is about to marry my brother-in-law, Jesse Atley. I've come to escort her to our house for the ceremony."

Lilith stared at Daniel, then turned to look at Sari. Her sudden, incredulous smile did a little to calm Sari's nerves. Sari thought her enthusiasm was forced when Lilith responded, "How exciting! I had no idea you had a beau, Sari! Congratulations!"

Meredith stood silently, staring at Sari, and Chetley's only response was a low grunt and a shake of the head.

Daniel came the rest of the way into the kitchen, and lightly kissed Sari on her left cheek. "I don't want to rush you, but we are expected at the house soon."

Sari nodded and untied her apron. "I will be back for the supper no later than four thirty," she told Lilith quietly.

To the group's surprise, Meredith spoke up, "Well, Mrs. Wills, I ... well, Sari has everything all ready for supper tonight except the cornbread, and she and I were just talking about that. Because of her planning ahead, I'm certain I can get supper finished on my own. Under the circumstances, Sari shouldn't have to come back to work, I can take care of everything."

"You most certainly will not." The sternness in Chetley's voice made Sari freeze. She lifted only her eyes to watch the man's face as he continued. "I can't have the kitchen shorthanded."

Lilith glanced at Daniel's frown, then put her hand on her husband's arm, "Chet, I can lend a hand if needed, and it does look as if everything is prepared. I think it will be fine."

Wills studied his wife's face for a moment, then shrugged. "Fine, Miss Webber, you may take the rest of today off, without pay, but let's not make this a habit."

Daniel was clearly annoyed, but he tamped it down and said, "Yes, Sari, you only get to marry Jesse just this once, you hear?" He winked at her and smiled, then extended his arm for her. Shaking and near tears, Sari whispered thank you to Meredith then allowed Daniel to usher her out the door, through the lobby, and onto the front sidewalk. They were half way to the house before Daniel spoke. "Is he always like that to you?"

Sari couldn't find her voice so she just nodded. They walked another block before Sari cleared her throat and thanked Daniel for his kindness.

"I didn't help much," he replied. "What I wanted to do was punch him in the nose."

Sari smiled at the picture his words created in her mind, "I've daydreamed about that myself," she answered. The exchange served to lighten their moods. As they neared the house Daniel turned to the woman on his arm. "Sari, in just a little while, Claire and I and our sons will become family with you. I want you to know that we are happy about that, and want you to know we are here whenever you need us, for whatever you need."

Again, Sari nodded. Words wouldn't come.

Claire was on the porch waiting for them when they arrived. She hugged Daniel and then Sari. "How are you?" Claire whispered to her as they parted. "Are you alright?"

Daniel intervened with a slight shake of the head that Sari didn't see as Sari gave a small smile, "Yes, I am. Just nervous."

"She has good news, though, Claire," Daniel prompted.

Sari nodded, "Yes, I've been given the rest of the day off, so we aren't in quite the hurry I thought we'd be."

"That's great news! Daniel, would you mind going to meet Jesse and the pastor? We ladies need about half an hour to get ready. I told him I'd send for them when Sari arrived."

Daniel kissed his wife on the cheek and bounded down the stairs on his errand.

"There," said Claire, "Now we have a few minutes to get ready. Would you like to freshen up a bit?"

"That would be nice," Sari agreed.

"Great, follow me." Claire led the way to the upstairs bedroom she shared with Daniel. Sari stepped over the threshold and looked around. The walls were soft blue set off by shiny white trim and baseboards. Wide, white crown molding at the ceiling gave the room a rich feel. The thick cotton curtains and bedcover held a delicate print with tiny blue and yellow flowers on a field of white. The cherry furniture, which included a sleigh bed and two side tables, added to the rich, inviting feeling the room held.

"This is lovely," Sari said. "Like something from a picture."

"Thank you. It took a long time to find just what I had in mind in here. I wanted it to be a special haven for Daniel and me to retreat to."

Sari let her eyes dance around the room, taking it all in.

Claire stationed herself beside the bed. "Um, I hope you don't mind, but I guessed that since you didn't have much time to plan, that maybe you didn't have time to think about a wedding dress. I have a trunk of dresses that, since I became a mother and got a little rounder, I can't wear anymore, but I dearly love. I wondered if maybe you'd like to wear one of these this afternoon?"

Sari appreciated the way Claire phrased her offer. She'd never met such kindness. There was nothing in Claire's words or actions that made Sari feel embarrassed or ashamed, and with surprise she realized she trusted Claire's kindness as well. Sari followed the sweep of Claire's hand and noticed for the first time three dresses hanging on the door jamb behind her.

At some point in the next half hour, sounds of Jesse, Daniel, the pastor, and the boys returning to the house filtered into the bedroom, but Sari and Claire paid scant attention. In spite of her shyness, Sari allowed

Claire's warm enthusiasm to carry her into a comfort she hadn't felt since her mother was killed. Like old friends, they chose an outfit, giggling and laughing as Sari dressed and readied herself for her wedding. Sari chose a blue, ankle length dress with mutton sleeves and a tight but demure bodice. The long, full bow, tied at the back, reminded her of a picture of a princess she'd seen once in a story book. The best part, though, was a matching hat that included a short veil. For a little while, Sari knew she could relax and allow herself the illusion of looking stylish as she hid her face behind the thin tulle and netting.

Sari's hands were cold and clammy as she and Claire entered the parlor. Jesse was standing beside the pastor, an older gentleman with kind eyes and a bald head. Jesse was wearing a dark green jacket and brown pants. His tan shirt was buttoned at the neck. A bolo tie with a silver clasp made him look formal and businesslike.

When Jesse first saw Sari, he beamed. "You look beautiful," he whispered as she came to stand beside him.

Sari dropped her eyes and inwardly rejected his words. *I'm not beautiful*, she thought. Suddenly she felt out of place, phony. She fought against the desire to run and hide.

Sari had never attended a wedding, so she shut out the jeering, accusing voice in her head that urged her to stop this sham and concentrated on listening carefully as the pastor spoke. Claire, standing beside the bride as matron of honor, studied Sari's profile as first Jesse repeated his vows, and then as Sari made hers. *I hope this marriage isn't just a business deal or spur-of-the-moment whim,* she thought. *God, please put your hand on them and this union.*

Claire was touched when the pastor asked Jesse for the ring. From Sari's reaction, it was clear that Jesse hadn't told her about the gold band he'd bought. She watched as Jesse slipped the band on Sari's finger. When it was Sari's turn and Jesse produced a ring for himself, the surprise was complete.

The only outwardly difficult moment was when the minister declared them husband and wife and told Jesse he could kiss his bride. They were standing face to face, but as Jesse leaned in to kiss her, he felt Sari stiffen and pull back. Carefully, he took her hands in his and lifted them to his lips instead, kissing the back of each hand softly and with tenderness.

There were congratulations all around afterwards. The pastor stayed long enough to have a piece of last night's coffee cake to celebrate before excusing himself. Jesse and Sari, Claire and Daniel, and the boys lingered at the dining room table.

Daniel turned to Sari when he'd finished his coffee. "I said this earlier, Sari, but I'll say it officially. Welcome to our family. Even after Jesse leaves, we are still here."

Her answer was a shy smile.

"Hey!" Greg was still shy around Sari, but had warmed up some. "Does this mean she is going to live at your house while you are gone, Uncle Jesse?"

Sari's eyes snapped up to look at Jesse, confused at the boy's question, but before she could respond, Jesse answered. "Of course, it's her house too since we're married now." Jesse pointedly ignored Sari's reaction and pulled his watch from his pocket to study its face then looked up. "If you don't mind, Claire, I'm going to steal my bride for an hour or so. Since Sari doesn't have to go back to the Copper Pot, we have some errands to run together."

Claire nodded, "That's fine. I'll get dinner ready. We'll eat about six and continue to celebrate, alright?"

There was a flurry of movement. Daniel reminded the boys about finishing their chores and feeding the rabbits early, while Claire began picking up the dishes from the table.

The closeness she'd felt in the bedroom with Claire was eclipsed by the emotions swirling inside her. Sari tried to excuse herself to go change back into her own dress, saying, "I, well, I need to change my clothes. I wouldn't want anything to happen to Claire's dress."

Claire stepped close to her new sister-in-law, laid her hand on the girl's arm, then quietly confided, "Sari, I'd be so happy if you'd agree to keep this dress as a wedding gift from me to you. You look so very lovely in it, much prettier than I ever did because the color is perfect for you, and it would make me happy if you'd keep it and wear it sometimes."

Sari was touched beyond words. She hugged Claire instead of answering. Jesse held her coat and soon they were out in the brisk air.

"Claire was so excited that you accepted the dress. She wants you to feel welcome. She wants you to love them."

"How could I not love them?" she asked wistfully. "They are so perfect."

"Well, that's certainly not true, but then, you'll find that out soon enough." Jesse hesitated then continued, "I was thinking that we could go to your place and pick up what you need for tonight and take it home. Then tomorrow we could use the truck and move you in properly. Would that be alright?"

"Move me? I don't understand. Until your nephew mentioned your house, I thought you lived with Claire and Daniel." She recalled the conversation in the kitchen and let her confusion show. "I didn't realize I'd be moving."

Jesse turned to face her, "I'm sorry. We should have talked about this earlier. There is so much we don't know about each other. I don't live with them, I have a house just half a block from my livery."

Sari's voice faltered, "You have a house, meaning you rent rooms there?"

Jesse grinned, "No. I own the whole house outright. It's mine. Um, it's ours. When I bought the livery, the house was part of the package. It took me five years to pay off the banknote, and now the business, the barn and the house are mine."

"I, well, I had no idea. I just assumed that after dinner, you would walk me back to my room and then you'd go home to Claire and Daniel's. I never dreamed you'd want me to move in with you."

Jesse didn't know what to say. He breathed a prayer for wisdom, then started again. "Sari, I told you that I want you to be my wife. I meant it when I said that I wouldn't insist on anything physical between us, but no matter, in the eyes of God, the state of Wyoming, me and my, no, our family, we are husband and wife. My home isn't fancy, and it isn't nicely decorated like Claire has done up theirs, but I hoped you might live and be happy there from now on."

Sari didn't, couldn't answer. The day had already held too much, and she was overcome. Jesse wasn't sure what to do with this silence, but after a moment he coaxed her by adding, "How about this? We will go retrieve your things, I've just realized that I don't know anything about where you live either," he stopped, shaking his head. Then he continued, "Anyway, let's go get what you need for tonight. I will show you my home, I'll sleep downstairs, and we'll wake up tomorrow and decide what to do from there."

Sari nodded, not trusting her voice. Shyly, Jesse put out his hand. "Mrs. Atley, may I hold your hand as we walk?"

Underneath the veil of the hat she still wore, Jesse couldn't see either the tentative smile that responded to him, or the tear sliding down Sari's cheek.

When they reached McCaffrey, Sari indicated they needed to go left. "Oh, do you live at a rooming house?" Jesse asked, knowing that there were two boarding houses on this street.

Sari nodded, "Yes, at the Old Wyoming."

They passed several houses and the Presbyterian Church, then crossed 8th Street. An old man sitting on a front porch called to Jesse as they passed.

"It's a nice afternoon for a stroll, isn't it?"

"Why yes, it is, G-String." Jesse answered, then he guided Sari across the street to stop at the edge of the sidewalk.

"I haven't seen you much lately, Boy. Heard you went to the Army."

"Yes, Sir, I did. I'm just home on leave for a few days. Sir, this is Sari Webber, um, Atley. She is my wife." He turned to look at Sari, "Sari, this is Jack Fulkerson, a real legend around here."

They greeted each other, though the man stayed seated on his bench. "There are lots of stories about me in these parts," Fulkerson told Sari with a wink, "and I'd bet most of them are true."

Fulkerson asked Jesse about the livery business, and listened intently as Jesse talked about buying a truck.

"We'd have never gotten that cable for the tram up into those hills with a truck. If you ask me, nothing will ever equal a strong set of horses or mules to do the hard work a man's got to do."

"I'm sure you are right about that, and I kept my team of Belgian draft horses for that very reason," Jesse answered.

Jack was nodding his approval when the front door opened and a small woman emerged from the house. Sari was immediately impressed by two things, the woman's kind smile and her long, dark hair. It reached nearly to her knees and was dripping wet. "Oh, my, Jack. I had no idea we had visitors. I just had my head in the sink, washing this tangle, and I didn't hear you out here."

With a laugh, Jesse responded by introducing Sari. "Mrs. Lena Fulkerson, this is my wife Sari."

"It's nice to meet you, Sari."

The couples chatted a bit longer, then Jesse made their excuses. "We really didn't intend to come visiting. We were just on our way across the street and saw Jack here."

"Well, come back another time when you can stay," Lena answered as Jesse and Sari took their leave.

On their way across the street, Sari asked, "Isn't that the man you told me you admired for his horsemanship?"

Jesse was touched that she'd remembered he'd said that the day they'd gone to Lost Treasure Gulch. "Yes, it is." He wanted to say more, but now they were at the front walk to the Old Wyoming Rooming house, and other tasks intruded.

They approached the house, but instead of walking up the front steps, Sari led Jesse around the house to the side of the building. She stopped to unfasten a latch to what looked like a lean-to. She opened the door and stepped in. "Here we are," she said shyly. "It will just take me a few minutes to get ready."

She fumbled for a match and lit a lamp before inviting Jesse in. The small room was furnished with a cot, a small, three-drawer dresser with the kerosene lamp on top, and a wooden, straight backed chair. In one corner stood a small kerosene heating stove. A tattered braided rug on the floor and a plain grey, wool blanket on the bed were all the room held for decoration.

"The boarding house has electricity, but you
don't?" Jesse remarked with a frown.

Sari felt and heard a serious undertone in his
words and didn't answer. Jesse stared around him as she
pulled a brown leather valise from under the cot. He
hardly noticed as she added items to the case, then folded
two garments hanging on a hook on the wall and closed it.

"I'm ready," Sari said as she turned around. Jesse
didn't move or respond. Sari watched him for a moment.
His jaw was set and she could see the muscles there
flexing as he ground his teeth. His eyes were stormy. He
looked so fierce and angry, it frightened her.

"This is where you live?" his manner was dark,
quiet. "Where do you bathe, eat, um, take care of other
necessities?"

Sari felt wary and embarrassed, "There's a privy
just around the corner in the back that I use. I bathe
inside using a bathroom I share with the other boarders. I
eat at the restaurant." She paused, heart pounding as she
noticed the tense set of his shoulders. "Did I offend you,
Jesse? I'm sorry, but I don't understand why you look so
angry all of a sudden."

Jesse clenched and then relaxed his fists several
times before he looked at Sari. He thought about the short
conversation he'd had with Daniel before the wedding
during which Daniel had described Wills' demeanor
towards Sari and her admission that he was often rude to
her. He took another breath, then looked at his new wife.
Clearly, he'd scared her. His voice was gentler now. "Oh,
Sari, you haven't done anything to make me mad. I'm not
angry at you. I just don't understand. Who arranged for
you to live here?"

"Well, Mr. Wills gave me two options when I arrived
in Encampment. I could live here in this room the way I do
and pay only a dollar a week in rent, or I could live in one
of the rooms inside and pay two dollars. Since I only
receive two dollars a week from him, there was really no
question, especially when Mr. Wills holds out fifty cents
each week for the food I eat."

Jesse wanted to explode. He wanted to tear down
the room—which he knew he could do with his bare hands
it was that ramshackle—and rail at the sky and anyone

who would listen about how badly Sari had been treated. It occurred to him that he could take out his anger on Wills himself. One glance, though, at the woman standing before him and he knew he had to hold his temper. Fighting hard to gain control, he took several deep breaths and then forced himself to smile.

Jesse stepped past Sari, picked up the valise she'd left on the bed, and blew out the lantern. He extended his hand gently, "Sari, let's go home."

Jack Fulkerson raised a hand in greeting as they passed his porch. A few steps later, movement on the side of the house caught their attention. Lena Fulkerson was standing in the yard with a comb in her hand. She'd draped her long tresses over the clothesline and was intent on brushing them as her hair dried.

The newlyweds smiled at each other and walked on in silence for a while, then Sari began, "I didn't expect the blessings of today. I mean, I didn't expect a new dress and hat, or a ring. Or a new place to live."

"The ring is pretty plain, that's for sure. Does it fit alright? Because they had two others at Parkison's. Ed said we could come exchange it for a better size if we needed to."

Sari examined the ring, twisting it. "I've never owned or worn a ring before, but it seems alright. I'll have to see if it can slip off when my hands are wet, I do a lot of dishes at work."

They were back on safe turf, and Jesse's anger at Sari's living conditions rested on a back burner as he concentrated on Sari herself. Soon, they passed the livery and found themselves in front of a neat, well-kept house. Jesse stopped, turning so that Sari could get a good view.

"This is yours?" she said. Her voice came out as a squeak. The home in front of her was a two-story cottage. The house was pale green, the trimming white. Tall, turned wood spindles held up the wide porch roof. Shorter, matching spindles held a railing that spanned the entire length of the front. The ample porch, complete with a rocking chair and a porch swing, prefaced the entrance. The front door was painted a dark, olive green.

"Come, I'll show you inside."

Jesse left Sari's valise inside the front door and conducted a tour of the main floor. A narrow stairway stood off-center to the left. Its golden oak banister, polished and shiny, matched the hard wood floors at their feet. At right, a modestly sized parlor welcomed them. The room was furnished with a small settee and two wing back chairs along with two side tables and a center table. A rock hearth and fireplace on the far wall promised warmth on cold winter nights. Beyond the stairs and to the left, was a doorway leading to a smaller room. The door was open, and Sari could see that Jesse had a daybed and a desk along with several shelves full of books in there. There were no pictures hung, but even so, the room suggested itself as a comfortable place to curl up and read.

A short hallway straight ahead from the front door led them to the kitchen and dining area, one large room that encompassed the entire back half of the first floor. Sari loved this room immediately. She lingered, trying to absorb its welcome, imagining what it would be like to take such a room for granted.

Jesse leaned against the doorframe and watched her survey the room. After another moment, he offered, "Come upstairs, and I'll show you the rest."

As she turned around, she noticed a closed door beside the entrance to the dayroom. "What is in there?" she asked.

Jesse opened the door, reached in and flipped on an electric light switch, and then stepped back so that she could enter.

Sari wasn't sure which impressed her most, the fact that the house had electricity or the room in front of her. "A real bathroom?" It was a combination of question and sigh. "Oh, my. Look at that claw-footed tub, it's nearly deep enough to swim in!" She turned around twice, thrilled with the pedestal sink, the commode, the tub. A shelf held crisp white towels.

Jesse drank in her excitement, gaining confidence in his decision to marry. He let her stay for a minute then gestured towards the stairs.

Sari had to hold the skirt of her frock up as she

climbed the steep passage. At the top was a short hallway holding two doors.

"There are two bedrooms up here, though I hardly use one of them." He opened the left door to reveal a small, dusty space with several boxes and an old butter churn haphazardly in the middle. He closed that door and then opened the other.

"This is the bedroom." Jesse placed the valise he'd carried up beside the door and moved to the right. A bed enclosed by shiny brass headboard and footboard took up much of the room. There was a tall chest of drawers on one wall and a dresser with a large framed mirror on another. The two windows in the room were covered with lace curtains, allowing the space plenty of light.

Jesse moved to the left and opened a narrow door. "Here is the closet, the only one in the house. It's pretty big, though, so I think it will be alright. Since I won't be here, I already folded my shirts and pants and put them in the bottom two drawers over there. So, you can use it to hang your dresses."

"There's plenty of room," was all she said.

"I cleaned out the top drawers of the dresser here, so they are ready for your things." Suddenly uncomfortable, Jesse pointed toward the mirrored dresser and looked at the small throw rug under his boots for a time. "Sari, I want you to be comfortable here. I don't know anything about decorating, but I know this room needs some. You've seen Claire and Daniel's bedroom. I'd like it if you had a nice room to sleep in. I, well, I have a little money put aside in the bank and there's also some money I've saved in the peanut can on the floor of the closet. I was thinking maybe you could buy some new curtains and such for this room so that it looks pretty for you."

Sari tried several times to answer him. She opened her mouth, then shut it again. Finally, she chuckled at herself, "I probably looked like a fish out of water just then."

Jesse snickered.

Continuing, Sari tried to say what she was thinking. "I do feel like a fish out of water. Since the acc-," she stopped to regroup. "Since my parents died, I never allowed myself to think of things the other girls at Miss Milton's talked of and planned for, like husbands or homes. I took the classes to learn homemaking, but neither I nor the teachers ever believed I'd ever have someone to share a home with. I guess I'd made peace with what I thought my life would be. The last two days feel like a walking dream, and I'm not sure how to take this in. Jesse, how can I ever thank you for your generosity and kindness? I was amazed at your willingness to marry me. But I think you've gone too far to offer me your home to live in while you are away as well."

Jesse motioned for Sari to go in front of him, and they descended the stairs. Sari sat down in one of the chairs in the parlor and waited, sensing that Jesse needed time to think. When he spoke, it was with confidence and conviction.

"I'm at a loss to explain the past week's events myself, and I certainly can't foretell the future. All I can say is that I know in my heart and soul that our marriage is real. I'm not offering you a place to stay just while I'm away. No matter what happens, whether I come home or not, this is your home now. I am your husband now, and you are my wife."

As they continued their discussion, Sari slowly began to take in that Jesse was serious about their union and that the parlor in which she sat was to become her home. She knew that it would take more than Jesse's words to make it feel real, but by the time they walked down the sidewalk toward Claire and Daniel's for dinner, she'd made a start at understanding.

Claire's dining room table was set with fine china and crystal glasses when Sari and Jesse returned. The house smelled of rich spices from dinner and pine from the merry fire beyond the hearth.

"Oh Jesse and Sari, here you are right on time. I hope you don't mind, but I ran into Dawson when I stopped over to Ella's to get some eggs this afternoon. He was delivering coal to her. I invited him to join us tonight. It will make our party more festive."

Jesse had shared news of his upcoming wedding that morning with Dawson at the livery. His partner's congratulations had been cordial, but somehow awkward. Jesse felt Sari's back stiffen beside him at Claire's news, and he hoped that Dawson's inclusion would turn out well.

They took their time at dinner. Sari removed her hat when they'd come in to the house, so she wasn't able to hide anymore, but Jesse seated her on the end of the rectangular table on his right. There was no one beside her at that end and Claire sat across from her with such amiability that Sari was able to relax a little. Dawson sat at the other end of the table. It seemed to her that he was uncomfortable, and wondered if it was because of her or if he just wasn't used to this kind of outing. The family chatted about a dozen topics and Sari let the bubbling conversation surround her. She spoke little but didn't feel neglected or left out.

At the end of the meal, Jesse raised his water glass in Claire's direction. "Claire, this was a fine meal and an excellent wedding feast. My compliments to you!"

Sari agreed, "Yes, Claire, everything was perfect. I loved every bite, probably a few more than I really am capable of holding."

Claire shook her head, "I was so nervous cooking this meal. I've eaten at the Copper Pot, and I know what a talented chef you are, I am not nearly as gifted in the kitchen as you." Sari blushed, unused to such warm praise, and thanked Claire who continued, "I hope that you'll be willing to teach me a few of your cooking secrets."

Just then, Daniel excused himself. He returned quickly carrying a tray. While they watched, Daniel opened a wine bottle then poured rich burgundy into a glass and handed it to Sari. She was afraid even to hold the delicate goblet, and accepted it gently. Daniel handed another to Claire, to Dawson, then Jesse and finally poured one for himself. He made sure his sons each had a little milk left in their glasses, then looked at the group seriously.

"To Jesse and his bride. Sari, we are thankful to have you in this wild family. We welcome you with open arms and hearts. Jesse, we promise to do our best not to scare her off with our shenanigans before you safely return to us."

A chorus of "Here, here," and "Congratulations" rang out, mostly from Michael and Greg, as Sari took her very first sip of wine.

Claire took a second sip, then put her wine glass down. Sari admired how confidently she moved. Claire caught Sari watching her and smiled. "Sari, did Jesse give me correct information when he said you have Sunday evenings off?"

"Yes, the Copper Pot serves only two meals on Sunday."

"Well, we hope that you will agree to come to Sunday supper this week with us. And, for that matter, every Sunday evening."

Greg didn't wait for her answer before he asked, "Aunt Sari?"

Her new title took her by surprise and she let it ring through the room. "Yes, Greg?"

"Do you like to play checkers?"

"Well, I've watched the game several times, but I've never played myself."

"Good, then maybe I can win against you! I lose every game against Michael," Greg answered, causing the group to laugh.

"Will you play with me when you come over?"

Sari thought her heart would explode with his innocent welcome. "I would love to."

"As I was saying," Claire reasserted herself in the conversation, her voice upbeat and relaxed, "You might just get lonely at your house in the evenings, and I want you to always feel welcome here, any time."

"Thank you so much. I work long hours most days, but I'll plan on coming over Sunday."

The wedding party members moved to the parlor for a while after supper. Warm and relaxed, the celebration continued. Jesse told the family about meeting Jack and Lena Fulkerson that afternoon, and Dawson, finally relaxing, joined the conversation to share a couple stories about G-String Jack that made the entire group laugh.

When the conversation began to wane, Jesse stood up. "Thank you all for sharing this evening with us." He reached for Sari's hand and she stood up beside him. "I know you will all take good care of my new wife after I'm gone."

His comment began a round of hugs and well wishes and Dawson retrieved his hat and thanked Claire for inviting him. Jesse walked his friend to the porch. Before he stepped away, Dawson turned to shake Jesse's hand and quietly said, "Jesse, I said some mean things about, um, your wife when we first met her. I just want to apologize for my harshness, and assure you that it won't ever happen again. She's a nice person, and I was wrong to be so ugly."

Jesse accepted the man's apology with a smile, warmed by his honesty.

A few minutes later, after a last round of hugs and good wishes for the bride and groom, a quick and quiet conversation between Jesse and Daniel, and a promise from Sari to come Sunday right after she got away from work, the wedding celebration came to an end. Jesse helped Sari with her coat and the two started down the street.

Claire leaned into Daniel as they watched the newlyweds disappear into the chilly night. "God bless them both," she said, tears welling up.

Daniel encased her in the safety of his arms. Her voice muffled against his chest she continued her prayer, "God, please don't let this be the last celebration we share with Jesse, please bring him home. Please bless this hurried marriage, and show us how we can welcome his wife into this family."

14

Encampment, Wyoming

Wednesday, October 31, 1917

It was still very dark when Sari awoke. For a few seconds the shadows clung to her and she wasn't sure where she was. Then her new reality asserted itself. She fumbled with the lamp, unaccustomed to simply switching on the light instead of lighting a match, and looked at the wind-up alarm clock at her bedside. It was very early, she had two hours before she needed to be at the restaurant, but she was wide awake. Sitting up, she stretched and looked around the room. So much had changed in just one day. Yesterday she was Sari Webber, today Sari Atley.

She sighed. So much had not changed. She still had to go to work. Resigned, she dressed in her old, stained dress and made the bed. She wondered if she'd disturb Jesse's sleep as she started down the stairs, but soon realized that he was already up and had coffee perking in the kitchen.

She slipped into the bathroom and smiled, anticipating the future luxury of taking a long, warm bath in that tub.

Jesse was standing at the sink, looking out the window into darkness when she came into the kitchen. "Good morning," she greeted quietly.

He turned around. His hair was uncombed and his eyes were still sleepy. There was a red crease across his cheek. "Good morning. Would you like a cup of coffee?"

"No, thank you. I love the way coffee smells, but I just don't care for the taste," she told her husband. "You look as if you didn't sleep well. I should not have let you give me your bed."

"I actually did sleep a little, but then a million tasks crowded in and there wasn't any more room in my head for sleep. I was just thinking about all I need to do today."

"Is there anything I can do during my time off this afternoon or this evening?"

"There are a few things that we will need to take care of together today, before I leave tomorrow. First, I've been thinking about finances," he hesitated then asked, "Do you have a few minutes before you need to leave? Can we talk now? It seems like we have lots to discuss."

Sari smiled, "I have time." From habit, she sat at the table slightly slanted away from him.

He took a breath and sat down. Taking a drink from his brown coffee mug, he began, "Here's what I'd like to do. First, I need to go to the bank. I'll put your name on my personal account, and I want to arrange for you to have a monthly withdrawal. We'll set it up so you can pick it up at the bank once a month so that you have what you need."

Sari was shaking her head. "No, I can't. I mean. I don't expect you to—"

Jesse interrupted her with a kind but stern voice. "Sari, let's don't argue about this. It's too early in the morning." He gave her a mischievous grin. "Just nod and agree, okay, please?" He paused and waited for her to reluctantly nod, then continued. "You told me last night that you receive two dollars a week from the Copper Pot and that part of that goes to renting your room and paying Wills," he said the name as if it left a bad taste in his mouth, "for the food you eat. You won't be paying the rooming house anymore, but still, a dollar and a half a week just isn't enough to live on."

Sari started to protest again and Jesse ignored her. "You probably will want to continue to eat at the restaurant. In fact, that's a good idea since the cook is so talented," he smiled at her then continued. "But I want you to also have food here in the kitchen. You'll need supplies, clothes, who knows? I told you last night that I want you to feel welcome to do some sprucing up in the house because it certainly needs it. I know Claire would love to lend a hand. I want to make sure you have enough money to be comfortable."

She felt ashamed to say it, but knew she needed to, "I've never had money of my own before. I don't know anything about paying bills or keeping a house financially."

Jesse smiled. The admission that had made Sari feel ashamed didn't seem to disappoint him. "I understand. Another place we'll go to is Lordier Drug store

and Parkison's and the other stores I have accounts with.
I'll introduce you to them as my wife and make sure they
know you. Anything you need, food, clothes, or things for
the house, you can pay cash for or you put the purchases
on the accounts I have. I'll ask them to send any bills to
the livery in care of Daniel. Each week when he and
Dawson meet about the business, Daniel will pay the
house bills as well."

"So Daniel is taking over the livery?"

Jesse appreciated that Sari was settling in to the
conversation. He answered her confidently, "Not exactly.
Dawson has worked for and with me from nearly the
beginning. Just recently I asked him to be my partner. He
and I have it set up so that he gets a salary for working at
the livery. Dawson will deposit my portion into my bank
account. Daniel has agreed to serve as a sort of financial
manager for the livery. He and Dawson will make sure the
business bills are paid, and Daniel will make sure the
house bills get paid as well. For example, there will be the
electricity, coal, and water bills. I've worked out a deal
with Michael to make sure there is plenty of coal in the
coal bin for winter and that you have wood carried in for
the fireplace in the parlor, and to shovel the walks for you.
Daniel will help you and take care of paying for those
things, so you needn't worry. You'll only be in charge of
your own living expenses. If you have any questions or
something big comes up, you'll need to talk to Daniel, but
if you don't go wild, there will be more than enough money
for you to buy what you want."

A thick silence stretched through the room. Jesse
watched Sari for a full minute, then asked, "Are you
alright?"

Sari sat still for a few more seconds, trying to
frame her thoughts into words. She searched for a way to
explain herself. "I'm having trouble fathoming all this,
Jesse," she began. "I only vaguely remember what it was
like before my parents were killed. When I was sent to
Miss Milton's orphanage, I wasn't just parentless, I was
classified indigent. All the teachers and the girls were
aware that I was a charity case. The treatment I received
and what I came to expect were all based on that fact.
Most of the other girls had some sort of inheritance that

afforded them new dresses and treats from time to time, a birthday purchase, a gift at Christmas. I was given hand-me-down clothes and was never allowed to go on special outings because I couldn't pay for them. I was expected to be thankful and uncomplaining."

Sari stopped and took a deep breath, then went on, "Coming here to Encampment has been much the same. Not only do, um, did I have nothing, but I am indebted. I've learned that I can't expect anything, and it's been difficult to hold on to hope. I understand the disgust I saw on your face when you saw where I've been living." Her eyes were down, so she didn't see that Jesse started to protest. She continued, "After seeing this home and Claire's, it is clear why, from your point of view, you would think my room is a hovel. But please understand, that room represented to me a step up. It wasn't nice, but I paid each month for that room. It wasn't charity."

She fell silent. Jesse rubbed his face and tried to find something to say. He didn't want Sari to think his outrage at the way she'd been treated was ire at her. At length, Sari concluded, "Now, you are explaining how you are preparing for me not only to have money to spend, but you've just described an entire new way of life and new position in society for me. I'm having trouble taking that in. You've told me that this isn't charity, but there isn't one thing that's happened between you and me that I deserve or can repay and I'm struggling to understand your actions."

She met his eyes then, and he saw her tears.

Jesse sighed a prayer for help before answering her, "I'll be the first to admit that our marriage has begun differently than most, but even so, I think with any marriage, both people bring to it all they have, and that's enough. I don't think it makes sense for any couple to keep score about who added what. As of yesterday, when we repeated our vows, we are a unit, and everything is ours." He could see the argument growing in her eyes and put his hand up. "I've thought about this over and over. I have been the recipient of a lot of grace in my life, and there have been many times I have received what I didn't earn or deserve. I guess this is just one of those times for you to consider. You do not owe me anything except what you promised yesterday in front of God, our family, and the pastor. I don't owe you anything either, as far as that goes, but I want, and I'm stressing *want*, to share all I have with you." He let her think for a minute, then reached out and cupped her hands in his. "Sari, I've wrestled with understanding God's grace many times through my life. I don't claim to understand it fully now. I sincerely think God brought us together, and it's His grace and blessings that I'm sharing with you. Please just accept it."

Sari studied how Jesse's calloused hand gently covered hers and began, "One night, just after I arrived at Miss Milton's there was a huge storm. Thunder and lightning were so close there was no time between flash and crash, the whole building shook. The room was cold and as I lay there shivering—scared and so alone—I began to pray. I can't exactly explain it, but all of a sudden I felt warm, comforted. I knew it was God, and that He was there. I often remember that comfort and feel strengthened, hopeful. I'll admit, my fear is stubborn, Jesse, and my fear is what is holding me back right now."

Not knowing how to respond, Jesse squeezed her hands in his and lifted them to his lips. He left two soft kisses on the backs of her hands, then changed the subject.

"Another thing I want to do this afternoon is finish getting your things from the boarding house. We'll need to talk to them so that they know you won't be back."

"Yes, we will need to stop in there, but I already have all my things."

"What? I saw you fold up two dresses and add a few things from the drawers. That can't be all your belongings."

His tone felt accusing, and Sari fought feeling defensive again. "When I arrived at Miss Milton's I had the clothes I was wearing, a night gown, and my mother's Bible. When I left, she pointed out to me that she'd gone above and beyond her obligation, as I was leaving with three dresses, two nightgowns, underthings, an extra pair of shoes, and a light coat."

Jesse was dumbstruck. "But, but I'm sure you have keepsakes, pictures. Claire and I had a hard life growing-up, but she still has a few mementos, my mother's Bible, a jewelry pin, and I even have a toy train that was mine when I was small."

Sari stopped and faced Jesse. "Less than two weeks after the accident, when I still was in bandages and feeling wooly-headed, the bank held an auction. They sold all my father's livestock and equipment, the house and land, and they auctioned off all that was inside the house. They sold everything, furniture, dishes, pictures. They sold the clothes my mother sewed for me and my ragdoll. I left the ranch that day with this tiny key," she hooked the leather lace from beneath her collar and pulled. The small brass key dangled between them for a moment, then Sari continued, "I also managed to find and hide my mother's Bible."

Without thinking, Jesse stood up and pulled Sari up to him and into a tight hug. He did it quickly, but not before Sari saw the tears forming in his eyes. He could never have comforted her with words more powerful than the look on his face and the fierceness of that hug. They stood in the kitchen for a long time. Finally, Jesse stepped back. "I am not offering you anything as if you were some charity case. I am asking you to share what I have as my wife, my equal and partner. Can you try to accept that?"

She hesitated before finally answering quietly, "You are asking me to shuck off ten years of treatment and the factual knowledge that I'm physically scarred and blemished. I don't know how well I'll do, but yes, I will try to understand and accept what you offer me. And I offer you all that I can contribute."

He hugged her again, and they stood there, each learning the rhythm of the other's breathing and heart beat for several minutes.

Finally, Sari glanced out the window. The sky was pink and growing lighter. She stepped away and Jesse looked at his pocket watch. "I don't want to make you late for work." He reached for Sari's coat, noticing a frayed cuff and more than one patch. He helped her into it, and then donned his own.

"Are you going to the livery this early?"

"Yes, but I thought I'd walk you to the Copper Pot then go to work," he answered.

The morning was cold. A light skiff of powdery snow covered the grass. Sari shivered and pulled her coat tighter.

"I'm sorry you have a longer walk to work now, Sari," Jesse said.

"It's not too much farther," she answered. "I like to walk most of the time, except when the wind is howling."

They continued in silence. Sari started to turn down the alley so that she could go into the kitchen through the back door. Jesse grasped her arm softly and stopped her. "Today I want to walk you in, and I want us to go through the front door. Daniel told me about what happened yesterday when he came to pick you up. I don't much like it that others treat you with disrespect. That stops today."

Sari nodded, unsure of what he meant and wondering if Jesse would ever stop surprising her with his kindness. They stomped the snow from their shoes on the front rug and crossed the Copper Pot's small lobby. Chetley and Lilith Wills were standing together at the entrance of the dining room.

"Good morning Chet, Miss Lilith." Jesse held his hat in one hand and Sari's hand in the other. "I want to present to you Mrs. Sari Atley, my wife. I think you've known her by another name." He shook the hand that Wills offered him as Lilith gave Sari a quick hug. After the round of congratulations, Jesse, still smiling and jovial, continued with a quiet voice. "I know that my wife has an obligation to you, and she and I are committed to her fulfilling that obligation." He waited. Wills nodded his approval.

"However, it seems to me that the hours Sari has been working here at the Copper Pot exceed the limits of her obligation and strain the confines of fairness." His words took the other three by surprise. Jesse focused his eyes on Chetley and continued, "Asking anyone to work thirteen or more hours a day, six days a week and an eight-hour day on the seventh day each week without respite and for what you pay her hints at slavery and borders on inhumane."

Wills leaned forward frowning. "Now Jesse, this just isn't your affair. It's between us and Miss Webber and the bank in Rawlins.

Jesse continued, "It's Mrs. Atley now, and I disagree. My wife assures me that she's never seen any paperwork or signed a contract, and I have a feeling that maybe, unwittingly, there have been a few liberties taken in the deal at her expense. I need you to be aware that from now on I'm going to insist on a little more consideration. Starting tomorrow, my wife will be working from six in the morning until three in the afternoon, six days a week. I expect that she'll be afforded a lunch period in the middle of the day to eat and take a break. Sari will also have *all* of Sundays off, not just half a day, to attend church with her family and enjoy a day of rest. And, she will take on these new hours for the same pay she had been receiving."

Sari squeezed Jesse's hand, frightened at the scene unfolding in front of her. Wills' face flushed as he listened. He took a step forward so that he was looming over Jesse, but Jesse didn't move. His voice was quiet and menacing, "I don't know who you think you are, but you can't tell me what I can or can't do with my employees. She is indentured to me, and as such I can choose her hours as I see fit."

Jesse smiled. "Chet, it's interesting that you'd use that word. It's the second time you've described to me your business relationship with my wife that way. I'm glad you did though, because it gets us to the heart of the matter. While indenture is legal in Wyoming, the courts have taken a hard look at the arrangement, and have found in favor of several plaintiffs, especially females who were housed improperly and overworked as a part of their servitude. Now, as I said from the beginning, we acknowledge at this point the debt and will abide it. However, if you aren't willing to modify her hours and maintain a positive relationship with Sari, I'd be happy to contact my uncle at the Justice Department in Cheyenne and file a writ of recusal to have the entire arrangement vacated. Chet, it's your choice."

Lilith, who had been standing quietly by during the exchange put her hand on her husband's arm. "Chetley, we are lucky to have Sari, and I have worried about overworking her. We can manage if she has fewer hours each day. What Mr. Atley says makes sense and won't really add to our budget."

Sari realized she'd been holding her breath. She exhaled quietly, sending aloft a prayer for the situation.

Wills held on to his bully stance for a second or two longer, then stepped back. "All right, Atley, have it your way."

"Thank you, Chet, I appreciate your understanding." Jesse spoke as if no tension had ever existed between them. He glanced at Sari and smiled reassuringly, then back at the couple in front of him. "There's just one more thing. I'm not sure you know this, but I've been called up for military service. I leave for France tomorrow. My brother-in-law, Daniel Haynes will be here as support for Sari while I'm gone. Since my time is so short, Sari and I have a lot to do today to prepare, so I need to come by and pick her up at one o'clock, and she won't be back today."

Wills' eyes got large and Sari was afraid he'd begin yelling, but once again Lilith stepped in. "Sari, I'm sure you are beside yourself with the wedding and everything. Of course we want you to have the time you need. I'd just ask you to make sure Meredith knows exactly what she needs to do to finish up so that supper goes smoothly."

"I'll be happy to, Lilith." Sari's heart was pounding, but she tried to look calm as she met first Jesse's eyes and then Lilith's and Chetley's.

Wills gave Sari a withering look, then turned and stomped away. Lilith looked from Jesse to Sari, nodded, and followed her husband.

Sari felt rooted to the floor. Jesse squeezed her hand gently and she looked up. "I didn't know you had an uncle in the Justice Department in Cheyenne," she whispered.

Jesse didn't even try to hide his triumphant grin. "I don't. I made that up."

"So," Sari was stunned, "Your threat of a writ of recusal was..." she searched for the right word.

Jesse supplied it for her, "A bluff? Yes. But it seems to have worked."

Sari couldn't hide her shock. Jesse continued, "I hate how he's treated you, I just couldn't let it go on. I hope you aren't angry with me."

"Angry? No. Mr. Wills frightens me, that's all."

"I meant what I said about Daniel being here for you, Sari. If you have any trouble, or if Wills reneges on our agreement about your hours, I want you to talk with Daniel about it, alright?"

Sari nodded, but she knew she would probably never have the courage to involve Daniel in her problems. She met Jesse's eyes, and took a breath, "I really do need to go get breakfast started.'

Jesse squeezed her hand again then let go. "I'll meet you here about one o'clock."

To Sari's surprise, Meredith was in the kitchen already and had begun peeling potatoes for hash browns. "Thank you so much," Sari said. "I can't tell you how much I appreciate you starting this."

"It looked like there was quite a discussion going on out there. Was that your husband?" Sari thought she heard incredulity in Meredith's voice and it cut her deeply. She swallowed hard.

A few minutes later, Lilith and Chetley Wills came into the kitchen. Instantly, Sari's heart began to pound. Now that Jesse was gone, she wasn't sure what to expect, especially from Mr. Wills. Sari had just finished cracking eggs into a bowl and beating them, so she moved to the stove and placed a large cast iron skillet over the flame of a front burner. She waited for the pan to warm before pouring the eggs in and stirring them. For a short while, the Wills just stood and watched. Sari's fright increased, tension filled the room.

Finally, Wills cleared his throat and addressed Meredith, making sure Sari could hear him, too. "Meredith, you've been doing such a nice job here. Lilith and I are really pleased with your work."

Sari kept her back to them, continuing to scramble the eggs.

"Lilith and I have decided that we'd like to promote you, and put you in charge of the supper meal."

"In charge? But I, um, thank you Mr. Wills."

"Yes, from now on, we'd like you to come in around

eleven. You can help Sari with lunch prep and clean-up and also begin your supper preparations. Sari will make breakfast. You both can work together on breakfast clean up as well as lunch. While Sari cleans up lunch, you can begin prep for supper. When Sari finishes, she can help you. She will be excused at around three, but not until you confirm all her jobs are complete and you are ready for the supper meal. How does that sound?"

"I'll be happy to do whatever you need," Meredith answered. The kitchen became quiet. Sari transferred the finished eggs to a bowl so they could be served, then turned to place them on the counter. Chetley watched her and it seemed as if he were waiting for her to challenge him. Instead, Sari covered the eggs with a cloth and began slicing the potatoes Meredith had just peeled.

"Oh, and Meredith, I want you to work with Mrs. Wills in the planning of the evening menus. We seem to fix the same things over and over. Maybe we could add a few new recipes."

Sari turned back to the stove to fry the hash browns, thankful to be out of the conversation. She understood that this was the avenue Chetley Wills had found to save face and regain his pride after speaking with Jesse, but his words stung. She felt nervous about the coming days.

15
Encampment, Wyoming
same day - October 31, 1917

Jesse left the Copper Pot harboring a mix of emotions. He'd wrestled with his desire to talk to Chetley Wills about his attitude and treatment of Sari for nearly half the night, but he had been uncertain whether or not he should. His early morning conversation at the table with his new wife, however, solidified his anger and gave him motivation to act. Remembering how small and hopeless he'd felt at the hands of the relentless bullying of his uncle and thoughtless father, Jesse was convinced that he couldn't stand by and allow Sari to feel the same way for even one more minute if he could help it. He replayed the scene in the hotel lobby in his mind as he walked through town, praying that his actions hadn't made matters worse for Sari. He made a mental note to talk with Claire about it and ask her advice.

Though it was still early, Jesse passed the New Bohn Hotel, rounded the corner in front of Parkison's store, and turned west. He passed City Hall, then Lydia Willis' unfinished brothel on his way toward Jameson's hardware, knowing that Nathan usually arrived before dawn. He paused for a moment outside the entrance to take a deep breath and change his thinking from Sari to business. He steadied himself and then entered the store.

Nathan Jameson had his head in a nearly empty bin, reaching for the last few screws the bin held, when he heard the door close. He looked up and gave Jesse a genuine smile.

"Good morning!" he called as he walked a few steps to the sales counter and dropped the handful of screws in a small bowl. "I'd heard you were back and hoped I'd get to see you."

The men shook hands and Nathan motioned towards a tall stool in front of the counter. Jesse nodded and slid onto it, pulling his boots up on the stool's low foot rest. Nathan pulled up his own stool, facing Jesse from across the counter. He met Jesse's eyes and leaned in on his elbows.

For as long as Jesse could remember, Nathan Jameson had been one of his favorite people. Jesse looked up to the man for his work ethic and God-centered life. He sat now, looking into Nathan's weathered face, and remembered a time when he was fourteen or fifteen. Nathan stopped by the house to see Jesse just a few months after they'd moved down from the mountains. He offered Jesse a job hauling some freight from Encampment to Hog Park. It wasn't a large contract but it was a huge commitment for young Jesse and an even larger compliment that the man had chosen to trust him with the job. Jesse smiled to himself remembering how he'd told Claire, "That Mr. Jameson is exactly who I want to be when I grow up."

"So, Jess, tell me about your first experiences with the Army. How long are you home for?" Nathan brought Jesse out of his memory and into the present.

Jesse described his training in Kansas and how he'd been promoted to Corporal. They discussed the war in general terms, and then in more specific detail. Jesse, encouraged by Nathan's genuine interest and care, described how he'd been assigned as a farrier for the 2nd Cavalry Division, and in that position he'd most likely stay well behind the fighting lines, but would have a huge responsibility to the men who would be on the front.

As they talked, Jesse relaxed. It was good to be able to speak so freely with someone. He'd told Daniel and Claire about his experiences and what he was facing, of course, but he'd done it with guarded censoring so that they wouldn't worry. With Nathan, Jesse didn't feel that need. As he talked, he shared his fears and concerns honestly for the first time, and listened to the seasoned and considered reactions of his friend and mentor.

"So, you leave tomorrow to start this next journey," Nathan's voice was smooth and warm. "We've been talking nearly an hour, though, and I've been sitting here seeing that gold band on your left hand and wondering if you are going to tell me about it." His eyes were smiling.

Jesse examined his hand then looked up. "Well, fact is, I got married yesterday."

Nathan extended his hand and answered, "Congratulations, Jesse, I wish you all the happiness in the world. Is she a local girl or someone you met in Kansas?"

They shook hands and Jesse answered, "Thank you, Nathan. The answer is, well, neither I guess. She isn't from Encampment exactly, but she's been living here for a little while. I met her just before I left for training."

Nathan tried to read the face sitting opposite him. He didn't see what he expected from an excited groom, and wasn't sure what to make of it.

Jesse continued to hesitate, his discomfort apparent. Inside, his thoughts were jumbled. He wanted Nathan's respect and blessing, and he wasn't sure of how to begin to explain. Nathan misread the young man's hesitation. Trying to comfort him, he answered, "Jesse, many good marriages have begun with a little one on the way. God's good at forgiving, and if you love each other, you'll be alright."

Jesse's eyes got wide, horrified at the conclusion Nathan had jumped to. "She's not. We haven't even. Oh, no, that's not it at all!"

His reaction was comical and Nathan laughed. "I'm so sorry, Jesse, I misread your hesitancy to talk about it."

Jesse recognized the care in the man's voice but still felt embarrassed. "Well, I guess that's about the only logical conclusion under the circumstances, and I sure hope that the rest of the town doesn't think the same thing. I hope I'm not leaving her to face more ugly gossip by herself." The last he spoke quietly, almost to himself.

Nathan studied Jesse. He sent a prayer to heaven asking for wisdom. Then, tried again, "Jesse, my congratulations are genuine, as is the apology for my rude conclusion. I know you better than to have thought that of you. I am sorry." Jesse met his eyes then and smiled. "Tell me about how this all came about."

Jesse shrugged. "The story is a simple one. Sari and I met this summer. I thought about her the whole time I was gone to training. When I got back, we saw each other again. And I asked her to marry me. Time is short, so there wasn't much time for a courtship or engagement. We got married yesterday in Claire and Daniel's parlor, and now I leave in the morning." Jesse wished for a moment that he'd told the story differently, he'd made it sound austere, and Sari deserved better.

Nathan listened intently, glad that business was slow and that they hadn't been interrupted. "Some folks declare that it takes a long time to know when you've met the right person, but I'm not one of them, and it seems you aren't either. I knew my wife and I were meant for each other right away."

Before Jesse could respond, Nathan continued, "Wait, did you say Sari? Could that be Sari Webber, Ralph and Kathryn Webber's girl?"

"I'm actually not sure of her parents' names. They were killed in an accident when she was little."

"Oh yes, it must be the same Sari! I knew the family quite well. They were such joyous, kind folks, and that little girl! Always skipping and smiling. I'd known Ralph and Kathryn for years. I did work for them but we were also good friends. I had dinner at their place regularly. In fact, I was there just a few days before they were killed. It was such a shock to lose them." Nathan paused.

Jesse waited, interested to hear more and get a glimpse into Sari's childhood.

Nathan sighed, shook his head and let memory take over, "I'd contracted a job in the mountains near Baggs, cutting and milling planks for a new house and barn for a customer. I left after that dinner and was gone for three weeks. By the time I got back and heard the terrible news, I'd missed the funeral, they'd auctioned off the land and farm, and little Sari had been sent away. It was all such a shock. The way the aftermath was handled never sat well with me, somehow. I even tried to contact her but no one could tell me exactly where she'd been sent." Nathan shook his head again, then looked up. "Listen to me! I'm talking about hard things long ago when we should be celebrating. Congratulations! Welcome to married life."

Jesse stored away the memory Nathan shared to think about later, and shrugged again good-naturedly. "Discovering married life will have to wait. Honestly, Sari and I don't know each other very well yet, and I'm not sure how to be a husband," he said. "The truth is, I'm not going to have time to figure much of it out before tomorrow. Married life will have to wait to see if I make it back after the war."

A cloud seemed to pass over Nathan, a sadness shown from his eyes when he answered his friend, "Jesse, my wife and I met for the first time on the afternoon before our wedding." Jesse was surprised, this was news to him. "For several years before that, Andriette and I wrote letters to each other. We'd been connected by a mutual friend and began corresponding. We shared our hearts, our fears and thoughts with each other on paper before we'd ever looked in the other's eyes. I fell in love with her script and words long before I fell in love with her pretty face. In reality, by the time I did meet her in person, it wouldn't have mattered what she looked like. I was already committed, knowing how beautiful she was inside."

Nathan paused, and wondered at the odd look on Jesse's face. Then he continued, "I know you are going away, and I don't envy where you are headed, but you can learn to be a husband, and really get to know your wife while you are gone. Write to her Jesse, write often and with your heart, and let her be part of your life, prayers, and thoughts every moment."

Jesse let himself absorb the idea, recognizing Nathan's sound wisdom.

"That's good advice, and I'll do my best to follow it. I imagine that there will be times, though, when there won't be much to say since I won't want to tell her about the war."

"I disagree, Jesse. The war and how you fit into it will be very important for her to hear if she's to understand who you are."

Before he could answer, the door swung open and two dusty ranchers walked into the store. Jesse recognized them as hands off the A Bar A. He'd done some work for them in the past. The four men talked for a few minutes about the weather. Nathan asked, "How can I help you boys today?"

"We've got a list here of supplies we need, and we need to talk prices on having you do some milling for us, using our lumber."

"I'd be happy to help," Nathan answered, then looked at Jesse. "This might take a while, Jesse."

Jesse understood Nathan's words as an apology and regret that their conversation had been interrupted. "No problem, I've got to get going. Oh, I actually came in to talk to you about the hauling contract you have coming open. I'd like to bid on it if it's still open."

Nathan didn't hesitate, "The contract is yours, no question. After I talked to Wiley about it, I'd already decided that. I have the paperwork and contract right here." He stepped over to an orderly desk behind the counter and retrieved a small packet of papers. "Here are all the details and what I'm offering to pay. Look it over today, make any changes you think need made and sign it. Have Wiley bring it in and we'll get going."

Jesse grinned. "That's the easiest bidding process I've ever been involved with. Thanks, Nathan. I know Dawson will do the best he can. If you have any concerns, you can talk with him or with Daniel, who will be backing him up."

"I'll do that, Jesse. Know that you will be in my prayers every day until you get back from overseas. God bless you." He stepped around the counter and pulled Jesse into an awkward hug. "Handshake just wasn't enough," he said as they parted.

Jesse nodded then stepped away, leaving Nathan and the two cowboys behind him.

Back out on the sidewalk, Jesse pulled his pocket watch out. The hour he'd spent with Nathan had encouraged him and he was certainly glad he had the chance, but now he felt rushed to finish all the errands he needed to do. *Next stop, the livery so that I can go over this new contract with Dawson and get that planned out. After that, the bank and City Hall.* He ticked his list off mentally and headed down the street.

The morning was a minefield for Sari. The weather inside the kitchen was stormy. Chetley was in and out more than usual. He never said anything to Sari, but his presence made her nervous. Lilith was quiet and subdued, yet her frequent stops in the kitchen added to the tension. To add to it all, Sari caught Meredith studying her several times, but as soon as she noticed, the girl turned away.

Sari continued feeling drastically off-balance with her workmate. Sari couldn't let herself trust her, yet she couldn't deny that there had been times when Meredith had been very kind, including yesterday when she stood up for Sari to Mr. Wills and enabled her to have her wedding afternoon off. As much as Sari would have liked to talk with Meredith and thank her for covering for her yesterday, there had been no opportunity, and anyway, Meredith seemed to be avoiding Sari whenever possible.

Sari vacillated between feeling positively about Meredith and resorting to her own self-preserving habit of distrust. She tried to fend off the ugly thoughts crowding her head, but even so she suspected that Meredith was silently gloating at Sari's fall from favor and her own rise. Sari's confusion along with the shock of being newly married made for treacherous passage through the morning. Remembering her time at the orphanage, Sari made a concerted effort to do her work perfectly, staying alert and on guard for any slights or attacks.

Sari understood that Jesse's intent was to show her respect and kindness by standing up for her to the Wills. Despite her concerns, she truly was encouraged to know that her days wouldn't be the long, grueling marathons she'd become used to. *Off by late afternoon and a whole day free each week! What an unexpected gift that will be,* she thought. *If I can survive the other six days.*

Unannounced, a distant memory popped into her head. A lilting voice rang through her mind saying, "The Bible starts several stories with the phrase 'It came to pass'. Darling, remember that. Hard times come to pass, they don't come to stay. You just have to be brave and depend on the Lord to help you weather the storm until it's gone."

Sari stopped snapping the green bean in her hand and held on to the vision. For just a moment she could nearly see her mother's face and feel the soft touch of her hands on the scraped elbow that had brought a wounded, six-year-old Sari into the kitchen. She closed her eyes, to stop the forming tears and to better concentrate on the memory. Her hands hovered, calm for a few seconds longer. She breathed a silent thanks that such a worthy moment had resurfaced in her mind. Encouraged by her mother's timely advice, she took a deep breath and continued her work.

By the time Jesse came to meet her, Sari felt tired and worn. As the clock ticked the minutes by, she realized that the stress of the morning was slowly being overshadowed by her trepidation about the afternoon. She wasn't sure she was up to being paraded around town and made the object of attention as Jesse introduced her.

Jesse's warm smile as they left through the front door of the Copper Pot did little to assuage Sari's mood, but she smiled back, trying to hide from him and herself her discomfort.

"You look a little tired," Jesse said after a few steps. "Maybe you need to rest before we start our errands. Let's step into the Bohn and get something to drink, alright?"

Sari smiled again and nodded. When they were seated, Jesse studied his wife's face and began, "I got a little hungry about noon and had a sandwich with Daniel. Have you eaten? Let's order you some lunch."

Sari shook her head, "I'm fine, I had something in the kitchen." The fact was, she'd tried to eat, but her stomach was upset and she'd only had a few bites.

They sat at a small table at the far end of the dining room. Sari sat so that her right side was toward the wall. Mary Bohn approached them and greeted Jesse. "It's been so nice to have you back in town, young man. How long do you get to stay?"

"Hello, Miz Bohn. It's been nice to be home. Sadly, I leave tomorrow. Oh, Miz Bohn, I don't know if the two of you have met before, but I'd like to introduce you to my wife. This is Sari Webber Atley."

The reaction was immediate and genuine, "Wife! Really! How wonderful for you both! It's nice to meet you, Sari. Congratulations! You've made a smart match with this boy, I can tell you that. I've watched him grow up, and I've wished a hundred times that I was young enough to snag him!" Jesse laughed as the woman's eyes danced with kindness. "And if you are the Sari that is the fabulous cook from the Copper Pot that I've been hearing about so much, he's a lucky man to have you!"

Sari was floored. She'd never expected anyone to welcome her so warmly, and she hadn't realized that others might be talking about her cooking. She thanked Mary, feeling both embarrassed and pleased at once.

"Are you here for lunch?" Mary asked.

"No, just some refreshment before we do some shopping and errands," Jesse answered.

"I have a red velvet cake in the back, I'll bring you each a slice, my treat, as a wedding present." Jesse asked for a cup of coffee, and Sari ordered tea. Mary Bohn bustled off, leaving Sari wide-eyed. Jesse smiled and reached for Sari's hand. "I hope your day wasn't too rough. I've been worried that my demands this morning would come back badly on you."

Sari took a deep breath. Just knowing that Jesse had considered the aftermath of his visit helped her. She debated with herself for a moment what to say, and then decided that she needed to be honest. She told him how Mr. Wills had framed the new schedule as his own idea and a promotion for Meredith and hinted that it was a demotion for her.

"That sly dog," Jesse hissed. "I used to like the man, but he's grinding that up and spitting it out with his actions. I'm truly sorry for how this has affected you, I just wanted him to know that the way he's taken advantage of you has to stop, and that if it doesn't, he'll have me and Daniel to contend with."

Sari couldn't help but appreciate Jesse's intentions. "No one has stood up for me for a long time," she said quietly. "And that alone makes it better."

Their conversation was interrupted as Mary Bohn returned, proudly delivering them generous slices of cake along with their drinks, Sari's in a delicate china cup, Jesse's in a thick mug. After she'd served them, she hesitated. "Sari, I'm not one to go behind someone's back, and now that you are married, you might not continue working, but just keep in mind that I'd be proud to have you in my kitchen if you ever have a desire for change."

Sari thanked the woman, buoyed by the offer but knowing that her situation wouldn't allow her the freedom to make that choice.

Mary left them to greet another customer, and the couple enjoyed their snack. When both plates were empty and their drinks gone, Jesse once again reached for Sari's hand. "I wonder if we could contact the bank in Rawlins. I'd like to see a copy of your father's loan. It might be an idea to find a way for you to be able to change where you work. What would you think about that?"

Sari considered his idea. She'd asked about the papers the first time she met Mr. Bagley and was soundly dismissed. The idea of dealing with Mr. Bagley's pompous ugliness again made her feel shivery inside. Finally, she answered, "Do you think I could just write to the bank and request copies of the papers?"

"You could, but it might be better if we spoke to him directly."

They sat in silence, listening to the noises around them as customers came and left. Jesse watched Sari as she stared at the table. He thought she looked sad.

"Sari, are you alright? Don't worry, I won't contact this Mr. Bagley if you don't want me to. If you remember, I've already confessed my big mouth to you. I'll be more careful about butting in to your business from now on, I promise."

"I'm fine. There's just a lot to take in. I've just been thinking, though. You've been so unselfish and insisted that the focus is on me and my needs. In reality, we should be concentrating on you. I'm not the one going off tomorrow to fight a war. Jesse, what do you need?"

Jesse pondered her question. He paused, rubbed his hand over his eyes, and looked out the window up at the mountains, silent and steady in front of him. "Sari, since I got home last week, every time I do something, I wonder if it is the last time I'll ever do that particular thing. I hug my sister and wonder if she's going to get a telegram in the coming months telling her I'm not coming home. I shake someone's hand and think maybe I'll never see them again. I look at Bridger Peak up there, and I wonder if I'll ever stand on its summit again.

"To tell you the truth, for years, I've dreamed about having a wife, someone I love and cherish that I'll share my joys and fears with. I've pictured working hard with a special woman beside me, and looked forward to lavishing her with gifts and laughter in an effort to show her how deep my love is for her. Much as I try to ignore it, I leave tomorrow. I only have today. I want to taste a little of those future dreams while I can."

There were tears in Sari's eyes. "That's a beautiful dream, Jesse, and one that you deserve, but you don't love me."

He didn't hesitate, "But I might! We might love each other eventually!" He studied the surprise on Sari's face and continued, "I spent a little time this morning with a friend, a man I look up to. He told me that he and his wife did their whole courtship in letters, before they'd ever met in person. He says they fell in love through those letters. I'm hoping that can happen again, with us. Will you write to me and let me court you with my letters?"

Sari nodded. "I will. I think I'll like being courted in that manner."

Jesse nodded and looked away. His voice was even quieter when he continued. "In all likelihood, this is our last full day together ever. You say that you have nothing to offer me in return, no way to repay me. Here's how you can. Allow yourself to enjoy this moment. I want to show you off in town, to introduce you as my wife to Encampment, to take you into Parkison's and buy you a new coat, maybe some pretty dresses and hats, or anything else we see that you might like. I want to see you smile. To laugh with me and enjoy our time together so that I can remember it when I'm at war and facing whatever horrors that brings."

Sari felt small and ashamed, humbled at the cutting reality in his words. Her focus *had* only been on herself, not on Jesse. She inhaled slowly and pushed down on the fears that crowded her mind. She willfully dismissed her desire to hide. Slowly, she looked up and met Jesse's eyes. In the silence, she vowed to put him first for the rest of the afternoon, acting on her promise with a smile. "I didn't know shopping was on the agenda today." She hoped her tone was light and teasing, "but I warn you, if you follow through and insist on buying me anything, you have to agree to buy yourself something as well."

Jesse laughed as he stood up, "I'll consent in theory, but I'm not sure how a peach-colored ascot or a new derby hat would complement the Army green I'll be wearing from tomorrow on, so I'm not sure there's anything I need."

With new tenacity and a common purpose, their first stop was the bank. The teller greeted Jesse as they entered the lobby, and he returned the greeting with a wave. He turned to Sari, "I came in this morning and talked with the bank president. Everything is all set up, I just want to introduce you and make sure you understand how to get what you need and who to talk to, alright?"

Sari nodded and then noticed an older gentleman approach. He was wearing a crisp three-piece suit of fine gabardine. His brown eyes were surrounded by deep lines, but the eyes themselves looked young and happy. "Good to see you again so soon, Jesse," the man began, "I just finished writing up the perpetual withdrawal letter, I just need your signature. This must be your wife." He turned his attentions from Jesse. "Mrs. Atley, I'm C.H. Sanger, the bank president. I'm happy to have you as a customer here, and I want to extend a sincere offer to you if there is anything at all I can do for you while your husband is fighting for freedom."

Sari was taken aback. He was standing on her right, and she had no ability to turn her scarred cheek away from him, yet he had shown absolutely no negative reaction to her as their eyes met. "Ah, thank you. It's nice to meet you Mr. Sanger."

They followed the banker to his office at the back of the lobby. He motioned for them to be seated in two leather wing-back chairs that faced his enormous desk. When they were settled, Sanger began, "Mrs. Atley, your husband has shared with me his desire for you to have what you need while he is gone. This form shows you what he has asked me to have available to you." He handed her a paper and continued, "We've arranged for you to have a monthly withdrawal for your household and personal expenses. Of course, you are welcome to come in at any time to withdraw more as you need it as well. As we talked, we weren't sure how you would prefer to receive this stipend. Do you think you'd prefer to withdraw the entire amount once a month, or instead come in to the bank more often and receive partial disbursements?"

Sari glanced at the paper in her hand as he finished speaking. Her heart began pounding as she fought to understand. "Jesse," she said, turning so that she was looking directly at him. "This is too much. You can't give me this much money each month."

Jesse's eyes were patient but she could already recognize the stubborn set of his jaw. "It isn't too much. You are going to have house expenses, groceries. You are going to need clothes and shoes."

"But," she began to argue, but Jesse put his hand over hers and she stopped.

Jesse turned back to the banker, "Mr. Sanger, how about this? For now, we will arrange for Mrs. Atley to receive her withdrawal for October today, and then at the beginning of each month from now on. If she decides later that she'd like to change this arrangement, she will contact you."

"That's a fine idea," the man agreed. "Does that meet with your approval, Mrs. Atley?"

"Yes, that will be fine." Sari felt shy and timid as she answered, overwhelmed. She reminded herself that the afternoon wasn't about her fears, though, so she straightened her back and lifted her head.

Jesse watched her for a moment, then broke into a teasing grin. He turned back to the man behind the desk. "I am fearful that my frugal and careful wife might be too busy to remember to come in each month and receive her disbursement, so I'd count it a personal favor to me if, by some chance she hasn't come into the bank by, let's say the third of each month, that you will have someone deliver the cash to her."

Sanger nodded, catching Jesse's real intent and agreeing. "We'd be happy to oblige. Am I correct in thinking that you will still be cooking for the Wills at the Copper Pot, Mrs. Atley, to help you pass the time until your husband returns?"

"Yes, Sir," was all Sari could say.

"Excellent," he stopped and gave Sari a wink. "I

almost hope you don't come to the bank each month. It will be a wonderful excuse for me to enjoy one of your amazing meals at the same time I make the delivery."

Even Sari chuckled at his lighthearted answer. A few minutes later, after Sari had been introduced to Mr. Healey, the cashier, and received her first withdrawal, the couple was back outside.

Jesse checked his watch. "It's not quite three o'clock. Claire expects us around six for my going away dinner. We still need to stop at the boarding house and then go home to our house," he emphasized our and then smiled. "I have some things I want to show you there. For now, let's stop in at Parkison's. You've been in there before, haven't you?"

"Yes," Sari responded. "But only a few times. I've never met the owner."

"Ed Parkison? He's quite a guy. He owns several stores including one here, another in Medicine Bow and another in Colorado. They came here from Denver. He's a real innovator. The first store they built here, it burned down in 1912, was heated with steam. He ran a steam pipe under the street to their home and heated both the store and the house with the same boiler."

"Does his wife work at the store with him?"

"Ella? I've never seen her there. She keeps their house and cares for their children. Did you know that Claire and Ella are close friends?"

"Well, I did hear Claire talking about her friend Ella, but I didn't make the connection."

Since Sari had emptied her room earlier, it only took a short time to conclude Sari's residency at the boarding house. A short walk later and they were at Parkison's. A small bell jangled happily as they entered the store. The lighthearted sound set the tone for the next hour. Sari wondered at the genuine pride she heard in Jesse's voice as introductions were made but didn't have time to reflect on it. The couple chatted with Ed Parkison and his clerk, Denver Suttles, for a few minutes. Soon, though, Ed made his apologies explaining he had a meeting to attend.

"Are you shopping today, Mrs. Atley?" Mr. Suttles asked as his boss retreated to the back room. Sari looked up at Jesse and back to the clerk. Jesse answered for her, "Yes, I wonder what you have in overcoats in my wife's size."

Though Sari was continually conscious of how much money Jesse was spending on her, she also couldn't help getting caught up in the fun of their shopping trip. He chose several dresses for her, insisting that she add everything, hats and gloves and shoes, to go with each of them. A mound of garments and accessories grew on the counter, which included new work dresses as well as several church outfits, before Jesse was finally satisfied that Sari was fully attired.

Politely, Jesse wandered away to give Sari privacy while she choose some undergarments. Sari noticed from across the store that he lingered for some time in front of one display. Mr. Suttles bustled away to wrap up the purchases when her shopping was concluded. Sari went in search of Jesse.

She found him in front of a gramophone. Unnoticed, she watched as he carefully rubbed his hand across the glossy wood grain of the cabinet. Eventually, he looked up and met her gaze with a sheepish grin.

"I look at this thing every time I come in here. Even if I didn't love music, I'd love this cabinet. The mahogany has such beautiful grain."

"I didn't know you liked music," she answered.

He continued to stroke the cabinet as he answered, "There was no music when I was little. After Mama died, I went to live for a while with Haddie and William Foster. They love music. Nearly every night after dinner, the whole family would gather and sing. William played the guitar, and he taught his children. I remember once we were working together weeding the garden and Haddie began singing. Everyone joined in. It seemed magical to me. I've loved music ever since."

He started to turn away from the display but Sari stopped him with a hand on his arm. "Jesse, you made me a promise that you'd buy something for yourself. I haven't seen any orange ascots, but how about this?"

Jesse shrugged her off. "I sure can't carry this with me tomorrow."

"That's true," came the answer. "But it will be here waiting for you when you return. Along with me."

Jesse stood silently until Sari added, "Besides, I have a generous allowance in my bag that my husband assures me is mine to spend as I want, isn't that right?"

He smiled as he anticipated what she was going to say next.

"So, I'd like my first purchase to be a wedding present for my husband, who loves music."

Jesse chuckled and nodded. "Mrs. Atley, I can't argue with that logic. Your money is indeed yours to do with as you please."

Their purchases were cumbersome, especially the gramophone and with several recordings Jesse chose. Mr. Suttles offered to have Jonah, their delivery boy, take care of them, but Jesse declined. It only took a few minutes for him to run over to the livery to get the truck. The couple laughed as they carried their new treasures into the house a few minutes later. While Sari worked upstairs to put away all her new clothing, Jesse set up the gramophone in the parlor. It didn't take long before the house was filled with music.

Sari came down the stairs slowly. The music was lively, happy and full of energy. She'd never heard anything like it. Jesse stood watching the needle ride through the grooves of the record. He turned and smiled as she came to stand beside him. "This is Mozart's piano concerto number 21."

"It's indescribable," Sari answered. They stood there for several minutes, letting the music surround and fill them. Without speaking, Jesse turned and took Sari's hand. He pulled her towards him and began to move. They didn't dance exactly, but they allowed the music to guide them together around the room. When the recording ended, they stood together. Hating to break the dearness of the moment, Jesse finally whispered to Sari, "Thank you. I will relive this day and this moment many times in the next months. You have given me so much to delight in."

Sari leaned her head on his chest and tried not to cry. "I also will relive today, I've never before experienced the generosity or care you've shown me today."

The weather changed overnight. Instead of yesterday's clear, sunny skies, the morning brought skies overcast and threatening rain. Jesse, sharply dressed in his uniform, helped Sari don her new wool coat getting ready to leave for work. "I'm sorry I'm not going to have time to walk you to work this morning," Jesse told her. "Claire and Daniel will be here in about half an hour, and I still have a few things to do."

"It's alright." An awkward dullness settled over them both. Jesse rubbed the toe of his boot back and forth across the floor while Sari fidgeted with the pocketbook in her hand. "Thank you for yesterday," Sari whispered after a pause. "I love all the beautiful things you bought me."

Jesse understood she meant more than just the shopping trip. He studied her for a moment, surprised that Sari was facing him without trying to hide her face or sidestep his gaze.

Jesse replied, "I knew you were uncomfortable, especially at Parkison's, but I really enjoyed helping you pick out some nice things. I hope you will be able to indulge yourself every once in a while after I'm gone." Sari gave an unconvincing nod and he continued, "You heard me warn Claire last night that you might need some company to help with shopping," his eyes teased her. "Claire loves pretty things. I think it is because we had so little when we were growing up. She'll be a good influence on you."

Sari glanced at the clock hanging on the wall behind her and took a breath. "I need to go. I don't want to be late after all that's happened."

Seconds ticked by. Finally, Jesse leaned over and kissed his wife tenderly on the forehead. He closed his eyes and lingered, his lips barely brushing her skin, and inhaled. She smelled sweet. He had a flash of fear about what was ahead of him, and he tried to memorize this moment for later use.

Sari also savored the moment, surprised at how easy it was to stand here with Jesse so close, and recognizing the threat of tears heralded by the ache in her throat.

Too soon, Jesse stepped away and they let the moment pass. Slowly, he turned the doorknob and pulled open the door, allowing the new day, and the ominous future it held, to flood in.

16
Encampment, Wyoming
November, 1917

It was still early when Sari awoke. Without opening her eyes, she relished the softness of the sheets and the warmth of the blanket and quilt cocooning her. Her mind and the world were quiet, calm. In the tranquility, alone and safe, Sari considered the week she'd just lived. *I've been a wife for five days, but Jesse has been gone for three of them. I have a new family, a sister- and brother-in-law and two charming nephews who have gone out of their way to be gracious and welcome me. I have a beautiful place to live. And, I have the entire day off.* That thought brought a smile to her sleepy face. Not counting two winters ago when she had a terrible cold and was remanded to the sick room, she couldn't remember a day without obligations.

Sari opened her eyes, and looked around the room. The growing dawn painted it with a soft pinkish hue and though she tried to hold on to the contentment and joy she'd just felt, other more assertive emotions enveloped her. *Claire and Daniel have invited me to their house around four o'clock. That's hours from now. What am I going to do with this day?* Briefly, she considered going to church but dismissed the idea, knowing that she just couldn't face anything else new for the moment.

She dressed, taking time to admire the gabardine and lace included in her new wardrobe. She made herself breakfast, lingering over tea and the view of the mountains out the window. She wandered through the house for a while, touching carefully, learning, absorbing. Thinking it might sooth her, she cranked up the gramophone and set the needle on the Mozart concerto they'd enjoyed together, but she only listened a minute before the music assailed her with loneliness and she turned it off.

The day crawled by. Sari felt restless and out of place. Eventually she sat in one of the wingback chairs in the parlor with her Bible. In the quiet, her thoughts bounced between her newly experienced blessings and her worries. For a long time she thought about Jesse. She read in Ephesians about marriage, considering how Jesse's care, concern, and generosity towards her were exactly what Paul told husbands to do in chapter five. She read and reread the passage, wondering how she could do her part to submit to and honor him while he was so far away.

Eventually, another set of verses on the page caught her eye. "Let all bitterness, and wrath, and anger, and clamor, and evil speaking, be put away from you, with all malice: And be ye kind one to another, tenderhearted, forgiving one another, even as God for Christ's sake hath forgiven you."

Sari's thoughts turned to Meredith. In the quiet of her solitary afternoon, Sari finally listened again to her coworker's words on the afternoon Jesse proposed to her, allowing them to echo through her mind. *Have I been mean to Meredith?* At first, she denied it. *No, I'm not mean. She's the pretty one who surely just acted nice sometimes to manipulate me or mock me.* But as she prayed, wrestled with herself, and pondered, she began to understand how perhaps her own fear of being the recipient of still another act of meanness might have colored her view of Meredith's treatment of her. Sari replayed scene after scene in the kitchen and realized that there had not ever been a time that Meredith had been anything but helpful and kind to her. Sari felt ashamed, and after confessing to God, she resolved to talk with Meredith and seek her forgiveness as well.

Hours dawdled. No matter what Sari tried to do to fill the time, her thoughts returned to the elements of her new life. By mid-afternoon, she was tired and weary. She'd just returned to the parlor from the kitchen when she heard voices on the porch. "I get to ring the bell."

"No, let me!"

Sari opened the door before the job was delegated, to find Greg and Michael pushing each other. Looking a little ashamed, they each straightened up and smiled. Michael elbowed Greg and then spoke, "Aunt Sari, Mama sent us over to check and make sure you have enough wood for your stove and to walk you to our house for supper."

Greg interrupted, "She said to tell you she knew that we were coming early, and there's no hurry if you aren't ready to come over right now."

"She told us to wait another half hour, but we were so excited to see you, she finally gave in and gave us permission to come."

The boy's exuberance touched and delighted Sari. "You are welcome to come in and check my stores of wood, and I'll be ready right away," she answered. Greg whooped and the boys hustled to the kitchen, and then out the back door to the wood pile.

Sari went upstairs to get a handkerchief and her pocketbook as they accomplished their chore.

Contrasting with the restless loneliness she'd felt most of the day, her evening was filled with warmth and comfort. The boys jostled for her attention on their stroll between the two homes, talking non-stop. Before they went into the house, they showed her the two pet rabbits they housed in a comfortable hutch behind the house. Inside, Daniel smiled warmly and Claire greeted Sari with a tight hug. She'd hardly gotten her coat off when Greg invited her to play checkers.

Claire put her hand on her son's head and shrugged to Sari, "Greg has been so excited since the other night when you said you'd like him to teach you the game. None of us are going to get a moment's peace until he gets his chance. Do you mind?"

"Not at all," Sari began, but Greg grabbed her hand before she could finish, leading her to a small table in the parlor already set up with the checker board.

They played several games, all the time with Greg explaining the game while Michael whispered strategies in her ear.

"Boys," Daniel had been sitting in a nearby chair, sometimes refereeing, sometimes encouraging Sari while also glancing at a copy of the *Saratoga Sun.* "Boys, I'm thinking you don't want to overdo it on checkers with Aunt Sari. You don't want to wear her out the first day, do you?"

"But Papa," began Greg until he saw the look in Daniel's eyes. "Yes, Sir, you're right. Thanks for playing Aunt Sari. You did really well for a beginner."

His guileless complement garnered snickers from Michael and a smile from Sari. "Thank you, Greg," she answered formally. "You are a good teacher. Why, maybe with a few more sessions of practice, I'll win one once in a while."

Greg giggled, "Well, I kinda hope not."

Claire called them all in to the dining room not long after. When the meal was finished and the boys were busily helping Daniel with the dishes, Claire and Sari relaxed together in the parlor. "I hope Greg and Michael don't overwhelm you," Claire said. "They are so excited to have you as their aunt."

"They are very sweet boys, Claire, and I appreciate all you and Daniel and the boys are doing. You are very kind."

"Now that we have a few minutes of peace, can I ask you how you are doing? Are you comfortable at the house?"

Sari wanted to answer truthfully, but stopped herself. She didn't want Claire to think her whiny or ungrateful. After a hesitation, she met Claire's gaze and answered, "I'm doing well, I think."

Claire, noticing Sari's tone and the tense set of her shoulders, was certain that 'doing well' was inaccurate, but she didn't challenge her sister-in-law. Instead, she changed the subject to the activities of Claire's garden group. In time, the conversation turned to crocheting and other girl talk, and the moment passed.

Monday morning had barely arrived. Only a hint of light shown in the east. The night had brought frost, and since the sun had not yet sent its first warming rays into the Encampment Valley, Sari's shoes crunched as she stepped down the sidewalk on her way to work. Jesse had been gone for five days. They'd been married seven. There were lights on in the windows of the house across the street, and Sari thought she saw someone peering out. She'd never had neighbors before, and wondered if the people around her would welcome her.

On her walk, Sari considered again how easy it would be to convince herself that the events of last week were an odd dream. Except, of course, for how she continued to wake up in his house, and how the pretty, new clothes he'd bought her still populated the drawers and closet, and most importantly of all, how the gold band on her hand attested to her new life.

As she rounded the corner and turned north onto Freedman, Sari let herself relax into the memory of last evening's supper with Claire, Daniel, and her new nephews. Being surrounded by their warmth was a treat she had never expected.

When she turned into the alley leading to the kitchen of the Copper Pot, Sari sighed. Chetley Wills was not happy with the new arrangement between himself and his 'indentured servant.' While he was abiding by the new hours Jesse required, Wills displayed his displeasure in a variety of new demands, cutting remarks, criticisms, and withering looks at every opportunity. Sari took a breath and squared her shoulders as she entered the kitchen. She felt that there was nothing to do other than weather the storm named Chetley Wills.

The morning was going well. Supplies for the week had been delivered right after she'd finished serving breakfast. She hurried through cleaning the kitchen and dishes and was nearly finished putting the groceries away. Lunch, chicken noodle soup, was simmering on the stove and the biscuits were ready for the oven. Sari congratulated herself. *It's a quarter to eleven and nearly everything is done,* she thought. She indulged herself with a sliver of leftover cobbler as she leaned against the counter.

Sari swallowed the last of the cobbler and was brushing crumbs from her hands when she heard noise outside the back door. At first, she paid scant attention as she reached for the broom. The alleyway often sported traffic and voices from both Englehart's mortuary and hardware store and J.H. Schmidt's Harness Shop next door. This noise, however, was not part of the normal workday din. Instead of being at the end of the alley, clearly the speakers were right outside the kitchen door. It only took a moment before Sari was able to identify one voice as Meredith's. The other was certainly a male voice. Both were charged with emotion and growing louder with each exchange. Caught between curiosity and respect, Sari began sweeping. She purposefully tried not to hear what was being said, but as their volume increased, Sari couldn't help but catch a sentence or two.

"What would I tell Aunt Nell?"

"I thought you said you cared for me,"

"But I do!"

Sari didn't know what to do. Clearly this was a private discussion, but Meredith sounded so distraught. Sari wondered if she shouldn't help somehow. She stood unsure, broom in hand, in the middle of the kitchen when Chetley Wills entered the kitchen and loudly asked, "What in the world is going on out there? We can hear yelling all the way up to the front desk." His voice was loud and harsh and his abrupt entrance made Sari jump.

Hoping to give the occupants of the alley a moment of warning, Sari stepped as nonchalantly as possible between Wills and the back door and answered in a clear, strong voice, "Good morning, Mr. Wills. It seems that there are some workmen down at the hardware store getting a little loud." She was surprised at herself, and wasn't sure where the lie came from. Even more shocking was what slipped out next, "Meredith just went out to carry out some trash. She was going to check on the situation."

Sari's confident answer derailed her boss just enough. A second later, Meredith entered through the back door. She was disheveled, her dress rumpled. Tracks of tears were evident on her cheeks. She shrugged as she came in, "It looks like everyone's left," she answered with a quick look at Sari. She stopped next to Sari and regarded Wills. "Good morning, Mr. Wills. I haven't seen you yet this morning. How are you?"

His annoyance deflected, Wills stammered, "I just arrived." Then he recovered to take aim at Meredith. "Miss Tucker, I certainly hope you are going to comb your hair before you go out to the dining room. You look absolutely unkempt."

Sari saw the effort it took for Meredith to smile. "Yes, Sir. I certainly will. Sari, thanks so much for working with me this morning to clean out underneath the stove. Whew, what a mess."

With a grunt, Wills left the kitchen. In stunned silence, Sari and Meredith stood frozen for several heart beats. Then Meredith turned to her partner, "You just saved me. Thank you so much!"

Sari wasn't sure how to respond. "You're welcome, but, Meredith, are you alright?"

Tears threatened, and Meredith swallowed hard. "I don't think I am, but I can't afford to lose this job, so I better get myself pulled together for lunch."

Sari's hand shot out as Meredith turned away, stopping her. "Wait, it's clear that something is very wrong, and I'd like to help. Later, while we are doing dishes, will you confide in me?"

Meredith nodded and whisked away. A few minutes later, she reentered the kitchen with her hair smoothed and tied back. Her face was pale, but clean, her eyes less blotchy. A smile replaced the strain that had been there earlier. While they worked to finish and serve lunch, Sari marveled at how proficient Meredith was at recovering her composure.

The lunch period was busy but smooth. Before Sari realized the time, Lilith stood in the door of the kitchen and told her employees, "The last of the diners have just left. I am on my way home for a few hours, and Mr. Wills is out for the afternoon. Alma is at the front desk. Before you both take a break today, Mr. Wills wants you to scrub the dining room floor."

Sari groaned silently and nodded in response. He always found a way to have the last word.

Alone in the dining room, Sari and Meredith worked together to move all the tables and chairs into the foyer. Soon they were on their knees side by side. They worked in silence for a few minutes, until Sari worked up her courage to begin talking. "Meredith, the first thing I want to say to you is that I am sorry. I've thought a lot about what you said to me the other day about how I've been treating you."

"I was just being silly, I didn't mean—"

"No, you weren't silly. I haven't been anything beyond barely polite to you, and I am sorry for that. I do want us to be friends. I never intended to be the reason we aren't. I hope you'll accept my apology and that we can begin anew, right now."

Meredith rinsed her scrub rag in the soapy water wringing it out as she answered, "I don't have many friends right now," Meredith said. "I surely would appreciate being yours. I've admired you since I first met you."

Sari was shocked. "I can't imagine a reason to admire me, especially after I've treated you the way I have."

Shoulder to shoulder, now in a more companionable silence, the two continued their task. Meredith spoke next, "I'll bet you could hear everything that we were saying out in the alley this morning." The question under the statement filled her voice with shy trepidation.

"I tried not to listen, but yes, I did overhear some of your conversation, but only a bit. Nothing made much sense." Sari scooted backwards, pulling the bucket with her and added, "I hope that everything is going to be alright."

It took a few moments before Sari realized Meredith was crying.

"Is there anything I can do to help?"

Meredith sniffed and shook her head. "I don't think so. Everything is so horrid right now. I don't think there is any help."

They continued scrubbing, moving the soap bucket as they travelled backwards across the floor. They finished one length and relocated to start again. Finally, Meredith quietly began, "I have a beau, and honestly Sari, I love him so much that sometimes I don't think I can breathe without him. We grew up living close to each other and last summer he was on a fencing crew my father hired. He's so sweet and nice. But, my father is very strict and I knew he wouldn't approve of me talking with him. He didn't let my older sister go to dances or picnics until she was nearly eighteen and here I am only just sixteen.

Anyway, after the fence was built and the crew moved on, he'd sometimes come around to see me. I'd meet him out at the pond or behind the barn. We'd talk and—" Meredith sat back on her heels and smiled at the memory. "He's smart and kind. He'd hold my hand. Once he brought me a bouquet of wildflowers." She sighed and then went back to scrubbing.

"One evening he shined a light in my bedroom window just after I'd gone to bed. I got dressed and slipped out to the barn. He said such sweet things to me that night. It's the first time he told me he loved me. He said he couldn't stay long because he had to go away for a while, but he just had to see me. When it was time for him to leave, he asked for a kiss. I told him no, that it wouldn't be proper, but he told me he just needed one kiss to get him through the time we'd be apart. It was one kiss. He closed his eyes and everything. But just as he was finishing, my father burst in."

Meredith's voice broke as she described the scene that followed. Her beau escaped into the dark amid shouts, curses, and threats. Meredith had been dragged into the house by her hair. The next morning, her father refused to even look at her. Instead, he insisted, speaking to Meredith's mother with Meredith standing right next to her, that he "wouldn't harbor a harlot." He demanded that before the end of the day, "the girl needs to be gone."

Pleading and crying and attempting to explain fell on deaf, cold ears. Her mother, while tearful, sided with her husband. Meredith put her clothes into a gunny sack and walked to Encampment.

"It took me all day. It's nearly twenty miles out to the ranch, and I hadn't had anything to eat."

"Where did you go? Do you have family here?"

"My aunt Mary Nell lives here. At first, she didn't want to let me stay. She and my father are a lot alike. She finally gave in since I had nowhere else to go. She agreed that I could stay, as long as I found work and was able to pay her rent and food money."

"And that's when you came to work here."

"Yes. Uncle Paul works at Rosander's brick kiln. He and Mr. Wills are acquainted, and he asked if maybe there'd be a place for me."

"I see. And it was this young man out in the alley this morning."

"Yes. He's been back for a couple of weeks. He told me he'd gone out to the ranch to see me, but of course, I wasn't there. I'd been so worried about him, and he says he was frantic to find me. Anyway, I ended up seeing him one evening on my way home from here."

Sari wasn't sure how to continue the conversation. They were nearly finished with the floor when Meredith went on, "I invited him to come over and meet my aunt and uncle. I thought if Aunt Mary Nell met him then maybe she could convince my father that he, and I, are honorable."

"That's reasonable. How did it go?"

"Not well. Uncle Paul called him a ruffian even before he came in the house. He accused him of being part of a group of boys who damaged some property at the kiln a year or so ago. They wouldn't let him in and my uncle and aunt ordered me never to see him again."

Tears slid down Meredith's cheeks as she dropped her rag in the bucket and stood up.

Sari stood up and stretched her back, then searched her new friend's face. She knew the answer to her next question before it was spoken, "But you haven't stopped seeing him, have you?"

"No! How can I? We are in love! I've been meeting him in the mornings before I need to come to work. I didn't lie exactly. I just haven't told my aunt that my hours have been changed."

Meredith carried the bucket out into the alley to dump it while Sari rinsed out the rags. Just as she was finishing, Lilith appeared in the doorway. "Girls, the floor looks good."

"Thank you," answered Sari, "We'll give it a few more minutes to dry and then replace the tables and chairs."

There was no more time for Sari and Meredith to talk for the rest of the afternoon, but Sari's thoughts didn't stray far from her workmate and her situation.

Supper preparations were nearly finished and Sari's work day was ending. She had just finished washing a pot when she heard voices behind her.

"Can I help you?"

"I, well, I came with a message for, um, Mrs. Atley."

"For Mrs. Atley? Oh, yes, Sari! She's just back there," Meredith smiled at their visitor and pointed, before she continued out into the dining room with an armload of clean tablecloths.

Michael nodded a shy thanks and crossed the kitchen, "Aunt Sari, I'm sorry to bother you at work, but Mama asked me to bring this plate of cookies for you."

Sari rinsed the bowl she'd just washed and wiped her hands on her apron. "Thank you, Michael. This is very sweet of her and you. Please tell your mother thank you for me, this is a very kind treat."

With a big smile he answered, "Greg helped bake them. Mama said to remind you about dinner on Sunday and that if you need anything, just let us know."

Pleased and surprised at Claire's gift, Sari thought about her new family as she walked through the streets of Encampment on her way home a few minutes later.

Sari glanced at the house across the street as she approached her new home. One of the curtains moved, and Sari wondered again who lived there. A moment later the front door opened and a young woman stepped out. She smiled broadly and waved at Sari as she stepped off the porch and made her way down the sidewalk.

"Hello there!" the woman called as she crossed the street to join Sari. "I've been hoping to catch you the last couple of days."

Sari smiled shyly and returned the greeting.

"My name is Beatrice Reid, Bea for short. I've just recently moved to town to live with my sister and her husband. I think you are new to the neighborhood, too, right?"

Sari nodded. As she drew closer, Sari could see that her neighbor was young, perhaps a year or two younger than Sari herself. "Yes, um, hello. I'm Sari Webber, oh, um, Sari Atley." She felt flustered. "I'm just married and not used to my new name yet," she explained.

Bea giggled, "That's alright, I imagine it would take me a while to learn a new name, too."

By virtue of Bea's warm smile and infectious good humor, Sari felt herself relax.

"You just moved in here, right?"

Again Sari nodded, "I've lived in Encampment for several months, but just a few days in this house."

"And your husband, he's that tall, really handsome man that owns the livery, right?"

Sari smiled at Bea's description. "Jesse does own the livery, but unfortunately he was called up to the Army. He left last week for France."

"Oh dear, how can you bear that? I can't imagine sending anyone off to fight a war. I'm so sorry."

Sari wasn't sure what to say, but before she had a chance to respond, Bea continued, "I'll bet you are lonely! That's a big house to live in alone. What do you do all day?"

"Well, I work, so that helps," Sari answered. "I'm a cook at the Copper Pot."

"Golly. I envy you! I've talked about finding a job, but Harriet and Royce, that's my sister and her husband, say that school is my job. Bah, school is so easy I barely have to think about it, and it doesn't earn me any money, either." She did a little dance, then added, "But Harri says what I need to learn most is patience. Gee, it's cold out here for just this sweater. Anyway, Harriet and I would like to invite you over one afternoon. We'd like to get to know you."

Bea's energy was endearing, and Sari was struck by her exuberance. "I'd like that," she answered honestly.

"Great! How about tomorrow afternoon, say about four?"

They agreed to the meeting and said their farewells. Sari watched her neighbor bound across the street, up the steps, and into her house.

She smiled to herself as she entered her own.

Jesse's quiet, empty house enclosed her as she shut the front door. Sari removed her new coat and hung it on the hook behind the door, then turned to face the evening. The peace and calm that surrounded her supplied her ample time and opportunity to consider her newly introduced neighbor as well as Claire and Meredith. She felt hopeful that all three women presented the potential for friendship.

17
New York and beyond
November, 1917

Jesse's three-day journey from Wolcott Junction to New York served as a buffer between one life and the next. He had no illusions that what lay ahead wouldn't change him and modify the Jesse he'd always been into someone new. He'd spent a lot of time watching the miles slip by and praying that whoever he became from now on would be someone the original Jesse would like and be proud of.

He saw very little of New York City. A harried sergeant manning an Army kiosk at one end of the station looked hastily at Jesse's orders and directed him to a repurposed hay wagon half-filled with other new arrivals. Before long, Jesse was bouncing over city streets, winding through tall buildings on his way to a makeshift camp along the waterfront.

That night he slept, or at least dozed, in a tent among other members of the 2nd Cavalry Division on a narrow canvas cot with a scratchy wool blanket to cover him.

Jesse was told to report to a tent beside a corral of Clydesdales after breakfast the next morning. As he stood under the dusty green canvas with three other men, his attention turned to a tall, barrel-chested soldier approaching. The man ducked his head as he entered, then began speaking. "Boys, I'm Staff Sergeant Bonner Wiggins." He stopped long enough to make eye contact with each man. "Look around you. You are a specialized set of men—all farriers—and you've been assigned to my battalion. I've been wrangling horses and mules for the Army for the last fifteen years. I am proud to say I was with General John J. Pershing and the 7th Cavalry on the Pancho Villa Expedition earlier this year on the Mexican border. Though old Pancho himself got away, we secured the US border and let everyone know that we aren't to be messed with. Before we joined this war, the US Cavalry boasted having over fifteen thousand men in fifteen regiments. Now there are nearly twenty-eight divisions getting ready to see action. We have a proud tradition of supplying the Army with horseman. We have machine gun and rifle mounted troops.

"Now you boys will answer to me, but I won't be hovering over you like a mother hen, I have too many four-footed and two-footed greenhorns to contend with. This afternoon, you each will be assigned to your own company. That will give you about a hundred and fifty men and their mounts to take care of. While we are here, you four will have to share this forge tent. When we get to France, you'll each be on your own. You'll need to recruit two or three of the riders in your assigned companies to help you as grooms and to aid you with moving and setting up your field forges. You have control over those men, so when you start working, keep an eye out for strong and able soldiers to recruit for your team. We'll begin drills to practice set up and take down in a few days. For now, get acquainted and get the forges heated up, we have stock that needs tended. I'll be back in about an hour and we can get started." He met each man's eye again, then nodded and left them.

They introduced themselves and set to work. Knowing that they'd soon be sent to their own companies, paired with the demands of getting ready to deploy kept the four farriers from forming anything deeper than a cursory working relationship.

Jesse was introduced into his company the next day, and spent several hours each afternoon for the next week watching Lieutenant Jones, the company commander, put the men through drills and practices. Jesse also made sure to eat in the chow hall at the same time as his company so that he could get to know the men who populated it. Within a week, Jesse had his team of aides, satisfied they were men he could trust to maintain cordial attitudes and a willingness to work hard. Then he settled into his role as their leader.

The youngest of the group, Private Danny Griffin, was just twenty. He came from a cattle ranch in Montana. As time progressed, Jesse recognized that Griffin's most valuable skill was his experience helping a local vet when he was in school. Knowledge about keeping the horses healthy and recognizing trouble early would be invaluable. The second man was about Jesse's age. Isaiah Rex, from

Arkansas impressed Jesse right away with his skill on horseback and his quick wit. Fred Baird, the only married man is Jesses' platoon, hailed from New Mexico. In comparison, he knew far less about caring for horses than the other two, but Jesse appreciated how willingly he took on hard work and how easily he asked questions and took suggestions and direction.

Time swirled quickly, and they all had to learn fast. Within a few weeks, his three-man team was capable and efficient. They'd practiced moving the forge enough to assure Jesse that they would be ready when needed. The days marched on and soon the battalion began loading gear onto the huge transport ship. When their equipment was stowed aboard, Jesse and his team joined the others to concentrate on loading the stock.

Passage to France took a relatively uneventful eight days. The forges were packed and cold, but Jesse was happy to pass the time taking shifts to tend the livestock or staring at the vast ocean around him during off hours. Though he'd never seen it before, Jesse decided he liked the sea. It reminded him in many ways of the Red Desert west of Rawlins, a stark region comprised of miles and miles of sagebrush and sand. On first inspection, the surface of the ocean looked devoid of life and forbidding like the desert, but as they cut through the waves and the days, Jesse saw enough to sense that just underneath the surface was a world teeming with life he'd never imagined.

On the day before they docked, Staff Sergeant Bonner stopped Jesse as he was in the chow line for the midday meal. "The lieutenant needs to talk to you. He wants us both to meet with him after chow."

Jesse had been summoned before by his officer, and he wasn't concerned. It hadn't taken long for Jesse to recognize that there were three kinds of officers. The first two were newly acquired by the Army and had been recently commissioned as a result of their education. With their inexperience obvious to all, some of these leaders were faltering and nervous. Their indecision kept their soldiers from trusting them. Jesse had sympathy for them and hoped that with more experience they'd become effective leaders. On the other hand, Jesse had little respect for the other category of new officers. Instead of letting their uncertainty show, they allowed the bars on their shoulders to go to their heads. They were capricious and bossy and full of ego. The men under them not only distrusted their authority but also resented them.

Thankfully, Jesse's lieutenant was among the third category of officers. Lieutenant Jones was a stocky man in his early thirties. He was a graduate of West Point and a career military man. Like Bonner, the man had seen action in Mexico. His quiet self-assurance and decisive manner exuded confidence, and Jesse trusted him.

Lieutenant Jones was studying a map when Bonner and Jesse met him. He greeted them and told them to stand at ease. "Atley, I'll get right to the point. Your sergeant here tells me that you have distinguished yourself as our best farrier. He tells me that you do excellent work and that you are a squared-away soldier."

"Thank you, Sir," Jesse answered.

"When I told the Sarge that I needed a man for a special project, your name was the first and only suggestion he had for me." He didn't wait for a reply, but continued on. "I received a radio message this morning. There's a big battle brewing in the north of France, and while US troops are not going to be involved in the fighting, higher command has been notified by French forces that they have an urgent need for support. One of their mounted battalions caught heavy fire recently, and they lost men in a poison gas attack. They need replacement troops right away, and we've assured them of our help."

Jesse met the officer's eyes and nodded, ignoring the spark of dread ignited in his belly.

"The offensive is in its final planning stages. When we dock tomorrow, you, your platoon, and your moveable forge equipment will be high priority for unloading. You will be re-loaded immediately on a train and sent to the north of France, a place called Cambrai. Your platoon will be on loan to the French Army for as long as they need you, then you'll be sent back to join us wherever we are. I have your orders here." He turned and rifled through a stack of papers on the table. Jesse scrambled to absorb what he was hearing. The lieutenant turned around to face Jesse, his eyes on the papers in his hand.

Without looking up, the officer continued, "Atley, from what I know of the campaign, it isn't going to be an easy fight, and while you and your men won't be engaging the enemy, you will be in the thick of things. I have confidence that you and your men will represent the United States well."

"Yes, Sir, we will do all we can." Jesse's voice was steady, and he was thankful for it.

There was a small smile on the officer's face when he looked up. "I've had limited contact with the French, but I have a few impressions. You will be under their command, but you go there as a courtesy, so you don't need to feel subservient. The French officers I've encountered have an air of superiority about them. Don't let that intimidate you."

"No, Sir. Thank you for the advice."

"One more thing. I have the authority to give field promotions as I see fit. Staff Sergeant Bonner confirms to me that you are an exemplary soldier. I want to send you to our allies with your head high and a little clout, so I am hereby promoting you to sergeant. I've got a copy of your promotion paperwork here for you, and I've already sent the originals in to admin. If you see my yeoman when we finish here, he will help get your new stripes sewn on your uniforms so that you are ready to go when we dock tomorrow. You have the afternoon to meet with your platoon, apprise them of this assignment, and get them squared away and ready to deploy."

"Yes, Sir. And thank you." Jesse snapped to a salute and felt Staff Sergeant Bonner do the same beside him. Lieutenant Jones returned the salute and dismissed them.

It was late that evening before Jesse finished preparations. He was tired, but he forestalled his cot a bit longer in favor of finding a table in the mess hall so that he could write to Claire and Sari. In the first days after he'd left them, his letters to his sister and his wife had been nearly identical. He had tried to write to each of them every two or three days, describing his days and sharing news. Soon, though, the repetition became laborious, and he knew he couldn't continue it. In the end, he decided that writing to Claire once a week or so would be enough

since he assumed that she and Sari would share news.
When he sat down to write to his sister, he pictured her
sharing his words with Daniel and the boys around her at
the dinner table. His letters were intentionally newsy and
upbeat. He glossed over the frustrations and tried to add
funny things that happened.

Writing to Sari took more thought. On the train
trip to New York, Jesse had often replayed his
conversation with Nathan Jameson, recalling what Nathan
told him about falling in love with his wife through their
letters before they'd ever met. Jesse pondered that advice,
prayed for guidance, and finally decided that writing to
Sari needed to be something different. Even though he
would probably only be able to mail her an envelope once
a week or so, he decided that he'd try to write to Sari every
night. Certainly, he described for her what was happening
each day, but instead of glossing over the negative and
sharing only the positive, he committed himself to writing
candidly. At first, his words were hesitant, stunted. But as
he became accustomed to the routine, he became freer
with his thoughts. He recognized that writing each night
made his letters take on a diary quality, and he decided
that was alright, as long as he kept Sari in mind. So, every
night when he sat to write, he began by praying for her.

Sitting alone at a table in the empty dining hall on
the night before they were to dock, Jesse pictured Sari
and prayed for her. When his letter began, it told of his
meeting with the lieutenant and shared about his
promotion. He admitted to himself and to Sari that he was
nervous about the coming days. He ended the letter
assuring her that he would continue writing, but that he
had no idea if and when he'd next be able to mail
something to her. As he sealed the envelope, he sent
another prayer heavenward, asking for God's protection
for his wife and for himself.

18
Encampment, Wyoming
mid - November, 1917

Sari's thoughts were on her husband as she left
the restaurant at the end of the day. *Jesse's been gone for
two weeks,* she reflected. Her life was so different. She had
friends—she'd spent three evenings with Harriet and Bea
and enjoyed their company very much. As she and
Meredith solidified their friendship, the kitchen at the
Copper Pot became a welcome occupation as long as the
Wills stayed aloof. Sari also had a family. She smiled
thinking about the two wonderful Sunday evenings she'd
enjoyed at Claire and Daniel's home. It was precious time.
The warmth and laughter, easy banter, and even serious
discussions of the news after listening to the wireless, all
lifted Sari up and helped her recall what being part of a
family felt like. In their company, Sari began to relax and
be herself, not the orphan, not the indebted serf of the
bank and the Wills, not even the beholden, misfit wife of
Jesse. Within the safety of their acceptance, she didn't
have to hide as much as she was used to doing.

After that first long, desolate Sunday by herself,
Sari began attending church with her new family.
Confident in one of the dresses she and Jesse had
purchased at Parkison's the day after their wedding, and
with her face safely concealed behind the veil of her
matching hat, Sari sat next to Claire on Sunday mornings
truly rejoicing in the Lord, happy that the God of Pastor
Abraham was loving and gracious, not angry and vengeful
like the god at Miss Milton's church.

Contrasting with the joy she discovered in being
with her new family, the new positivity of working beside
Meredith, and the fun of spending time across the street,
the time she had alone in Jesse's house continued to be
difficult for her. She felt as if she was an intruder, jumpy
and nervous and haunted by the fear that at any time
someone was going to knock at the door and demand she
leave. She'd promised Jesse that she'd try to make the
house her home, but try as she might, each time she
walked in, she felt out of place. Something like a cold ache

grew in the pit of her belly each time the door clicked behind her. The empty rooms taunted her, declaring to her that the only reason Jesse was willing to marry her was because he believed he wasn't coming back. Here, with no smiles and no work to distract her, she couldn't avoid the feeling that she didn't belong.

While she continued to eat breakfast and lunch at the Copper Pot, Jesse had been wise in predicting she'd need to eat at the house as well. Her shorter hours dictated making evening meals for herself. In Jesse's kitchen, Sari used pans, plates and utensils as she needed to, but she was always careful to replace each object back in the drawer or cupboard where she found them. Sometimes, she shook her head and wondered at the incongruous placement of a particular item, but even when she was sure there was a more convenient way to configure the kitchen, she didn't allow herself to change anything. This was Jesse's kitchen, Jesse's house, not hers.

Other than the drawers Jesse left empty for her and the closet where her dresses were hung, every other spot in the house remained his. Only when she had a good reason did Sari even open a drawer or cupboard.

Lonely evenings paced by. Sari's normal routine included making herself something to eat, then sitting in the parlor to embroider or read. Near bedtime, Sari often allowed herself a long soak in Jesse's deep tub before she climbed the stairs to end her day reading. One evening she garnered her courage after eating a fried egg and toast for dinner, and ventured into the dayroom downstairs where Jesse slept before he left. She intended to explore the bookshelves, hoping to find something to read. A pair of Jesse's work boots sat neatly at the end of the daybed and one of his shirts lay carelessly across one of the chairs. The intimacy of his discarded clothes unnerved Sari, and she fled the room, closing the door behind her. After that, she stayed in the kitchen, parlor, bathroom and bedroom, not venturing into the second bedroom upstairs or the downstairs dayroom again. The only room she made any changes in was the bathroom. Here, she allowed herself to populate a small stand next to the sink with her own toiletries, hairbrush, and comb.

Tonight, because of an invitation she'd received to Claire and Daniel's, Sari wasn't relegated to spending the entire evening alone. Sari felt more buoyant. Lightly, she climbed the stairs to change out of her work dress.

It was dark already and a stiff wind stung her face when she left the house. A few minutes later when she turned up the sidewalk to her sister-in-law's house, Sari's nose was cold and her fingers felt stiff in the evening air.

The front windows glowed with invitation, promising welcome and warmth. Claire had not yet closed the living room drapes, and Sari could see that Greg was hunched into one of the wing back chairs reading a book. The light in the room flickered, and Sari knew a fire was dancing beyond the hearth. Thankful that she was welcome in this loving home, Sari shook her head slightly in amazement at this blessing.

"You are right on time," Claire greeted her with a smile when she answered Sari's knock. "I hope you won't be offended by dinner tonight. It is just a plain meatloaf and boiled potatoes."

"I haven't had meatloaf in a long time. It smells wonderful," Sari replied. "My meatloaf always turns out dry," she admitted.

"I can't believe that's true," answered Claire as she took Sari's coat to hang behind the door.

In the kitchen, Sari noted that there were only four places set at the table. Claire shrugged and answered the unspoken question, "Daniel has a meeting tonight. There's been some issue with the electrical production plant, and he's trying to find a solution. Actually, I'm glad. I'll have you all to myself after we finish dinner."

Sari drank in the conversation at dinner as she feasted on Claire's meatloaf. The boys dominated the table with descriptions of their trials and triumphs at school. Michael crowed about a perfect score on his most recent history test. When Claire asked Greg about his day, the boy was less pleased.

"Well, Mama, the truth is I am still having trouble with arithmetic, and some of the other kids teased me today when I gave the wrong answer. Mr. Armitage says he'll help me tomorrow, but I'm not sure I'll ever get it." His face was a study in dejection.

"I used to be pretty good in arithmetic, Greg," Sari ventured. Inside, her heart trembled with compassion for the boy. "Maybe I could help you for a little while?"

She looked up to see Claire's nod.

"Son," Claire was addressing Michael, "How about you and I do the dishes tonight together and give Aunt Sari and Greg some time to work on his problems?"

Michael grimaced but nodded. He wasn't happy at taking an extra turn at kitchen duty, but a strong look from his mother warned off any thought of mutiny.

Soon, Sari was sitting next to Greg at the cleared dining room table. A math primer was open in front of them along with a tablet of paper.

Sari asked Greg to explain to her what he didn't understand. After a few false starts, she was able to see the issue. With a reassuring smile, Sari began, "Greg, you are showing me that you can do any of this figuring, and I'm impressed at how well you know your multiplication tables."

"I know those things, I just can't do these story problems." It was the first time Sari had ever heard the boy be whiny.

"I think I can show you a trick. Read this problem out loud for me."

He shrugged and began reading a short story about a farmer and gallons of water for his horses. When he was finished reading, Sari asked him to draw a picture of what he'd read. At first he balked, but she demonstrated what she meant. Soon, a smile spread across the boy's face.

"Oh, now I see. He needs this many gallons for this horse and this many for that horse every day." As he spoke, he diagrammed his thoughts. "That means we have to add these together then multiply by seven for the week!"

"Exactly!" encouraged Sari.

Armed with a way to illustrate the facts of the problem, it only took a few more minutes for Greg to complete the page that had been his nemesis at school. With an excited hug and a sincere thanks, Greg skipped out of the room just as Michael and Claire finished the dishes.

After bringing out a steaming cup of tea for them both, Claire slid into the chair across from Sari. "What you just did for Greg was wonderful!"

Sari shrugged. "All he needed was to organize his information," she answered.

"I can't tell you how many nights Daniel and I have struggled to help him with his figures. He knows the facts but he just can't see what to do with them."

Sari agreed. "I think having him draw an illustration helped. It will help him see the problems differently."

Claire reached for the letter she'd placed on the table. "This came today from Jesse. It doesn't say much, he wrote it just two days after he left while he was still on the train. Would you like to read it?"

Sari said yes and accepted the page from Claire. The letter was short. Jesse told of seeing a huge herd of wild horses out the train window near Laramie and the struggle the train had in getting up Sherman grade between Laramie and Cheyenne. He'd written the letter while on a stopover in Omaha, Nebraska on his way to New York. Sari could almost hear the wind blowing across the vast, flat cornfields as he described them. Jesse ended the letter with two requests: first, that he share the note with Sari and second, that they both write to him. He assured them that the address he'd given them before he left would be forwarded to wherever his battalion was.

When she finished and looked up, there were tears in Claire's eyes. "I miss him so much," she whispered as she scrubbed the tears from her cheeks. "I hate this war."

Sari was filled with an odd mix of emotions and considered how she felt. She was sure she didn't miss Jesse like Claire did. She'd spent such little time with him. Yet, there was a hole in her life that hadn't been there before.

Claire sat up straighter and put her shoulders back. "Well, now, that kind of silliness doesn't help anything, does it?" she gave Sari a self-depreciating grin. "You, my dear sister, look a little pale tonight. Are you alright?"

Sari didn't mean to answer the way she did, and as the words escaped she was amazed at herself. "I'm healthy, no aches or pains or sniffles. I guess that there are just been too many changes for me lately, and I'm having some trouble getting my balance."

Claire leaned forward, elbows on the table, arms crossed, and waited for Sari to continue.

"I don't know what Jesse has told you, but before I moved into his house, I had a small room attached to the Old Wyoming Rooming House on McCaffrey." Claire shook her head, this was news to her. Sari took a breath and continued slowly. "It was a very small place, and not very nice. Sometimes, after work, I felt lonely in that room, but more often, once I closed the door to the outside world, I felt safe, secure, even a little happy. I could let go and be myself, drift away, get lost in the pages of a book or focus on an embroidery project and just not worry about anything."

Claire pictured her own attic room in Rapid City and understood. She didn't speak, but wondered if someday she'd share her own experiences with the new friend in front of her. Sari couldn't guess her companion's thoughts, but Claire's kind eyes and sweet silence encouraged her to continue. "Now that I am at Jesse's, I can't seem to find that safe harbor." She dropped her eyes and rushed on, "Please don't misunderstand. I am thankful to Jesse for his generosity at letting me stay there, and the house is beautiful and comfortable, I just— well, I just don't really belong there." The words hung in the air between them and at once Sari regretted them, fearful of how they'd sound to Jesse's sister.

"Several times you referred to the house as "Jesse's", and I can understand that, but, I'm certain, because Jesse told me so, that he wants you to feel like the house is your home. I'm wondering if you are having the same trouble Greg was having with his story problems."

Sari tilted her head to one side and regarded Claire with doubt. "I don't know what you mean."

"I think you need to see this situation from a different perspective. It's only been a short while since you moved in, and feeling at home takes time, I understand that completely. But, it isn't going to get better if you continue to think of the place only as Jesse's house.

Jesse's name is on the deed to the house, but, remember, it's your name now too." She could see that Sari was listening. "You and Jesse didn't have much time together before he left, and you've said that you don't know him well. That's fact. Another fact is that probably Jesse will be gone for a while—I can't even think about any other options. In the meantime, unless you decide to move back to your room at the boarding house, that house is your home. It's up to you to decide to make it your safe harbor."

"But I feel like I'm snooping when I open a cupboard." Sari knew she sounded shrill and didn't like it, but Claire seemed not to notice.

In spite of herself, Claire snickered. "I just feel frustrated when I open those cupboards. Jesse has absolutely no sense of how to organize anything. The last time I was at his house I needed a spoon for my tea. I found a screwdriver and a pencil in the silverware drawer along with only about half the spoons. Lord knows where the others are."

"The screwdriver and pencil are still there. The other spoons are on the top shelf of the pantry," Sari answered as Claire continued to chuckle. Claire's levity was contagious and Sari smiled, but then she turned serious. "I didn't move them thinking that's where Jesse chose for them to be."

Now Claire laughed aloud. Sari started to feel slighted, then replayed her last words in her head and heard how silly they were. Claire confirmed that no meanness was intended as she added, "Oh Sari, that's a classic new bride's mistake. Jesse didn't intend for any object to be in any drawer or cupboard in that house. He does what Daniel and probably every other man does. If he moves something at all, he just stuffs it in the first available space he can find."

They giggled again, and Sari considered Claire's observation.

After a moment, Claire offered a new idea. "Sari, tell me, if you hadn't married Jesse, and instead were living in the house as a renter, or if you lived there as a favor to him as his caretaker, just to look after it while he was gone, would you feel more comfortable? Would you be able to organize drawers and enjoy the challenge of putting things right?"

It took her a full minute to answer. "Well, yes, maybe I would. If I had been hired to be the housekeeper in his absence, I think I'd feel it was my job to put things right and make it as nice as I could in preparation for his return."

Sari saw Claire's point right away, but before she could comment further, Claire added another point of view. "Okay, now let's suppose that you'd purchased the house, and that it was yours. What would you do then?"

"I see what you are pointing out. If the house was mine, then of course I wouldn't hesitate to remove that screwdriver or rearrange the furniture in the parlor."

Claire smiled, warm and encouraging. "That's right, and Sari, honestly, both scenarios are true. As his wife, you are the house keeper, you are in charge. While we both are going to pray constantly that Jesse soon comes home safe and sound, in the meantime, you do own the house and you need to take charge of it."

The honesty and simplicity of Claire's words soaked deeply into Sari's heart. The air in the room was so friendly, homey. After a pause, Sari replied, "Claire, I think you've just shown me that I need to give myself permission to enjoy living at Jess—I mean to live in my house."

Claire nodded and reached out to touch Sari's hand. "That's a good way to put it."

After a few moments, Claire became serious. "I know feeling more at home will be a good start for you. I would love to help in any way I can. In fact, if you are interested, I have some linen curtains that I think would fit the windows in your bedroom. I'll look in my cedar chest for a table cloth I think you'd like as well."

They talked for a few minutes about decorating. Claire offered Sari a refill on her tea then asked. "Is there anything else I can do to help you find that balance you mentioned?"

Sari hesitated, vacillating between trusting this new friendship or finding a way to shut the conversation down. She wasn't sure she'd made the right decision when she began, "Feeling at home in the house is only a part of this, Claire. It's everything. Having a new home, having this ring on my finger and a new name. Jesse even talked with the owners at the Copper Pot and insisted on a new work schedule for me. He's arranged for me to have an allowance for spending money. He took me shopping and bought me more beautiful clothes than I've ever owned. There's no way I deserve any of his kindness, or yours, and I don't know how I can ever repay all that's been given me."

Claire didn't hurry to answer. "I've never been in your situation certainly, but I think I can understand how you can feel." The doubt in Sari's face was clear, so Claire continued. "Someday maybe I'll tell you about my life before Daniel and I met. But trust me, for a long time even after we married and moved here, I lived in fear that others would discover that I didn't deserve him, the life I have, or their friendship. For me, it was a matter of forgiving myself and trusting in God's redemption. Coming to understand the depth of His love for me, as well as Daniel's, took a lot of prayer and," she chuckled as she went on, "a couple of pretty loud arguments with Daniel before I began to believe it."

Finally, with Claire's gentle eyes watching her, the weight of it all became too much for her to hold alone, and she continued, "Claire, I know that I'm ugly. I know that people are repulsed when they look at me."

"So you don't believe you deserve kindness because of the scars on your face?"

Sari's answer conveyed to Claire the depth of her conviction about its truth. "Of course, my scars are the reason. Why and how would any normal person want to subject themselves to being in the company of such foulness? I know that the accident that scarred my face wasn't my doing, yet it has always seemed as if the marks I bear are some way an indictment of me. My life changed so completely after the accident. Not only were my parents, with whom I was very close and whose love for me abounded, ripped from me, but everything else I knew and loved was gone as well. I went, in just a short time, from being the center of my parents' world to being hidden away in the kitchen of an orphanage, cared about by no one and subject to horrified looks and cruel comments."

Sari stared at the table as she spoke and in the silence that followed. It took all the will power she had to slowly look up. What she saw surprised her. Claire was crying, silent tears sliding down her cheeks as she replied, "So you don't believe you deserve kindness because of the scars on your face?"

The questions and Claire's tears gave Sari enough courage to finish, "It isn't just that my pretty face was gone. I began feeling, and still do, like my scars are an indication that I'm worthless through and through, that I have nothing at all to offer anyone. My ugliness is just the outward confirmation of that."

Claire was quiet a long time before she spoke. *Sari has been trapped in this story for so long, she can't hear how wrong it is,* she thought. "It's ironic, Sari, that God brought the two of us together." Claire stated quietly but with conviction. She brushed away a tear and rubbed her nose with the back of her hand. "When I met Daniel I knew I was attractive. Actually, I thought I was beautiful, and others did as well. But, when I was honest with myself, I also knew that despite all my outward loveliness, I was rotten and ugly on the inside. I couldn't believe that anyone could love me, least of all someone as wonderful as Daniel. It wasn't until I understood that the God of all creation cared for me, that He had, in fact sent Jesus to die to pay for my sins, that I could even begin to understand Daniel's love. Once I understood God's love, only then could I accept Daniel's. Now here we are, you and me. I don't know what Jesse has said to you in your private moments together, and I am well aware that you two barely know one another. But. I do know my brother, and based on what I've seen in his face when he looks at you and in his actions, I'm convinced he cares deeply for you. His feelings don't stop or start with how you look."

Now Sari brushed away tears, but she didn't interrupt. Claire closed her eyes and pleaded silently for help, then continued. "The reality is, Jesse chose to marry you because he wants to be married to you. Be assured," she gave Sari a guilty smile, "that I questioned him thoroughly on his motives." Claire was relieved to see Sari nod. "Based on my own struggles, I can see that until you can accept that Jesus loves you for who you are inside and out, no matter what, you won't be able to let your marriage be real for either of you."

"But, I do, Claire. I am a believer, and I do know God loves me."

Claire seemed to change the subject with her next question, "Sari, when did you accept the Lord as your Savior?"

"Well, I was," she searched the ceiling for a moment before answering, "It was the winter before the accident. My mother had just finished telling me the story of Peter walking on water with Jesus. I began asking questions, and she helped me pray to become a believer."

Claire nodded. "I could certainly be wrong, but I wonder if somehow, with all you went through after that, you didn't start thinking that God was just as, um, put off by your injuries as the people around you seemed to be?"

Claire's words slammed into Sari so hard she wasn't sure she could stay upright. It only took one heart beat for Sari to recognize the truth and wisdom of Claire's observation and to understand that she'd just been given something vitally important.

Sari swallowed and tried to breathe. She swallowed again. How could she explain to Claire that what she was feeling was similar to the sensation of being in the dark for a very long time and then lighting a bright lantern? It wasn't her eyes that were blinking, trying to become accustomed to the glare, it was her heart.

Finally, knowing she needed to say something and also knowing she would need time to assimilate the new, vivid brightness of understanding inside her, she met Claire's eyes and said, "I think you might be righter than you can imagine. Thank you. I have a lot to think through, and I'd like to change the subject now if we could. I wonder, though, do you think we could talk again about this?"

Claire answered without hesitation. "Yes, any time you want. In the meantime, I am going to be praying extra for you, alright?"

Sari nodded. When Claire reached across the table and took her hand, Sari was happy to feel the steadying warmth and return it with a squeeze.

With effort, they safely steered their conversation to the new Ladies' Aid Society forming in Encampment. Claire had barely begun to describe how the ladies were planning to mimic US Vice President Marshall's wife and begin sewing surgical dressings and hospital garments for the Red Cross when they heard Daniel's footsteps on the back porch. He looked so tired as he entered the room, his face pale and lines beneath his eyes. Sari didn't stay long after his arrival. She left with a dish filled with leftover meatloaf and potatoes and a strong hug from Claire.

When she turned on the light in the parlor and shut the front door, Sari knew she'd also arrived with a shift in her thinking.

19

Encampment, Wyoming
mid - November, 1917

Sari was again thinking about the meatloaf dinner she'd shared with Claire and the boys and replaying the conversation they'd had when she stopped in at the post office after work the next day. She was surprised and pleased when the postmaster handed her a letter from Jesse, postmarked New York. She tucked it safely into the pocket of her coat, waiting to read it until she was alone.

Once at the house, she sat at the kitchen table and stared at the letter a long while before opening it. She read it twice, and then a third time before she returned the pages to the envelope and began walking aimlessly between the kitchen and parlor. In the letter, much as in the letter Claire received, Jesse detailed his trip across the country, telling about the scenery and adding some light and astute descriptions of the passengers he travelled with. Then, he went on to describe the camp in New York where he was staying.

As she read on, however, Sari realized that this letter was quite different from Claire's. It was much longer than Claire's and Sari was sure this letter hadn't been written all at one sitting. Sometimes the writing was hurried and a little messy. In other sections, his words seemed more deliberate and considered. Jesse's words to her didn't stay light and airy as Claire's had. He departed from merely relaying his experiences and let her glimpse what he was thinking and feeling. He related a little about himself, admitting briefly to her that he was anxious about what the future held. At the end, he pledged that he would write as often as he could and asked that she please write to him.

At first she felt disjointed and uncomfortable with the intimate tone of the letter. Despite being married, they were nearly strangers. She was nearly convinced that their marriage was simply an example of someone's kindness to another, but Jesse's letters and Claire's unconditional acceptance spoke differently and she was confused.

Restless, she tried to distract herself with her embroidery, but she couldn't concentrate. She replayed Jesse's letter and Claire's words over and over. Eventually, her thoughts turned to prayer, nearly wordless seeking. She didn't feel better when she whispered "Amen."

She rambled through the rest of the evening. At last, she slipped into bed, weary and downcast but wide awake. She ignored the Bible beside her on the table and picked up the *Life* magazine that Claire had given her. *I know you are there, God, and I'm trying to believe that You haven't rejected me.* Her thought wasn't a prayer, more to herself, *And I know Your Bible is filled with answered prayers, but for so long it has felt like I'm just not someone You talk to.*

Trying to escape her worries, Sari concentrated on the magazine in her hand. This edition was a month old, dated October 4, 1917, but she didn't mind. The cover held a drawing of a rotund cook in what made her think of what a kitchen on a Naval ship would look like. He had a spatula in his hand. Three airborne pancakes were lined up for landing on a frying pan he was holding. Sari liked his relaxed and mischievous grin and his unkempt white shirt and apron.

As she leafed through the magazine, she wondered if an Army cook made pancakes for Jesse. Ads for tires and White Rock Mineral water were interspersed between the articles. One news piece caught her attention and she read about how two Kaisers in Germany replied to the Pope's suggestion of peace. She lingered for a few minutes at an ad for Velvet tobacco. The ad was adorned with pictures of Br'er Rabit and Br'er Fox. The sight of those two cartoons reminded her of a small volume of Uncle Remus stories her mother read her when she was small.

A few pages later God spoke to her.

Toward the back of the magazine Sari's eyes glanced at a short article that began with Colossians 3:23. "Whatsoever ye do, do it heartily, as to the Lord, and not unto men." The verse wasn't new to her, but the words from that page spoke new meaning to her nearly as loudly as if she'd heard a voice.

She couldn't explain later how her thoughts converged with a clear vision of what she needed to do.

Instantly she knew, though, that this was the answer to her prayer and the advice she needed to guide her. *Live heartily, do your best, do it for God. For whatever reason, I've been placed right here right now,* she thought. *I can continue to question the why of that, or I can use what I've been given to do something positive.* Now wide awake and no longer weary, Sari got out of bed and went downstairs. She stoked the fire in the stove and sat at the table while the tea kettle slowly got hot. While she waited, she replayed the last few weeks and began to feel ashamed of herself. The kitchen listened as she explained, "I've been moping around and complaining since Jesse asked me to marry him. I've been so caught up in wallowing in self-pity and in the feeling that I don't deserve anything that I haven't seen either the blessings I'm receiving or the opportunities I'm facing."

She made herself a cup of tea and paced the kitchen, continuing to process her new perspective. Her tea was nearly gone when her thoughts expanded. "It's not just since I met Jesse that I've acted this way." Guilt pushed on her. "I've been so focused on myself and my own trials that I haven't made any room for anything else. I was mean to Meredith, oh dear, how many other possible friends have I pushed away instead of welcoming them? Oh, God, I'm so sorry!"

Sari went to her knees right there in the middle of the kitchen and began praying. Instead of the polite, arm's length prayers she was accustomed to, she pulled God to her with complete abandon. She confessed her selfishness and pitiful attitude, then asked for help to leave that thought pattern behind. Much later, when she climbed the stairs for the second time that night, she felt renewed. Armed with a forgiven spirit and a plan, she slept well.

Holding tightly to her goal to put others first and do her best at every task, Sari arrived at the Copper Pot's kitchen the next morning with energy and a light heart. Lilith noticed the change in her morning cook right away and returned Sari's positivity with positivity of her own. At breakfast a few days later, Lilith mentioned it to Chetley. "It isn't as if Sari is working any harder or accomplishing more in the kitchen. She's always been quick and efficient, but there is a change in her."

"I know what you mean. Yesterday she asked how my day was going," Chet told his wife.

"Yes, that's a part of what I'm seeing. Instead of hanging her head and keeping her eyes low, she's standing straighter and actually smiling sometimes."

Sari's evenings also became time she enjoyed instead of dreaded. She decided that since she was, in fact, Jesse's legal wife, she needed to act like it. To be a good steward of the home he'd left for her to live in, she embraced the responsibility of creating a home that Jesse would appreciate more than the bachelor digs he'd left. Right away, Sari began the task of cleaning and organizing. She tackled the kitchen first by removing everything from the cupboards and drawers so that she could scrub and clean thoroughly. Next, she started organizing.

It was nine o'clock on the fourth evening of her effort when she dried her hands on her apron and stood back to survey her accomplishments. Sari sat down, satisfyingly tired, and admired how pretty the table looked with a new coat of lemon oil on it. The room smelled fresh and sparkled from ceiling to floor, inside and out. The window was clean, the curtain washed, ironed and replaced. Stove, icebox, sink and counters, and floor all shone. Dishes and glasses, all newly washed and dried, rested on crisp new shelf paper. Everything had a logical spot. Smiling, Sari had moved the pencil Claire remembered from the silverware drawer to the desk in the parlor. After some debate, however, the screwdriver was stowed at the back of the silverware drawer. With a nod to Jesse, Sari decided that maybe she'd need it someday.

The shelves of the narrow pantry, unseen behind the door next to the ice box, were clean but quite empty. "Now that I've uncovered a well-equipped and sparkling clean kitchen," she told the pristine room, "it's time to add some staples to those shelves."

The next evening, after a stop at Parkison's at the end of her workday, Sari filled the house with the warm scent of snickerdoodles. The batch sat in uniform rows cooling on a dishtowel as Sari enjoyed a dinner of Campbell's chicken soup and crackers. As she washed the dishes, she listened for a knock on the door.

Since two days after Jesse left, Michael, often with Greg in tow, came over twice a week to carry in and stack firewood beside the parlor fireplace and to check on her supply of coal in the cellar coal chute. Just last week, when it had snowed during the day, Sari returned to the house to find that her walks had been neatly shoveled. She felt guilty at having the boys work for her, but when she'd tried to tell Michael she didn't want to impose on him, he merely shrugged and answered that he and Greg wanted to help. "Anyways, Aunt Sari, Papa says that helping you is a way for Greg and me to give Uncle Jesse and the war our support. Plus, we like coming over to see you!" With that assurance, their short visits became a highlight of her evenings.

Michael arrived while Sari was washing dishes the night she'd baked cookies. Without Greg that day, he greeted her and went right to work. Sari was drying the last dish when he returned to the kitchen. "Aunt Sari, this room looks so different. It's even nicer than Mama's kitchen now!"

Sari thanked him with a wide smile.

"The coal chute is full, and so is your wood box in the parlor. I shoveled the ashes out of the fireplace and laid a new fire for you. All you need to do is put in a match."

"Thank you, so much, Michael," she answered. "I baked you a treat, would you like some milk?"

"Yes, please!"

They sat together at the table. Sari asked about his school day and they chatted comfortably. Sari was pleased to hear that Michael had befriended Bea at school. "She's older than me," Michael told her, "but she doesn't act all snobby like some of the other girls. She played tag with us yesterday. She's easy to be with and she's funny."

Sari had to agree with Michael's assessment. The fact that Bea was a year younger than Sari didn't seem to hamper their friendship.

Michael finished his milk and a third cookie when Sari said, "I'll wrap up some for you to take home and share with your mom, dad, and Greg."

"That would be great," he answered brushing a crumb from his chin.

A few minutes later, Michael slid his arms into his coat. He turned to leave, then remembered, "Oh, Aunt Sari, I have a note here from Mama for you."

The note told Sari that the family had been invited to Daniel's boss' house for dinner on Sunday, so they wouldn't be able to have her over. "P.S. I am so sorry to cancel," Claire finished, "I'd much rather visit with you!"

Sari was touched at the postscript, and asked Michael to wait. On the back of the note, she wrote, "I understand. I hope you have a fun evening."

"Here you go, Michael. Could you return this to your mother for me?"

"Sure." With a quick hug, the boy was gone and Sari had the house to herself again. She closed the door and surveyed the kitchen and realized that for the first time, she didn't feel lonely or anxious.

After work the next day Sari stopped at the house across the street on her way home. Since her family would be busy on Sunday, Sari decided to invite Bea to spend the afternoon with her. Bea accepted immediately and both of them spent the rest of the week looking forward to their time together.

Sari was comfortable with the routine she'd settled into. Evenings alone were much less desolate now that she had friends to divide her time with. Just as she had from the beginning, each evening, before she climbed the stairs to get ready for bed, she sat down at the small secretary desk in the parlor and picked up her pen to write to Jesse. At first she felt shy, but the more she wrote, the easier it was to tell him not only about her days, but also some of her own thoughts and feelings. She described what she'd done in the kitchen and tried to put into words how she'd gone from feeling out of place to looking forward to coming home after work. She told him about the advice Claire offered and also how God had changed her thinking with the Colossians verse.

Sunday evening, two weeks later, Sari lingered on the sidewalk outside Claire and Daniel's for a few moments before she went inside, relishing her new-found feeling of belonging. Finally, with the cold creeping into her toes, she mounted the steps. She knocked only once before the door flew open. "Hi Aunt Sari," Michael greeted her before yelling into the kitchen, "Mama, Aunt Sari's here!"

Supper was nearly ready when Sari entered the kitchen. She helped Claire dish up the meal while Greg finished setting the table and Michael went to the carriage house at the back of their lot to retrieve Daniel.

It was a relaxed meal, full of gentle discussions that included what the boys were learning at school and the water supply project Daniel was presently concerned with. When they'd finished, the boys were excused but the three adults lingered. Daniel sipped a cup of coffee as Claire reported that she'd received a letter from Jesse on Friday.

Sari nodded, "I got one as well."

"Is yours from France?"

Again, Sari nodded.

"Then I'm sure he told you that he's a sergeant now."

Sari told her that he had and Claire continued, "I am proud that he got a promotion to sergeant, but it makes me nervous that he's going into battle so soon." Claire finished her statement with a frown.

Daniel reminded them, "Yes, but before you let yourself worry too much, keep in mind that he's in a support capacity. He's not going to see action."

Their talk about Jesse's letter eventually reminded Claire of the news she'd been waiting to share. "I got another letter to tell you about. Daniel, you'll be surprised to find out who it was from." He looked at her quizzically and shook his head. "Lela!"

It took Daniel a moment to respond. "Lela? From Rapid City?"

Forgetting Sari for a minute Claire continued, "Yes, but really, Daniel, she hasn't lived in Rapid City since just a few months after we left. She lives in Baltimore."

"Okay, yes, of course."

Claire met Sari's gaze, "Oh Honey, I'm sorry, I should explain. When I lived in Rapid City, before Daniel and I married, I was friends with two ladies," she hesitated at the word, but then recovered herself and continued. "Estelle and Lela and I were pals. Now here's the fun news. Daniel, are you listening?"

Daniel had been easily distracted through dinner and both women wondered what was occupying his mind. "Yes, Claire, I am waiting patiently for your news of Lela." He said it comically, and Sari giggled. She enjoyed these moments with this couple so much.

"Anyway, the news is that something to do with her husband's business is taking them to San Francisco. Lela looked at a map and realized that their trip across the country will take them right through Wolcott and Rawlins. She's talked her husband into delaying for a day or two so that they can come here and see us!"

"Really?" Something in Daniel's tone denoted something less than excitement, but his smile was warm.

"It will be a short visit, but I am looking forward to seeing her again."

"How long has it been since you've last been together?" Sari asked.

"Let's see, we left Rapid City in December of 1897 and I've not seen her since then, though we write four or five times a year to keep in contact." She stopped to add up the years then added, "Oh my, can it have been twenty years already?"

"When will they be through here?" Daniel asked.

"Sometime in mid-January. She promised to send me a telegram a few days before they arrive."

Daniel finished his coffee and stood up. He poked his head into the parlor and called, "Greg, I think it's your night to help with dishes. Come on, Son. I think we should get after it."

Sari heard a little grumbling roll in from the front of the house, but soon the table was cleared and the soft murmur of voices from the kitchen created a calm background noise.

Claire invited Sari into the guest room. "You look tired, I know you have long days and I don't want to keep you too late, but I found the kind of shirts we talked about for Jesse's Christmas present this week while I was at Parkison's. I bought four of them." She pulled out a stack of white undershirts that were wrapped in brown paper. "Are these what you were picturing?"

Sari rubbed the soft cotton flannel between her thumb and forefinger. They'd agreed to work together and send Jesse a Christmas package. Sari was a little uncomfortable sending him undershirts. It seemed too personal even though he was her husband, but clearly he wouldn't be wearing anything other than his uniform, and warm undergarments were practical.

"These are wonderful. You put them on my account at the mercantile, right?"

Claire nodded, "Yes, I did."

Sari continued to rub the fabric, lost in thought. "I'd like to find something else to add to the package, I'm just not sure what."

"I've been thinking the same thing." Claire agreed. "I have these warm socks for him, and both boys are writing him letters. I bought some penny candy, the kind he used to love when he was little, but I can't think of anything else that wouldn't just be in his way."

Sari closed the brown wrapping around the shirts and retied the string. "You know I considered a Bible, but after you told me about the one he has, I searched the house, and I can't find it, so I'm quite certain he did take it with him. He wouldn't need two."

After a few moments, Claire shared a thought, "You know, Daniel and I got married on New Year's Eve. That Christmas, I bought him a pocket knife. He cherishes that knife and still carries it with him. I know Jesse has one, but it's old and not special in any way."

"That's a wonderful idea!" Sari knew instantly a pocket knife would be the perfect gift for Jesse. "I'll stop at Parkison's tomorrow after work and see if they have any. I know we decided that we needed to get this parcel mailed right away, so I'll bake the cookies I wanted to add tomorrow night and drop them off to you on my way to work the next morning. Thank you."

20

near Cambrai, France
December, 1917

"I dunna think this blooming battle is ever gonna end." Jesse had become used to the grousing demeanor of his tent-mate, British Corporal Willem Perry. He'd also become accustomed to the man's thick brogue and his penchant for swearing. Today, Jesse was too tired and too harried to give his fellow blacksmith's comments much consideration.

"Hey, Uncle Sam, wha' day is't?"

It was a nickname he'd acquired when he and his platoon arrived at the multinational camp near Cambrai. It took several heart beats before Jesse processed the words as something he should respond to. "Uh, I think it is December first," he answered finally, ending with a grunt as the horse he was shoeing tried to dance away from him. He cautioned Private Baird, who was holding the lead rope, to keep the horse steady and kept on working.

"Eleven days, then, of this hellishness," came a delayed response. "I canna help thinkin' if it weren't the Frenchies in charge, we migh' not have lost so much ground to the Krauts yesterday."

Jesse didn't answer. He didn't have the time or inclination to debate. Jesse knew that in reality, it was British General Julian Burg, in charge of five mounted divisions as well as three tank divisions for this battle, who was making the decisions. He knew also that the ground the allies had gained on the first day of the battle on November 20th had not been secured as it should have been by the cavalry forces. Since they hadn't been deployed quickly enough to exploit the gaps created by the tanks, the advantage was lost. Now, after the German counterattack yesterday, all the ground gained was lost and there was speculation that the troops in the front trenches were going to need to fall back soon or take the chance of being overrun by the enemy.

He concentrated on the hoof in his hand. He finished trimming it and checked to make sure the shoe was good and tight. After getting clear of the skittish gelding, Jesse nodded at Private Baird and turned to use a ladle to dip into the deep basin and refill his metal drinking cup. He took a drink, then stretched his back and limbered up his neck as he rested. Baird led the gelding out of the forge tent just as a courier in a French uniform entered.

The courier spoke a moment with Corporal Perry, who was closer to the entrance. Jesse stared in their direction, letting his mind coast, and didn't pay much attention until he saw his British counterpart point towards him. He watched the courier wind his way through the stall gate and approach him.

"Are you Atley?" the Frenchman's English was barely understandable, but Jesse appreciated his effort.

"Yes, I'm Sergeant Atley."

"I have some mail for you." The words came with an extended hand holding an envelope and a postcard.

Jesse took it with a stunned thanks and the courier retreated. He stared at the mail in his hand. He'd been warned that mail service would be slow at best once they arrived in Europe. In addition, before he'd left the ship, Lieutenant Jones' yeoman assured him that they'd hold any mail for him so that he could get it when he returned to them. How these found him was a mystery, but one that warmed him heart and soul. He read the post card first. The Red Cross printed them and made them available to soldiers. No postage stamps were needed. Jesse flipped over the card and smiled.

> We sailed first to Liverpool, England, then to South Hampton. Landed in Cherbourg and marched all the way into Paris. They saw fit to let us ride a train from there. Have been in training now for several weeks. My Ma wrote, says she's heard you are in France also. Maybe we'll run into each other. Wilber Toothaker

Jesse laughed at the grousing in Wilber's note. Then, he savored his first look at the envelope he held. He let his eyes rest on the flowing lines of Sari's handwriting and pictured her small, delicate hand. He concentrated for a moment and the commotion of the forge faded, replaced by the memory of that soft hand resting in his as they walked together in Encampment.

His respite didn't last. Hoarse shouts and the clanging of a bell brought him back to the present as controlled chaos descended on the camp. A poison gas attack on French troops was responsible for Jesse's temporary assignment away from his American company to the Battle of Cambrai, and the threat of another attack hovered over the battle camp constantly. Jesse was familiar with the meaning of the bell's toll and had participated in drills and practices dozens of times. He knew, somehow, in the pit of his stomach, though, that this was not a drill.

Jesse stuffed Sari's unopened note, along with Wilber's card, into his pants pocket while he took in a deep breath and held it. He swiveled his head around to the work bench to locate his small-box respirator. He ran to the bench, and, nearly shoulder to shoulder with Perry, slipped the box filter over his head, letting it dangle like a macabre necklace on his chest. Urgently, he fitted the rubber mask over his face and cinched up the straps. Once the mask was secure, Jesse looked around again and had an instant of sheer panic before he located his long-sleeved jacket. There was no way of knowing what kind of gas they were being attacked with. The Germans may have sent simple tear gas, but it was more likely the attack included more hazardous chemicals such as phosgene, chlorine, or even mustard gas. The respirator would help protect him from the first three, but mustard gas not only threatened the lungs, but also put wicked blisters on any exposed skin. Jesse pulled on his jacket and buttoned it up to protect his neck, then he bent down and stretched his socks over the ends of his pant legs. He fitted his helmet over the gas mask. Finally, he pulled on gloves, checking as he did that none of his skin was exposed. He gave Perry a thumbs up and waited for the man's gesture in reply. Then, they moved together towards an adjacent locker and filled their arms with as many over-sized masks as they could carry.

Mounts for the cavalry were kept in a variety of corrals and paddocks around the camp. Jesse and his platoon were assigned care of the forty horses in corral six. Corporal Perry and his grooms tended a similar number in corral seven. Jesse led the way, on a run, out the tent flap and across to the corral.

Later, in nightmares and memory, Jesse would recall the scene more as a disturbed ant hill than as anything human. Men around him, bug-eyed in goggles and covered in drab green, dashed in every direction. Jesse combed the chaos for the three men in his platoon. With a rush of relief he saw they were already inside the corral ahead of him. He ducked under the rail.

The horses had also been through countless drills but that didn't stop them from being nervous with the commotion and the fear and adrenaline of their handlers. Jesse slowed his pace and quieted his movements as he distributed the masks. When his arms were empty except for one mask, he turned to the mare closest to him and stroked her side, then worked his way up to her head, rubbing her ears and getting a good hold on her lead rope before sliding her gas mask into place. She tried to fight it, but he held her tightly and she gave in and accepted it. When he had her mask secure, he located a pile of masks that had just been delivered by one of the French grooms. He repeated the process again and again until every animal around him was masked. He estimated they had completed the job in less than fifteen minutes.

Jesse moved to the edge of the corral and ducked back under the rail. He turned to face the livestock and lean against the fencepost to catch his breath. He was having trouble seeing, so he used his gloved hand to wipe away the dust and grime clinging to the lenses of his goggles. When his actions only helped a little, he realized that the problem was with fog on the inside. With a frustrated oath, he blinked his own eyes and willed the haze to clear, knowing that it wouldn't. Squinting, he located the individuals of his platoon, then let himself stop moving long enough to pay attention to the horse in the corral in front of him. The Army had experimented with several kinds of safety gear for the horses. The masks they currently had only covered the horses' mouth and nose.

Their eyes were unprotected. Jesse watched as a gelding near him snorted and blew in the mask he wore. The buckskin tossed and shook his head. He wasn't alone. Other mounts were pawing the ground. A gentle sorrel mare stood apart from the rest, legs splayed, trying to rub the side of her head on her outstretched foreleg. Jesse watched more closely and began to see that the eyes of many of the horses were watery and beginning to redden.

There was no question, then, about this being a false alarm. Jesse squelched fear down and concentrated on the animals. By the minute, they were becoming more and more uncomfortable and agitated. After a few moments of hesitation, he had an idea. He motioned to Griffin to follow him and set out on a dead run back to the forge tent. There, he grabbed as many towels and rags as he could find and dumped them into a trough of water. He yelled to explain what he wanted, but conversation behind the masks was so difficult it was his gestures and pantomime that communicated his idea to the private. Soon, he had a handful of wet, wrung-out cloths draped over his arm. He left Griffin behind him to wring out the rest and bring them. When he arrived back at the corral, Baird and Rex, watched Jesse and quickly understood his plan. They grabbed rags from the pile and the three men began tying them over the horse's eyes. The roan that Jesse first caught shied and tried to avoid Jesse's help, but as soon as the cooling water began to quench the itching and burning of his eyes, he settled down. It didn't take long before all of the mounts in corral six stood calmly, more relaxed and comfortable even though blinded by the compresses over their eyes. Jesse looked up from his final horse, noticing that Perry had his grooms in the next corral following Jesse's lead.

It was a long afternoon. After the mounts were settled, Jesse and his men filled buckets with water, and, using a sponge, they methodically re-wetted the makeshift blinders to keep the horses calm and comfortable. The sun was nearing the horizon when a breeze began. It was light and unpredictable at first, but once the breeze became a wind the danger of any lasting gas was carried away and the all-clear trumpet sounded.

Jesse's hair was dripping with sweat and his face red when he finally pulled off his respirator and took a deep breath of fresh air. He knew in his mind that the air he sucked in through the box filter hanging from his neck was safe, but even so, it seemed stifled and stale compared to the fresh air he now breathed.

Jesse whispered a prayer of thanks and wanted to go collapse onto his cot. Instead, he knew there were several hours more of work ahead of them. Resigned, he organized his platoon with a couple quick commands. Then he ducked under the corral rail once again and began removing the blinders and the breathing masks from a paint horse nearby.

It was nearly midnight when Jesse shucked off his socks, shoes, and outer shirt and lowered himself onto his cot. The hard roll and chunk of cheese he'd managed to grab from the mess tent earlier was only a memory in his belly. His stomach rumbled, but he ignored it. After all the masks and blinders had been removed, the horses all needed to be fed, watered, and curried. Then the soldiers had cleaned and inspected all the masks, human and animal, and stowed them at the ready for the next attack. Sari's letter was forgotten as Jesse's need for sleep prevailed.

He awoke very early the next morning, his heart racing from a dream in which he was alone, trying to fit human gas masks on dozens of horses. When the dream cleared, he lay back and tried to go to sleep, but knew right away he wouldn't. He got up quietly and pulled on his clothes. There was a clean uniform in the trunk beneath his cot, but he didn't even consider it. No one had offered laundry services in over two weeks. Jesse's only consolation was that the others smelled as bad as he, and the horses didn't seem to care. Outside his barracks tent, Jesse gazed at the stars, points of light in an inky black sky.

He walked through the quiet camp until he came near the mess tent. Availing himself of the light from a lantern that burned by the door, Jesse retrieved Sari's unopened envelope from his pocket and read her words. He smiled broadly at the way she'd described her renewal of the kitchen. She gave him a vivid picture of the room transformed with her touch. He closed his eyes, wishing he could sit at the table and enjoy it. Then he continued reading an update about how the Wills were treating her and that she'd begun attending church with Claire and Daniel. The end of the letter, though, touched him deeply.

I think often about the day you took me on the drive up to Lost Treasure Gulch. We were looking at those trees the sheep herders carved. You talked about the scars. Instead of hearing your interesting story, all I heard was the word scar and I reacted poorly. Recently, Claire and I had a heart-to-heart talk. Honestly, her words were hard to listen to at the time, but they made me examine myself, and since then I've been praying and thinking. Thanks to those trees, you, Claire, and God's patience, I've come to understand a truth I'd never seen before. Those trees aren't ugly, they are an interesting record of life and events. Then this occurred to me and became clear. Jesus has scars! Instead of being ugly, His scars are beautiful monuments to how much He gave for us and how much He loves us. And Jesse, here's what I've learned: while I've never stopped believing in God, I didn't feel His love, and I didn't think He thought much about me. You and Claire have helped me see that Jesus loves me. He loves all of me, and He isn't ashamed of me or repulsed by my looks. He's so busy loving me, He doesn't see any ugliness. He loves me just how I am. I can't begin to tell you how this understanding has changed me. If it hadn't been for you, it seems to me that I could have lived my entire life without ever grasping this. I am so grateful to you and Claire, for seeing past my scars even though I myself was never able to, and for showing me your kindness and care. Please be safe. Be confident that I am praying every day, thanking God for you and asking Him to protect you.

Jesse rested his forehead in his hands, hoping that no one would walk by until he got himself under control. Scrambling with his emotions as the camp around him came to life, Jesse wiped his face with his hand, carefully refolded the letter, and returned it to his pocket. As he aimed toward the mess tent, a thought both warmed and chilled him. *Maybe that is it. Maybe that's the job God put me on earth to accomplish. Now that it's done, maybe He's done with me on this earth.*

The poison gas alarm sounded again just two days later. Like before, the horses initially reacted with fear. This time, though, the men were more confident about their own equipment and how to better manage the situation. Jesse and his platoon didn't wait for signs of distress. They applied the wet blinders to the horses' eyes as soon as the masks were all in place and saved themselves and the horses a lot of trouble. Jesse was gratified to see that the horses settled down more quickly, confident that their handlers were protecting them.

Eight days later, Jesse and his platoon wearily climbed the steps to board a supply train heading south. The nearly month-long battle at Cambrai ended as the French and British forces fell back to regroup and re-strategize. It was clear to the generals and to the soldiers in the field that a fighting cavalry would not serve the allies well in this new era of trench warfare, barbed wire, tanks, and machine guns. Corporal Perry, when he shook Jesse's hand and said farewell, told him that he'd just received the news that the company he was attached to would be transformed into an infantry unit, and that Perry himself was to be reassigned to a cavalry division in Morocco, where mounted regiments were having success.

Jesse and his platoon had gotten no information from their battalion beyond orders to return to their unit, which was now encamped south of Paris. He wondered if they would trade their mounts for boots and become infantry as well. As he settled into his seat, the train groaned and steel wheels began lurching down the tracks. Jesse let go of his concern, knowing he didn't have the energy to worry about it.

Across the aisle, Private Griffin was already asleep, his head bouncing against the glass of the window in rhythm with the train's sway. In the seat behind Griffin, Privates Baird and Rex settled in. Rex had his nose in a dime novel. Jesse watched as Baird pulled his cap down over his eyes and stretched his legs out in an attempt at sleep. Jesse didn't need a mirror to know that the stress of the past weeks along with the long hours and constant fear surely made his own face as haggard and grey as those of his platoon. Hidden in the gaunt eyes of the Americans was a twinkle of relief and joy, however, and as the miles increased their distance from the front, Jesse began to relax a little. Finally, the monotony of the train's rhythm lulled him to sleep.

21
Encampment, Wyoming
mid - December, 1917

There were only two other customers in the store when Sari arrived at Parkison's. With her workday finished, Sari hoped to finish her Christmas shopping for Jesse and then go home to bake cookies so that Claire could get his package mailed in the morning. Mrs. Oliver, a second clerk in the store with Mr. Suttles, smiled as she patiently helped an elderly lady choose thread and ribbon for a project. Kindly excusing herself momentarily, Mrs. Oliver met Sari's glance and said, "Hello Mrs. Atley. May I help you?"

"Good afternoon, Mrs. Oliver. I'm doing some Christmas shopping when you have time."

"It may be a few minutes until I'm free, but Mr. Suttles just went into the back room for a moment. He can help you right away." As she finished speaking, the older gentleman came around the counter. He was a slender man about Sari's height. He wore gold wire-rimmed glasses. His balding head was tan and spattered generously with dark freckles. Until he'd moved to Encampment to join his wife, Sari knew that Mr. Suttles had been a miner in Colorado, though she had trouble picturing him in that role.

"Good afternoon, Madam. What may I help you with?"

Sari was happy Mr. Suttles was available. Since the first time they met, she'd been impressed with his gentle, kind smile and felt comfortable with him. "I'm shopping for two things today. First, my husband," those words still made her falter, "is away in France. I'm hoping you can show me the pocket knives you have available. I'd like to purchase one for him as a Christmas present."

"Yes, Ma'am. I'm sure Mr. Atley would like that gift very much. I sure do miss seeing him around here."

"You've known him a long time, haven't you?"

"Yes, Ma'am. I've lived in and out of this area many years, I've watched him grow from a quiet and gawky kid into a superb man."

"That's kind of you to say."

"I'm not sure we're going to find anything suitable, but our knives are over here." He led the way through the store to a counter in the back. "These are what we have right now. But I know we are expecting more within the next few weeks."

He removed several knives and laid them out for Sari to see. There were five knives of varying size and shapes. Sari was disappointed. These were all plain and utilitarian, not what she'd had in mind.

Mr. Suttles noticed her hesitation and winked at her. "Though I'm not sure Mr. Parkison would appreciate my saying so, I was in Jameson Hardware last week. They have some really pretty, fancy pocket knives there. You might want to check with them."

With a chuckle and a conspiratorial grin, Sari thanked Mr. Suttles and agreed that she'd like to check there before she decided.

"Understood. What else can I show you?"

"Do you have any cookie cutters? I need some for Christmas cookies."

"Oh, yes we do. I think you'll like these."

Before long, laden with three metal cutters and armed with directions to Jameson's Hardware just three blocks west, Sari was back out in the cold.

A pesky wind gust tried to grab the door from her hands as she entered the building a few minutes later. Struggling against the unseen force, Sari closed the door and turned around to gain her first view of the inside of Jameson's Hardware. No one was at the counter, and she found herself alone in the room. The air was filled with the warm, clean smell of freshly cut pine and cedar. The walls surrounding her were rough wood adorned with nails holding a variety of offerings, including straps and tools, leather pouches, and items Sari couldn't identify. A calendar with a large picture of a tractor was tacked to a wall fronted by a scarred wooden counter. Sari surveyed the high surface, noting the two tall stools in front of it. Sitting atop the counter among a jumble of boxes, were a hammer, a hand saw, and a glass bowl filled with penny candy.

It was that bowl that demanded a memory take shape, and Sari knew she'd been here before. She could nearly taste the sweet root beer flavor of the hard candy from the bowl. She knew without looking that there would be candy that looked like kernels of corn somewhere near the bottom among the other treats. She closed her eyes and thought she could hear the sound of her father's laughter as he sat on one of the stools and chatted with other men.

Tears threatened, and she willed them away in favor of the delight the memory afforded her.

She didn't know how long she stood there, lost in the joyful memory of being in this place with her father, before a movement grabbed her attention. A tall, broad-shouldered man rounded the corner and entered the room from behind the counter. It took him a moment to spot Sari standing at the door, giving her time to search his face. She knew his eyes, the soft, warm brown and the kindness harbored there were familiar, though she didn't recognize the wrinkles. He opened his mouth to speak to his customer, but no words emerged. From habit, Sari stood in partial profile to him, shielding her scars, but somehow, though he hadn't seen her in more than eight years, he knew who was standing in front of him.

"Welcome home, Sweet Pea," he said softly.

Without another thought, she rushed forward so that he could enfold her in a secure hug.

Their reunion was a bittersweet mixture of happy and sad, since neither could escape mourning the absence of Sari's parents. Soon though, after an extended embrace mixed with tears and laughter, they both relaxed into contentment.

They reminisced for a time, and Nathan congratulated Sari on her marriage. At first, they were careful to concentrate on fun memories far from the accident. Inevitably though, the topic did turn to the sad. "I've spent lots of time wondering if I shouldn't have tried harder to find you and bring you home here with me." Nathan admitted. "I hope you'll forgive me for not acting on those thoughts."

Sari was touched. "Of course, I forgive you. It all happened so fast that I doubt if there would have been anything for you to do."

"I never stopped praying for you and thinking about you. I can't change the past, but I'm warning you, I'd like to make spending time with you a habit now that you are back."

Sari nodded. "I would like that more than you could know. It's funny. I suppose I should have recognized the name Jameson, but when I was a child, I only thought of you as Uncle Nathan."

"An uncle by choice, not blood relation. I loved your dad as if he were my brother. I cherish the memories of times I spent with him, and you and your mother."

"My memories are scant, I think. But now that I am back here sometimes an event or a moment comes back to me that I didn't know I remembered."

"And now here you are, grown up, married and ready to make your own memories."

Sari gazed at the man before her, a man who had been so important to her as a child, and felt thankful that her winding journey had returned her to this shop.

Just as she began forming words to try to tell him, a noise in the back of the building derailed their attention.

"I'm expecting a delivery. Let me go check on that."

Sari nodded and slid onto the seat beside the counter. She reached into the candy bowl, rummaging through to find a candy corn. She could almost see her own child-sized hand searching through the choices.

A moment later Nathan returned. "That's Dawson in the back. Do you know that the day before he left, Jesse and I contracted for him—well, actually Dawson—to do hauling for me between Saratoga and here?"

"I heard a little about that, though I don't really have much knowledge about the business. I, well, I haven't actually known Jesse very long." It felt like an admission of guilt, and Sari dropped her eyes.

"Every marriage takes time to grow."

Sari nodded and looked up.

Nathan's eyes were on her, filled with encouragement and care. Another noise from the back got Nathan's attention and he shrugged, "I hate to say this, but Dawson is going to need a little help in a few minutes."

Sari nodded, then remembered what she'd come for. "Oh, Uncle Nathan, my new sister-in-law and I are preparing a Christmas package for Jesse. We should have already mailed it, I'm afraid, and I was thinking I'd like to send him a pocket knife as a present. Parkison's has a few, but they suggested you might have better ones to choose from."

Nathan grinned, happy at how she'd addressed him, then turned aside and reached underneath the counter. "I do have some, and actually, this past summer, I had them on the counter when Jesse came in, and he admired one." He lifted a tray to the counter, selected one of the knives and handed it to Sari.

It was about four inches long. The knife's two blades were folded into the intricately carved handle. Sari admired the elk head carved on one side before flipping it over to study the geometric design on the back. She liked the weight of it in her hand. Gently, Nathan took the knife back and opened it for her so she could see the sturdy blades.

"Jesse saw this one and liked it?"

"Yes, he looked at it for a long time before putting it back on the tray. Told me he'd consider it. Then the draft lottery was announced and his focus moved elsewhere."

"I'll take it," Sari decided. She chuckled to herself. This was only the second time in her life she'd ever purchased anything without agonizing first over the price, and both times it was to purchase a gift for Jesse.

Nathan closed the blades and reached a second time below the counter. He wrapped the knife in a square of brown paper and tied it with string. Sari paid him then carefully placed the small bundle into her purse. The door opened behind her as a new customer came in, fighting the door as she had.

"I'm on my way home to bake cookies for Jesse," Sari told Nathan. "Can I stop in again soon for another visit?"

"I look forward to it, Sari. In fact, this old bachelor isn't much of a cook, but I won't poison you. How about you come see me tomorrow evening about this time, and we can go to my house and I'll make us something to eat?"

Sari didn't hesitate, "I'd love it, but let me bring something."

"Alright, I say you bring us some bread and a few of those cookies you are going home to bake, and I'll make some stew."

They ended their reunion with a strong hug and Sari left feeling light and happy. Though the wind did its best to jostle her as she walked home, she ignored it, reveling in the reconnection she'd just made.

At home an hour later, Sari sported a bright red apron and a flushed face. The cookie cutters Mr. Suttles had sold her were perfect. She'd chosen three shapes: a tree, a star, and a gingerbread man. As she removed the first batch of cookies from the oven, she smiled, satisfied. *Dusting these with a little powdered sugar will make them perfect,* she thought.

When the front door bell sounded, Sari dusted flour from her hands and walked toward the front of the house. Only last night Michael had been over to renew her firewood and coal supplies, so she wasn't expecting him.

Dawson Wiley, his hat in his hand, stood on the porch. "Good evening Mrs. Atley. I hear I just missed you at Jameson's a little bit ago."

"Mr. Wiley, hello. Yes, I was there when you came to deliver. Please, come in."

"I can't really stay," he interrupted himself, "Man something smells good in here!"

Sari nodded. "I just took some cookies I was baking to send to Jesse out of the oven. Would you like to be my official taster?"

"Yes, I would, thank you."

Dawson followed Sari to the kitchen.

"Won't you sit down?"

Dawson tried to hide his discomfort and sat gingerly on the edge of the kitchen chair she indicated.

She used a pancake turner to scoop up a star and a tree, placing them on a small plate before serving her guest. Dawson thanked her. He closed his eyes after the first bite, clearly enjoying the sweet treat.

Embarrassed, he finished the cookie and looked at

Sari. "These are delicious, Jesse is going to be plenty thankful to get a box of 'em."

Sari thanked him, and they sat for a moment in awkwardness.

"Oh," Dawson said with a chuckle after a moment, "That was so good I nearly forgot why I came. The reason I stopped over was to give you this." He reached into his coat pocket and handed her a small package. "Nathan Jameson said to tell you that if you have room, he'd appreciate it if you could add this to the box you are mailing."

Sari accepted the package with a nod. "Uncle Nathan is a thoughtful man."

"Uncle? I didn't know you had any family here," Dawson responded.

Sari nodded again, "He isn't actually my uncle, just a close friend of my father's. I used to call him Uncle Nathan when I was little, and I guess that's what feels right even now."

Again, there was a lull. Then, Dawson turned. "I won't bother you any more, thank you for the cookies, they are wonderful."

"Thank you, Mr. Wiley, and thank you for dropping this off. Um, how is everything going at the livery? I'm sure it isn't easy doing all the work that both you and Jesse shared."

"I think it's going pretty well. I'm plenty busy, but I'm keeping up with all our contracts and such. Now that Daniel is helping me with the ledger, I get a little more sleep at night than I was."

Dawson thanked Sari again for the cookies and took his leave. Sari watched his uneven step, wondering about his limp as she followed him to the parlor.

Sari closed the front door and went back to the kitchen and her cookies.

Dawson turned the collar up on his coat. He'd been nervous about stopping at Jesse's house. He'd barely spoken to his partner's wife when he'd met her at the Haynes' that night for dinner. He still felt guilty for what he'd said about her to Jesse, but now that he's begun to know her, he understood better how Jesse could want to marry her.

The temperature was falling as night edged in. *I'm tired clear to my bones,* he mused as he walked home. *I had a good lunch. Maybe I'll just have some bread and butter and go to bed.*

All hope of an early night fled when Dawson rounded the corner and saw his brother sitting on the porch steps of his small rented apartment, a ragged duffle bag next to him.

"Howdy, big brother," the greeting came while Dawson was a few steps away.

"What are you doing here, Evan? Did you lose another job?" Feeling even more tired at the sight of his visitor, Dawson's impatience saturated his voice.

"Aw, Daw, don't be like that already. I didn't get fired, if that's what you mean. It's just that now cold weather's set in, there isn't as much work available, and it's just too darned cold to be living in a tent down at the river any more. I'm like to freeze to death."

Dawson entered his small apartment and turned on a lamp. Evan followed him into the small space and shut the door. Dawson shucked off his coat and hung it on a hook. Then he rubbed his face and turned to his brother.

"Evan, I'm tired, and I don't have any money I can lend you."

A flair of temper crossed Evan's face, but he quickly masked it. In a measured voice he answered, "Dawson, I just need a place to stay for a while, until I can find work again." He hesitated, then added, "Please."

Dawson felt his own temper rising. He gestured at the small room they stood in. "Just where do propose you'll stay? I have one room and a bathroom. There's one bed that's also the sofa, the chair, and when I pull up that little table, it turns into the dining room."

Evan ducked his head and answered quietly. "I haven't anywhere else to go."

"You could go out to the ranch and help Ma and the girls."

"Daw, it's just not the same since Pa died. And anyway, Ma doesn't want me there."

"The only reason Ma suggested you leave the ranch is because you weren't pulling your weight. She was feeding you and cleaning up after you, and you weren't doing anything to help her or the girls."

"She just didn't understand how sad I was that Pa died. I just couldn't get my feet under me, and she didn't care."

"Evan, you aren't the only one who lost a loved one when he died. Ma lost her husband, and the girls lost their Pa just like you, yet they had to keep going."

"But I was closer to him than anyone else."

Yes, you were, closer than I ever was for sure, answered Dawson to himself. *You were his pride and joy at the exclusion of all others, and he ruined you.*

Dawson was tired of this fight, they'd gone over it so many times. He took a deep breath and answered, "I'm tired. I want to go to bed. If you can find room on the floor over there, you can stay, but just for a few days."

"Few days? Daw, it's nearly Christmas. Nobody is hiring this time of year. At least let me stay until after the New Year arrives."

Against his better judgement, Dawson shrugged again and didn't answer directly. "You need to add some groceries to the kitchen before you eat any of my food, and clean up after yourself."

22
Encampment, Wyoming
mid - December, 1917

Claire's nose was running and her hands were cold as she knocked at Sari's door. *That's funny,* she thought as she waited for the door to open. *This has always been Jesse's house, but I just thought of it as Sari's.*

Before she could ponder that further, Sari welcomed her in. "Claire, you look frozen! Give me your coat and go sit by the fire and get warm."

Claire handed her coat to Sari and turned toward the parlor, surprised to find a young woman sitting on the settee.

"Oh, I hope I'm not interrupting, I didn't know you had company."

Sari guided her sister-in-law towards the fireplace as she made introductions, "Claire, this is my neighbor, Bea Reid. Bea lives with her sister and brother-in-law right across the street."

"So nice to meet you. I think you go to school with my sons," Claire answered.

Bea returned the greeting with a smile. "Yes, I know Mike. He and I have worked together on a couple of projects in civics class. I've heard a lot about you from Sari."

"It's mutual," Claire acknowledged. "I've been thankful knowing Sari has friends nearby."

"We were just having some hot cocoa. Would you like some?" Sari asked.

Claire nodded, "Yes, absolutely, thanks."

While Sari was gone, Claire and Bea chatted comfortably. The conversation continued when their hostess returned with Claire's warm mug and a plate of cookies.

"You are becoming pretty famous for these cookies, you know," Claire told Sari. "Daniel reserved a few of those you brought us and took them to City Hall yesterday. To hear him tell it, Mayor Rankin and one of the clerks nearly came to blows over the last one."

237

Sari was pleased at the compliment. "Since there's only another week before Christmas, I thought I was probably done baking them this year, but they keep disappearing, so now I think I'll bake another double batch to bring over Christmas Eve."

"I'm glad to hear you say that, since the men at my house certainly prefer yours to mine."

The women laughed and chatted until Claire's cup was empty. When Sari offered her more, she declined. "Actually, I only intended to stay for a minute. I wanted to talk to you about going with me to the Ladies' Aid Society meeting on Thursday evening. Bea, we would enjoy having you come as well."

Bea thanked her and asked, "What do they do there?"

"Well, we all are trying to find ways to do our part for the war effort. We meet at the Presbyterian Church reading room in the old Fowler M.E. Church building on Rankin. There are groups working on two projects right now. Some of us are sewing hospital gowns to be sent to the Red Cross for field hospitals. The other group is making scrapbooks."

"Scrapbooks? That sounds odd," remarked Bea.

Claire fumbled for a moment in the pocket of her skirt. "I actually cut out an article from the *Encampment Echo* to share with Sari about it. Here it is," she handed the paper to Sari.

Sari glanced at it and began reading aloud,

The Red Cross is asking for scrapbooks that would be of interest to recuperating soldiers. These scrapbooks are to be filled with pictures, cartoons, very short stories, good and new jokes (especially those originating in the army). These can be cut from magazines or papers or gathered elsewhere. Ideas included Kodak pictures of animals and scenes of places of interest. Buy blank books at the 10-cent store and paste items in. The pictures and stories should always be cheerful.

"That's a good idea. It will give them something nice to think about," commented Bea.

Sari remained quiet as she studied the paper in

her hand. A log shifted and when she finally spoke it was with a quiet, somber voice. "I found a stack of old magazines and papers in the downstairs bedroom. I wonder if he'd mind if we used those?"

Claire answered lightly, "I doubt he will ever think of all the junk he had stored around this house when he sees how beautiful you've made it. By the way, I love how you rearranged the furniture in here."

Sari pushed away the worry she was feeling about Jesse and all the soldiers and thanked Claire.

"Is that a new table by the window?"

"No, I found it upstairs in the extra bedroom. I washed it and put a table cloth on it."

"It looks lovely there."

Claire stood up then, "I really need to get home. It sounds like maybe both of you would be interested in coming on Thursday?"

"I am, and if it's okay, I'd like to invite my sister Harriet also."

"I think that's a great idea. How about you, Sari?"

"Count me in. I'll bring those magazines with me. Do we need to go to Parkison's for the blank scrapbooks?"

"I don't think so. I'll check with the president of the society, Mrs. Sproat, but I think I heard Mrs. Rankin, the vice president, say the society had purchased a number of the scrapbooks already. I'll let you know."

As Claire walked home that evening, she couldn't help thinking about how much Sari had changed since the first time they'd met. *I see more confidence in Sari nearly every time I see her. I can't say I understand all the reasons for the changes, but I need to remember to tell Jesse about it in my next letter.*

It seemed to Sari that everyone and everything at the Copper Pot the next morning had been touched with some sort of mischief. Jar lids wouldn't budge, the sink was running slowly, and people were testy. Sari wasn't pleased with how the three coffee cakes she'd just taken out of the oven looked. She tasted a sliver of one, to assure herself that they were edible, nodding at the taste while frowning that they hadn't raised like usual. Her attention was diverted by voices just outside the kitchen.

"But Mr. Wills, why? Have I done something you disapprove of?"

"No," came the terse answer. Sari began washing dishes as the voices continued, "Your work is good, but the war has put a damper on business, and I just don't need you anymore."

Sari felt the news in the pit of her stomach. She hardly knew Jennie, the middle-aged woman who cleaned the guest rooms, but she did know that the woman's husband had been injured at one of the mines and was unable to work.

"I'll do anything you need, Just don't let me go."

"I'm sorry," came his answer, though there was no remorse in his voice. "There's nothing more to talk about. I'll have your pay for you at the end of today."

Sari felt like crying for the woman.

Across town, Dawson felt like crying as well, but for completely different reasons. His morning had also started badly. He'd gotten an early start, knowing he had four jobs to complete for customers before the day was finished. *Honestly, I left early to avoid Evan,* he thought angrily, *I never should have let him stay even one night. All he does is sit around all day and then go to the bar every evening. When I asked him to buy some groceries, he told me he was dead broke, but he seems to have enough change in his pocket to come home late and unsteady.*

At the livery, Dawson crawled under the truck. The oil hadn't been changed since Jesse left. He pushed an old tub underneath the truck's oil pan and unscrewed the plug. A sludge of thick, used oil slowly filled the tub until all that was left was a few drips oozing out. Dawson, hands now covered in oil, wrenched the plug tightly back into place. Using an old rag, he mopped up the drips and slid out from under the vehicle, pulling the tub gently behind him. Once clear of the chassis, Dawson slowly got to his feet, then reached down and lifted the tub. He usually poured the used oil out on the ground in the alley behind the livery, and he started that way, trying not to slop out the oozy contents. He made it to the alley and was almost to his dump spot when he stepped on an unseen rock and his ankle rolled. He shifted his weight to his bad leg, which buckled under him. He went to the ground on one knee, dumping the entire contents of the tub down the front of his shirt.

He let go a long and vehement series of cusswords, and tried to wipe away the muck, knowing that there was no use. Frustrated and angry, Dawson blotted as much as he could from his shirt and trousers, then slammed the door of the livery closed behind him and headed home.

He stomped up onto the step of his apartment, angry and cold. He hadn't dared to put on his coat and ruin that, too. He kicked off his boots, hoping they could be salvaged, and wrenched open the door to his apartment.

And stopped dead still.

Evan, who Dawson had last seen sleeping soundly on a bedroll on the floor, was now laying on Dawson's unmade bed. In itself, that was excusable. But Evan wasn't alone, he held a blond-haired girl tightly beside him.

Dawson's surprise was so complete, it took a minute for him to register the identity of his brother's companion.

"Meredith?" Dawson's voice was filled with surprise and shock. Instantly the girl reacted. She shrieked and jumped up. Looking around like a frightened rabbit, she pulled together her unbuttoned bodice and grabbed her cloak, then rushed past Dawson and out the door.

Evan stood up more slowly. His shirt was unbuttoned, his hair unkempt. He gave Dawson a sly grin and a shrug. "Good morning, Brother." He wasn't disconcerted and made no motion to follow the girl.

"What in the hell is this?" Dawson was trembling with rage. "In my house? With Meredith?"

"Simmer down, Dawson. You're going to give yourself a heart attack. You gave up on that girl and moved to town."

"I never 'gave up on her' as you say. Evan, you know I cared for her."

Evan shrugged dismissively. "Well, I've had my eye on that one for a long time myself." His laugh was tinged with meanness. "Her daddy doesn't know the favor he did me when he banned me from their ranch and sent the girl to town to keep her away from me. He made it so much easier for me to continue seeing her."

Dawson's punch caught his brother along the jawline. Evan's head cracked back and he flopped onto the bed. Dawson stepped forward before Evan could catch himself, landing a second, round-house punch on the side of his brother's head.

The blow made Evan's ear ring, and the room spun a few times.

Dawson stepped back, "Get up. You have disrespected me and that naïve girl. You have about thirty seconds to gather your gear and get out."

"Get out? Where do you propose I go?"

"Honestly, Evan, I don't care. Maybe you should be a man and join the military instead of dodging the draft and loafing around here."

"Oh sure, you're one to talk. You and your crippled up leg are safe and sound here, now aren't you?"

"I have this crippled leg because of you."

Evan laughed with mockery and derision. "Yeah, that was a fun day, daring you to ride that stallion Pa and I both knew you'd never stay on, and then watching the great Dawson, bronc rider supreme, land in a heap."

Dawson fought down his urge to pummel the figure in front of him, knowing that if he allowed himself even one more punch he might not be able to stop.

"You have less than a minute before I go for the marshal. I'm sure he and Meredith's pa wouldn't appreciate you taking advantage of someone so young."

Normally Evan would have argued, but the grim set of Dawson's jaw told him he'd exhausted any grace left from his brother. He gathered his belongings. Dawson stood in the middle of the room, watching in silence. When Evan reached the doorway, Dawson quietly finished the conversation with a promise, "Evan, you've always done what you wanted. Pa stood up for you and made excuses. I won't. Ever. You aren't welcome here anymore. I want you to leave Encampment and leave Meredith alone.

Joining the military would be my suggestion, but whatever you decide to do, do it far away from here. Stop by and say goodbye to Ma, but don't stay. I'll be checking with her, and with Meredith. If you don't leave or you come back, I'll go to the marshal."

Evan slammed the door behind him. Dawson stood in the silence, feeling a mixture of anger, revulsion, and relief. He slowly unbuttoned his shirt and dropped it with his oil-stained pants on the floor before going to bathe and begin his day again.

Lunch was nearly ready, and the dishes were washed. Sari had successfully endured the trials of the morning, thankful that the restaurant hadn't been too busy. At about a quarter to eleven, Sari heard Meredith come in the back door. She turned with a greeting, "Good morn—," she broke off at her first sight of the girl. Meredith's eyes were swollen and red, her face pale and splotchy.

"Oh my, are you ill?"

Meredith dropped her head and answered quietly, "No, I've just had a difficult morning."

Sari hugged her friend and whispered, "Are you fighting with your Aunt Nell again?"

Meredith nodded her head, letting Sari's incorrect conclusion suffice so that she didn't have to make any admissions. "I just want to forget all about it," she answered back.

"I'm so sorry. I think it must be something in the air today, everyone seems to be out of sorts."

The day dragged by. When she'd dried the last lunch dish, Sari looked up at the clock. It was after three, though she felt tired enough for it to be midnight. While nothing bad happened the rest of the day, it had been a quiet, stern, and tense afternoon. Sari looked around to see what else she needed to finish before she left for the day when a shadow fell across the alley door.

"Well, Mr. Wiley, this is a surprise," Sari said. "Is everything at the livery alright?"

Meredith's head snapped around at Sari's greeting. She felt so frightened she was nauseous.

"Good afternoon, Mrs. Atley," Dawson replied shyly. "Everything is fine at work. I actually, well, I came to talk for a minute with Meredith."

Sari was surprised. "I didn't know you two knew each other." Since Meredith was behind her, Sari didn't notice that all color had drained from the girls' face and that she was trembling.

Dawson noticed and was afraid that Meredith was going to collapse. He answered Sari kindly, "Yes, my family's ranch shares a fence with Meredith's family. Our mothers are very good friends and we often spent holidays together when we all were small. I've known Meredith for a very long time."

"That's wonderful. I had no idea."

"Um, Meredith, could I just talk with you for a minute? It's alright."

Sari misunderstood Meredith's reticence and nodded to her reassuringly, "I've got everything else done. I'll take over at the stove. You go ahead."

Meredith wiped her hands on her apron and quietly followed Dawson out the back door and into the alley. They stood facing each other, though Meredith refused to look up and meet Dawson's eyes.

Unsure of what to say, Dawson began, "I just wanted to check on you and see if you are alright."

"I'm fine," was her mumbled answer.

"Meredith, I want to apologize. I've known for a while that Evan was seeing someone, but I had no idea it was you, or I would have stopped it long before now."

Meredith's head came up, there was fear and anger in her eyes. "Stopped it? I don't want anyone to stop it. Evan loves me, and I love him. I just want everyone to understand that and let us be together."

"Meredith, you are young, too young. Evan is nearly four years older than you. He's taking advantage of you, leading you astray."

"Don't say that!"

Dawson took a deep breath and gathered his thoughts. "I didn't come to argue with you or to lecture. I just wanted to make sure you were alright and to tell you that I've warned Evan that if he stays around here, I will go to the law."

Meredith put her hands over her face and began crying, "You are ruining everything." She turned around and rushed back into the building, leaving Dawson standing alone in the alley.

23
Encampment, Wyoming
Tuesday, December 25, 1917

Claire relaxed by the fireplace, warm and satisfied. Her embroidery lay idle in her lap. Stockings were once again empty. All the presents had been opened. Christmas dinner, cooked, served, and now cleaned up, had been a joyous meal filled with laughter and love. Outside, the sun edged its way closer and closer to the mountain horizon, long shadows stretched across the world outside her window. Claire recalled the screams of delight of her sons earlier in the afternoon as they enjoyed the sleds they'd received for Christmas. She pictured Daniel's grin as he took his own turn down the hill a few blocks from the house. After a few trips each, she and Sari left the three men to their cold, snowy fun and came in to warm up. Now, they sat in contented quiet by the toasty fire. Christmas day was coming to a close and Claire felt warm inside and out.

Sari's attention was on the crochet hook and yarn in her hands. *Seven weeks,* thought Claire. *Seven weeks Sari has been with us.* While the situation was still quite new, the relationship between Sari and Claire felt easy, right. Claire watched her, thankful for how her kind spirit augmented their family. *Does she look sad?* Claire wondered.

Sari felt her sister-in-law's stare and looked up. She let her hands relax in her lap. "Thank you again, Claire, for inviting Nathan over for dinner last night for Christmas Eve. It was a special treat for me."

A log in the fireplace shifted and sparks scattered in a flurry.

"You're welcome, but it wasn't just for you. We enjoy his company as well. You've been spending quite a bit of time with Nathan lately haven't you?"

"Yes. I've been to his house and he's come to dinner a few times, I spent an evening at Miss Lillian's house with Nathan and his sister and her family just last week. I didn't realize it until then, but Nathan's sister, Abby lives not far from me. They are such lovely people."

"I don't know any of them as well as I'd like. Now that we have a reason to get together, I hope our friendship with them grows. See how good for us you are?" The complement was genuine, and Claire saw Sari's small grin before she dropped her eyes back to her hands.

"Claire, thank you. After Jesse left, you could have just ignored me, but you and Daniel have been so gracious."

"Sari, the more I get to know you, the more I understand Jesse's desire to marry you. We are thankful to have you here."

Claire looked at the opened gifts under the Christmas tree and, changing the subject, told Sari, "Thank you for the crocheted scarf you made me, the color goes so well with my coat, and it will be so warm."

"You are welcome. I love the book you gave me. I've heard of Mrs. Child's *The American Frugal Housewife*. I'm glad to have a copy of my own."

"I got a copy right after Daniel and I married, and I use it often. That's why I wanted you to have one. I know there are lots of recipes, and you probably don't need those, but there are also remedies and hints on all kinds of household topics."

"I like the sub-title, 'Dedicated to those who are not ashamed of economy.' I noticed it said the book was first published in 1833. Good advice never gets old."

They sat in peaceful quiet for several minutes, then Sari offered, "This is the first Christmas I've celebrated by giving and receiving gifts in a very long time. I had so much fun making things and shopping."

"You did a wonderful job. Everyone loved what you gave them." With a nostalgic tone, she continued, "Jesse loved, loves Christmas. He was always the first one up to open presents." Claire wiped a tear away and continued, "I wonder what he's doing right this minute."

"I read in the paper that for the past few years on Christmas there were unofficial truces called. They say that in 1914 there were football games between the German and Allied soldiers, and that they came out of their trenches to enjoy the holiday together."

"I've read that as well. It seems a bit macabre to play a ball game one day, then go back to trying to kill one another the next."

"I know, but I guess it's better than fighting on Christmas."

Claire sighed, "I read that the Allied generals have forbidden that sort of truce to happen this year. The article also stated that it seems animosity has increased and there is much less chance of anyone's willingness to have peace, even for one day."

The room was quiet for a time. "Oh, I almost forgot," Claire didn't want to cry so she turned the subject and her thoughts away from Jesse and the war. "I got a letter yesterday from my friend Lela, and we've firmed up our plans. She and her husband will be here on January sixth. They are staying here with us. On the seventh, if the weather cooperates, Daniel has volunteered, at my urging, to take Richard to the Platte River for some fishing. Lela says he's an avid angler. The boys are excited to go along. That means Lela and I will have a day for catching up and girl talk."

"That sounds great. I know you've been looking forward to having time for just the two of you."

"It will be fun to reconnect. I am hoping that you will come over after work to meet her and have dinner with us. I've told Daniel I'll plan supper for around seven."

"That's very kind of you, but don't you want to keep her all to yourself?"

"Well, I'm looking forward to her visit, but I admit I'm a little nervous as well. It's been a long time since we were close chums. I hope we still have things to talk about."

"I understand, and yes, I'd love to come over."

"Great. Come right after you get off, and then we'll have time to talk and then get supper ready together."

Sari picked up her hook and crochet thread. The ladies worked in silence for a few minutes before Sari asked, "Claire, Daniel seems distracted and tired. Is he doing alright?"

"Yes, I think so," she answered. "With so many men gone from the community to fight the war, more and more responsibility and work has been heaped on those left here. Daniel has been covering not only his position at work, but also that of two other men. He's exhausted."

"I understand. Even though the war is on the other side of the planet, it has even affected us here in Encampment."

Moments later the sound of boots stomping and loud voices broke the peace as the sledders came home.

24
Encampment, Wyoming
January 7, 1918

Glamorous. It was the best description of Lela that
Sari could come up with. *She doesn't have fine features or
a perfect visage, but somehow she is beautiful. Captivating.*

Claire, Lela, and Sari had been together in the
parlor for over an hour. The conversation, full of laughter
and smiles, tripped through a wide range of subjects from
current events and politics to raising children and
managing a house.

"You know, Claire," Lela began. "The only wedding
I'd ever been to when Richard asked me to marry him, was
yours."

Claire chuckled, "You poor thing. Our wedding was
so plain and simple, though I thought it was perfect at the
time."

"It was perfect. And when Daniel surprised you by
hiring a photographer, Estelle and I were beside ourselves.
It was the most thoughtful and romantic thing we'd ever
heard of."

Claire smiled, then left the room. She came back a
moment later holding a small picture in a cardboard
frame, and handed it to Lela.

"I had no idea a photographer was coming, and I
was too stunned to react, I think. It was at Daniel's
insistence that we took that picture."

Lela studied the picture a few moments longer
before handing the frame to Sari. It was a picture Sari had
never seen before of Claire, Lela and another young
woman. Claire, the most conservatively dressed of the
three, stood in the middle with her arms around her
friends.

Claire took the frame from Sari when she handed it
back and said wistfully, "Even after all these years, I miss
Estelle."

"She was definitely the light source in any room,"
responded Lela. "She and I stayed close. Even after
Richard and I got married, we only lived a short distance
away from each other."

"It haunts me that she waited so long to get treatment."

"Yes, I agree, and she and I talked about that. She knew she was sick and guessed at the cause, but she'd heard so many horror stories about people who had been treated with mercury, she refused to even go to the doctor. By the time I heard about the new remedy of arsphenamine, I think it is also called Salvarsan, and talked Estelle into going to the doctor, she'd already lost her eyesight and had so much trouble thinking, it was too late for anything to be effective."

Sari wasn't sure if she should, but quietly she asked, "Did she have cancer?"

Lela looked up sharply at Claire. Something unspoken, perhaps an apology, flew silently between them. It was Claire who finally answered, "Our dear Estelle had syphilis." The answer fell flat between them.

Sari was horrified at herself, "Oh Claire, I am so sorry to have pried where I shouldn't have."

Claire squared her shoulders and then leaned over to pat Sari's hand. "It's alright. Really." Claire smiled at Sari encouragingly and the room became quiet.

Lela took a final sip of her tea, then drew in a quick breath. "Oh Claire, I nearly forgot, I brought you a present!" She stood up and looked around. "I left it in my satchel, I'll be right back."

Sari's earlier embarrassment quickly changed to curiosity when Lela returned and put several items on the table between her chair and Sari's. Lela turned to Claire and asked, "Do you remember how we used to have so much fun on Sunday afternoons looking through magazines and trying new hair styles and makeup?"

Claire nodded. "You both used me constantly for practicing the latest trends and fashions," she answered with a giggle.

"Well, I know you don't wear much make-up these days, but I found this great pot of rouge, and as soon as I saw it, I knew it would be the perfect color for you. It's much too pale for me."

Instead of handing Claire the small jar, she unscrewed the top, then knelt down in front of her friend and rubbed her finger first in the pot, then on Claire's cheeks. "See, isn't that perfect?" Lela looked to Sari for confirmation.

"Yes, yes it looks very natural. Claire, it gives your cheeks a nice glow."

Then, to Sari's shock and horror, Lela scooted over in front of her. Reaching for another container, Lela ignored how Sari recoiled in her chair and said with a gentle voice, "Sari, if you look carefully at my face, you will see several pock marks from when I had smallpox as a child. If I didn't have makeup on, you'd also see that I have a birthmark on my forehead and several nasty liver spots on my nose and chin." She watched Sari's reticence for a moment, then added, "And we both know that Claire over there has a crooked nose and too many freckles."

Claire laughed and nodded, "Yes, it's true."

Lela returned her attention to Sari. "Now, I don't want to offend you, but I wonder if you'd let me try something?"

What Sari really wanted to do was run away. Instead, she swallowed back the lump in her throat and gave a nearly imperceptible nod.

Lela mildly smoothed Sari's hair back behind her ears and opened a compact. Sari watched the woman's hands as they lifted a round pad and dusted it on the packed powder. She began applying it to Sari's scarred cheek. Lela repeated this action several times, lightly patting Sari's whole face. When she was satisfied with the application, Lela reached for a smaller jar. Inside was a thick, dark brown powder.

As she dipped into this with her pinkie, Lela began talking, "Close your eyes, dear. Now the whole trick with makeup is to apply it so that no one knows you are wearing it. You need to use just enough to get people to look at what you want them to see, but never let anyone be able to notice you have it on. The products you choose are important also. I like this Helena Rubinstein powder, but this little bit of colored paste I'm putting on your eyes is from a company called Max Factor. There, now you can open your eyes. The final touch is a little lipstick. This one is from a newer company from France called L'Oréal. Never put lipstick on heavily. Make it look like you've just stained them a little, not painted them."

Lela sat back and surveyed her work. "Claire, what do you think?"

Claire stared for a minute, blinking hard to combat the emotion she felt. The change was profound. "That makes quite a difference."

Lela stood up with a smile. "Claire, get me a hairbrush and a tie."

Addressing Sari as she moved behind her, Lela continued, "Sari, like I said, fashion is all about making people see what you want them to see."

Claire was back at Lela's side and handed her a silver hairbrush. Wordlessly, Lela combed Sari's hair, sweeping it up into a high pony tail but leaving some small, tender curls free at her temples and the nape of her neck.

"You have absolutely gorgeous eyes, and I wish my hair was as thick and wavy as yours."

Sari sat frozen in her discomfort. After a short time Lela and Claire stepped back. Both women gazed at Sari for a moment. Finally, Claire broke the silence.

"Sari," she said with a whisper, "why don't you go look for yourself in the mirror."

Sari was afraid to move. She wasn't sure how to read the look on Claire's face. Woodenly, she stood up and made her way to the bathroom. *If I had known this was going to happen, I wouldn't have come,* she berated herself as she walked down the hall. *I never asked for or wanted this kind of attention.*

Certain that she wouldn't like what she saw, Sari stood in front of the mirror but stared into the sink beneath. She pulled in several breaths before she had the courage to lift her eyes. What she saw shocked her. Nothing had changed, yet everything was different. Her scars were still there, still visible. Yet, the powder had softened the cruelty of the deep fissures and muted the mottled pigments. Her eyes, with just a little help from the darker shadow, appeared rounder, more dynamic. Her hair, which she had always used as a veil to hide her shameful scars, bounced daintily, framing her face. She smiled tentatively before noticing Claire and Lela standing in the doorway watching her.

Carefully, Lela continued the lesson she'd begun in the other room. "Do you see how the powder helps smooth all the colors into one, and that makes your cheeks fade into the background as your eyes become more noticeable? The color on your lips works the same way. What people will see when they look at you will be your beautiful eyes and smiling mouth. The rest of your face just won't matter."

Sari could see the words were true. She was so stunned at the difference that it was hard to breath, hard to think.

Sari reacted by hugging Lela. She held her tightly and whispered, "Can you show me how you did this, in the mirror, so that I can do it for myself?"

With renewed laughter and comfortable chatter, Sari washed her face and they began again with Lela coaching Sari as she learned to apply the products for herself. "I'll leave these cosmetics with you, Sari. As a gift to a new friend."

When Sari tried to protest, Lela put up a hand and answered, "No arguing."

Sari thanked her humbly when Claire added, "I know Lordier's Drug downtown carries Helena Rubinstein, but I'm not sure of the others. I'll bet, though, that we can both find rouge and lipstick there or at Parkison's when we run out." The friendly collusion helped Sari feel comfortable.

All the while Lela and Sari worked together at the mirror, Claire stood in the doorway of the bathroom. She added encouragement and approval, and silently prayed for Sari. Claire couldn't deny that the hints and help Lela offered Sari were for the good. She felt ebullient when it became clear that her sister-in-law's reaction was one of gratitude and acceptance.

When Lela was satisfied that Sari had succeeded on her own, she hugged her, then held her out by the shoulders. "Honestly, beauty begins with confidence. If you act shy and timid, or if you hang your head or think you aren't pretty, others will think that, too. But, if you walk into a room or meet another person with assurance, then others will be more comfortable with you. The colors in these pots don't change you on the inside, but they help a little on the outside."

Sari nodded, tears welling up. "I don't know how to thank you for your bold kindness."

"Well," laughed Lela, "Subtlety has never been a trait I'm accused of!" Turning to Claire, Lela put her hands on her hips, "And now, Missy, it's your turn. I've got a great idea for your hair!"

Sari relinquished her spot in front of the mirror and replaced Claire in the doorway. When, later that evening, the entire family sat down for dinner, Claire and Sari both sported makeovers. Daniel quickly complimented his wife's new hair style, and while he didn't say anything to Sari, she caught him watching her throughout the evening with a smile that touched her heart and her confidence.

It was nearly nine thirty when Sari entered her quiet home after dinner. It had been good to meet Lela and Richard. She'd enjoyed dinner with everyone very much. She couldn't ignore, though, that Lela's advice and tutoring had made the day remarkable. Sari stood in her quiet bathroom and studied the mirror in front of her. She couldn't deny that Lela's powder and colors did much to hide the ugliness, but as she watched herself in the glass, she noticed the truth and import of Lela's advice. *If I duck my head like this,* she thought, *I look different somehow than when I put my chin up.*

Though it was late and she knew she needed to get to sleep, she felt excited, keyed up. It didn't take long for her to realize that more than anything, she wanted to write to Jesse.

Her first paragraphs were newsy updates. Finishing that, she was hesitant, not knowing how to begin describing her thoughts. Then, putting aside her shyness she wrote:

> *A friend of Claire's and her husband were in Encampment visiting today. Lela is a gorgeous woman, and she took the initiative to share some beauty tips with me. I was frightened to be the center of her attention at first, but she and Claire were so dear, and the time ended up being very warm and helpful. Her suggestions resulted in a*

marked change in my appearance, and with encouragement from both Lela and Claire I think there's been a distinct difference in me.

Jesse, you told me that you wanted to marry me because you wanted your life and going to war to mean something. You convinced me that the pension and insurance that would come should you not return would give your life some sort of meaning. You seemed to only consider the good result that would occur with tragedy. What you could not and did not consider was how quickly and completely your actions would improve my life now. By marrying me you have provided me with a home and a family and a whole new start. I'm sure you know the beautiful character of your sister and her family, but I doubt that you anticipated the wholehearted welcome they've given me.

At the orphanage I was 'the ugly girl in the kitchen'. When I moved here, I was the 'that poor deformed girl' to some and a lowly debtor to the Wills. In both places I was an outsider with no hope. I was not liked and honestly, I did not like myself. You have changed that. You have given me not only a home and a family, but you've also given me a name and an identity beyond the scars on my face. Because of you and the love of your family, I understand now that I am not my scars, but that my scars are simply a small part of me. I can't thank you, Jesse. There aren't words. All I can say is that I look forward to the future when you arrive, safely, back here in Encampment and see what your grace and kindness have accomplished.

Tears were falling as Sari finished writing. She folded the pages and sealed the envelope before she went upstairs to bed.

The next morning, Sari stood before the bathroom mirror and debated with herself. One side of the argument was that she should only use her new cosmetics for special occasions, and not 'waste' them on work days. The other voice in her mind countered that by applying them each morning regardless of the upcoming day's activities, she would help herself feel confident. *The truth is, you often stop at the post office or the store on your way home.* She stared at the small compact and continued justifying. *And, what about when you end up serving customers in the dining room?*

On the way to the Copper Pot a half hour later, Sari smiled to herself. *Now, just don't forget to stand up straight and meet people's eyes.*

The morning was hectic. The weekly grocery shipment came earlier than normal and the delivery driver was new and unsure of where to leave the boxes. Sari nearly scorched the eggs she was scrambling as she directed his efforts. Then, a few minutes later, Lilith came into the kitchen with a bowl of oatmeal Sari had just sent out.

"The child who got this is unhappy that it has raisins in it. Fix it, please." She sat the bowl on the counter and retreated.

Sari grimaced. Lilith wasn't often so terse, and fleetingly Sari wondered if she'd done something to annoy her boss. She turned to the more immediate issue and grimaced again. The entire batch of oatmeal had raisins, so Sari grabbed a spoon and painstakingly removed each raisin she could find from the child's bowl. When she was certain not even one remained, she squared her shoulders and delivered the oatmeal to the dining room.

The mother at the table looked tired and weary as she gave Sari an apologetic smile. Fighting her habit of dropping her eyes and chin, Sari smiled back and addressed the child, "Here you go. Does that look better?"

The child remained petulant and didn't answer her, but the father graciously added his thanks. Again, Sari returned his attention with a smile before turning toward the kitchen. Mr. Wills was watching her from the table closest to the kitchen door. He was sitting at the table with Lilith and another person whose back was towards Sari. Wills' face was stern, but he gave her a small nod, then gave his attention back to the gentleman

sitting opposite him. A familiar voice made Sari glance at
Mr. Wills' table as she entered the kitchen, and she
realized that the gentleman sitting with Chetley and Lilith
Wills was Mr. Bagley from the Rawlins bank.

Seeing him made her heart pound. Worry swirled.
What can this mean? She asked over and over, afraid of
finding the answer. Her earlier confidence evaporated and
she felt her shoulders hunch as the hollow pain in the pit
of her stomach grew.

Thankfully, the breakfast rush was at an end, and
the kitchen was quiet. Sari occupied herself with washing
a few dishes and continued preparations for lunch. No one
came into the kitchen, though Sari kept an eye on the
door, thinking that at any moment she would be
summoned and confronted by the banker.

Sari didn't mean to eavesdrop. There were shelves
by the kitchen door though, and she needed to put away
the morning's delivery. She worked quietly and quickly,
transferring apples and bags of rice and beans to their
proper spots on the shelves, when voices from the dining
room drifted in. Lilith's voice grew louder and more shrill,
and it caught Sari's full attention.

"But Henry, all Mr. Cramer has to do is read the
contract, and he won't sign it. No one would sign a loan
with an interest rate that high."

Sari shivered as she heard the answer from Mr.
Bagley, "Little sister, you worry too much."

Sari froze. *Mr. Bagley is Lilith's brother?*

Bagley continued, "That's the beauty of it. I know
for a fact that Cramer is illiterate. He can't read the
contract."

Sari moved away from the door, fearful that they
might know she had overheard and horrified at what she'd
just learned.

She felt as if she needed to do something with the
information she'd overheard but had no idea what. Taking
advantage of someone who couldn't read was disgraceful
and shouldn't be allowed to happen. As she pondered all
she heard, it also occurred to her that if Mr. Bagley was
willing to take advantage of one rancher, perhaps there
were others. She turned the information over and over
without finding any recourse.

When Meredith arrived, she had to greet Sari three times before her coworker responded. Sari was so consumed by the conversation she'd overheard, she hadn't noticed Meredith was in the kitchen.

"Things look peaceful here," Meredith remarked. "Have you had a good morning?"

If you only knew, Sari thought, but she answered evasively. "Things seem alright. I think everything is nearly ready to go. What can I do to help you start dinner preparations?" Sari took a breath and willed herself to stand up straight and not think about anything except her job.

They chatted as Meredith washed her hands and tied on her apron. "I'm making pork chops with mashed potatoes tonight, so there's not much to do this far ahead."

"We got apples in today. Maybe we should make cobbler."

Meredith smiled, "I think that's a good idea."

Retrieving the bin of apples and a paring knife, Meredith began peeling. Sari watched her, thinking how glad she was that they were now on such friendly terms.

"How are things, Meredith? Are you getting along better with your aunt and uncle?"

The girl nodded. "Yes, I guess. Of course, now that Evan is far away they have nothing to be angry about, plus I feel better because I am not lying to them anymore."

Sari had been so surprised when she finally realized that Meredith's beau was Dawson's brother. She'd never met Evan, but from all she'd heard, she couldn't imagine two brothers more dissimilar.

"Oh, so they know he's gone?"

"Yes, I told them. Uncle Paul says that joining the Navy was a good idea, and that service will make a man out of him. I didn't argue with him, but I know he's already a good man. You know, Evan promised that as soon as this war is over and he can, he'll come home and marry me." With a shine of hope in her eyes, Meredith described how they would buy a house and be happy forever. "We'll show my family how wrong they are about him."

They'd peeled nearly all the apples when Meredith looked up. "Oh, Sari, I'm excited to ask you this. I've talked about you with my aunt and uncle. Last night Aunt Mary Nell suggested we have you to dinner one evening. Do you think you could come over on Sunday?"

Sari was pleased at the invitation and accepted with only a little hesitation. Later, on her way home, she smiled at herself. *Not long ago, I would have never accepted,* she supposed. *Meeting new people has become a much less arduous prospect than it used to be.*

On Thursday evening, Sari sat with Claire, Bea, and Harriet in the reading room of the Presbyterian Church having cookies and punch at the end of their meeting. "Ladies," society president Ellen Sproat interrupted the quiet conversations. "I just wanted to thank you for your hard work in the past few weeks. As of right now, we have completed twenty-five scrapbooks and about forty hospital gowns. Mrs. Rankin and I will get everything packed up and taken to the post office this week. We might be a small group from a small town, but we are surely doing our part for the war effort. Unless there are any other ideas, I suggest we continue on this course during our meetings until the first of April. Then, I think we need to spend one or two of our meetings discussing the Victory Gardens we can all plant for the summer."

There was universal agreement among the members, and soon after, the meeting concluded. Sari pulled on her coat and gloves before remembering she needed to talk with Claire privately. "Bea, I need to have just a short minute with my sister-in-law."

"No problem," came the answer. "Harri and I will wait at the door for you so we can walk home together."

"Great, thank you." Sari crossed the room and joined a small group of women that included Claire, Mary Bohn and Alice Peryam.

"I haven't gotten to talk with you all evening," Mary said to Sari. "I was just talking with Alice about the marvelous book collection they have at the Roadhouse."

Sari had only met the older woman standing next to Mary briefly before, but her kind eyes and warm smile welcomed Sari into the conversation. Alice's voice was soft and kind as she explained, "W.T. and I are avid readers. We wanted to make sure our children had plenty to read as they were growing up. Now we have more books than the Rawlins library."

Shyly, Sari asked, "Do you ever loan them out?"

"Yes, we love to share. You are welcome to come by anytime. I'd love to have a visit with you and get to know you better. In fact, how about you and Claire come by on Tuesday afternoon?"

Sari glanced at Claire, nodding. "I'd like that very much. Could we come about four thirty?"

"That would be perfect," came the answer. "I'll look forward to it."

At that, the group separated, and Sari walked toward the door with Claire.

"Since I've learned to drive our Ford, if you come over Tuesday when you get off work, I will drive us to the Peryam's."

"That will be fun. I've never ridden with you driving. It will be an adventure." They laughed and then Sari added, "Harriet and Bea are waiting for me. I just wanted to let you know not to count on me for Sunday. I've been invited for a meal with Meredith Tucker. She lives with her aunt and uncle, Mary Nell and Paul Baker. Do you know them?"

Claire's face changed into a hard mask at the question. She quietly nodded. "Yes, I know Nell."

Sari noted the hardness in Claire's voice and the grim line of her mouth. "Is something wrong?"

Claire paused before she answered. "No, Sari. Mary Nell and I used to be friends, but we aren't any more. Just be guarded with Nell."

Sari nodded, unsure of what that meant, but they'd reached the entryway and there was no opportunity to ask.

Mary Nell and Paul Baker's dining room was small. Dark rose damask wall paper on all four walls and thick, heavy brocade drapes created a stifling, closed-in atmosphere. Paul sat to Sari's left. His hands and face were clean, but his cambric shirt was dusty and worn. He ate with a purpose, his forearms resting heavily on the edge of the table. Other than his initial greeting when they were introduced, he took no notice of the guest at his table. Sari passed a cut glass butter dish to Meredith, who sat opposite her. Then, she sat down her fork and glanced toward the woman on her right. Mary Nell was staring at her. Nell was tall and thin. Sari guessed that in her youth she may have been pretty, but her years had added deep frown lines to her sallow complexion resulting in a severe, haughty, and formidable air. Uncomfortable because of her placement in respect to the lady of the house and also the stiff feeling pervading the meal, Sari smiled shyly and busied herself with the napkin in her lap.

After grace had been offered and the meal began, Meredith introduced several topics, but despite her efforts to foster the table's conversation, the discussion remained clipped and stilted. Eventually, she gave up and the group ate in near silence.

"Mrs. Baker," Sari put her fork down on her empty plate and looked again at Mary Nell, hoping that the complement would soften the woman. "This salad is unique and very delicious. Is the dressing mayonnaise?"

Looking as if she really didn't want to answer, the hostess finally nodded slightly and responded, "Yes. It's called a Waldorf Salad. My cookbook says it was created by the chef at the Waldorf Astoria in New York in 1893. It's simple, really, just apples, celery, walnuts and mayonnaise."

"It is wonderful." Sari looked across the table at Meredith and continued, "Maybe we should consider adding it to our menu sometimes."

Ignoring the complement, Mary Nell addressed Sari, "Meredith has told me a little about you. I understand you are recently married?"

"Yes, Jesse and I married on October 30th."

"Is that Jesse Atley, the man who owns the livery?"

"Yes, that's right. Have you met him?"

"I knew him as a child when we lived in Dillon." Before Sari could reply, Nell continued, "One would think that a young woman *such as yourself* would choose to remain in her home, taking care of her household instead of working out in public." Sari felt as if the air had been sucked from her lungs by Mary Nell's insinuation, her sharp tone and her icy stare. It was clear what the woman was referencing.

Sari fought against her desire to hunch inward and drop her head. Instead, she took a steadying breath and ignored the slight. She answered with kindness and a straight back, "My husband and I married just before he left for France. He is a farrier for the Second Cavalry Regiment in France. Being alone affords me plenty of time to both work at the restaurant and take care of my duties at home."

"Well, in my opinion, you'd be better suited at home."

Sari clamped down on her irritation and purposely misunderstood her intent. "Well, it's true that this Great War has necessitated changes we never would have predicted. I don't suppose any of us expected most of our men to be sent away or anticipated the sacrifices the war would demand. Few if any foresaw the need to create new habits such as 'Meatless Mondays' or 'Wheatless Wednesdays' to help support the war effort."

Meredith, in an effort to stave off an argument, tried to salvage the moment. "It is sure hard to come up with good meals at the restaurant while we adhere to the government's suggestions. Oh, talking about helping the war effort, Aunt Nell, Sari has been telling me about the Ladies Aid Society and what they are doing to help. Tell her, Sari." Meredith's voice was a combination of encouragement and desperation.

"Yes, well, we have been creating scrapbooks to

help comfort the men who are confined to hospitals.
Others are sewing hospital garments."

"I'm sure both are necessary."

"Maybe you and I could start going, Aunt Nell?"

"Am I to assume you attend these meetings with
your sister-in-law?"

The question seemed to harbor a threat that Sari
didn't understand. "Well, yes. Claire originally invited me,
and we usually attend together."

Nell shrugged and made eye contact with
Meredith. "I will continue to support our country in many
ways, but I just can't in good conscience spend time
cavorting with the likes of Claire Haynes, Meredith. You
will need to trust that I have your best interests in mind
as I forbid you from it as well. Now, you will excuse us,
Paul and I are in the habit of resting on Sunday
afternoon. Mrs. Atley, it was interesting to meet you."

Within seconds, Meredith and Sari were alone.

"I'm sorry, Sari. I apologize."

"It's okay. It's not your fault." Sari remembered
Claire's look when Mary Nell's name was mentioned, and
wondered if she dared ask Claire more about it.

Meredith refused to allow Sari to help her remove
the dishes from the table. In just a few minutes, Sari
found herself strolling home.

It was a crisp and clear January day. Ice-crusted
snow piled into dirty mounds against walls and fence
posts, but the sky was pure, deep blue. The sun, a well-
defined orb above the summit of the Sierra Madres, gave
off very little warmth. Sari replayed the callous overtones
of her hostess, and waited for the old, familiar pain and
shame to come. The surprise was that it didn't. Certainly,
the moment had been uncomfortable, and she knew
she'd do all she could to avoid Mary Nell Baker in the
future, but the overwhelming shame and embarrassment
and the resulting guilt and remorse she normally felt
were absent.

Considering this, Sari tried to piece out the
change. *I don't focus on my scars and my face the way I
used to. Beginning with Jesse and certainly as a part of
the Haynes family, my face doesn't define me anymore.
Since my scars have stopped being so important to me,*

*comments and barbs about them don't bother me nearly
as much.* The sudden awareness made her nearly giddy.
The world around her became more vivid, beautiful.
Later, in a letter to Jesse she would describe the feeling
as a new and holy freedom.

Throughout the next week, though Sari tried to
console her friend and assure her that her aunt's
behavior was not her fault, Meredith was sad and quiet.
Thursday afternoon found them working together
chopping vegetables for chicken soup. "Meredith, I know
you've said that you are okay, but you don't seem that
way in your actions. Are you still worried about last
Sunday's dinner?"

"No, not really. I know you don't blame me for
how petty Aunt Nell was to you, though it's hard for me
to know that you endured her at my invitation."

"I know you didn't intend for the afternoon to go
the way it did. I hope you can just let it go. I surely have.
How has she treated you this week?"

"No different than before, if that's what you mean.
She hasn't mentioned your visit at all. She barely talks to
me, anyway."

Sari had been considering her offer all week,
"Meredith, I'd need to write and ask Jesse how he feels
about it, but what if you were to come move in with me?
I have an extra bedroom."

"Oh, Sari, that is so sweet, but I couldn't. I thank
you for the offer, and I've actually considered moving into
one of the boarding houses, but I don't think that's a
good idea. I'm trying to save every cent I can so that
when Evan comes home, I have a little money to help us
get started. Things at Aunt Nell's aren't fun, but overall,
it's okay. Don't worry."

"I have been worried. You seem so sad all the
time."

"I'm not really that sad. I miss Evan a lot, and I'm
concerned that I haven't heard from him. I've also just
been feeling tired. I don't think I've been sleeping well."

"Well," Sari finished with the carrots she was chopping and wiped her hands. "My offer remains if you decide differently."

Meredith gave her a quick hug and turned to tend the chicken stock on the stove.

Sari left the Copper Pot that afternoon a little later than usual. She ducked into Parkison's to buy a few groceries, then, with her grocery bag over her shoulder, she stopped in at the post office. She'd been receiving a thick letter about once a week from Jesse and it had been nine days since one arrived.

"Mrs. Atley, I just got a letter for you. It looks like it's from France."

She accepted it from the mail clerk with a smile and then studied the envelope. This one felt thick in her hand. There was no stamp, soldiers weren't required to pay for postage. The bottom left corner held the handwritten notation: *Censored by Lieutenant Jones, US 2nd Cavalry Division.* Sari knew that security was important, and it wasn't as if he wrote anything intimate, but she always cringed at the thought of someone else reading their mail.

Looking forward to savoring Jesse's news, Sari tucked the letter safely into her coat pocket, thanked the clerk and turned in time to see Bea arrive. They chatted amiably for a few minutes and Bea promised to stop over for a visit on Saturday evening. As Sari turned to leave, Bea turned to the clerk. "I'm here to pick up mail for my sister and her family."

Sari waved and stepped outside. She'd only gone half a block when Dawson rounded the corner and came into sight, walking quickly and with his head down. He'd nearly passed her before he looked up.

"Good afternoon, Mrs. Atley."

Sari laughed, "Good afternoon! You were certainly walking with a purpose."

Dawson shrugged. "Yes, Ma'am. I was thinking about all I still need to do today."

"Is business that good, then?"

"Well, yes, I'm staying very busy with hauling and livery services. I think Jesse would be proud of how things are going."

"But you still have another delivery this evening to do?"

"Well, no. What I was thinking about was how I'm going to get the ledger up to date."

"Oh I see. Daniel is helping you with that isn't he?"

Dawson hesitated. "Well, the truth is he's been too busy, and we haven't met for a couple of weeks. It isn't his fault. He's had just too many things at his job pulling at him."

Sari pictured Daniel's tired eyes the last time she saw him, and knew that he was stretched too thinly for his health and happiness.

"Mr. Wiley, is there anything I could do to help take off some of the load at the livery? As Jesse's wife, I'd be happy to help if I could."

Dawson sighed and put his hands out and palms up. The gesture let Sari know that her offer was welcome but that he had no idea what she could do. He shrugged and dropped his arms to his side with a crooked grin. "If you know how to do bookkeeping, I'd put you to work in a minute."

Sari smiled back. "I will talk with Daniel on Sunday and see what can be done. I don't know about keeping a ledger, but perhaps I could learn. Thank you for all the hard work you are doing." She knew her encouragement wasn't much of a help to the man, but it was all she had.

Dawson nodded and they parted a moment later. As he walked away he thought about Jesse's wife. *I was so wrong about her,* he thought.

Sari continued on her way, her mind filled with new concerns. When she arrived at home, she hung her coat and hat up, then put away her groceries. Remembering that she had a meeting later, she decided not to light a fire in the fireplace. Instead, she went downstairs and adjusted the damper on the coal furnace to give the house more heat.

Back upstairs, she kicked off her shoes and
tucked them underneath her dress as she sat on the
couch. Finally, she was ready to read Jesse's letter. It
was dated December thirty first. He wished her a happy
New Year and told about how quiet the fighting had been
since Christmas Eve.

> *It's a strange sort of quiet, though. It feels like
> even the countryside is holding its breath, waiting
> for the fighting to resume. It's been very cold. Not
> as cold as Encampment, surely, but with the added
> humidity, even forty-five degrees feels pretty bitter.
> The day after Christmas I received the box you and
> Claire sent me. Thank you. The socks and
> undershirts are a god-send. Today, because I knew
> I'd be outside with a group of sick horses, I wore
> two undershirts beneath my uniform shirt, and I
> stayed nicely warm all day. Another good thing
> about my new undershirts is that when I wear
> them, my dog tags, the two aluminum identification
> disks I wear around my neck at all times, can go
> between my uniform and my undershirt. Doing that
> makes the things more comfortable. I don't know if
> you are aware, but Nathan's gift was a small metal
> canister to keep matches dry. Certainly a good gift
> around here. Please thank him for me.*
>
> *Thank you also for the cookies, which arrived
> in perfect condition and were delicious! Mostly,
> thanks for the knife. It is so fine I hate to use it, but
> be assured I will keep it in my pocket at all times. I
> mean that, since we all are now ordered to sleep in
> our clothes to be prepared for an attack.*
>
> *Most of my days I spend tending horses or
> working at the forge. I've heard the Lieutenant say
> that in many ways for the war effort, a horse is
> more important than a man. I hate to think that is
> true, but training and transporting, plus feeding
> and caring for the horses is time consuming and
> expensive, so I suppose it is true. We use the
> horses mostly for* XXXXXX.

Sari frowned at the redacted lines of Jesse's letter.
Clearly, the censor didn't like Jesse talking about how
the horses were utilized at the front. After three lines that
were blackened, Jesse continued.

I don't know what you are reading in the news. No matter how bad the news sounds, don't worry about me. I am much more fortunate than most soldiers, who are living nearly constantly in the trenches. I've talked with many of them, and I count my blessings that I'm not fighting trench foot - which is when a man's feet stay wet in their shoes for so long they begin to develop sores - or any of the many ailments that get passed around in such close confines. I have my own, warm bunk in a tent I share with my platoon, and I am getting enough to eat.

Sari, I need to get some sleep, so I'll close. I think of you every day, and pray God is taking care of you.

Sari read the letter three times. Then sat, warm and safe in her and Jesse's home and prayed for her husband.

That evening, at the conclusion of the Ladies' Aid Society meeting, Sari asked Claire if she'd have a few minutes to talk.

"Yes, of course." Claire answered. "I had some cloth and supplies to carry this evening, so I drove the car. I'll drive you home and we can talk."

Within minutes, Sari had the teapot on and she and Claire sat together at her kitchen table. They'd already talked about Jesse's letter and the news of the day.

"We haven't talked since before your dinner at Meredith's house. How did it go?"

Sari described the laborious meal, ending with what Mary Nell said to her about staying home. Claire's eyes flashed with anger as she listened.

"I should have done more to warn you about that woman. I am sorry."

Sari shook her head. "You made it clear there was something between you."

Claire's voice rose as she answered, "Yes, there is something between us. She was a good friend of mine, but then she became involved with the Temperance movement and became very judgmental." Claire broke off and took a breath before going on. "As the years go by, she has become harsh and disparaging about anything and anyone who does not fit her idea of perfection. Again, Sari, I am so sorry I didn't give you more information."

They sipped their tea in comfortable quiet for a few moments.

"There is something else I'd like to talk with you about, Claire."

"As long as it doesn't have anything to do with Nell Baker, I'll be happy." Claire's sense of humor and perspective were back and Sari moved on.

"I know we have talked about how busy and overstretched Daniel is right now. I've been worried about him."

"I am, too. He seems to be carrying more than he can manage, and I don't know what I can do to help."

Sari cleared her throat. "I don't want to add anything to that load, Claire, but earlier today I ran into Dawson Wiley. He mentioned that he is behind with the livery's book keeping. He told me that he hadn't been able to meet with Daniel for a while."

Claire sighed. "I asked him about that last week and he just glared at me. He really hasn't enough time in his days."

"I understand that, and I'm wondering if there is anything I could do? I have plenty of time in the evenings that I could use to do the business paperwork, if only I knew how."

After considering, Claire answered, "A long time ago I did book keeping at a hardware store in Rapid City. I wonder, if you and I sat down with Dawson and the ledgers, if we couldn't figure out the system?"

"It seems to me it would be worth a try. I'm certainly willing to learn if you could teach me. That would take something off of Daniel."

"I'll mention it to Daniel tonight and see what he says. I'll let you know on Sunday."

Sari waved at Claire as she drove away a while later, then noticed in passing that Bea's bedroom light was on. Shivering with the chill of the night, Sari closed the front door and turned off the porch light before going upstairs to get ready for bed.

Across the street, Bea and Harriet were sitting up, side by side under the covers and propped against the headboard of Bea's bed, talking quietly.

"You haven't had a nightmare for a long time," Harriet said. It was more of a question than statement.

"No, I haven't," Bea assured her. "I think the one I had last night was the first one since I've been here." Bea shivered, though she wasn't cold. She thought about waking up last night, crying and fighting to breathe. She shuddered again with the memory, trying to release the fear and urgency she'd fought in her dream.

"Are you homesick, Bea-Bea? Are you unhappy here?"

"No!" her answer was louder than she'd intended. "I love it here. I love living in town and away from the farm. I don't want to ever go back out there to stay. Of course, I miss Ma, but I sure don't miss the ranch and all my outside chores, or the wind howling. Or the lonesomeness."

Harriet scooted closer so that their shoulders were touching. "I was just trying to consider anything that might be weighing on your mind that would spark a nightmare."

"I'm not worrying about anything, Harri, least I don't think I am."

After the sisters were quiet for a few minutes, Harriet glanced at Bea, "What are you thinking about?"

Bea leaned her head on her sibling's shoulder. "I was concentrating on happy things, like this room and how pretty it is. My dressing table is my favorite spot in the whole house, other than the chair in the living room where I curl up to read."

Harriet smiled and nodded her head. "It is a nice room. I see you've put your wooden box out on the top. Do you think having it out might have prompted your bad dream?"

She was quiet a long time. Finally, Bea replied, "It could be that I suppose. I've always kept it hidden in a drawer. I've never shown it to anyone but you. I just thought it looked nice with my brush and comb on it."

"It does, yes." Harriet waited a little longer.

"Could be the box did remind me of the fire. You might be right. In the morning maybe I'll put it back in my drawer."

"Was it the same old dream?" Harriet asked tentatively, unsure if talking about it would help or hinder.

"Yes, I was back upstairs, trapped in my bedroll, and the fire was all around me. No matter how much I screamed, no one came."

"It's strange to me that you dream that. We were all safely out before any of us even saw the flames. You never were close to the fire."

"I know, and I tell myself that, but it doesn't seem to keep that dream from coming."

Bea and Harriet were quiet then, both transported in memory back to the trip they'd taken with Pa and Harlan to explore the house and land the family had just acquired. The men were gone until nearly dark working on fences the day they'd arrived, and when they did return, they were tired and hungry.

"You girls did a good job of fixing supper." Pa offered the rare compliment as he pushed back from the wobbly table the girls had found and brought in from the barn.

Harriet beamed. "Did you get all the fences checked?"

Their brother Harlan snorted, "It's going to take a lot more than one afternoon to do all the work Pa wants done."

The girls cleared the table and began cleaning up as they listened to Pa and Harlan discuss how they were going to proceed in the morning.

"We only brought food for a few days, so we'll see how far we get by tomorrow night. Then we'll decide how to go from there," Pa finished. He stood and stretched. "I'm tired and we're going to start early tomorrow. Harlan, help me carry in some wood and stoke up the fire to help keep the chill off for tonight, then let's get to bed," he added.

A few minutes later, Harriet and Bea climbed the stairs. The room seemed so large and wondrous. They didn't mind sleeping on the floor. They were nearly tucked in, and Harriet was ready to blow out the candle they'd used for light when she noticed Bea tucking the blanket over something near her feet. "What's that?"

Bea hesitated before revealing the shiny box she'd found earlier in the day. She told her sister the story of finding it in a hidden panel in the wall, and after some discussion, Harriet agreed that the treasure was rightfully Bea's. Smiling, Bea fell asleep hugging the box as if it were a favored doll.

Grown-up Bea broke the silence she and Harriet had immersed themselves in. "I don't remember much about the night of the fire beside sitting out by the fence watching the flames dancing in the windows."

Harriet nodded. "You were so little, so I'm not surprised. Pa and Harlan figured later that either there was something in the chimney that caught fire, or embers ignited the roof. I just remember waking up coughing and hearing Pa and Harlan yelling at us to get out. I grabbed your arm and we started down the stairs but you broke free and went back for the box and gave me a fright. I grabbed you again and we stumbled outside. It wasn't until we were safely away that we began to see the flames."

"I remember thinking how cold I was sitting there in the dark when just nearby was all that pretty warmth."

"It was kind of pretty, in a horrid way," Harriet agreed. "We were sure a rag tag group that arrived home the next afternoon. All our food had burned up, and you and I were in our nightdresses when Ma first saw us, since I didn't grab our clothes. It took a week before we washed the smell of smoke from our hair."

"One good thing came of the fire, though," Harriet added, wanting to lighten their memories, "Pa felt so bad that the house was destroyed and we all didn't get to live in it, he and the older boys spent time that summer doing some fixing on our house. They painted the outside and Pa even let Ma pick out wallpaper for the dining room."

A few minutes later, Harriet yawned. Bea assured her sister that she was calm and ready to turn out the light. "Call me if you can't sleep," Harriet said as she kissed Bea's forehead and slipped out of her sister's bed.

Alone in the dark room, Bea snuggled down and waited for sleep.

26
near Amiens, France
mid – January, 1918

"What a way to start the day," Jesse spoke to
Private Griffin as they leaned side by side against the
corral fence and watched the wagon pull away. Since
November, Jesse and his platoon had been installed with a
large battalion just east of Amiens, an area of hot fighting
east-northeast of Paris.

It was barely dawn, the sun was still well below the
horizon and only a mere hint of day relieved the darkness.
"I thought that mare was doing better yesterday
afternoon," remarked Griffin. "I couldn't believe it when I
came on watch and she was down."

"Yeah, I thought she looked better when I checked
her last evening also, but by the time you called me, her
breathing was so labored. She just couldn't fight any
more."

Griffin rubbed his face with a grimy hand and took
a slow breath. "I know just how she feels. I get pretty tired
of this daily battle myself."

Jesse punched the man on the arm in comradery,
"Don't get any ideas about me putting you down just
because you've missed your beauty sleep. I'm not doing it,
no matter how much you whine."

Griffin chuckled as he pushed himself away from
the fence. "Rex will be here any minute. I'm going to go get
some chow and then head to bed if you don't mind."

"Actually, Lieutenant Jones sent Rex out on a
message run about half an hour ago. I don't expect he'll be
back before the end of the day. You go on, though. I'll
stay. I need to check that roan we got yesterday anyway."

"Another message run? That's the third time this
week."

"Well, Rex is darn good in the saddle, and Jones
knows it. When there are messages that just can't wait or
go over the radio, somebody's got to take it."

"Guess you're right. I'll see you later."

Jesse watched him walk away, then forced himself
to move. It wasn't that he was tired exactly, he'd slept well

even though he'd awakened early. *No, he thought as he walked across the enclosure, I'm just weary. While it seems there is war all around me, I'm here in this oasis where nothing changes. I've read all the books in camp and done every chore I can find. Every day is just like the last.* The noise of rumbling wagons caught his attention. He stopped and faced the road. Standing at attention, Jesse watched as the caravan passed. The first two were ambulances. Jesse noted that each carried more men than they were designed to transport. He winced at the occasional moans and cries he could hear over the din of the wheels and engines. The next three wagons carried silent cargo. *I wonder how many bodies are concealed beneath those tarps?* he thought.

Since fighting stopped at nightfall when darkness kept targets obscured, crews were dispatched each night to collect the wounded and the dead. Jesse knew that many of those who succumbed weren't killed by bullets, but by infections and diseases. The trenches, damp and cold and cramped, were dangerous places even without enemy rounds whizzing overhead. For Jesse, who was always up early, watching the ambulance wagons return each morning from their grim task was a painful but stark reminder to count his own blessings. He had a sudden memory of standing under the stars and full moon on the prairie outside Encampment, asking God to spare him from killing another person. He recognized how his prayer had been answered and was humbled. *Thank you, God,* Jesse prayed, *that I'm here with the horses, not being asked to kill. Thank you that I am safely bored instead of in a trench, or on that detail, retrieving bodies.*

He resumed his path as the last caisson passed him. Shaking his head and taking a breath, Jesse fought against the desolation pressing on his soul as he approached a roan standing alone near the water trough. Jesse rubbed the animal's warm, silky neck then checked the saddle sores on his back. "Easy there, fella, it's all going to be alright," he crooned quietly, unsure whether his words were for the horse or himself. He continued to murmur as he examined the horse's injuries. Satisfied that there was no infection, he gave the roan a final pat and turned to the next animal. By the time he'd satisfied himself that the rest of his brood fared well, the camp was waking up. The smell of coffee and bacon nudged his belly. He climbed between the corral rails and set out for the mess tent.

Late that evening, Griffin was playing solitaire on his cot and Jesse was just finishing a letter to Sari when Rex stumbled into the tent. He was covered in mud and blood, his uniform was torn. "Oh my God," Griffin exclaimed, his cards forgotten. He rose and grabbed Rex's arm. "What happened to you?"

Rex righted himself. "Sorry, I tripped over my own feet. Actually, I'm alright, better than I look."

Jesse asked again, "What happened?"

Rex sat heavily on his bunk and began pulling off his boots. Jesse, reassured that his tent-mate, platoon member, and friend was alright, settled in to listen. One part of Rex's personality was his ability to tell any event with a storyteller's skill, and Jesse had no doubt that they were about to hear an exciting retelling.

"Jones sent me with a high priority dispatch for a British tank division set up about ten miles north east, out near Frechencourt. There weren't supposed to be any enemy troops in the area according to the information they had. I was ridin' that chestnut stallion you know I like. The sunrise was grand and the countryside quiet. I made it to the tank camp easily and delivered the packet. No problems, but the Cap told me he'd have a return message for me to take, but not until late this afternoon. No problem. I grabbed something to eat, and then found a corner in the mess tent to take a nap."

He paused as he shucked off his shirt, looked at it with disgust and dropped in on the canvas floor. "I'm about out of uniforms," he said with a grim smile peeling off his trousers and adding them to the heap.

Griffin kicked the pile aside and began collecting the cards from his bed and the floor. "So far this doesn't explain your current appearance."

Rex grimaced as he pulled on a clean pair of pants. Jesse noticed a growing bruise the length of the man's thigh as he went on. "Well, I slept, then ate again, then kicked around until about four when the Cap called for me. He had a satchel for the Major. He warned me it was real important, and said that a platoon had encountered a small bit of resistance near Cardonnette, so I should go wide to the south. The first six or so miles were a breeze. The shadows were beginnin' to crawl long when, out of nowhere, something dusted up the rocks right in front of me. It took me a second to realize what was happenin', and before I reacted, several more followed. By then, both the stallion and I were sufficiently spooked.

"I kicked him hard then and we made a run for it. I knew I had about three miles to go so we rode hard and I kept my head down. About a mile farther, my heart finally stopped pounding so hard I couldn't think, and I reigned him in a little. By then, the chestnut was laboring. Even though we slowed down, he was wheezing and stumbling. I let up on him, thinking at first he was just tired, but then his head went down and I realized a bullet had got him. Poor son of a gun gave me all he had without complainin', then his legs buckled and he went down. I had little warnin' and I didn't get my foot out of the stirrup before he rolled on his side and just died. Worst of it was I was pinned under him and had no idea where the Germans were. Stuck there, I could see that a round got him through the chest. I fought that poor horse's carcass for what seemed like a long time before I edged myself out from under him. I could hear voices a ways off, so I lit out of there like my pants were on fire, dodgin' and keepin' cover until I could see the lights of camp."

Rex inspected his arms and hands, then grabbed a towel from the end of his cot. "I gotta go clean up."

Jesse watched him duck under the tent flap, thankful that he'd made it back safely.

"It's what I've been saying all along," Griffin's voice was gruff. "They got no business sending any of us out on runs like that without an escort. The sidearm pistols they give us are pea shooters that wouldn't do much against the shells out there." He roughly shuffled his cards and began dealing himself another hand.

Feeling unsettled and tense at Rex's close call, Jesse looked at the envelope on his green wool blanket and decided a walk to the mail tent might feel good. While he didn't disagree with Griffin, he knew that his platoon was only called upon as couriers when no one else was available. He'd actually enjoyed the runs he'd been sent on, though admittedly he'd encountered no danger. He'd welcomed the opportunity to leave camp to see the bucolic French countryside, getting a respite from doing the same tasks over and over. It had given him something to write about in his letters to Sari. He'd have to be careful retelling this one, though. He didn't want Sari or Claire to know just how close he was to the Germans.

27

Encampment, Wyoming
February, 1918

February attacked Encampment with wild winds and blowing snow. It was a short walk to Claire's, yet even bundled up with only her eyes exposed to the outside, Sari's toes were cold and her legs were tired from leaning into the steady gale when she stepped up on the porch. Greg held the door tightly so the wind couldn't grab it and Sari squeezed past him and into the house.

Dawson Wiley was already sitting at the table with Daniel and Claire. They'd met together twice before, once with Daniel and once without, and Sari felt more and more confident about her abilities to enter transactions in the ledgers.

They'd worked for over an hour when Sari smiled and snapped the oversized leather volume shut with a satisfying snap. "There," she said in triumph. "We are completely caught up on paperwork and I'm feeling quite confident that I can take this from here."

Daniel lifted his mug of hot cocoa and gestured first toward Dawson and then to Sari and Claire. "Here's to the three of you. I've already apologized that I wasn't able to meet with you weekly, Dawson, as we'd agreed before Jesse left. But, thanks to the ladies here, an even better plan has evolved."

After a round of clinking mugs, laughter, choruses of "Cheers," and "Here, here", Daniel continued. "Sari, it's amazing to me how quickly you've caught on to all this. Now that you have this under control, I have no doubts you can handle the ledgers by yourself from here on out."

Sari was pleased at the accolade. "It's been all your and Claire's tutoring. She's made it so easy to understand."

Daniel nodded, adding, "Now, with you doing all this time-consuming work, it will be easy for me to find time to continue to pay the bills for the business and the house. Though I'd like to do it with you, Sari, so you can learn that as well."

Dawson raised his cup again in Sari's direction and added, "And now I can sleep at night and not worry about anything other than saving receipts and doing what I know how to do."

Claire sighed. "Have you told Jesse that you've taken over the books, Sari? He'll be so proud."

Suddenly feeling shy, Sari responded quietly, "I told him in my last letter. I waited until I felt confident that I really could learn to do it before I mentioned it. Oh! That reminds me, I got a letter from him today, and he tells the most wonderful story in it! I wanted to share it with you three tonight."

She jumped up and left the room to retrieve the letter from her coat pocket. "I want to read this to you all, Jesse tells it so well." She rifled through several pages then began reading,

I don't know if the news there is covering anything about the air war that is raging here and in England. While I wrangle horses, the real war is being fought in the air. Yesterday I talked to a soldier who just arrived from near London. He says that it is common to watch heated battles being fought overhead. A couple weeks ago he watched as two British fighters were in a dog fight with several German planes. I didn't know this, but most fighter planes carry two men, one man is the pilot, the other is the gunner. Well, during one hot fight, the pilot of a Bristol F2B British fighter banked into a steep dive to avoid being shot by a German. The gunner, a guy named Captain John Hedley, wasn't ready and he was actually thrown out of the airplane during the dive.

Sari paused when she heard Claire gasp. "I can't even imagine flying up in the air, but falling out?" Claire shivered as Sari continued.

Well, the pilot, a Captain Jimmy Makepeace, saw what happened. Quick as he could, he twisted that plane around and managed to get beneath his falling gunner. I'm sure God helped him, but the gunner managed to grab on to the plane and crawl back into his seat. He was unharmed.

Sari looked up. There were tears in Claire's eyes. Dawson looked dazed as he told them, "That gives me goose bumps. I watched some barnstormers perform one time in Cheyenne for the Frontier Days Rodeo, and I just can't stomach the idea of flying."

"I wouldn't mind taking a ride in an airplane," Daniel shared. "What I can't get over is how that pilot could think and react so fast that he could maneuver the plane underneath the man while he was still falling."

The group was quiet for a moment when Daniel observed, "Our world is changing so fast. This war started out being fought on horseback but it's going to end with who has the best planes, submarines, and the toughest tanks."

Sari glanced at the clock on Claire's kitchen wall and began gathering her things. She stacked Jesse's letter and her pencils on top of the ledger book and stood up. "It's getting late, and I promised Bea I'd stop over on my way home, I need to get going."

"I have the truck," Dawson volunteered, "Can I drop you off?"

Sari agreed, and before long she was sitting beside Dawson in the pickup. She was thankful for him, and happy that they'd become comfortable enough with one another to be on a first name basis. As he carefully maneuvered the slick streets, Sari made a decision. She and Dawson had never discussed his brother or mentioned the day that Dawson had come to the restaurant to see Meredith, but she knew her workmate had received no word from her beau since he'd left. "Dawson, I'm right that you have a brother who's gone to the military?"

"Yes, Evan left in December to join the Navy." Dawson tried not to picture the anger in his brother's eyes the last time he saw him.

"Have you heard from him since he left? Where is he stationed?"

"Evan and I have never been close. I haven't heard from him, no. But, my ma got a post card a while back from the Navy saying that Evan was assigned to a destroyer. Then, just a few days ago she got a letter from him. He's patrolling the waters near England on a ship that hunts U-boats and protects bigger ships."

"That sounds exciting and dangerous."

Dawson didn't answer and Sari saw in his look that the conversation needed to end. He pulled up in front of the house. Sari thanked him and got out of the truck, hugging her books and papers tightly against her so the wind wouldn't snatch them.

Instead of going home when Dawson drove away, Sari crossed the street and knocked gently. Royce answered the door and ushered her in. "We were just enjoying a cup of hot cider," Harriet told her after she'd handed Royce her coat and piled her things on a small table by the door. "Would you like some?"

"Anything warm is welcome," Sari answered. "It is so cold outside!"

Bea, after a quick hug, invited Sari to sit beside her on the sofa. Soon, the four were exchanging pleasantries and news.

28
Encampment, Wyoming
March 31, 1918

Sari carefully deposited her Easter treasure on the counter when she came in the back door in the late afternoon. Above, hanging on the wall, a calendar advertised Parkison's Store. *Easter Sunday, March 31, 1918.* She pondered that date. *It seems as if the past five months have taken only a blink to pass, while at the same time the memory of my life before seems so far away and unreal.*

Shouts of "Hosanna" and "He is risen indeed!" along with songs of praise still echoed in her mind from the morning's rousing church service. Sari had never taken part in an Easter Sunday service with so much joy. While the pastor hadn't glossed over the horrors of Jesus' crucifixion, he had chosen to focus his congregation on the eternal hope of the resurrection. In the midst of the trials of war, it was a sermon well received.

She put a match to the logs Michael had set for her earlier in the week, and soon a fire was happily warming the room. Sari settled in for a quiet evening to herself, happy for the solitude after a noisy, laugh-filled afternoon. She'd enjoyed a beautiful Easter dinner after church with Claire, Daniel, the boys, and Nathan Jameson. A plate of left-over ham and scalloped potatoes awaited her in the ice box, though she'd eaten so much at Claire's table she was certain she wouldn't need to eat again until tomorrow.

Sari smiled as she picked up her latest crochet project, a tablecloth in fine ecru thread. As she worked the stitches, she recalled the fun and conversation with her family.

"Hey, Aunt Sari!" Greg had exclaimed when the family was settled in the parlor after they'd eaten. "I think the Easter bunny came for you!" The mischievous twinkle in his eyes and crooked grin told Sari how excited he was about the gift.

"What?" she answered. "But I didn't set out a nest for the bunny to fill."

Greg giggled, "We did it for you! I made yours out of a little box and some tangled string I found in the carriage house, and Mike added a ribbon Mama said we could have. We put yours next to ours. Look!" Sari knew that the boys were much too old to believe in the magical properties of the Easter Bunny, but she also knew from their Christmas celebration that the family continued the traditions of both Santa Claus and the Bunny just for fun. Greg pointed to a space beneath the china hutch, and Sari spied the small nest.

Daniel laughed, "Why don't you hand the nest to your aunt, Mr. Greg?"

The boy popped up quickly to oblige. With exaggerated pomp and circumstance, he handed Sari a small parcel filled with a chocolate rabbit and jelly beans. A lace book mark was tucked in along one side.

Sari, sitting in the warmth of her own parlor, let the memory of that small surprise fill her. She closed her eyes and breathed a prayer of thanks for her vast and unexpected blessings. In the quiet, her thoughts roamed, finally resting on Jesse. She wondered again at how Jesse's proposal had changed not only her circumstances but her life. Thinking of Jesse, she turned to prayer, for his safety and his warmth tonight.

After a while, Sari resumed her handwork and found herself humming quietly to herself.

A sudden, insistent knock at the front door made Sari jump. She put her project in the workbasket beside her chair and moved quickly to answer the door.

Meredith stood huddled against the cold on the front step. Sari opened the door and shivered at the chilly wind that came in with her guest. It wasn't until the door was closed and she had the girl's coat in her hands that Sari actually looked at her friend. What she saw frightened her. Meredith's hair was matted, tangled from the wind. Her face was red from the cold but Sari could see that her eyes were swollen and her face mottled. Clearly she'd been crying.

"Oh Sari, I'm sorry to burst in, but I didn't know where else to go."

Assuming that there'd been another argument between Meredith and her aunt, Sari calmly insisted that her friend come in and sit by the fire to warm up. She hurried to the kitchen and returned with a cup of warm tea. Meredith accepted it gratefully, then glanced up at Sari. "Oh Sari, I have been walking for at least an hour, trying to find some sort of solution to my problems. Everything is just so hopeless."

Sari sat down on the settee beside Meredith and took her hand. "Did you and Nell have another argument?"

Meredith's laugh was tinged with acrid bitterness. "No. Everything is fine at the house. We went to church this morning, then had a nice dinner."

"Then, what's happened to make you so upset?"

She took an uneven breath and began, "Aunt Nell invited several people to share Easter dinner with us. Without mentioning anything to me, she included the Drakes. Do you know them?"

"I know of them, I've met their son. Donovan Drake is a friend of my nephew Michael. They are school chums."

"Yes, I suppose they would know each other. The family used to live near us before they moved to town. I knew Donovan and his older brother Crispus then."

"From what I know they are a nice family."

"They are," Meredith agreed with sadness in her voice. "Mrs. Drake isn't like Aunt Nell, she's gentle and never gossips. Mr. Drake owns several buildings here in Encampment and in Saratoga. Both brothers are polite and kind. Honestly, when I was in school, I always had a little crush on Crispus. He is tall and handsome." Sari didn't reply, waiting for her friend to continue.

"I was actually enjoying the dinner. That is, I was until Mr. Drake brought up how happy he is Uncle Paul and Aunt Nell have agreed that Crispus may court me." At this admission, Meredith put her face in her hands and began to cry.

Sari wasn't sure how to respond. She gave her companion a minute, then quietly said, "Meredith, this sounds like good news. The Drakes are nice people, upstanding in the community, well respected. You've already said you liked him. It sounds like your aunt and uncle have encouraged a good prospect for you."

Her words only made Meredith cry harder. Sari was at a loss. She waited as Meredith produced a wilted hankie and finally wiped her eyes and blew her nose. Then, with a look of abject sorrow, she looked into Sari's eyes and explained, "It would be a wonderful prospect, and I would be so fortunate to even consider a future with someone like him. But." She closed her eyes and as a tears continued to stream, she added, "But what they don't know is that I'm going to have a baby. Evan's baby."

In an instant Sari understood the recent paleness of her friend's face, her moodiness and sadness. Sari felt sick.

"If you want me to go, now that you know, I will. I wouldn't blame you for not wanting to associate with me."

Without hesitation Sari answered, "Don't be silly. You are my friend, I won't abandon you."

"Even though it's clear I'm a hussy?"

Sari felt sure of her answer, "But you aren't. How many girls have been taken in by love and then left desperate?"

"Oh Sari, I didn't really want to give in to him. But, he was so insistent. He told me he loved me and that we'd be together always. I kept saying no, but he convinced me that it would be alright. I only said yes a few times."

Sari was sure she was correct when she asked, "Dawson caught you two together, didn't he?"

"That was the worst day ever. Evan convinced me that he couldn't live without seeing me, so we began meeting at Dawson's place in the mornings after Dawson left for work. It was so nice to have time together. At first we'd just talk, hold hands, and dream about the future. But then, Evan insisted that if I really loved him, I'd let him kiss me. And then. Well. The morning Dawson surprised us, I'd given in, again, to Evan. He'd finished with me and I'd gotten nearly dressed when the door flew open and Dawson was there. I was so mortified."

"That's the day Dawson came to see you at the restaurant."

"Yes. I was so frightened when he came in, but he was kind. He apologized for the actions of his brother, and told me that I shouldn't trust or believe anything Evan told me. Imagine, his own brother telling me that my love was a liar. I was so angry at Dawson for the mean, hateful things he said about Evan."

Sari squeezed Meredith's hand gently as she asked, "And now. Evan has been gone for nearly four months. How do you feel about what Dawson said?"

Her crying began again as she admitted, "I just don't know what to think. He promised to write, but I haven't heard a thing. I saw Dawson the other day, and he told me that his mother had received several letters from Evan, so I know he could write if he wanted to." They sat in silence together until Meredith added, "I'm afraid Sari. What am I supposed to do?"

The conversation turned to speculating on Meredith's options, though both knew there weren't many. "I surely can't let Crispus court me. I won't do that to him, but how do I stop it? I've assured Aunt Nell that my relationship with Evan is finished. I can't let her know about the baby. She'd turn me out, or worse, the very moment she found out. So far, my clothes cover my growing belly, but I don't know how long I can keep it a secret. I have no place to go and I don't make enough to pay for a room, even if there was a rooming house or place here that would allow a girl in my state to stay. Sari, what am I going to do?" she asked again.

Sari responded without much thought. "You will always be welcome here."

Meredith shook her head, "No, I can't bring shame on you. You and your family are well-respected in Encampment. I couldn't tarnish that by allowing you to take me in."

The conversation evolved into a circular mire of maybes and possibles until Sari finally suggested, "Meredith, my sister-in-law is level headed and much wiser than I. Would it be alright with you if we talked with her about this to see if she has any suggestions we haven't considered?"

Meredith hesitated. "Well, the truth is, the whole town is going to know soon, the evidence isn't going to be easy to hide for long."

When she left Sari's that evening, Meredith had stopped crying and had squared her shoulders. "Thank you for being my friend. I actually considered just walking off into the mountains and letting myself freeze to death or be eaten by wolves or coyotes."

Sari heard the sincerity with which the words were spoken and shivered inwardly. "Be strong, my friend. We have a few weeks before your condition will be at all noticeable, and by then we will have thought of something."

Later, with strong hugs and a silent prayer, Sari watched Meredith lower her head against the cold night and trudge off.

Bea left a note on Sari's door Wednesday evening inviting her to supper before the Ladies' Aid meeting the following night. Happily accepting, Sari found herself on Thursday evening sitting with a plate of trout, creamed corn, and baking powder biscuits in front of her and lively conversation around her. Royce regaled them with a story of how he had apprehended a sheep rustler that morning.

His female audience was sufficiently, and rightfully, impressed with his police work and the charming way he told the story. "I live a sheltered life," Sari admitted when the story was done. "I guess I don't realize that there are criminals around us even here."

Royce nodded. "There really isn't that much crime. Most of my days are pretty mundane."

Harriet handed him a serving bowl and told him, "There is only a little corn left. Finish it for me, alright?"

Royce accepted the task and emptied the bowl. He took a spoonful and Bea asked, "Did I hear you say you had to go to Rawlins tomorrow, Royce?"

"Yes, and I might be gone a couple of days. I am doing some investigating, and I have several people to talk to."

"Oh, that sounds serious," Sari remarked as the last of the corn disappeared.

"I'm not sure if it will come to anything. I'm looking into some land deals that seem suspicious, but so far I can't prove any laws have been broken."

"I don't understand how there could be a crime involved with land," Bea told them. "Land is land, isn't it?"

"Well we had a rancher last fall who came in to report a problem with a piece of ground he'd purchased. It had been surveyed, and he'd ridden the entire perimeter with the seller to locate all the survey markers before the sale was complete. After the sale, though, he claimed that one of the landmark points, a large rock with the survey point chiseled into it, was on the opposite side of a small creek than it had been when he'd ridden the land with the seller."

"Why would something like that matter very much?" Harriet asked.

"In this case, it makes a lot of difference. Water access and water rights are vital in our dry country, and if that creek is not on that parcel of land, the rancher really can't run cattle on it. The seller, who still owns the adjoining property, put up fencing to restrict livestock from getting to the stream."

"Is the land near Rawlins? Is that why you have to go?" asked Harriet.

"Well, no. That parcel is east of here, but since that rancher came forward, we've heard of several other land deals that seem crooked, and I need to go talk to the land company and a bank in Rawlins to see what I can find out."

Sari's head snapped up. "The bank in Rawlins? Do you think the bank has anything to do with it?"

Royce nodded slowly. "I can't give any details about this. I'd appreciate it if you ladies wouldn't talk about it. But, yes, Sari, it seems that several of those suspicious deals have one of the two banks in common."

Sari felt like she'd been kicked.

Harriet hadn't noticed Sari's reaction as she stood up and began clearing the table. "We have about thirty minutes before we need to leave for the church. Sari, would you like a refill on milk or a cup of tea while Bea and I clean up the kitchen?"

Sari was still reeling from Royce's report. She murmured a quiet, "No, thank you."

Royce got up and patted his belly. "I'm going to go read the newspaper in the living room if that's alright with you." He kissed his wife on the cheek, thanked her for a fine meal, then started for the front room.

"Um, Royce, could I talk to you for a moment?"

The seriousness of her voice arrested him. He turned and nodded. "Sure, will you join me in here?"

They sat across from one another. Sari was instantly nervous and unsure. She didn't want to tell him the extent of her personal experience but felt she needed to give him a bit of background.

"I, um, well, I am acquainted with Mr. Bagley in Rawlins, Royce." Royce's eyebrows raised at the name. "I have had some dealings with him myself regarding a mortgage my father had when I was very small. It is a debt that I inherited."

Royce leaned forward in his chair and she continued, "It is probably nothing, it isn't about moving survey markers or anything. You will probably think I'm silly to even share this, but recently I overheard a conversation that you might be interested in." He nodded and Sari took a breath. "As you know, I work at the Copper Pot. Recently, Mr. Bagley was at the restaurant, and I found out that he and Lilith Wills are brother and sister." She could tell this was new information to Royce. "Well, I didn't mean to, but I overheard them discussing a bank loan." Royce nodded again, encouraging her.

"I didn't hear much, but it sounded as if the loan had a terribly high interest rate. When Lilith told him there would be no way he could get anyone to agree to a loan like that, Mr. Bagley answered that since the borrower couldn't read, it didn't matter."

Royce leaned even closer. "Sari, this is important information. Can you remember if you heard the name of the borrower?"

Sari closed her eyes and replayed the scene in her mind. "Yes, I think it was Conner—no, no, it was Cramer. Mr. Bagley said, "Cramer is illiterate, he can't read the contract." Then the three of them laughed."

Royce sat back and rubbed his face with his hand. "Have you talked about this conversation with anyone?"

"No."

"Did anyone else hear it?"

"I don't think so. The dining room was empty except for them, and I was alone in the kitchen."

"Sari, this might be an important lead. Can I count on you not to discuss this with anyone? Not anyone?"

"Yes, of course."

Just then, Harriet and Bea came into the parlor. "There you are. Are you ready to go?"

Sari glanced at Royce and then stood up, "Sure."

Later, when she was back in the quiet of her home, Sari thought again about her conversation with Royce and reviewed the dealings she'd had with Mr. Bagley. She also thought about Jesse's admonition to get copies of her father's loan. Right then, Sari sat down and wrote to Mr. Bagley, requesting copies of the loan documents.

29

Encampment, Wyoming
April, 1918

Claire decided to walk to Sari's instead of driving. The early April evening was cool but pleasant after she'd been in the hot kitchen most of the day. The note she'd received from Sari was odd. It only said, "Can you come over tonight after dinner? I need to discuss something with you." Everything had been going well lately, Claire thought. They both were hearing quite regularly from Jesse, and though he was in France with the war all around him, he continued to reassure them that he was out of harm's way. His letters were mostly positive, and he sounded well. She couldn't help worrying that Sari had heard something troubling.

She knocked on the door. Sari answered right away, ushering her in and taking her coat. Claire followed Sari into the kitchen. A young woman was sitting at the table.

"Claire, I'd like you to meet my friend and co-worker, Meredith Tucker. Meredith, my sister-in-law, Claire Haynes."

Meredith stood up and offered her hand, "It is nice to meet you Mrs. Haynes, I've heard so much about you from Sari."

Claire returned the greeting and the ladies sat down at the table. "Please, call me Claire. I think we've met before, a long time ago. You are Nell Baker's niece, correct?"

Meredith smiled, "Yes, I am."

They chatted amiably while Sari poured tea from a porcelain tea pot into three matching cups.

Conversation lagged while they sipped the hot tea and nibbled at cake. Finally, Sari began. "Claire, you know how much I appreciate you and respect your opinion. I hope you don't mind, but Meredith is in need of some help and insight, and we are hoping you are willing to offer yours."

Claire could tell Sari was suddenly uncomfortable. "Of course."

Sari looked at Meredith expectantly. In response, Meredith put her hands in her lap and dropped her eyes. Claire sat quietly, listening and observing as Meredith's story and predicament slowly came to light. She let the girl talk for some time, explaining and justifying, then, deflated and discouraged, Meredith sat quietly waiting.

Claire breathed a silent prayer before she spoke, "Meredith, how can I help you?"

Meredith heard no accusing and no condemnation in the woman's voice. The kind willingness she did hear broke her. She looked at Claire, tears streaming, and pleaded, "I don't know what to do. By my count, the baby is due to be born in late September. It's been easy to hide my belly under heavy winter clothes, but I'm getting bigger every day, and the weather is warming up. Soon I won't be able to wear heavy skirts and shawls. As it is, Aunt Nell has already mentioned a couple of times that I must be eating a lot at work since my face is getting rounder."

"So your aunt is unaware of your condition."

"Oh Lord, yes. I can't tell her. She and my Pa don't put up with sinners."

Claire let that statement pass.

Claire asked, "And you've heard nothing from the child's father?"

New tears came as Meredith answered, "No, I haven't heard a word from him since he left just before Christmas. But, I know that he has written to his mother several times."

"Does he know about the child?"

"No. I don't have an address to write to him."

The clock ticked quietly, disturbing the silence. Softly, Claire asked, "Meredith, what do *you* want?"

"I want to let Evan know about the baby. He said he loved me. He promised he'd come back and marry me after the war. I want him to come home and for us to be a family."

Claire knew of Evan Wiley. His misbehavior was no secret in Encampment. She couldn't imagine that knowledge of a child on the way would change him, but there was always hope that he'd grown up and matured enough to come home after the war and do the right thing. "I think that you absolutely should contact him. Sari, do

293

you think you could ask Dawson for his brother's address?"

Meredith answered for her, "I know Dawson, and he knows Evan, um, courted me. I can ask him."

"Good. I'd suggest you write a letter to Evan and tell him about the baby as soon as possible. Ask him to write to you immediately so that you will know if he will stand by you." Claire watched Meredith's face, then asked, "Under the circumstances, and with everything you know about him right now, what do you think will happen when he receives the news that you are carrying his child?"

Sari sat quietly, studying the strained look on Claire's face.

Meredith began to answer, "He'd be happy—" then she stopped herself. She dropped her head onto her arms and started sobbing. After a moment she went on, "I want to say he'd be happy and want to marry me right away." Her voice was muffled, and they strained to understand her. "But I'm afraid he wouldn't."

She looked up. Claire was astonished at how young and innocent the girl appeared, though her answer was the first insightful thing she'd said so far. "I'm fearful he will either ignore me or make some excuse about why it wasn't his fault and say he can't help me." Meredith continued.

Claire took a relieved breath. *Now,* she thought, *now we can begin to speak rationally.*

With the steadying influence of Claire's matter of fact attitude, and Sari beside her for support, the conversation slowly became less emotional and more rational. "It will take several weeks for you to write to Evan and get an answer back." Claire said. "While we wait to hear from him, we'll pray and hope that he'll surprise you. Also, though, I think you'd be wise to look into what other options there are."

"Options? Are there any, really?" Tears began again.

"Yes, options. Dear, I know this is difficult, but stop feeling sorry for yourself and start thinking. What possibilities are there for you?"

Meredith palmed the tears away and sat up. "I could move to somewhere big, like Cheyenne. I could tell people my husband was killed overseas. No one would know."

"Yes, that is an option. You would have to figure out how you could support yourself and who would take care of the child while you were at work. What else?"

"I, well, I could give the baby away."

"Yes."

Sari leaned forward, her arms on the table. She wished there was something she could do to ease the pain and fear Meredith was feeling.

"I hear there are ways to stop a pregnancy." Meredith's voice was hollow and desperate. Sari gasped when the words were unleashed.

Claire stayed silent. The comment took her back to Rapid City, and she recalled how one of her friends there had managed to cause a miscarriage for herself with a very hot, long bath and a bottle of gin. That girl had been only a few weeks pregnant, though, and Claire knew it wouldn't be effective for Meredith now. Then, she remembered how another woman had taken a concoction of Brewer's yeast and pennyroyal tea to end her more advanced pregnancy. *Oh yes,* Claire thought ruefully, *there are ways of ending your child's life, dear girl, but I'm not about to share them with you or even let you entertain this idea.*

With a stern and serious tone, Claire looked at Meredith and replied, "I will not be part of any discussion that includes murdering an innocent child."

Meredith dropped her head back down on the table, though her sobs did not recommence. Without raising her head Meredith told Claire and Sari, "I didn't mean it, I couldn't. It's just I feel so hopeless!"

Claire looked at Sari. Then, she took a strong breath and answered, "Meredith, you are still small enough to hide your situation from others, so we have a bit of time. While you wait to hear back from Evan, it seems to me that we would be wise to do some research. Sit up, now, and let's make some plans."

Meredith raised her head. Sari nodded to her and smiled encouragingly. Meredith smiled weakly back and looked to Claire. "What do you think I should do?"

"I know that when we lived in Denver, years and years ago, there was talk of a home for unwed mothers. I will write to Daniel's sister in Denver and get some information."

Claire continued, "Before the war, our Ladies' group was a civic organization. We made blankets one year for the Wyoming State Children's home. I think it's actually called the "Wyoming Humane Society for the Protection of Animals and Children." I believe that the home used to be in Wheatland, but has now moved to Cheyenne. We could also write to them and inquire about services they offer for mothers and the procedures for accepting children for adoption."

Meredith stared at Claire, then slowly nodded. "I don't really think that I want to give away my baby, but, well, we could find out about it, I guess."

Before long, with the efficiency of a business meeting, Claire had turned the gathering from an emotional scene into a focused group with a mission. Each of them took on a letter to write, and they agreed they'd meet again in a couple of weeks to share what they'd learned.

"You won't tell Aunt Nell, will you?"

"Your aunt and I rarely speak to one another. No, your secret is secure with Sari and me."

"Good. Thank you. I just don't know what Aunt Nell or my Pa would do if they found out, but I'm afraid if they do. Religion is so important to them both, and they've been convinced for a long time that the devil has a hold of me. I know I'm a disappointment to them both and to God, and that I'm doomed to hell. I just don't want them to hurt my baby."

Claire's voice was soft and gentle, "I don't believe that having a child out of wedlock makes you unredeemable, Meredith."

"But Aunt Nell has told me that loose women are doomed. Since I came to live with her she had made me pray with her each morning. She tells me how bad I am because I disobeyed my Pa. She makes me read the Ten

Commandments out loud and talks to me about how fornicators should be stoned. She makes me repeat Bible verses every day to teach me that sinners go to hell, and I know she's right."

Meredith looked at the two women at the table then recited, "Psalm twenty-six, verse five: *I have hated the congregation of evil doers and will not sit with the wicked. And Psalm one, verses one and six: Blessed is the man that walketh not in the counsel of the ungodly, nor standeth in the way of sinners, nor sitteth in the seat of the scornful. For the Lord knoweth the way of the righteous, but the way of the ungodly shall perish.* First Corinthians fifteen thirty-three: *Be not deceived, evil communications corrupt good manners.* And then, Romans six, verse twenty-three: *The wages of sin is death.* It's right there in the Bible, I know I'm going to hell. I'm beyond help. If she found out about the baby, I don't know what she'd do."

Claire was clearly angry. "I'm sure that she hasn't made you memorize James three, verse seventeen or Ephesians two, though has she?" Meredith responded with a confused look and Claire continued, "In James we are told *The wisdom that is from above is first pure, then peaceable, gentle and easy to be intreated, full of mercy and good fruits, without partiality and without hypocrisy.* Your aunt's hypocrisy and finger-pointing keeps her from understanding God's love. You can't let her make you think you are beyond God's grace."

Meredith shook her head, "But I must be, Aunt Nell says sinners go to hell."

"But dear Meredith, we are all sinners. God does hate sin, but Ephesians two says God is rich in mercy and that by His grace we are saved through faith. Meredith, your aunt hasn't told you the whole story of God. That Romans passage you recited, that isn't the whole verse. The whole verse says *The wages of sin is death, but the gift of God is eternal life through Jesus Christ our Lord.* We all deserve death because we are all sinners, but Jesus came to offer us salvation. He died for us so that we can live with Him. I encourage you to read the Bible for yourself, not just the verses Nell pushes on you. Read Matthew, Mark, Luke and John. Those books tell the story of Jesus' life and His perfect love and forgiveness."

It was clear that talk of forgiveness and grace was foreign to Meredith, and it gave Sari an idea. "Meredith, it has taken me a long time to understand God's grace and forgiveness, and I know I'm still learning. Believing that God loves us when we are so undeserving is hard. What if you and I read the gospels together and talk about them? I'll bring my Bible to work, and we can find time to read a chapter, then talk about it while we are working together."

Meredith smiled for the first time, and nodded. "I'd like to know about a God who loves me and doesn't just want to damn me."

Standing at the front door a few minutes later, Sari watched Claire hug Meredith then hold her for a moment by the shoulders and tell her, "Meredith, should your aunt find out about your condition, or if anything makes you feel unsafe for you or your baby before you have all the information you need to make a good decision for yourself and your child, I hope you will come immediately to either Sari or me. We will stand with you through this, and will offer you all the help we can."

Meredith answered her with a tight hug, then another for Sari.

It was nearly closing time, and Nathan was tired. He'd helped Dawson unload a large shipment of lumber and his knees ached nearly as badly as his back did. He stretched, feeling old and tired, when the bell jangled, telling him someone had come in up front. He stepped around the corner and felt better with one glimpse of the new arrival. Sari was leaning against the front counter, peering into the candy dish. "You are nearly out of root beer barrels," she teased without looking up.

Refreshed just by her presence, Nathan gave her an exaggerated shrug, then came around the counter and added a hug.

"How's my favorite almost-daughter?"

Sari loved the name he'd coined for her. "My feet are tired and I cut my finger paring potatoes today, so I'm a little crabby," she answered.

"Oh, sorry, I don't need any crabs, I have plenty of my own."

Laughing, Sari scooted onto the stool at the counter and sat down. "I actually came to pick up that invoice Dawson left here the other day. I need it to update the ledger for the livery."

In a moment, Nathan handed it to Sari, then sat on the stool beside her. "Are you working too hard? You certainly have a lot of responsibilities, what with keeping the books for the livery and working long hours at the restaurant."

Sari loved the concern in his voice. "I'm fine. Don't worry about that. I enjoy doing the ledgers, it's a fun challenge. But, please don't ever stop worrying about me completely, it's so nice to know you care."

Nathan understood, "I can't imagine how alone you felt when you were sent away where no one knew you."

Sari shuddered before answering, "I'm thankful that part of my life is over. I am so blessed to have you and Jesse's family, and a few friends. Being alone is the hardest thing in the world, I think."

"I agree." Nathan put his hand of Sari's shoulder. "Don't go away, I have something for you."

"For me? Another receipt?"

"Just wait." Nathan disappeared into the back room for a moment, returning with a rectangular package wrapped in brown paper. "You might know that my sister and her husband are moving to Cheyenne. She and my mother are going through the attic at Mother's and they found some things of mine. This was in one of the boxes."

Sari accepted the parcel and carefully removed the paper cover. Behind the glass of an old picture frame were her mother and father and an eight-year-old Sari with a perfect face. Sari could almost smell her mother's lilac cologne as she absorbed every detail. Her father sat on an oak Queen Anne chair in front of the fire place in the family's sitting room. He wasn't smiling, but his eyes were merry as he held hands with the unscarred child standing on his left. Her mother, standing on his other side with her hand on her husband's shoulder, wore a simple, dark floor-length skirt and button-up blouse with mutton sleeves.

Sari sat transfixed for a time, studying the images of those three people she loved and missed so dearly. She was transported back to the day a travelling photographer had rumbled his wagon into the yard. She'd been so surprised when her father agreed to sit for the portrait. Sari remembered how hard it was to stand still for so long as the photograph was taken. She'd wiggled on the first exposure, and they'd had to try it a second time. "How did you come to have this?"

"Your mother gave it to me and asked me to make this frame for it. I never got the finished product delivered to her. As soon as I saw it, I knew you'd like to have it."

Words failed her. Instead, she hugged Nathan tightly as she cried. "I know just the place I can hang this so that I can see it every day. Oh, Nathan, thank you."

Nearly four weeks after Sari, Claire, and Meredith had first met together, the three women sat once again at Sari's table. "I guess I expected this," Meredith sniffled. Claire and Sari, despite the girl's tears, were impressed at how stoic Meredith appeared. She'd just read them the letter she'd received from Evan. "Getting his letter and reading his words didn't cut as deeply as I thought they might." Meredith sat at Sari's table, nursing a cup of warm milk. "Having him claim that he can't take responsibility for 'it' since he isn't assured he's the father was a low blow, though."

She stopped, staring at her hands. "Now I can't wait anymore. Crispus has come for dinner twice, and Aunt Nell keeps giving me funny looks. Yesterday, Lilith stared at me for a long time as I was cutting up chicken for dinner. I think she was about to come talk with me when Mr. Wills called her."

Sari reached over and put her hand on Meredith's arm. "I think you'll be pleased about what Claire has discovered."

The hope and trust Claire saw in Meredith's eyes made her want to cry. She cleared her throat and smiled. "Yes, I received a letter Monday from Mrs.

Young, the matron at Cottage House in Denver. She is willing to take you as a resident as soon as you want to go."

Meredith asked quietly, "What kind of a place is it, do you think?"

"Well, the good news is this, I asked Daniel's sister Addie to go there so that we would know more. Her letter about that fact-finding trip arrived yesterday. You are welcome to read it, but since Sari hasn't had a chance to read it either, I'll fill you both in. Cottage House was established in the 1880s for girls just like you. They call them "betrayed, misled or unfortunate."

Sari was watching Meredith as they listened. "That's encouraging, it sounds as if they are sympathetic not blaming."

Claire continued as Meredith nodded slightly, "It is on Fairfax Street in the southwest of Denver. Addie says it's a brick, three-story building with a garden and a separate laundry building. She was impressed with Mrs. Young and how clean and welcoming the place is. She described her as motherly and kind. The house has a medical license, so the residents give birth right there, helped by a female doctor as well as a male doctor and several female assistants. Everyone she met there, including several of the girls, seemed happy and healthy."

Meredith slipped her hands into her lap, hoping that Sari and Claire wouldn't see that they were shaking. "It sounds like a good place, but I don't have any money. How would I pay them?"

"They charge three dollars per week while you live there, but they understand if you can't pay right away. All they ask is that you *try* to pay them back after you leave."

Sari asked what Meredith was thinking, "I wonder how they pay the bills?"

"The brochure I received along with Addie's letter says that the Women's Temperance Union is a sponsor. They also receive food and donations from several businesses. While you are living there, they

will also help train you for a job, so that after you've
delivered you can support yourself."

"But what about the baby?"

"Meredith, Cottage House encourages unwed
mothers to give their children up for adoption. They
work with parents who want to adopt, helping you
take care of the legal issues associated with all that."

"But I don't know if I can just give away my
baby. What if decide I want to keep her or him?"

"They do support adoption, but they won't force
you into anything you don't want. Addie spoke at
length with Mrs. Young about that."

The room was quiet for a long time. Claire and
Sari waited. Claire's heart broke to look at Meredith.
Finally, she looked up, "I'm scared to go so far away
and live with strangers, but I'm more scared of Aunt
Nell and my Pa, so I think I should go to Cottage
House."

"I think that's a prudent choice. Addie has
offered to meet you at the train station and take you
to Cottage House, if that would help."

"Wow, that would be very kind. Yes, I think
that is what's best for me and for the baby." Meredith
said with conviction. "But, what will I tell Aunt Nell?
Or the Wills? When will I go?"

On Sunday morning, Meredith carried out the
plan they'd devised. Claiming a head ache, she stayed
in bed until her aunt and uncle left for church. As
soon as they were gone, she dressed and packed her
belongings into a carpetbag Claire had given her.
Leaving one letter for her parents and aunt and one
for the Wills explaining that she was leaving but with
no other details, she slipped out of the house. Claire
and Sari drove her to the train depot on the outskirts
of Encampment. After tears and hugs, they watched
the train pull away.

30
Encampment, Wyoming
mid – July, 1918

"Sari, is that a new dress? It looks so pretty on you," Claire remarked as the family came out of the church after Sunday services.

"I ordered it from Sears and Roebuck, it arrived last week." Sari answered, shyly adding, "It's a present from Jesse. In one of his letters he insisted that he wanted to get me a blue dress to match my eyes. But of course under the circumstances he couldn't buy it himself. After I ordered it, I sent him the page from the catalog to show him what he gave me."

Even Daniel, who was standing with the ladies chuckled at Sari's story. "You two are always giving gifts to one another. Have you heard from Jesse since you mailed him that copy of Zane Gray's new novel?"

"Yes, he got *Wildfire* last month. He wrote to say he liked it, and has already shared it with one of the men in his platoon. I also sent *His Last Bow*, the latest Sherlock Holmes novel by Arthur Conan Doyle in that same package. He didn't like it as well."

"I don't blame him. I'd rather read about cowboys than detectives myself."

"It's funny," Claire noted, "You wouldn't think a man would have time in the middle of a war to read a book, but I think Jesse has read more since he got to France than he ever did growing up."

Sari tried to recall how Jesse had phrased it, "He says that a great deal of the time is concerned with staying awake, with brief periods of terror and chaos mixed in."

"It makes me sick to think about it," Claire said quietly.

Daniel wanted to derail the train of thought they'd embarked on, so he changed the subject. "Sari, how is your Victory Garden doing?"

"Well, I'm managing to keep most of the weeds out, but I'm not sure it's getting enough water. I've been getting home late from the restaurant, and I'm often tired and forget to go check on it."

"I hate that you are back to working fourteen-hour days again. I thought Jesse helped you get that schedule stopped." Claire had been concerned for several weeks with how pale and tired Sari seemed.

"Well, since Meredith, um, moved away, there hasn't been anyone else but me doing the cooking. Mr. Wills did agree to changing the times we serve meals, so breakfast isn't quite as early and dinner service ends at 6:30, but my hours have lengthened."

Daniel leaned toward Sari so that their shoulders were touching. "Do you need me to help you intervene? I promised Jesse I wouldn't let that man take advantage of you again."

Sari appreciated the concern in Daniel's offer. "I think it's alright. I did put my foot down about not working on Sundays. He didn't like it, but he agreed."

"Just remember I'm here if you need me."

"Thank you," Sari answered. Claire and Daniel still did not know the real reason Sari worked, and she was happy to keep it private. The argument about Sundays she'd had with Mr. Wills had been filled with threats of dire consequences, but when Sari didn't give in, Wills backed down. Sari knew that without the confidence she'd gained from Jesse, she could never have advocated for herself without giving in. Even though she was working much more, it felt like a win to her.

"Anyway," Claire responded, "Is there anything we can do to help with your garden?"

"You know, I probably could use a little help with watering."

"I'll start sending Greg over in the mornings to do that for you." Daniel put his arm around Claire. "Are you ready to head home, my dear?"

"Yes. Sari, I have a pot roast for dinner tonight. We'll see you later, right?"

"Of course. I made a cherry pie. When the cherry man came to the Copper Pot the other day, I bought some for myself, they looked so wonderful. How about if I bring it tonight?"

"Perfect."

The house was hot when Sari got home. The July sun seemed relentless, especially with the absence of a breeze. She changed her clothes, opting for a light gingham frock, then chose two books from her bedside. Armed with *Collected Sonnets* by Edna St. Vincent Millay and *A Short History of England* by G.K. Chesterton, she retreated to the front porch in search of a cool spot to rest. She smiled as she carried the volumes through the house. Thanks to Alice Peryam at the Roadhouse, Sari had a seemingly endless supply of great books to read. Once or twice a month, Claire and Sari made the short drive to Riverside to visit Alice, exchange books, and visit. Sari thought Alice Peryam was delightful. The mother of six sons and one daughter, Alice was full of stories. When Claire and Sari had been there last, Alice entertained them with a memory from the late 1870s when her second son, Ben was an infant. "There was this Cavalry captain stationed with his wife at Fort Steele. She was a pretty little thing, but for some reason they were unable to have children of their own. They took one look at Benjamin and offered me ten thousand dollars on the spot if I'd give him to them. I remember her large brown eyes as she told me that it would be easy for me to have another child, and that they'd take real good care of Ben."

Sari sat down on the porch smiling as she heard again in her memory Alice's tinkling laughter at the end of her story.

Sweating, Sari chose the Chesterton, and settled in.

She'd been reading for close to an hour when she heard Bea call her name. Looking up, she waved. "Come on over, I have lemonade," Sari called.

Both Bea and Harriet crossed the street together and then settled themselves on Sari's porch. "Whew, it is a little cooler over here. You are on the shady side of the street," Bea spoke as she wiped the beaded sweat from her upper lip.

Harriet fanned herself with a dainty lace fan and agreed. "Yes, we have that huge tree in our yard, but it doesn't seem to help much."

Sari excused herself, and came back a few moments later with a tall glass for each of them. "I haven't seen Royce today, is he working?"

"No, he has the afternoon off. He is currently snoring on the couch, that's why Harri and I decided to come see you, to get away from the noise." The ladies relaxed into light gossip and chatter.

The sisters asked Sari about Jesse. She'd just begun telling them about his latest letter when a brand new, shiny, Maroon-colored Ford Model A came down the street and stopped in front of the Rogers' house. Sari fell silent as they watched a man dressed in a black suit emerge from the driver's seat, step up the walk, and knock at the door. Before Harriet could react, Royce opened the front door and had a short conversation with the man.

"I think that is Councilman Englehart. This must be something official," said Harriet quietly.

"I thought Mr. Englehart was the mayor," Bea countered.

"He was up until May, then he went on the council and Mr. Rankin became the Mayor. I think the voters have helped them exchange positions several times in the past few years," Harriet clarified.

Soon, Englehart and Royce, now dressed in his uniform, appeared on the porch. Royce looked across the street, said something to his companion, and walked across to the ladies.

"Good afternoon Sari," Royce began. She smiled as he went on, "The telegraph office just got word of a casualty in Europe."

Sari's heart dropped and she felt instantly cold.

"Evan Wiley has been killed. George and I are going to drive out to his mother's ranch and take them the news."

"That's awful," Harriet said. "What happened?"

"A ship he was on took fire from a German U-Boat. It sank. He didn't survive."

The initial relief Sari had felt that it wasn't Jesse was replaced by grief for Meredith and Dawson. "Evan's brother Dawson lives just a few blocks away," she told Royce.

Royce nodded. "We are on our way there first. We'll take him out to the ranch with us if he wants to go. Harriet, don't wait dinner for me. I don't know how long we'll be."

In silence, the women watched as the car drove away.

Sari struggled the next day at work to keep her mind on what she was doing. She had never met Evan, so she wasn't grieving him, but she cared for Dawson and felt the pain of his loss.

Meredith was another matter. When Sari shared the news with Claire last evening, Claire summed up both of their feelings, "I can't help but wonder if this isn't actually a blessing in disguise for Meredith. I think she was still harboring hope that he'd come back to her after the war."

Now, as the afternoon dragged by, Sari's thoughts were on the coming evening. She and Claire agreed they had to give Meredith the sad news as soon as possible. They considered sending a letter, or even asking Daniel's sister Addie to go to Cottage Home and tell Meredith in person. In the end, they finally decided that they would telephone her instead.

Monday evenings were usually easy, and tonight business at the Copper Pot had been especially light, so by six forty-five, Sari was thankful that she was nearly ready to leave. *I'll head straight to Claire's to use her telephone. When we've talked to Meredith, maybe I can stop thinking about it,* she told herself.

Sari finished the last of the dishes and dried her hands. When she turned around, Dawson was standing at the back door. His hair was disheveled, his clothes dusty. He looked weary and worn.

"Dawson," Sari stepped forward. "I am so sorry to hear about your brother. How is your mother?"

"Thank you. She's taking it pretty hard."

"Is there anything I can do?"

"Where is she, Sari?"

The question surprised her. "What?"

"I know you know where Meredith is. You are her closest friend." Sari stammered, unsure how to answer. "Sari, listen, I'm not blind. I caught Evan and Meredith together at my house, I can guess why she left town. I've known her since she was a child. To tell the truth, I wanted to court her but her father didn't see me as a suitable match for her with my bum leg. I care about her and I can guess how this news is going to distress her. Please, I just want to talk with her. Where is she?"

Sari didn't want to betray the secret and she hesitated. Dawson tried again, "Evan was always favored by both my parents. My mother is beside herself right now, she lost my father and now her son. She has a right to know about the grandchild she has on the way, and I want to make sure that Meredith and the child are cared for. Evan may have been a roughneck, but family needs to look out for family."

Probably Sari gave in more because of how much she respected Dawson than any other reason, but quietly she responded, "Meredith is living at a place called Cottage House in Denver. It is a home for unwed mothers. I've received several letters from her. She is healthy and happy there. They are teaching her secretarial skills along with how to be a good mother."

Dawson let out a breath and nodded. "Thank you. Does she know, a—about Evan yet?"

"No. I am planning to go to Claire's this evening to telephone her with the news."

"I see." Sari thought Dawson wanted to say more. Instead, he fidgeted with his hat as he went on to tell Sari that he needed to take a few days off from the livery. "The navy didn't recover Evan's body, so we have nothing to bury, but my mother wants to put a headstone for him next to my father's out at our family cemetery plot on the ranch. I need to get a stone cross for him and I've talked to Pastor Abraham about coming out on Saturday to say a few words for Mother to hear, and he's agreed. I'll send messages to our clients explaining why their deliveries will be late, I don't think there will be any problem."

"Of course you need to take off. I'm sure our clients will understand. Perhaps you could talk with Nathan Jameson about having one of his men help out if something needs done. I'll ask my nephews to take care of the horses while you are gone."

Sari watched Dawson walk away a few minutes later. Then she walked to Claire's to call Meredith.

31
near Amiens, France
late - July, 1918

On the surface, the officers acted as if everything were the same, but just underneath, the current of anticipation was strong enough to let every man in camp know something big was coming. Fighting continued, but without much energy from either side. Though the German army was outnumbered by Allied troops, the war had degenerated into a war of attrition. Neither side seemed motivated to change that. But then at the end of July, General Pershing himself, along with General MacArthur, arrived to oversee the relocation of the bulk of the 2nd Cavalry Division farther east. It was Pershing's decision as well that kept Jesse's platoon and a small contingent of soldiers behind. They were tasked with acting as support for the British, Australian, French and Canadian forces that were building on the outskirts of Amiens.

"It's been three days since 'ole Pershing abandoned us here," Rex groused as he sat at chow next to Jesse. "I already was feeling like an extra wheel on a pony cart since they've mechanized nearly all the divisions, but now they've left us behind, too."

"I'm not too upset about that," Griffin, who was sitting across the table next to Baird argued. "From all the whispering, it sounds like Pershing is gearing up for a huge offensive, one that will include cavalry as well as mechanized forces. I'm happy to be staying out of it."

Jesse agreed, "After you took fire and had that horse shot out from under you, Rex, I'd have guessed you'd be happy to stay back."

Rex groaned. "It's not that I really want to get into the fight, I just want to get this whole ugly mess over with so we can go home."

Jesse had heard this rant from Rex before. Trying to change the subject, he asked Baird, "Did you finish reading *The Treasure of Hidden Valley* yet?"

"I'm nearly done with it. It's pretty good."

"I haven't heard of that one. Who is the author?"

The question came from a Canadian sergeant eating nearby.

Jesse answered, "Author's name is George Emerson. He isn't very well known."

"Well then where'd you hear of him?"

"Truth is, I knew him. He was part of a group of men who pretty much founded the town in Wyoming that I come from. Though this book is a fictional story, it is set in the mountains I consider home, and many of the characters in it are real people I know. My wife sent it to me."

Rex snickered, "Yeah, I noticed the handwritten dedication at the front, *To my husband – so you can read about your mountains even when you are far away. Love Sari* I was glad she didn't get any mushier or add hearts and kisses."

Good-natured ribbing about the books and cookies Jesse often received continued as they finished breakfast. Rex and Griffin were both single, and they enjoyed watching Jesse's face redden when they teased him. Jesse didn't take offense, he knew they quietly envied the steady stream of letters and treats he received and shared.

After breakfast, Jesse sent Rex and Griffin off to feed and water the horses as he prepared to do some repair work for one of the Australian tank brigades. He leaned against the door jamb, trying to catch some fresh, cool air as he waited for the forge to heat up and thought about Sari. There was no doubt that their correspondence had changed. At first, her letters were overformal, almost stilted, and he knew his had been as well. Now, though, there was a comfort and intimacy in Sari's letters that warmed him and encouraged him. Admittedly, since he'd left Wyoming, he'd had a few bouts of something close to regret about their quick marriage. *Close to,* he emphasized in his thoughts, *but not actual regret. I don't think I could ever be sorry I married her. I still know it was the right thing to do. I just didn't spend much time thinking about how it would be if I did make it back home. We didn't pretend to know or love one another. Now, though, it feels different. I look forward to her letters, and I feel hopeful that if I do see the end of this war and head home, I might just be going back to someone who will welcome me as her partner and husband.*

He'd worked up a sweat at the forge when a shadow in the doorway made Jesse look up from the metal brake he was using to bend a sheet of tin. Not recognizing the silhouette there, he nodded and continued his task. When he'd finished the bend and assured himself that the metal would fit over the angle iron he'd forged earlier, he put both pieces on the work table and turned around. He grabbed a towel to wipe the sweat from his face and approached the figure at the door.

"You Sergeant Atley?"

Standing closer, Jesse could see that the soldier was a British corporal. "Yes, I am."

"I've been asked by me leftenent to find ya and request that ya come to the headquarters tent of *Lieutenant* General Sir Charles Kavanagh of the British Cavalry Corps as soon as ya can."

"Well, Corporal, usually one of my men takes courier missions, both of them are fine riders. You can find them just across here over near Corral B."

He started to turn when the corporal replied, "Beggin' yer pardon, sir, but they's asked specifically for Sergeant Atley. No ones else."

Jesse studied the man for a moment, then nodded. "It will take me a few minutes to change. If you'd go across and ask one of my men to saddle the big sorrel gelding, I'd appreciate it."

"Yes, Sir."

Jesse was both irritated at the interruption and thankful for the relief from his routine. A few minutes later he wound around through a labyrinth of tents before he finally located the headquarters tent for the British Cavalry Corps.

He identified himself to the sentry and was immediately escorted to a desk in the back. In contrast to the austere and easy to disassemble and transport furnishing of an American battalion leader, the office Jesse was shown was replete with a large, shiny oak desk. A matching book case sat to one side. On the other were two brocade, wing-back chairs surrounding a delicate oak table set with a complete silver tea set. Jesse felt disoriented, as if he'd traversed from the war in France to a manor in London with just a few steps.

"Sergeant Atley of the American Cavalry Corps to see you Sir," the corporal announced as they entered.

"You may present him, Corporal."

"Yes Sir. Sergeant, this is Lieutenant General Kavanagh, commander of the Cavalry Corps."

The man sitting at the desk looked up. Jesse guessed him to be in his mid-forties. His face was thin and horsey, his brown eyes resembled those of a basset hound, droopy and turned down. The man's nose was his most prominent feature, long and straight ending with a substantial knob above a thick, unruly mustache.

"Good of you to get here so quickly, Sergeant. I have a courier pouch that needs to go to Esnouveaux," he began. "I would send one of my own men, but they are all occupied relaying messages concerning our upcoming attack. General Pershing assured me that your corps would be available as needed."

"Yes, Sir. I'm available. Beg your pardon, though, I am unfamiliar with Esnouveaux. Do you have a map?"

"Of course." The Colonel gestured behind Jesse as he came around his desk. A large map was posted on the wall. "We are here, and there is the Esnouveaux training center, southeast of Paris."

Jesse studied the map and tried to keep the irritation from his voice. "Sir, that's a long trip, perhaps 250 miles or more. It will take me about four days on horseback if I take an extra mount. I didn't come prepared for an extended run."

Kavanagh nodded. "I apologize, Sergeant. I didn't specify. I don't need a rider, I need a man of rank and dependability. You will take the train from the station at Amiens, through Paris, then on to Esnouveaux. The orders affixed to the front of the courier pouch give you priority boarding and seating."

"Yes, Sir, thank you for the clarification."

"Well, then." He pulled a gold pocket watch from his breast pocket, studied it for a moment, then snapped it shut. "It's just after ten now. The train for Paris you'll want is scheduled to leave Amiens at eighteen hundred hours. You'll have to change trains there for Esnouveaux.

Put this directly into the hands of the leader of the AEF. I expect there may be return correspondence as well."

"Yes, Sir." Jesse repeated. He saluted and made a sharp about face. He'd glimpsed the colonel's watch and knew he had plenty of time to take the gelding back, pick up an extra shirt and his shaving kit, and leave for Amiens.

An hour later, Jesse caught a ride into Amiens with a French transport truck. They dropped him and a French soldier at the edge of town. "Sorry we can't take you all the way to the station, Sergeant," the driver told him in broken but understandable English. "We need to get these medical supplies delivered right away."

"No problem," Jesse answered. "I can get myself to the station."

"It's about a mile and a half that way," the driver answered, pointing.

Jesse thanked him and shouldered his rucksack. "Where are you headed, Private?" The young French soldier who'd disembarked with Jesse was carrying a satchel and a roll of papers.

"To one of the headquarters buildings," he answered with perfect English and a lilting French accent. "It is very near the train depot, so I can make sure you get to your train safely if you'd like."

"That would be very kind. We came through here on the train, but I was in the stock car tending horses, so I didn't see anything." Jesse put his hand out. "I'm Jesse Atley."

"Enchanté, Sir. My name is Etienne Degris."

They walked for a short way before the private began telling Jesse about the buildings they were passing.

"You know Amiens very well."

"Merci. But, I should. This is my home. My parents live only a few blocks north of the city square. My école only a few blocks away."

Jesse enjoyed the continuing tour. The young man was clearly proud to share his home with him.

They'd walked about half a mile when Etienne stopped at a busy crossroad. "We have been walking on the Rue Saint-Fucien," he said. "If you look just there," he pointed a distance down a crossroad at a brick house.

"You mean that brick house with the cupola at the edge?"

"Yes, that's it. That was the home of Monsieur Jules Verne. Do you know him?"

Jesse was surprised. "Yes, I've read several of his books. I didn't know he lived here."

"Oui, this was his home until he died in 1905. He served on our city council. I met him many times at the boulangerie."

"Wow. That's quite amazing. My wife loves Jules Verne's books."

"If I may, what time does your train leave?"

The change of subject was abrupt. "Well, the Colonel said six o'clock."

"Bon! Then you have time. To go to the train station, we should turn and go there." He pointed in the opposite direction of Jules Verne's home. "But I would hate for you to leave my Amiens without seeing the Cathedral de Notre-Dame. It is only a few blocks that way. Would you like to go?"

"But, do you have the time to show me?"

"Mais oui! I only need to get to the headquarters before lights out. I will stay with my parents tonight."

Jesse agreed and before long, the imposing walls of the cathedral came into view.

Etienne explained, "The cathedral de Notre-Dame is the tallest Gothic cathedral in France. It was built in the 1200s."

Jesse thoroughly enjoyed the tour and short venture into the cathedral. He was impressed at the size and magnificence of the structure and the detail of the stained glass.

As they turned away from the cathedral on their way to the Gare du Nord station, Etienne made a suggestion. "I know a small café just up the street. Perhaps you would like to stop and have something to eat before we get to the station?"

"That sounds great," Jesse answered.

There were four small tables on the sidewalk. Etienne led Jesse to the far table and sat down. The matron was a plump, rosy woman who spoke no English, so with Etienne's help, Jesse ordered bread and cheese and a bowl of onion soup. He sat, relishing the rare opportunity to let go of the war and enjoy the adventure of exploring France. He realized he'd had a wonderful afternoon, and began framing the letter he'd write to Sari to tell her about it.

"I'd love to bring my wife here someday. This is such a beautiful place."

"You must! And," Etienne rummaged in his satchel, retrieving a small piece of paper and a pencil. "I am writing down my name and address for you. Also, the names and address of my parents. When you come back, after we have kicked the Germans out of France and peace is restored, I would very much enjoy acting as host and guide for you and your wife."

Jesse was impressed with the young man's zeal and his kind, genuine offer. He took the paper and knew that they'd made a connection that would last, if they both survived the war.

"Thank you, I hope we will meet again."

"May I make just one more suggestion?"

"Of course."

Within minutes Jesse found himself in a small stall filled with books and trinkets. Etienne stood at the door, speaking familiarly with the bookseller as Jesse perused the shelves. Most of the books were in French, so when a copy of Verne's *From the Earth to the Moon* in English caught his attention, Jesse removed it from the self. The volume was a bit tattered, but that stopped mattering when Jesse opened it to the first page. Written in flowing script beneath the title was written, *"Je vous adresse mes meilleurs vœux- - Jules Verne"*. Jesse stared at it in amazement for a moment, unsure if that was actually Verne's signature. After showing it to Etienne and the proprietor of the store, he was assured that it was indeed the author's signature, and that the inscription in English was "Please accept my best wishes." Neither Frenchman was overly impressed with Jesse's find and Etienne assured him, "Nearly every volume here in Amiens has Monsieur Verne's inscription." With Etienne's help and encouragement a fair price, lower than Jesse feared, was agreed upon and the book was quickly wrapped in brown paper and string and tucked into his pack.

A few minutes later, Etienne helped secure his ticket on the train, and Jesse was thankful yet again for his companion. "Before the war, the trip from here to Paris takes only an hour and a quarter." Etienne told him. "Tonight, you will not be so lucky, my new friend. The conductor is telling me that they are scheduled to stop outside of Beauvais to take on some troops and that they expect to be delayed also at least four or five hours waiting for supply trains to move on the same tracks. I asked, and he does have a private berth available if you are interested."

Jesse hesitated. "I don't have much money with me. How expensive is that?"

After a quick conversation, Etienne assured Jesse, "Your courier orders cover all your expenses. I confirmed you wanted a private compartment."

Before long, Jesse bid adieu to Etienne, with the mutual hope that they would meet again, and boarded the train.

His compartment had a chair and small table, a narrow bunk, plus a sink and lavatory. Impressed with his good fortune, Jesse settled in. The train began its trek and he watched as open, rolling and hilly farmland shared the landscape with dense forested areas. He searched the passing countryside, trying to picture the scene before it was marred with trenches and other proof that war surrounded them. The sun was below the horizon and night was settling in when a porter knocked on the compartment door. With a mixture of languages and gestures, Jesse was eventually provided with some stationery and a fountain pen along with some water and a sandwich.

Jesse enjoyed the next hour as he recounted his tour of Amiens to Sari in a long letter. He felt refreshed just having something other than war and horses to write about. He finished the letter describing the book store and how nonchalant the others had been regarding Verne's inscription in the book. Trying to find the right words, Jesse watched himself in the reflection of the train window for a moment before he finished the letter. At last, he added the paper containing Etiennne's addresses into the envelope with a quick explanation in a P.S. Then he tucked the envelope into the book. He carefully re-wrapped the gift with the string and brown paper and addressed it, intending to make sure to mail it when he arrived at Esnouveaux. It wasn't long after that before the train's motion rocked him to sleep.

32
Encampment, Wyoming
August, 1918

Sari relished Sundays. It was pure luxury to remain in bed when she awoke without having to hurry up and prepare for work. Often, she reached for a book and spent time reading. This morning, she took a long, warm bath and allowed extra time to fix her hair and apply her makeup. She was dressed and ready for church with half an hour to spare, so she made herself a second cup of tea and stood looking out the kitchen window. She thought about the last letter she'd received from Jesse and his description of the ambulance wagons full of casualties rumbling by his tent. "I have all this because of him, and he suffers," she said aloud. Giving up meat two days a week, joining the Ladies' Aid Society, buying war bonds, growing a Victory Garden—all the ways she tried to support the war effort were so very paltry in comparison to what Jesse and all the soldiers were going through.

Claire and Daniel were waiting for Sari near the steps of the church when she arrived. With a quick hug from Claire and warm greetings from Daniel, the three entered the sanctuary and found seats on the left side toward the front. Michael and Greg straggled in a few moments later and sat down beside Daniel. Sari took a deep breath as the piano began playing, trying to dispel the guilt she felt as the recipient of the many blessings she had.

While they were singing the morning hymns, Sari caught a glimpse of Dawson sitting a few pews behind her. She'd never seen him at church before, and so his presence in the congregation was a surprise. *He got the news about his brother's death only three weeks ago, maybe his grief brought him to the Lord,* she thought.

"I needed that sermon," Claire told Sari as they filed out after the service. "It's easy to forget how mighty God is with this war going on." She sniffed and shook her head, trying to let go of her worry. "You haven't seen the news this morning, have you?"

Sari shook her head. "I haven't. I usually read the paper at the resta—" She broke off as the crowd in front of her cleared enough that she could see Dawson shaking hands with the pastor. "Oh my, Claire. Look who is with Dawson."

A few quick steps and Sari folded Dawson's companion into a strong hug. "Meredith! What a surprise to see you!"

Meredith hugged Sari, then stepped back, beaming. Her pregnancy was obvious beneath a grey cotton tent dress, and Sari thought at once how adorable she looked with her round face and rosy cheeks. Dawson cleared his throat and quietly said to the group, which now included Claire and Daniel as well as the minister, "I was just telling the pastor that my wife and I have moved into a house we just purchased on Heizer Avenue, across the street from the Lamberts. We are looking for a church to worship with." The look that Dawson gave Sari was a combination of hope and pleading.

There was a small pause as everyone considered the news before Claire recovered and said, "Your wife! Oh how marvelous!"

Hugs and handshakes sent the small group into happy chaos for a few minutes. Finally, Claire continued with a smile, "Dawson, I hope that you and Meredith will come for dinner this evening to our house. We'd like to celebrate your marriage."

Dawson looked at Meredith, who gave him a slight nod and shy smile. "We'd like that."

Plans were confirmed. As they watched the new couple walk away, Sari said quietly to Claire, "Dawson told me that family needed to take care of its own, but I didn't think he meant marrying Meredith."

"It's an honorable choice," Claire answered. "I won't fault either of them for it."

Sari agreed. "Dawson's serious, steadfast personality will be good for Meredith. He will protect her and help her mature."

Claire nodded. After a pause asked, "Do you have plans this afternoon? I could use help getting supper ready if you are willing."

"I'm willing."

319

"Great. Just come home with us now. I was going to invite you to come early anyway. Daniel and the boys are taking the horses out for a ride this afternoon, and I thought we could spend time together." Sari could tell something was worrying Claire, but she decided to wait and ask about it later.

"There, the chicken and noodle casserole is in the oven and you've snapped the green beans and sliced cucumbers and onions for the salad."

"They should be good with milk and vinegar over them as a dressing."

"Perfect." Claire dried her hands on her apron and left the kitchen. A moment later she was back. "I don't even want to show this to you," Claire said as she handed Sari the newspaper in her hand.

The room was quiet as Sari read the report of the Battle of Amiens. It described how under a heavy fog at four twenty-five on the morning of August ninth a major offensive began just east of Amiens. The reporter detailed how the opening salvo was a long barrage of tank fire that sounded like thunder and lasted a full four minutes. Sari cringed when she read of the hundreds of RAF planes in 'overwhelming numbers' that joined the assault as well as the observation balloons aloft to report troop movements. News of the battle was positive, many German soldiers were taken prisoner and the Germans were pushed back nearly nine miles in a short time.

Sari finished reading, then studied the map that accompanied the article showing the battle front east of the city. She had no idea exactly where Jesse was stationed. All she knew was that it was near Amiens, and that knowledge made her feel ill.

Finally, she looked up, her eyes brimming, to see Claire standing nearby, watching her and fighting her own tears. "The reporter who witnessed the beginning of the assault is so proud and excited. It's hard to understand that sort of thinking when what he describes means people are dying."

"I thought the same thing," Claire agreed.

"I wonder if we'd understand better if it were our town, our land."

"Maybe," Claire assented, "I can't even imagine that. I just wish it didn't take so long for news to get to us. I want to hear his voice, Sari, I want to hug my brother and know he's safe."

Sari stood up. She put her arms around Claire, holding her tight as she cried.

They'd put the paper away, dried their eyes, and found solace in baking a "Trench Cake" by the time Daniel and the boys returned and the newlyweds arrived.

The meal felt surprisingly comfortable. Sari watched as Claire and Daniel and the boys, without any hint of doubt or recrimination, accepted the couple's marriage. She had been the recipient of the same grace and welcome herself, and she found herself celebrating the ability to join them in passing it on.

When they'd finished eating, Claire suggested, "Daniel, why don't you take Dawson and the boys out on the front porch. We'll be out in a bit with dessert." Michael and Greg grinned and bolted from the table, excited to be released from clean-up duty. Dawson and Daniel were close behind them.

Soon the ladies had the kitchen to themselves. Suddenly, Meredith seemed shy and uncomfortable. Claire recognized her distress and told her, "Meredith, we are so glad things have worked out for you the way they have. Dear, please sit down. Let us clean up while you rest. You must be exhausted most of the time in this heat."

Meredith looked relieved and plopped down thankfully, "I'll be glad when the baby arrives, then maybe my feet will quit swelling up. Yesterday, I couldn't even get my shoes on."

Overall, Meredith reported, she was feeling pretty well. According to the doctors and Mrs. Young at Cottage House, her pregnancy had been quite an easy one so far. She reported that living at Cottage House had been a good experience for her, except for the looming fear that she would have to give up her child.

"I prayed and prayed that God would make a way for me to keep this little one," she told them as she patted her round belly. "Then, after Mrs. Young reminded me that I needed to make a decision and start the paperwork for adoption if that's what I was going to do, Dawson arrived. At first, they told him he couldn't see me, but he was real polite and insistent, and they called me in. Dawson explained how he was the baby's father and that he had made a mistake, and that he'd come for us, to marry me and take us home to be a family. When he told them he was a partner in a livery and that he'd purchased a house for us, well, then Mrs. Young wished us well and we went right then to the courthouse and got married."

"And now you have a home of your own." Claire was cutting generous pieces of cake as she spoke.

"Yes, when we came back from Denver, Dawson took me out to his family's ranch. Mother Wiley was surprised to see us, and she scolded Dawson about the baby—we haven't told her the truth, but after a while she calmed down and congratulated us. I stayed with her until this last Friday. It took that long for Dawson to get everything ready for me."

As Sari listened, she couldn't help but wonder if Meredith hadn't truly begun to believe that Dawson was her child's father. "So, have you seen your parents or your aunt?" Sari asked the question with trepidation.

"I wrote Ma and Aunt Nell letters telling them our news and asking for their support. Aunt Nell hasn't answered. Ma sent a note saying she'd try to come visit after the baby comes, as long as Pa doesn't find out."

"I'm sorry," Claire put her hand on Meredith's arm. "Let's not dwell on the negative tonight, shall we? Here, help me take the cake out to the porch."

Dawson and Daniel were talking about a new contract for the livery when the ladies came out. Claire served the cake and settled on the railing next to Daniel.

"This isn't your normal recipe is it?" Claire could tell Daniel was disappointed that it wasn't a rich, chocolate cake but was trying to sound complimentary.

She laughed as she answered. "No, this is a recipe I got from a magazine. It doesn't have eggs or butter in it. I'm trying to conserve for the war effort."

"Well," Daniel was good naturedly suspicious of the treat.

"It's called a Trench Cake," Claire explained. "The British Government put out the recipe suggesting wives and mothers send cakes to their boys in the trenches. Since they are made with only a few ingredients and with no butter or eggs, they aren't frivolous to make and they last a long time without spoiling."

"What's in this exactly?" Meredith asked.

"Brown sugar, raisins, shortening, water, cinnamon, cloves, baking powder, salt, flour, and powdered sugar," came Claire's answer. "It's very simple, and not bad, really."

Daniel nodded. "It actually is good." He didn't mask the surprise in his voice and the group chuckled.

Sari motioned for Claire to remain seated as she gathered plates a few minutes later. "I'll just stack these in the kitchen," she told Claire, to mollify her.

When Sari returned, the group was discussing current local news, intentionally avoiding the latest reports from Europe.

"Here's something interesting," Claire added. "I got a letter yesterday from my brother Marcus. He used to work for the Pinkerton Agency, but when President Taft was nearly assassinated in 1909 and the Secret Service was expanded, Marcus was recruited to work for them. Right now, he lives in New York City and works with a unit that investigates counterfeit money rings."

"I didn't know that," Sari replied. "That's so interesting."

"Yes, he's a really tough man who's had an exciting life," added Daniel. "I respect him a great deal."

Claire was clearly pleased at her husband's praise. "Well, anyway, in Marcus' latest letter, he mentioned that Boston and New York have had some serious trouble with that terrible influenza that hit Spain this spring. Marcus says that it started in Boston with just a couple of men who were sick, and within just a few days, thousands were ill."

Dawson shook his head. "That doesn't make sense. If it's so bad why hasn't there been anything in the papers about it?"

"Marcus told me not to trust the news reports on this. Since President Wilson signed the Sedition Act, the papers don't dare publish news about it."

"The Sedition Act?" Sari hadn't heard of it.

Daniel answered, "The Sedition Act makes it a punishable crime to speak, write, print or publish anything disloyal or, in plain fact, negative about the government. Have you noticed the poster up at the post office?" Sari shook her head. "Look at it when you next go. It says that anyone who is spreading pessimistic stories should be turned in to the Justice Department. People are interpreting that to mean negative factual stories as well as propaganda. It's outrageous."

"I read that poster," Dawson agreed. "It says that even cries for peace or anything that belittles the war effort should be reported."

"It's a horrible slight to the first amendment," Claire fumed.

Daniel interrupted her, "Yes, it is, but our president felt something was necessary to make sure that we, as a country, remained united in the war effort."

"The end result, though, is that Marcus says the news of this awful epidemic is being squelched, and that's dangerous. He's promised to keep me informed."

Dawson glanced at Meredith, grinning. "You look as if you are about to fall asleep," he said softly.

"It has been a busy few days," she answered. "I guess I am pretty tired."

Dawson stood up then helped her up. "Thank you so much for having us to dinner, we appreciate it a lot."

There was no mistaking his deeper meaning. Sari could see in his eyes that he'd been concerned that his marriage to Meredith would be disparaged, and the acceptance he'd met instead boosted his confidence and dispelled his fears.

As Sari and Claire stood together at the sink finishing the dessert dishes after the couple left, they discussed the situation.

"What do you think about their marriage?" Sari asked.

Claire answered slowly. "Dawson and Meredith have invented a new reality for themselves. I understand their decision to omit Evan from their story."

As she dried the dishes Sari nodded, "I feel alright about accepting the story as they tell it. The truth about the baby's father would only complicate things, I suppose."

Claire agreed. "Many of us have made choices when we were young that we regret. It seems that God's grace and mercy are at work here more than anything else."

"With very few family members to support them, I feel like it is up to us to step in," Sari offered.

"I completely agree. She's so young and inexperienced. Since she's the youngest in her family, I'll bet she hasn't been around babies or children often. She's going to need kind advice and encouragement about being a mother."

Sari dried a pot and put it on the shelf above the stove. "Claire, I read in a *Ladies' Home Journal* that a new tradition is starting among women back east. Friends are hostessing parties called 'showers' for new mothers. They serve special tea cakes and mints, and those invited bring gifts for the baby and mother."

"That sounds like fun. I'm sure Meredith would appreciate being showered with gifts and friendship. Who would we invite?"

Sari loved Claire's willingness and enthusiasm. "Do you think we could invite the members of Ladies' Aid, and also some women from the church?"

"Yes, of course! I'll ask Ella Parkison to make a cake, and I'm sure that Alice Peryam will come as well."

"We could send out invitations and make it festive and special. I'd be happy to have the party at my house," Sari concluded, then stopped. "Claire, this whole town will know that Meredith was expecting long before Dawson married her, if everyone doesn't know already. Do you think a party is appropriate?"

Claire frowned. "There will always be the mean-spirited—like Mary Nell Baker—who judge and gossip.

Maybe by inviting a good many ladies and celebrating the birth of this innocent child, we will discourage gossip and ugly chatter and promote Meredith's acceptance into our town's society."

"I think it's worth the risk." Sari said after she considered it. "Let's set a date right now, then I'll recruit Bea to help me make the invitations."

"Great. I'll talk to Ella. This is going to be fun, Sari."

"I hope so."

They looked at the calendar and settled on a Tuesday evening three weeks away.

Claire and Sari were excited at the prospect of a festive gathering. "I'll talk with Meredith and tell her our plans for a shower." Sari mused. "You know, I think I'll invite her to come to the Ladies' Aid meeting this week. We can introduce her as a married woman and people can get to know her."

"That's a good idea. If she and we don't act guilty or ashamed, then others will be likely to accept her as well."

Daniel wrapped his arms around Claire when she slipped into bed beside him that night. "How can your feet be cold when it is a warm summer night?" he teased.

She snuggled in close, laying her head on his chest, listening to his heart beat. "Daniel, Marcus' warning about influenza has me a little spooked. Thousands of people died in Spain as a result of this disease. If the papers aren't covering the progress of it here in America, how will we know how to keep the boys safe?"

Daniel considered her fears. She thought he'd fallen asleep when he answered, "Maybe it would be a good idea to have a plan in case the outbreak comes here. The boys and I haven't been up to our house in Dillon yet this summer. What if I take them up for a few days, to make sure everything is secure up there and that we have plenty of wood cut and stacked? I could even take some staples like canned goods, flour, salt, and things we can store in jars and pots, so that if we needed to, we could escape to the mountains."

Claire loved how practically and calmly her husband approached problems. "I don't want the boys to be afraid."

"We won't tell them why we are doing it. We'll just go up like we have in the past to have some fun."

Claire fell asleep, relieved and secure in Daniel's embrace.

On Tuesday, in the lull of the afternoon, Sari slipped away from the Copper Pot intending to stop briefly at Meredith's and then at the post office while Lilith kept an eye on the pot roast.

With Dawson's directions from Sunday evening, Sari easily found the house on Macfarlane that he'd purchased and moved his bride into. Meredith greeted her at the door, and Sari was surprised as she toured Meredith and Dawson's new home. Sari'd expected sparse furnishings, but was instead met with a warm, inviting, and fully furnished place. By way of explanation, Meredith described how her mother-in-law's ranch included not only the home she raised Dawson and his brother in, but a second that had belonged to Dawson's grandparents.

"Dawson and I were surprised when his mother suggested we consider using some of the furnishings from his grandmother's house. The family hadn't even been in the house for years. When his grandmother died, Dawson's mother covered all the furnishings with heavy sheets, then they closed up the house, and that preserved mostly everything."

"This is a beautiful home, Meredith," Sari said, meaning it. "You have it arranged and decorated so well." They moved into the parlor, and Meredith offered Sari a glass of water.

Meredith nodded and became serious as she replied, "Thank you. Thank you for being my friend and not scolding me for keeping the baby and marrying Dawson."

"I, well, I only want what is best, for you and, well, the baby and Dawson also. When I encouraged you to go away, and even to consider adopting the baby out, that was my goal. As it is, I'm glad you are home, I've missed you terribly in the last weeks."

Meredith stood up suddenly and pulled Sari up into a hug. "Oh Sari, I felt so alone there, even though everyone was kind. I didn't tell the whole story about when Dawson came. At first, I said no to his offer. I was afraid of Aunt Nell and the gossips in this town, and I didn't want to come back here. I was afraid Dawson would let me down just like Evan had. I feared keeping my baby and also giving it away. I felt so lost. Dawson seemed to understand all that. He told me that ever since I was a little girl, he had cared for me. He talked about how jealous he'd been of Evan and how angry he'd been that Evan didn't treat me respectfully. He convinced me that if we, he and I, worked together, we could grow our friendship and the feelings we've always had for each other into something good and lasting. He persuaded me that we could make a life for ourselves. I've come back determined to be the best wife and mother I can be."

Sari was impressed at the conviction she heard in her friend's words and also with a new undercurrent of maturity and responsibility that she'd never seen before in Meredith. "I believe you, and I know that you can and will succeed if you stay strong."

A few minutes later Sari reluctantly told Meredith, "I can only stay a minute more. I'm only on my break. I have two things to talk with you about before I go, though. First, I want to invite you to come with me to the Ladies' Society meeting on Thursday. It will be a way for you to be introduced into the community of ladies in Encampment."

"I don't know about going to a meeting. Look at me. I'm a newlywed and as large as a house. I'm not sure everyone will understand like you and Claire."

"Claire and I talked about this and we think you should come. If you are kind and confident, and hold your head up, soon everyone will forget about any questions of timing they have. Come on Thursday evening, Claire and I will be with you to face the ladies and begin to show them who you are."

"Women like my aunt will never forget."

"That may be true, and we can't control that, but many will welcome you, you'll see. Please come."

Hesitantly, Meredith agreed. "I'll try it once and see how it goes."

"Great," Sari exhaled with relief. "Now there's something else." At first Meredith balked at Sari and Claire's plan to hostess a shower for her. Eventually, though, Sari's enthusiasm for the celebration won her over.

"I really have to leave," Sari announced a few minutes later. "I have to get back to work."

On her way to the post office a few minutes later, Sari prayed for Meredith and Dawson, asking God to continue to grow them into a strong couple and to quiet the rumors and gossip.

Sari ducked into the post office and all thoughts of Meredith were temporarily forgotten, replaced by the surprise of receiving a small package in the mail from Jesse. The postmark assured her that ten days ago, Jesse was fine. *A lot can happen in ten days, though,* she told herself, *and with the news of battles so close, how can we know that he is alright today?*

As always, she decided to delay opening the package until she got home. The anticipation of uncovering the contents helped her through a busy afternoon filled with finicky customers and several jibes and sneers from Mr. Wills.

That evening she bathed, then fixed herself a light supper. She liked to make opening Jesse's letters tiny celebrations, and felt that a parcel deserved even more. Finally, she settled into her chair and as Mozart played on the gramophone she carefully untied the string and pulled off the tape to reveal a worn book.

Sari was thrilled. She'd never read *From the Earth to the Moon.* She sat the envelope with Jesse's letter aside at first, and examined the volume, stopping abruptly at the sight of the book's inscription and Jules Verne's signature. "Oh, my," she said aloud, awed. She adored the book for several minutes before laying it aside and opening Jesse's letter. Smiling through most of it, she felt as if she could almost see the flying buttresses of the cathedral, taste the bitterness of the French coffee he'd enjoyed at the bistro, and had walked with Jesse through the aisles of the tiny, dusty book store. She was delighted that he was able to translate Verne's inscription for her. When she got to the end of the letter, though, her tears began to fall.

> *My dear Sari, when I saw this volume I knew I wanted it for you. My first thought was that it would be a perfect birthday present for you. Then I realized that I have no idea when your birthday is. There's so much we don't know about each other. Perhaps, I've missed it, or maybe it is coming soon. Either way, please accept this with my heartfelt wishes that you have a wonderful day. And so you know, my own birthday is April 7th. Love, Jesse*

"It's May sixth," she whispered. She read and re-read that paragraph, savoring the care and kindness it revealed. She stared at his closing for a long time. It was the first time he'd ended a letter that way, and she wondered, *Could he really mean it?*

33
near Amiens, France
August, 1918

Jesse returned to camp outside of Amiens late in the evening on August sixth. He was awakened by the roar of large guns and the drone of aircraft overhead just after four the next morning. For the next three days the camp was a controlled, noisy war machine bent on supporting the five hundred tanks, nineteen hundred planes and balloons, and seventy-five thousand men engaged in the battle. News that the Allied forces punched through over eight miles into the enemy's lines buoyed them all, though watching the steady stream of both Allied casualties and German prisoners reminded them of the cost.

Rumor had it that Commander Rawlinson was ecstatic at the success of the campaign, though they all knew that this was only the first step in defeating the German army. Six days later, Jesse and his platoon received orders to relocate. It didn't take long before they found themselves rejoined with American forces outside the town of St. Mihiel, two hundred miles nearly straight east of Paris and just a hundred miles south of Luxembourg, Belgium.

As he settled into the new camp, Jesse learned that the Germans in this area caused continual trouble for the Allies by disrupting supply lines and communications. The United States Army was called upon for help by the Allies, and they had given General Pershing the St. Mihiel sector. Pershing had big plans for a large offensive, led by his four American divisions, to push back the Germans in the area.

Just as before, Jesse and his platoon were tasked with caring for the horses, using the forge for repairs, and occasionally running messages. While specific plans were not announced to the troops, Jesse had insight into the planning of the operation through his courier duties. Often, after delivering a message or packet of papers, he was asked to wait for return messages. During those times, conversations between commanders and advisors were sometimes conducted in Jesse's hearing so that he was able to get a picture of the magnitude of the upcoming campaign. Twice, Jesse delivered messages to General Pershing himself. Jesse was impressed with the man. Pershing's kind eyes and warm, easy smile welcomed Jesse as he entered the headquarters tent while his decisive and confident demeanor reassured all around him of his capacity to lead the forces successfully.

It was clear that Pershing was involving himself in every aspect of the offensive. His detailed orders and objectives let each commander know exactly what to do in each contingency. Certainly, there were those who disparaged Pershing's detailed management, but most were encouraged.

Jesse, on his second trip to headquarters, overheard two commanders discussing Pershing's plan. "When communications break down, which we know they will, I feel confident that I'll still know what General Pershing wants."

"Yes," answered Colonel Patton, the commander of all tank forces, "We all have such a clear vision of the larger picture for the battle, we will be able to make split-second decisions instead of waiting for confirmation from higher up. That should give us a tactical advantage we haven't had before in battle."

None of Jesse's courier trips were as enjoyable as his train trip to Esnouveaux from Amiens. Assignments now entailed hard, fast riding and little time to relax, but even so, he did often enjoy them. The French countryside was pleasant. He admired the thick woodlands offset by open farmland. Occasionally he'd pass a farmer in a small field or a house with a yard filled with chickens and children. It seemed incongruous to him that a family would remain in the area, tending sheep or gathering vegetables with the war looming so closely. He tried to imagine what he'd do if a war came to his home, wondering if he'd run away and become a refugee or hold on to hope and remain in his home, trusting the soldiers and God to protect them.

The offensive at St. Mihiel began on September twelfth. Commanders and soldiers alike knew that the battle would be fierce since the Germans were so deeply entrenched in the area, and they all knew that winning this battle was vital to the outcome of the war. For the first three days, Jesse stayed at the forge doing repairs, trying to keep dry from the torrential rains that hampered them, and feeling overwhelmed by the workload. Griffin and Rex were kept busy mostly with courier duties, leaving Jesse and Baird with care of the horses.

Rex came in after dark on the second night of the offensive. "You just wouldn't believe the mess out there," he told Jesse. "Our Renault tanks are made to cross six-foot trenches without trouble, but the thick mud makes the edges of enemy trenches collapse to eight feet or more. Tanks are getting bogged down and stuck. Then, when infantry comes up to support a tank, the machine gun nests and barbed wire that the Germans have in place cause holy hell out there."

On the morning of the sixteenth, despite the continuing rain, news was positive. Allies were gaining ground. Both Rex and Griffin had been called out for courier duty. Jesse fed and tended the horses. At mid-day he was dusting himself off and preparing to go grab something to eat when a corporal approached him with a call for a runner. Jesse didn't hesitate. He put on his coat and strapped on his sidearm, then he saddled a strong, black gelding. He grabbed his canteen, some bread, and a slice of meatloaf before reporting to the communications tent. He was directed to General Vanmeter's desk.

"Sergeant, I need this delivered to the battalion commander who is set up south of Richecour. He's right here," he pointed at a dot on the map about twenty miles east of camp. "The colonel and his three-man crew are behind the German front, though their line is broken and flimsy there. Keep your head low and stay quiet on your way."

Jesse nodded, hoping that he looked more confident than he felt. He checked the map and left camp.

For the first three miles he kept his mount at a trot. The road was packed and the day cool, so the pace was comfortable for both of them. The farther south and east he travelled, the sloppier the road became, however, and his pace slowed. It began raining with a fine, soaking mist as he passed the small town of Montsec. He showed the sentry there his orders and continued on the road. The route became even more challenging about a mile later, and several times he dismounted to lead the horse though the muck. He spotted fighter planes overhead several times, and the low, menacing thump of artillery grew louder and closer as he neared Richecour. Jesse left the road and stayed just at the edge of a thick stand of trees for cover. He hesitated to enter the village as the Montsec sentry had warned him that there were German patrols seen in the town itself recently. He skirted around it inside the trees along the edge of a field that had once been corn but was now just a barren land filled with shallow, but empty trench lines. South of Richecour, Jesse melted back into the woods, moving slowly and quietly. A small, swollen creek lined with brambles and scrubby bushes gave him some aggravation before he spotted a good place to cross.

The sun slipped quietly below the low hills to the west as Jesse edged up to the tree line. He breathed a sigh of relief at the sight of an American truck protected by a machine gun nest at the edge of a large clearing.

Jesse picketed his horse just inside the tree line to give him a chance to graze, then walked the short distance to the outpost. He showed his orders to the sentry who pointed at a tall man a few feet away. He made his delivery after a smart salute to the officer. Standing at attention beside a truck, Jesse watched as the colonel removed a set of maps and spread them out on a small table. His review of those maps afforded Jesse time to catch his breath. He realized then how tense he'd been for the last few miles of the trip, and willed himself to relax. His respite was short lived, however.

The colonel looked up and opened his mouth to address Jesse, but his words were drowned out as a dreaded but familiar whistle pierced the quiet, followed instantly by a large explosion just on the other side of the

truck harboring them. Jesse instinctively covered his head
with his arms as the concussion threw him to the ground.
Another explosion followed, falling only a few feet from the
first, and there was no doubt that more were on the way.
The dust and smoke were thick, and Jesse's eyes were
gravelly. Staying low, he got to his feet and looked around
to the sound of machine gun fire. Two gunners manning
the machine gun nest at the rear of the truck were firing
blindly into the twilight, unsure where the German tank
was located. The third man in the detail, the man who'd
acted as sentry when Jesse arrived, joined them and was
searching for a target using large field glasses. Jesse
blinked hard and looked frantically around. The colonel
lay a few feet away. His eyes stared into the growing night
without seeing.

Jesse fought the fear and nausea he felt at the
realization that the colonel was dead. He turned his head
away from the gruesome sight and took a step towards the
fortified safety of the gunner's nest. Then, thinking about
the maps and plans in the information he'd just delivered,
Jesse scrambled backwards on his knees. He shivered as
he slipped the papers from the officer's hand, then he
stuffed them back in his leather bag.

He turned once again toward the safety of the
gunners' fortification. He'd taken two quick steps when
the nest disappeared in a chaos of fire and smoke. The
force of the blast bashed Jesse backwards, knocking all
breath from his lungs. Though he was wearing his helmet,
his head hit the ground with such velocity that stars
exploded behind his eyes. Then another blast rocked him.

It was a direct hit on the gunners. Nothing
remained of the fortification but a crater in the ground.
Dazed, Jesse gathered himself slowly, trying to ignore the
reverberating, pounding ringing in his ears and the hurt in
his back and side. He could hear nothing else. He
attempted to take a deep breath but the resulting pain
was so sharp he abandoned the effort. Rolling over, he
pulled his knees under him and gritted his teeth against
the queasiness and pain. Once he regained his feet, the
world spun around him and he had to hold on to the side
of what was left of the truck beside him in order to stand.
The smoke and dust settled around him.

Jesse was vaguely aware that he wasn't thinking well. Something urgent nagged at him that he couldn't quite grasp. Trying to clear his thoughts, he wiped his face and eyes, realizing distractedly that his helmet was gone. Death and destruction surrounded him. For a brief, terrible moment he thought maybe he was the last person left in the world. The horror of that thought prompted his sluggish mind and body into action.

Neither the ringing in his head nor the pain in his body subsided, but rational thought slowly returned. Bending down carefully to retrieve his helmet, Jesse also picked up his courier bag, pulling the wide strap over his head and under his right arm to secure it. Then, he sat his helmet on his head, fastening the chin strap. As he did so, he scanned the clearing. His heart skipped a beat as he watched three lights bounce toward him in the growing darkness.

Running in a crouch, Jesse headed for the trees where he'd left his mount, hoping the animal was safe. Moments later, thankful that the horse was still there, Jesse raged at the effort and pain it cost him to get his foot in the stirrup and his body in the saddle as the gelding side-stepped with wild, panicked eyes. He gathered the reins and gently kicked his heels into the mount's sides, guiding it into the trees. He rode low, hunched close to the gelding's warm shoulder, and together they picked their way through the trees.

Jesse's intent was to retrace his route and go north at the small ford he'd found earlier, but in the rising darkness he missed it. Afraid to turn back, he continued to follow the creek, realizing it was taking him farther and farther south, and concerned that the small stream had slowly grown wide enough to be considered a river now.

He stopped once, when the queasiness overwhelmed him. He slid from the saddle to throw up, then washed his face in the cool stream. His ears rang and ached as he fought his growing vertigo. Remounting was a challenge accomplished through gritted teeth. Fighting fear and growing weariness and doing his best to push through the pain in his side and the ringing in his head, he continued on.

He didn't hear or see the patrol, but when the horse's head came up, suddenly alert and wary, Jesse scanned the trees around him. Their first shot went wide and sent Jesse and his mount instantly into a gallop. The second shot travelled through the calf of Jesse's left leg and into the horse. The horse stumbled, and Jesse, fighting the searing pain, knew they were going down. Reacting with cowboy instinct rather than thought, Jesse launched himself off the horse as it fell. He hit the ground hard with his shoulder and rolled, coming up on both feet. Ignoring everything except the desire to get away, he ran for cover.

It was a mindless, rash, and reckless action as he tried to gain as much distance between himself and the shooters as possible. Although his eyes were accustomed to the dark, and he had little trouble navigating through the woods, he knew he couldn't evade the soldiers for long with only one good leg and without being able to hear them over the continued ringing in his ears. He considered making a stand against the patrol with his sidearm, but knew he was outgunned and wouldn't last long in a shootout. He stopped briefly, hidden in shadow, concentrating on locating his pursuers. He couldn't see farther than a few feet. His only chance, he reasoned, was to hide.

He would have liked to climb high into one of the trees, but the pain in his leg precluded that option. He pulled out his handkerchief and tied it tightly around his calf. As he did so he noted that the bullet had travelled through the meaty back of his leg. *Painful, yes,* he decided, *but not horrific. Thanks, God that it missed the bone.* He began searching for a suitable hiding place. A glance behind him told him that he was in real trouble, lights danced behind him as the patrol continued their search.

Desperate, Jesse looked at the river and made a decision. Quickly he pulled his knife from his pocket. He didn't think about the carved elk's head on Sari's gift as he cut several willow branches then returned the knife to his pocket. He set his jaw and stepped into the cold water near a large tree. The deep, harsh voices of his pursuers were loud enough now that he could hear them, German boots thudded on the mossy ground nearby. Within a minute, he'd installed himself near the tree trunk, deep in the shadow. Thankful that the river bottom here was soft mud, he slid down into the water so that all but his face was below the surface, then he arranged the willow branches in a tight thicket above his head, hoping that he couldn't be seen.

He'd barely gotten settled when the beam of a flashlight scoured the creek bank right beside him. Exhausted, cold, and beyond emotion, Jesse fleetingly recalled his premonition that he'd not survive the war. With calm resignation, he sunk lower into the muddy water and prayed.

34

Encampment, Wyoming
early - September, 1918

Keeping the plans for Meredith's baby shower as
her focus in the next days helped mitigate Sari's
frustrations at the Copper Pot and even her worries about
Jesse. Bea was happy to help with the invitations, and she
also made some crepe paper decorations for Sari's parlor.

As the time approached for guests to arrive on the
afternoon of the party, Sari and Claire were both nervous.
"I hope we have a nice turnout," Claire remarked as she
surveyed the room. "Everything looks very pretty, and we
have plenty of food."

"The invitations asked the guests to arrive at three,
and I told Meredith to come over at three thirty. That will
give us a chance to greet our guests and get everyone tea
or punch before she comes in."

"I've been praying all day that this turns out well,"
remarked Claire with a wink. "You look really pretty, Sari.
I like your hair pulled back like that."

The compliment was unexpected. "Thank you. I
feel really exposed. I know the face powder I'm now
wearing all the time helps, but Lela's suggestion that I pull
my hair back so that people can focus on my eyes still
makes me uneasy." As she spoke, Claire noticed how
Sari's hand went protectively to her ragged cheek. The
movement was a familiar indication Sari was upset or
uncomfortable.

"I'm proud of you for your courage," Claire
answered her. "You really do look nice."

With that, Harriet and Bea arrived with a quiet
knock on the back door. Bea carried a market basket over
one arm filled with crepe paper flowers.

Claire smiled at the overfilled basket. "Let me help
you put these around the room. They are so pretty."

Sari told her companions that she needed a few
moments to get the game ready. When Claire asked for
details, Sari quickly explained, then added, "I hope this
idea works."

To Claire and Sari's joy and relief, half an hour later, the parlor began filling with Encampment's ladies, dressed in their Sunday finery. Claire had just handed Alice Peryam a small glass of punch when Sari got their attention.

"Ladies," she began quietly, "Before Meredith gets here, I'd like to enlist your help with a little surprise I have set up. I have some small pieces of paper and some safety pins over here. I'm hoping that each of you will write down one piece of advice that you have for the new mother, and be sure to sign it. When she gets here, I'm going to give Meredith this apron and ask her to wear it tonight." Bea held up a yellow apron adorned with embroidered pink and yellow flowers as her audience smiled and admired the stitching. "Then, as the festivities begin and you each have a chance to talk with her, I'd like you to pin your advice to her apron. Towards the end of our gathering, we will ask Meredith to read each piece of advice. I have prizes for the ones she likes the best."

Everyone was enamored with the party game, and soon each woman had paper and pencil in hand. Beside Ella Parkison sat her daughter, Milly, dressed in a starched blue dress with matching bows in her hair. "Mama, can I write one?" she asked,

Ella began shaking her head, but Sari shyly intervened. "If it's alright with you, Ella, I think it would be a great idea for Milly to participate." Turning to the girl Sari continued, "I'm sure you have lots of ideas about what a good mother is like since yours is so sweet."

A moment later, Meredith arrived. It was clear from her surprised look as she entered the room that she hadn't expected such a turnout. She was blushing and fighting tears when Claire welcomed her. It took Sari and Meredith a few moments to get the apron tied comfortably around Meredith's ample belly, and by the time the deed was done everyone was laughing. Several of the women shared quips about the size of their own baby bellies, and the room became relaxed and festive.

When everyone had finished with their finger sandwiches, cake and punch, and after Meredith had opened all the generous gifts she'd been given, Sari asked her to remove the notes pinned to her apron one at a time and read them aloud. Advice ranged from how to best launder diapers to ways to help with teething and tummy upsets.

When asked to choose her favorite, Meredith faltered. "Actually, I have two, is that alright?"

"Yes, of course," smiled Sari.

"Well, my first favorite is this one, *Always pray for your child when you put him down to sleep.*" Shyly, she explained, "I only recently became a believer and I don't always think about when I should pray. Claire, thank you for this."

Claire nodded. "I understand, praying isn't always what we think of when we are busy as moms or wives, but I believe that saying a prayer does two things. First, you are asking God to watch over your baby, and second you are connecting with Him yourself. Both are important activities."

Alice added, "Speaking as a mother with children who are grown, I can tell you that they never stop needing us to support them with prayer."

Several of the ladies shared their thoughts. When the room quieted, Bea refocused them and asked, "Meredith, what is your other favorite?"

Meredith smiled. "While Claire's advice is important, I think this other one is the most practical. It says, *It's okay to spank sometimes, but just not too hard.*"

Milly Parkison clapped her hands, "Hey that's mine!"

One of the ladies remarked, "Why Milly, you are always so well-behaved. I can't imagine that you have any experience with this topic."

Milly became very serious. "Well, sometimes I do get into trouble and need a spanking, but Mama is always real nice about it." The ladies laughed at her innocent wisdom.

Later, after the guests had gone and Meredith had driven off with Dawson, the livery's truck laden with gifts, Sari and Claire tidied the house then sat together, resting at the kitchen table.

"This turned out wonderfully, don't you think?" asked Claire.

"I do. I didn't hear an unkind word or feel a moment of judgement among us."

"Yes, everyone was so gracious. I hope this is the beginning of a new and wonderful life for Meredith and Dawson. Now she knows that even if her family is still too self-righteous to accept her, she has a group of us in this town who do."

After the excitement of planning and hostessing the shower, life settled into a tense dullness for Sari. *From the Earth to the Moon* lay crooked on her bedside table. She straightened it after smoothing the bed covers, frowning as she did. She'd read it twice in the last four weeks. The story was engrossing, certainly, but in all honesty, she'd read it the second time mostly hoping to feel closer to Jesse. The package had been the last contact either Claire or Sari had gotten from him, and they were worried. According to news reports, the Battle of Amiens began on August eighth and was followed a month later by the Mihiel Offensive led by John J. Pershing. When she'd studied the map from the paper, she could see how close the two areas were, and considering that Americans were involved in the September battles, she felt certain Jesse was close to the action.

The calendar hanging in the kitchen mocked her as she ate her breakfast. It was Friday, September twentieth, nineteen eighteen. Six weeks with no letters.

Sari wiped crumbs from the kitchen table, then she wiped it again. She knew she was procrastinating. Working at the Copper Pot was an increasing trial and it became harder and harder to push herself out the door each morning. She told herself again and again that, since she'd been at the job for over a year now, she was much closer to having her debt paid off, but some days that didn't encourage her much.

Business had been slow lately. The war seemed to hang in the air, pushing down hard so that people were not traveling or eating out like they had been. Mr. Wills' sour attitude grew in direct correlation with the decrease in customers. As she closed the front door behind her, Sari wondered if he took his anger home with him and made Lilith the victim of his sharp tongue and mean comments when there weren't employees around.

Sari was lost in thought as she turned onto the sidewalk and began her trek to work when Bea called her. "Good Morning!"

Sari looked up and returned the greeting, "You're up early this morning," she called.

"Yes, Harri and I are going out to the ranch to see Ma today. We haven't been out there in a long time."

"Have fun," Sari called as she began her walk toward the restaurant.

The encounter dispelled the gloomy beginning of her morning, and Sari was still smiling at her friend's greeting as she stepped in the back door of the restaurant. She was able to hold on to her positive mood for most of the day, until late in the afternoon, when she looked up from kneading bread to see both Mr. Bagley and Mr. Wills standing in the doorway watching her. Instantly it seemed as if much of the breathable air had been sucked from the room.

Sari greeted them, carefully draped a clean towel over the bread dough, and dusted off her hands, moving slowly to give herself time to breathe and to think. She walked closer to the men and stood quietly.

"Mr. Bagley just stopped by to check on your progress here, Sari," Wills told her.

"Good afternoon, Sir," Sari began. Then, timidly she began, "Mr. Bagley, when we first met, I asked you for a copy of my father's loan papers. Then, months ago I wrote to you at the bank with the same request, and I haven't yet received them. I'm asking again, could you please send me a copy of the loan and also a list of payments that have been made since I began working here?" She hoped her voice was a mixture of confidence and politeness. She wanted to keep the conversation friendly.

He cleared his throat and nodded, "The language on those documents is difficult for someone as yourself to readily understand, so taking the trouble to have copies made for you, which is a laborious task, probably will not help you understand your obligation any better. If you insist, however, I'll see what I can do."

Sari hated his patronizing words and tone.

Wills glanced from Sari to his companion and then told her, "Sari, I was just telling Mr. Bagley here that unless business picks up real soon, I'm going to have to cut your hours."

Sari felt the words like a blow to her stomach. Bagley surveyed her sharply, then told her, "Please keep in mind that Mr. Wills has been doing you a favor by employing you, and that your debt is not his responsibility. Should cutting your hours, and thereby your income, become necessary, you will still be responsible to the bank for the full monthly payment."

Sari felt ill. A sudden, vivid memory of the day Jesse had stood up to Mr. Wills about her hours jumped to mind and instantly anger, hot and courageous, flared inside her. Sari met the man's condescension with a sort of confidence. "It will be impossible for me to meet my obligations without being fully aware of what they are. I have never been told exactly what my work here is worth to you. How do you suppose, then, that I will know what payment I need to make to your bank should Mr. Wills become unable to pay it for me?"

Bagley looked uncomfortable, he glanced at Wills before answering, "Now don't get all hysterical, Mrs. Atley. We are only trying to prepare you for something that could happen."

Sari concentrated on keeping her voice steady as she answered, "If my hours are reduced, I will not have the money."

Bagley gave Wills a disgusted look before he answered her. "Now, really, Mrs. Atley." As he said her name, he emphasized the word *Misses*, "Do not expect me to believe that you do not have a comfortable income from your husband's company and his additional pay as a soldier."

"Mr. Bagley, we are discussing my debt, not that of my husband's. The two are separate."

"I doubt the courts would agree. Be advised, I will

not hesitate to foreclose on the livery or even on that nice little house you live in if you fail to meet your monthly obligations."

With that, he motioned to Mr. Wills and they walked confidently away. Sari's knees were watery and her eyes filled with tears. She held on to the edge of the table and breathed deeply until she was relatively confident that she wasn't going to be sick, then she moved to the sink where she dampened a cloth and wiped her face.

She finished the day in a fuzzy turmoil. Yes, she had been saving nearly all of the allowance Jesse had set up for her. She did have a nice sum, but she considered it Jesse's money and hated the idea of using it to pay her father's debt to the bank. She considered going straight to Claire and Daniel's house to ask for their help. She'd walked a block in that direction when she changed her mind. *How can I add to the worry Claire already feels about Jesse, and how can I add to Daniel's overworked burdens?* she asked herself.

Next, she entertained the idea of confiding in Nathan, who was always so kind and willing. She let go of that thought quickly, though, as she pictured his pale, gaunt face when she'd met him at the post office earlier in the week. His mother, Miss Lillian, was ill and failing, and with his sister gone to Cheyenne, providing care for his mother rested solely on Nathan. Resigned to facing this crisis alone, she walked home.

Feeling as if she were drowning, she paced the rooms of her home that evening, unable to eat, unable to sit down. At times she berated herself, *How could I have been so stupid to marry Jesse and put all that he'd worked so hard to achieve in danger of foreclosure?* Alternatively, she was convinced, based on the conversation she'd overheard and what Royce had told her, that she was involved in something shady. As evening turned to night, she found herself at the desk, preparing to write to Jesse as she did each night. With the pen poised above the paper, she hesitated, knowing that even if she did describe to him all her fears and conjectures, frustrations and anger, she probably wouldn't ever mail it.

She felt a deep loneliness settle into her core and realized that it was a familiar ache she hadn't felt for a long while, and knowing that it had been Jesse who banished her loneliness. She picked up her pen then. *Even if Jesse never reads this,* she thought, *just imagining myself talking this out with him will help.*

When the letter was complete, it was after two in the morning. Sari was spent and exhausted, but she felt better. She'd concluded that her best course of action was to talk again to Royce.

Sari felt like she was walking on eggshells around her boss for the next few days. The effort and the tension at work made her tired and weary. Feeling as if she'd been run through a wringer in body and mind, Sari was thankful when she made it home at last on Saturday evening. She felt buoyed that she'd have Sunday to rest and recover. She'd only been home a few minutes when there was a familiar knock on the back door followed by Michael's chipper voice, "Aunt Sari? I've come to check on the wood and coal."

Sari greeted her nephew gladly. Even in her weariness she could count Michael as one of the many blessings that accompanied her marriage to Jesse. Michael busied himself with refilling the wood box, then tromped down to the cellar to check the coal bin. He returned with a black smudge on one cheek and a report that her bin was still sufficiently full.

"Can you sit and have a glass of milk and a cookie?" This had become a ritual with them, and Sari made sure she always had a treat for the boy.

Through bites, Michael told Sari about his school day adventures.

"One of my classmates says that her uncle in Nebraska just came home from the war." He told her as he finished his milk. "She says that he had part of his arm blown off by a shell and now all he does is sit in the house and drink."

"That's so sad," Sari responded. "It must be awful for him."

"Another of my friends told me that he heard on the wireless about a man who was severely injured in the war and the Army wants to discharge him, but he doesn't want to get out. He wants to go back and kill more Germans. It sounds to me like that first man is pretty weak and the second man is very brave."

"It's hard for anyone to accurately judge what bravery is and what isn't," Sari began. "Maybe the first man is using a lot of courage just to get up and get dressed each morning."

"Papa says that good things and bad things happen to everyone and all God expects of us is to just do our best."

"I think that's very true, Michael. Maybe each of those men are doing their very best."

Michael sat thinking, then ventured, "Aunt Sari, I think you are really brave."

Sari had no idea what her nephew meant. He didn't notice her puzzlement and continued, "I mean, you don't hide like that first man and you aren't angry like the second man. You are just kind and nice to everyone so that no one notices anymore or cares if you have a few scars. I think that takes lots of courage."

Sari put her hand over his, "Michael you are a kind young man. I'm certain that my scars are nothing in comparison to the wounds of those men, but I appreciate what you've said to me."

After Michael left, Sari considered their conversation. Was it true that those around her really had stopped noticing or caring about her mangled face? Certainly, with the added confidence her face powder brought her and her growing familiarity with the people in town, she hadn't received many curious glares or disapproving glances for a long time.

Though it was only the middle of the evening, her weariness from the week was asserting itself, and she decided to go upstairs to bed early. She locked the back door and turned off the kitchen lights. She was half-way up the stairs when there was a knock on the door, and she turned around.

Dawson, looking harried, stood on the porch when she opened the door. "Sari, I've been sent to fetch you. Meredith is having pains, and I'm on my way to get the midwife. She says the baby's coming soon."

Her tiredness fled as she reassured Dawson, "You go on, I'll go right over and stay with Meredith until you return."

Dawson didn't offer any thanks. He just nodded and returned quickly to the truck.

Sari walked quickly through the quiet streets, shaking off her weariness in exchange for hope and happiness arriving in the form of a child.

Meredith was pale when she met Sari at the door but otherwise seemed quite fine. "My back aches, but my pains aren't too close together yet," Meredith told her, "But, it helps if I walk." So, Sari linked arms with her friend, and the two paced the small living room together.

"You've decided not to go to Good Shepherd hospital over on the east side of town then?" Sari asked.

"Dawson and I talked it over, but since Doctor Perdue was killed by his wife, the hospital only has nurses. I'd feel much better just staying here. We could call Dr. Irwin, but I just wanted a midwife instead."

Half an hour later, Meredith's discomfort had grown, and Sari helped her as she alternated between walking and reclining on the couch. "I hope Dawson gets back soon." Meredith was speaking in nearly a whisper now as tiny beads of sweat arrived on her upper lip and forehead. "I feel different. I think the baby's coming soon."

"Shall we get you to your bed?" Sari began to worry that the delivery might fall to her, and she had no idea what to do.

Meredith nodded and with effort she rose from the couch. Holding tightly to Sari, she shuffled to the bedroom.

Meredith lay down on her side, and Sari covered her with a sheet when they heard footsteps on the porch. Sari stepped back as Dorothy Peryam entered the room, followed closely by Dawson. The youngest child and only daughter of W.T. and Alice Peryam, Dorothy and Sari had met many times. Whether sharing tea at the roadhouse when Sari and Claire went to borrow books and chat, or at Ladies' Aid meetings, Dorothy was always quick with a smile and a kind word. Though she was just twenty-two, Dorothy had already gained a reputation in the area as a capable midwife, and many of the local women preferred her assistance in child birth to that of the two local male doctors.

Tonight, she was all business, Dorothy nodded at Sari, then began asking Meredith questions. Soon, she turned to the onlookers and smiled. "Sari, how about you go make our new father a cup of tea and let me and Meredith get on with our work of birthing this child?" Relieved, both Dawson and Sari retreated.

Dawson paced and fidgeted while Sari sat still, watching him, intrigued that while he knew the child was not his, he behaved as if it were. His care and concern were clearly more than just a duty for him. Minutes ticked by and the house became very quiet. Both Dawson and Sari strained at each noise they heard until finally, a small cry told them what they wanted to know.

Dawson bounded from the room, unable to wait a moment longer. Sari, not wanting to intrude, sat alone at the table praying for the new family. A few minutes later, Dorothy, looking a bit tired but sporting a relaxed grin, stepped into the kitchen and invited Sari to go in.

Meredith was tucked into bed, sitting up with a pillow behind her. Her paleness was gone, and she looked surprisingly well, though disheveled. Dawson sat jubilantly on a chair beside her, staring at the messy parcel of blanket and baby in his wife's arms.

"Sari, this is our daughter, Esther Opal. Would you like to hold her?"

The night was deep and dark when Sari finally said goodnight to the new family and walked through the silent streets toward home. Stars glittered above her, and the world seemed to be taking a deep, renewing breath. Sari absorbed the peace and hope the night offered.

In the next few days, Sari vacillated between hope and worry. Each evening after work, she stopped in for a brief visit with Meredith and Esther, reveling in the newborn's perfect beauty. Sari had never held an infant or spent time with small children, so Esther was a wonder to her. Hoping to help the new mother, Sari learned to change the baby's diaper. She loved how warm the infant felt in her arms as she breathed in her sweet, milky smell and marveled at the perfection of her nose and fingers. Sari wondered at how soft Esther's forehead felt when she kissed her, and she laughed at how she furrowed her eyebrows when she was unhappy.

Meredith was adjusting well to motherhood, and seemed content. While Sari was at their house, whether Dawson was present or not, Sari sensed an aura of tranquility that fed her soul.

But that was the only refuge in Sari's world. Since her discussion with Mr. Bagley and Mr. Wills, she'd had only perfunctory conversations with either of the Wills, and the atmosphere at the quiet restaurant was subdued and strained. She'd tried twice to talk with Royce about Bagley's foreclosure threats, but he had been out of the office when she stopped in at City Hall, and he hadn't been home another evening when she called on her neighbors. Harriet promised to give him a message that Sari would like to talk to him, but let her know he'd been working long hours.

Even at home, where Sari usually felt safe and comfortable, she was assailed with worries about Jesse's safety and her own finances. Once again, like when she'd just moved in, her evenings became endurance tests pitting her will and faith against her worries.

On Friday, the twenty-seventh of September, Sari awoke from a fitful night to find a light dusting of snow of the ground. The chilly house and gloomy sky enhanced her own disquiet. She left her house as the sky was barely awakening for the day and glanced across the street. Guilt sat on her shoulder, *I have hardly talked to Bea since Esther was born. She must think I'm the rudest friend ever.*

Only a few lights were on at the Copper Pot when she entered the kitchen. No one was around. Sari tied on her apron and began her morning preparations. An hour later, she stepped out in the alley to empty her garbage bin and was happy to see the sun had pierced through the gloom and the only snow remaining lay in hidden corners.

The day dragged. They'd only had three tables for breakfast, and lunch hadn't been much better. A pork roast and baked potatoes sizzled in the oven. The kitchen was clean. She glanced at a copy of the *Saratoga Sun*, and sighed, noting that the front page was filled with nothing but war news. "Sari," Lilith's voice called her from the dining room.

"Coming," she answered, dropping the paper in the trash.

Royce stood beside Lilith in the dining room, his face grave. Beside him stood Mr. Cox, the telegrapher. Sari anticipated their mission without a word. Cox nodded as he handed her the telegram. Sari had to read it three times before she could grasp the news it held.

We regret to inform you that Sergeant Jesse Atley, US Army, is missing. With courage and valor, he traveled behind enemy lines on September 12, 1918 carrying sensitive information, and has not been accounted for since. Any further news will be sent to you as soon as possible.

Sari continued to stare at the page in her hands, knowing that she'd look up into the sympathetic eyes and unsure if she could stand it. Royce stepped forward and gently touched her arm. He spoke to her formally, "Mrs. Atley, I'm certain that under the circumstances Mr. and Mrs. Wills will excuse you for the day. Might I accompany you to your sister-in-law's house so that you can share this news and console one another?"

Without looking up, Sari nodded. Silently, she removed her apron, donned her coat, and left with Royce.

Outside, Royce opened the door of the 1917 Ford Model T two-seated automobile parked in front of the Copper Pot and held Sari's arm as she sat down. He closed the door quietly and quickly had the vehicle started on the short drive to Claire and Daniel's. "I saw your brother-in-law at City Hall and gave him the news. He said he'd meet us at their house."

Sari nodded.

Claire was standing on the porch with Daniel beside her when they drove up. Sari stepped onto the porch and handed Claire the telegram. Claire's hand shook a little when she touched it, then she began to read.

Like Sari, she had to read the message several times before the weight of it broke through her unwillingness and settled at the bottom of her heart. She felt Daniel's arm around her, guiding her into the house and to a seat on the sofa in the parlor.

"But it doesn't say he's died," she whispered. "It says he's missing. That means there's still hope." She looked at Daniel, her eyes pleading.

Daniel couldn't share the glimmer of hope his wife held, but his instinct to protect her wouldn't let him speak the truth he feared. Instead, he kissed her forehead gently and pulled her close.

Sari followed the couple into the parlor. She stood, aware that Royce was beside her, but feeling adrift and alone. She hadn't spoken since she'd read the telegram. There was nothing to say now. She'd been married to the idea of Jesse for nearly a year, but in reality had spent mere hours in his company. As she watched Claire steel herself against the news and begin her season of mourning, Sari knew that her own grief would be different. Certainly she cared for Jesse and his friendship, but her deep sorrow would also include the loss of hope for a future unrealized.

Claire dried her eyes, stood up, and smoothed her skirts. She invited Royce and Sari to sit down and in the same breath offered to make coffee. "I have some coffee cake if you'd like some," she added.

Royce shook his head. "I can't stay, but thank you." He offered the family his condolences, then turned toward the door. He took a step, then looked back at Sari, "I know this isn't the right time, but Harriet gave me a message last week that you wanted to talk with me. I'm sorry I didn't come see you sooner. Do you still need to speak with me?"

"Yes, maybe now more than before," Sari answered quietly, realizing that being a widow could make her even more vulnerable to Mr. Bagley. She paused then added, "Perhaps we can talk in the next day or so?"

"Of course. I'll stop by your house tomorrow evening. How about that?"

35
farm near Richecour, France
mid – September, 1918

Jesse fought to understand why the woman who randomly appeared and disappeared within his haze of pain and fever had Sari's eyes but wasn't Sari. He couldn't shape thoughts solidly enough to ask, or even to wonder how he'd ended up in the small room that harbored him. In that first week, when he surfaced from the haven of blackness, his disjointed thoughts jumped from scenes of Haggarty Creek to dim memories of his cold, watery hiding place. Sometimes he relived his run from German guns, other times he was sure he was dodging bears or mountain lions in snowy mountains.

Other times, his body convulsed with coughs so urgent and severe that he thought he would suffocate. In those moments, pain was all he knew.

His fever broke on the eighth day and his head finally began to clear. The afternoon sun slanted into his room through a small window tucked into the peak of the wall opposite the narrow bunk he was lying on. His first truly rational thoughts since he'd lowered himself into the cold, inky water to avoid the patrol arrived, and he raised his head tentatively to look around. An old steamer trunk with a large, empty picture frame leaning against it populated a corner under the window. A rough wooden table and a marred chair sat near his cot. The room was otherwise bare. Clearly, judging from the dust, this space was rarely used.

Twisting his head farther, he could see the top of a set of stairs descending to his right. Carefully, Jesse pushed himself up with his elbow. The room tilted and spun for a moment, but he closed his eyes and let it pass. Encouraged, he sat the rest of the way up and immediately felt hot, stabbing pain. His chest ached and felt heavy. Deep breaths were out of the question. There was an annoying ringing in his left ear and his whole body felt dull. Pushing away the sheet and blanket that covered him, he surveyed the bandage on his left calf, then with massive effort, he reached out and ran his hand along the gauze. A memory surfaced, remote and indistinct at first, then finally clear and complete, of his horse dying beneath him and his desperate run through the forested darkness.

Fighting lightheadedness, Jesse clutched the mattress for support. His head ache became sharper. The longer he sat up, the more wicked the pain in his calf became. Feeling nauseous and fatigued, he lay back on the bed.

It took a little while to recover from his exertion, but when his breath returned to normal and his pain had receded, he began remembering and piecing together what had happened. He knew clearly where he had been and what had occurred, but was unsure of where he was now or how he came to be in this room and bed. He had some sense that time had travelled on without him, yet he had no idea how long he'd been ill. He flexed his hands and raised his arms. They felt heavy. His stomach rumbled, and he felt a profound emptiness that indicated he'd not eaten in a considerable time.

He turned his head when he heard noise on the stairs. A woman with blond hair carrying a small tray appeared.

Probably a bit older than Claire, the matron was pleasingly round with pink cheeks. Her eyes startled him. While not exactly the same shade as Sari's, the intensity of their blue hue was familiar. She glanced up as she approached the bed and smiled. "Good afternoon," she greeted him, her English understandable despite the thick French accent that carried it. She placed a tray on a rough wooden table nearby.

He stuttered out a greeting in return and was rewarded with a sweet smile. "I'm so thankful you are better. Your fever finally came down last night, and I was hoping you'd be awake." Jesse had to concentrate to understand her.

"Where is this?"

"This is my farmhouse. My name is Daphne."

"How long have I been here?"

"You've been here eight days. Today is Friday, September twentieth."

Jesse was shocked. He struggled to sit upright again, "Eight days! I can't be here this long! My commanders needed that information! They'll think I've deserted!" He threw the covers off and tried to swing his legs over the edge of the bed. Pain cut through every other thought, and he gasped before being overcome with an unrelenting cough. Daphne reached out to support him, then calmly but firmly nudged him back down.

Her voice was quiet and calm, "You see, you are badly hurt. Please, lie back down and we will do all we can to help you."

Her tone, coupled with the pain and sickness he was feeling, convinced Jesse to obey. He closed his eyes and concentrated on controlling his breathing. Eventually, he opened his eyes and once again thought of Sari as Daphne's blue eyes watched him. She let him recover before she stepped back.

"I'm sure you have many questions, and I'll do my best to answer them all. I wonder if you'd like to sip some consommé while we talk?"

Jesse's stomach rumbled again and he nodded. It took a few minutes for her to put pillows behind his shoulders and help him get situated with a cup of warm beef broth. Then she pulled the straight-backed wooden chair up next to his bed and sat down. He took a sip of the steamy soup and smiled as his hostess began.

"My husband and I own this farm. We are a long way from any main roads or places of interest. For most of the war we've been left alone. Even so, we've had both Allied and German patrols pass through our little valley. We've been careful to treat everyone with respect, and because of this we have been lucky and neither has paid us much attention. Usually, the fighting is farther away, though about two months ago it became clear that the Allies had started concentrating their forces just north and west. Right now, there are many Germans in this area. We've heard that a huge battle near Saint Mihiel in the past week has pushed the Germans back, but it's been quiet here except for a few patrols."

Jesse was relieved to hear the Mihiel offensive had begun and was doing well.

"The night you want to hear about started with three or four heavy explosions just to our north. We turned off all the lights and went to the cellar. Later, we heard machine guns and voices in the dark very close by."

As he listened, Jesse relived the attack he'd survived. The unseeing eyes of the colonel, the gaping hole where the machine gunners had been, the ringing in his ears, and the pain in his side and head. He thought about his frantic flight and felt again the stark fear when the gelding crumbled beneath him and he ran through the dark woods on his searingly painful leg.

Jesse blinked and looked up, realizing that Daphne had stopped talking and was watching him closely. He was sitting up straight again, his fists were clinched, his breath coming in quick gasps.

Slowly, he calmed himself and lay back into the pillows, exhausted.

"I'm sorry that I've upset you. Perhaps that is enough talk for now," she told him.

Jesse studied her kind face. He took a moment then answered her, "I'm alright now. The last thing I recall is slipping into the mud and water on the river bank to hide from them. How did I get here?"

She studied him a moment, then, reassured that he needed her answers, she responded, "Everything had been quiet for several hours, so at dawn, Maxim and Rayan, that's my husband and son, left me in the cellar and went out to look around. The Germans had gone. No one was around, but not far away from our barn they found a dead horse. It had been shot, and there was evidence that the patrol had been searching the area. They couldn't tell if the rider of the horse had been captured or not. Maxim was walking along the brook and he thought he saw something at the water's edge. He called to Rayan and there they found you. They carried you back here to the house. It took all three of us to bathe the mud off of you and get you dry and your wounds tended."

"You are taking an enormous risk helping me."

A look of defiance crossed the woman's soft face and she answered quietly, "We have been cordial to our occupiers only out of self-preservation. We do not like the Germans trying to steal our beautiful France. All the Allied soldiers are, to us, heroes." Her voice had grown louder as she spoke. She paused for a moment and took a breath. Smiling after a moment she shrugged and quipped, "You see, it is not only for you that thinking about the war causes emotion."

Jesse nodded and returned her smile as she continued, "In order to protect you, Rayan took your uniform and identification tags, along with a satchel of papers and buried them in the woods so they couldn't be found. I believe there was a weapon as well. We brought you up here so that you would be safe."

"Has the patrol been back looking for me?"

"Yes, they came again a day after Maxim found you. We offered them food and wine, all the time praying you'd stay quiet, and they would not search our house. They did search the barn to make sure you weren't hiding without us knowing it."

Jesse realized more deeply the danger harboring him had brought this family. Humbled and grateful, he thanked her, knowing his words weren't close to adequate.

Daphne stood then and took the cup from Jesse's hand. "You have been very ill. You need to rest now. No more talking. Sleep." She smiled briefly, then lifted the tray and retreated down the stairs. Jesse complied.

Later that afternoon, Jesse once again tried sitting up, but again the pain in his lower leg was intense enough to dissuade him. He laid back, grimacing when he heard Daphne climb the stairs. A young man entered the attic after her. He was tall and stocky with a ruddy face and his mother's blue eyes.

Pride was evident as Daphne introduced her son Rayan to Jesse. Jesse extended his hand and began with a hearty thank you for finding and saving him. The teen shook Jesse's hand and nodded as Daphne explained, "Sadly, Rayan does not speak English. I've brought him to help me redress your wound."

Jesse nodded in return and scooted up as she helped adjust his pillow. Daphne began unwinding the bandage from his leg as Rayan helped support his leg by lifting his foot up and holding it so she could work. The process was difficult and Jesse fought the pain with clenched jaws and breaths as deep as his aching lungs would allow. He saw the source of his pain when the bandage was removed. His left calf was twice the size it should be and horribly red. The wound itself was oozy, and as soon as the bandages were off Jesse's nose was assailed with a sour, sickly smell. Daphne dropped the soiled wrapping in a small bin and looked at Jesse. "You were covered in thick mud when Maxim found you. We did the best we could to clean you up and sanitize the wound but you were in such agony and fighting against us that I'm sure we weren't thorough."

Jesse tried to smile, though he wasn't quite successful. "I'm sorry I fought you. What have you been using on it?"

"At first I used a paste made with turmeric. When that didn't seem to be helping any more I made a poultice of honey and onion. Actually, it does look a little better, if you can imagine, and since your fever has come down it makes me think that we've kept you from sepsis."

Jesse nodded. "I agree. While I feel weak and tired, I don't feel sickly. Those are remedies I would have tried myself," he told her. Her response was a quizzical look so he continued, "I've spent my life so far tending horses, so I know a little about doctoring them." His smile was shy.

Daphne nodded. "Because of the fighting, our resources are limited. Do you have any suggestions?"

Jesse adjusted his position and, once again clenching his teeth, bent his knee and brought his leg up to get a closer look at his calf. Tenderly, he pushed on the area around the bullet hole, then he sat back. After taking a couple of breaths to allow the pain to ease, he asked, "The bullet went all the way through, right?"

Daphne nodded, "We flushed the gap with water and a little cognac to cleanse it."

Jesse smiled at the innovative use of the liquor, "Once back home I had an old roan who'd gotten into some rusty barb-wire. I couldn't get that sore to heal until I made a soak for him. I had him stand in a bucket filled with hot water and black tea three times a day, and it only took a few days for the infection to be gone. Another time I made a poultice with black tea and a slice of white bread for another stubborn infection on a little mare."

Before he was finished speaking, Daphne was nodding, "I've heard of this also, but didn't think of it." She turned to Rayan and after a quick exchange in melodious French, her son disappeared down the stairs.

When Rayan returned, his arms were laden with a new set of supplies and he was followed by an older man carrying a deep bucket of steaming water. The resemblance between father and son was pronounced. Another round of introductions ensued, and Jesse learned that Maxim, like his son, spoke no English.

Daphne served as translator and foreman of the scene. First in one language then the other, she explained that she wanted to try both of Jesse's suggestions. Daphne helped Jesse sit on the side of the bed so that he could immerse his damaged limb. They soaked Jesse's leg in the warm water and tea first. After he collapsed back into bed, she dressed it, this time soaking a piece of bread in tea water, dividing it into two, and applying them to both sides of Jesse's leg.

So began a pageant of sleep, exertion, and pain, soaking his wound and changing dressings, and fighting the low-grade fever that dogged Jesse. Daylight hours were easier, Daphne came and went, bringing hearty soups and stews along with comfort and conversation. Nights though, were long and filled with restless dreams and nightmares.

By the third day, the success of their ministration began to be apparent. Jesse's intermittent fever was much better and his pain was diminished. When Daphne finished unwrapping the bandage that afternoon, Jesse sat up. They shared a grin when the wound seemed less red, and the sick smell Jesse had noticed before was gone.

"I'll leave this unwrapped for a while for it will get some fresh air. I'll go to get some water to soak this—"

Rayan's voice, quiet and urgent interrupted her from below, "Maman, l'adversaire est là."

Daphne's demeanor changed instantly. "You must not make a sound," she whispered and was gone.

Jesse, virtually helpless and completely vulnerable, lay still. He tried to capture every sound coming from below him, picturing the scene.

Daphne glanced out the front window to see an armored car approaching as she descended the steep stairs.

"Depeche toi et aide moi, Rayan!"

They pushed the armoire in front of the attic door to hide it and replaced the rug in front, finishing as the armored vehicle pulled to a stop in front of the house. Rayan stuffed the rags they'd prepared as dressings for Jesse into a drawer. Both looked around, searching the room for any sign of the American.

Rayan stepped out onto the porch to meet the arrivals while Daphne pulled some scones from the cupboard.

Two German soldiers, young, haggard and dusty, emerged from the car, each holding a rifle. By gesture and broken phrases, the soldiers let it be clear they were searching for American soldiers.

Jesse heard their heavy boots on the floor below him and began to pray.

It seemed a long time before he heard a motor cough to life outside and then slowly move farther and farther away.

In caution, Daphne and Rayan didn't remove the furniture barrier from the attic stairs for over an hour after the German patrol was gone.

Two days passed after the German patrol had searched the house. Since then it had been quiet. Neither Maxim nor Rayan had seen any patrols come by. Daphne and Jesse began to relax, and both were relieved to see that their doctoring efforts were finding success. Jesse's wound was still very painful and raw but the redness had subsided. The heavy ache in his chest was better also, and he had fewer and fewer coughing fits as the days passed. Jesse was beginning to feel better overall. He couldn't put weight on his left leg, but with the help of a set of crutches Rayan produced one afternoon, Jesse was able to get up and move around some in his attic room. The steep stairs and fears that a patrol could return, however, kept him in the attic.

On the third day, Jesse sat upright on the side of his bed, wearing a cambric shirt and pair of cotton trousers that belonged to Maxim. The sleeves of the shirt were a little long and he had them rolled to just above his wrists. Daphne had just delivered lunch to the small table in front of him, then settled into the chair nearby to keep him company as he ate. It had become their midday routine since he'd become strong enough to sit up for a while.

Two pieces of thickly sliced bread topped with melted and toasted cheese sat in front of him. Unsure of how to proceed, Jesse used his fingers to lift the sandwich and take a bite. "Oh man," Jesse said after he swallowed. "That's delicious. What do you call this?"

"It's Coque Monsier."

"The ham is wonderful. What else is in there?"

Daphne smiled. "Well, ham and cheese, plus a sauce. The bechamel sauce has flour and milk with a little mustard, pepper, and nutmeg in it."

His only answer was a nod and another bite of the heavenly concoction.

Daphne watched him. She'd been careful not to ask too many questions of her guest, not wanting to pry, but the easy rapport that had grown between them gave her courage.

"When you were very ill, you called for someone named Claire. You are wearing a wedding ring. Is Claire your wife?" she asked.

Jesse studied his left hand a moment before answering Daphne. "Claire is my sister. I suppose it makes sense that I'd ask for her instead of my wife, since she raised me, and also because I'd only been married a week when I shipped out. My wife's name is Sari."

"You've been away from home a long time?"

"Nearly a year. It seems like a lifetime." Jesse paused and stared at the wall. Wyoming felt so remote, so fictional, compared to this moment. Had he ever not been tired or fearful about what was to happen next?

Daphne saw the faraway and worried look in her patient's eyes and tried to steer their conversation to something lighter. "Where in America do you come from?"

"In the middle of the country, the state of Wyoming."

"Why, you are a cowboy! When I was learning English I read some, I think they are called dime novels, about Wyoming and Montana. Are you a gun flinger?"

Jesse chuckled. "They are called gun *slingers*, and no. I'm a perfectly boring, law-abiding horseman."

Their conversation became easy then, as he described his life in Wyoming and told her about owning the livery.

The next day, when Daphne brought his lunch and sat down, Jesse began the conversation. "Daphne, I've been here many days and no one knows it but you. Do you have any mail service or any way to get a letter out? My unit doesn't know where I am—they may think I'm dead."

"Maxim and I have discussed this. Yesterday, Rayan went into Richecour. He and Maxim often go for supplies so we didn't think it would attract any attention. Rayan was able to get into town and get a few provisions, but the town is occupied by German forces. The grocer told Rayan that our entire valley is under German control. They are patrolling the roads and have many check points. I understand your need to contact your commanders, but right now, there is no safe way to do it."

"Does that mean that the Allies are falling back? Are the Germans succeeding?"

"No. Rayan heard that your General Pershing has been very successful just north of here, around Mihiel. It seems that the Allies are doing very well. The Germans are being pushed back all over France. They are holding on to our little valley in desperation."

This news relieved Jesse, but even so he was worried and frustrated.

"Maxim told me this morning that he will send Rayan to town every few days to get news. Try to be easy, worrying will only delay your healing, I think."

Days passed slowly. It took another two weeks before Jesse's low fever finally completely released him and Daphne was satisfied that his lungs were healing. Though his cough lingered, he began to feel stronger. The bullet wound in his calf slowly healed, though walking remained painful.

Maxim and Rayan both shook Jesse's hand after he made his first halting trip down the attic stairs to join the family for dinner. It was mid-October. Leaves turned from green to orange, and rumors flew among the farmers in the area about the status of the war. Since they were tucked deep into the valley floor, Daphne and Maxim had no radio, but they continued to get news every few days through trips to town. The Allies were pushing the Germans back toward the border, and hints of an end to the fighting began to circulate.

Jesse felt weak and frustrated from his long confinement. He knew that the only way to regain his strength was to get fresh air and exercise, but being spotted by a passing German patrol would be catastrophic not only for him but for his kind hosts. He began taking walks around the farm after dark. At first Rayan or Daphne accompanied him, but as his strength returned and he became more familiar with his surroundings, he felt confident enough to venture out alone. Walking briskly and enjoying the freshness of crisp fall nights served to restore Jesse's body and his spirits. Days, however, were long. He read the few books in English that Daphne treasured, then read them again. Slowly, he began doing small jobs around the house. He remodeled a cupboard in the pantry and built a bookshelf for the parlor. Once he felt strong enough, he spent time in the barn, repairing tack and helping care for the two horses the family owned.

In the weeks that followed, Jesse's strength returned, but his frustration grew. He thought nearly constantly about making his way back to his unit. His French improved daily, and in a halting conversation, Jesse and Maxim considered trying to send a letter out, but the German perimeter and the threat of discovery kept them from following through. Knowing that his family probably thought he'd been killed left him with a cold, hollow spot deep in his belly. He grieved for their grief.

To combat his frustration, Jesse poured out his concerns and worries in long letters to both Sari and Claire. As he wrote, reassuring them and himself that someday they'd be reunited and all would be well, his thoughts went again and again to speculating how Sari would feel if he did return. He couldn't help wondering if she'd welcome him and be willing to try to create a marriage and a life together or if she'd want to quietly divorce him. He knew that his hope was that she'd agree to stay. Remembering the kind, quiet wisdom in her letters, he knew that he'd come to love her and prayed she felt the same.

36
Encampment, Wyoming
November, 1918

Through the rest of October, news reports
described the successes of General Pershing in France,
but in Encampment there had been no more news from
the Army about Jesse. November came with low
temperatures but little snow, and though Claire continued
to welcome Sari for Sunday dinner and at least once more
through each week and the family tried to continue on, a
cloud of grief dampened everyone's spirits. Daniel seemed
pale and distracted, even more so than usual. Michael and
Greg continued to banter with one another, but even their
exuberance was subdued. On the surface Claire was her
normal, busy and confident self, though in unguarded
moments Sari could see that the effort taxed her sister-in-
law and a masked wretchedness lived just below the
surface.

Sari understood. To combat her own sorrow and
worry, Sari orchestrated a routine that kept her busy. She
did her best at work, focusing on creating meals that
saved money. She worked as conscientiously and
efficiently as possible. After work each evening, she
stopped in to see Meredith and Esther, cherishing the
sweet moments of happiness that enveloped them. She
was careful not to overstay, though. It would have been
easy to while away long hours with the new family, hiding
from the reality of her own life, but she kept herself in
check and forced herself to leave soon after Dawson came
home.

She did stay later one evening each week so that
she and Dawson could update the livery's accounts. Sari
was proud of the progress she'd made learning how to
keep the accounts current. She grew confident in her
abilities. Slowly she'd taken over paying the bills for both
the livery and for her own personal finances. Freeing
Daniel of his time and responsibility and becoming totally
responsible for herself gave her a great deal of satisfaction.
She still checked in with Daniel, especially when financial

decisions loomed, but even then she felt empowered by her new-found mastery.

Often, she spent one evening a week with Claire and Daniel, and each Thursday found her at the Ladies' Aid society meetings. At intervals, she'd go over to Harriet and Royce's after dinner to play whist or help Bea put a puzzle together.

The busyness of her days and evenings helped Sari endure the deafening quiet of being at home alone, but not entirely. Even soothing music from the gramophone couldn't always mitigate the thoughts that assailed her there in the solitude of her home. Sewing new curtains or crocheting doilies for the tables couldn't totally succeed in keeping at bay the emptiness.

Both Greg and Michael were fighting coughs, so instead of going to Sunday dinner at Claire and Daniel's on November tenth, Sari accepted an invitation to Royce and Harriet's house.

Bea proudly served a shepherd's pie she'd made herself, and the comradery around the table was pleasant and warm. After dinner, Royce invited Sari into the parlor while his wife and her sister did dishes.

A muscle in Royce's jaw danced and his eyes snapped as he updated Sari on his inquiries into Mr. Bagley and Mr. Wills. "I've found three foreclosures in the last two months that seem shady, in addition to the others I've told you about. I've talked this over with Marshall Helugs, and we sent a letter this morning to Douglas Preston, the Wyoming attorney general in Cheyenne, giving him all the information about what I've discovered. I included Bagley's dealings with you and let Preston know that I'm fearful Bagley is setting you, the widow of a war casualty, up for a foreclosure and asking if his office couldn't please look into it."

"Thank you, Royce, for how you've pursued this. I appreciate it very much."

"Well, it's clear that at the very least both Wills and Bagley are unscrupulous. I can't get over the fact that the day after you got the notification your husband was missing in action, Wills added to your duties by requiring you to not only cook but help the chambermaid so that he could reduce her hours. That was a cold thing to do to you."

The next afternoon, Sari was cleaning in room three when first one, then two whistles began blowing. She smoothed the coverlet over the newly-made bed and went to the window. She slid it open and leaned out, trying to see if smoke was rising from anywhere nearby, knowing that the sawmill whistles were often used to summon the fire department to help quench a fire. She saw nothing. The whistles continued. Occasionally a car horn added to the blaring sound.

She closed the window, made sure that the room was tidy and ready for the next guest. She gathered her supplies and returned to the kitchen using the back stairs. It sounded as if another whistle had joined the blaring of the first two as Sari quickly put her supplies away, smoothed her hair, and walked to the front desk.

Mr. Wills was standing behind the front desk next to Lilith and another man. Lilith, with tears streaming, looked up at Sari and smiled.

"What is it?" Sari asked, "What's happened?"

"The Armistice has been signed. The war is over!"

Sari stammered an incoherent reply, and Mr. Wills continued, "The Germans have surrendered. We've won!"

Sari listened as he elaborated to the growing group of guests and employees that France, Great Britain and Germany had signed an agreement to stop the fighting. "The armistice began at eleven this morning. The eleventh day of the eleventh month. Isn't that something?"

No one in the gathering had many details, so after a few minutes of listening to the excitement and joy of the group, Sari quietly sought solitude in the kitchen.

Not long after she returned to her duties, Gregory bounced into the kitchen from the alley. "Aunt Sari, did you hear the news?"

"Yes, I did. It's wonderful."

"Mama says to ask you to come over as soon as you can so that we can celebrate together."

"Tell her I will. I'll be there as soon as I can."

Greg added a hug to his reply of "Swell," and was quickly gone.

Mr. Wills came shortly after Greg left. "I'm

expecting a larger crowd tonight to celebrate this news, so be sure we have plenty of food ready. I'm certain business will pick up now. Maybe your little house is safe after all," Sari wondered at his tone. Was he disappointed? She thought he was.

Pushing Wills' heartless comment aside, Sari began peeling more potatoes and then increased the amount of carrots in the pot.

Claire served fried chicken and scalloped potatoes later that evening, and the conversation was light. Daniel's prayer before they began eating was filled with praise and thanks. The boys carried the conversation with excitement and looking forward to life out from under the pall of war. "Can we have pork chops this Monday, Mama, to celebrate the end of 'meatless Mondays'?" Greg asked. Claire answered with a quiet chuckle and a nod. Despite the lightness of the evening, Sari studied Claire's face and guessed that, deep down, they were both feeling the same way. Once the adults adjourned to the parlor and the boys were busy cleaning up, Sari tried to say aloud the conflict she'd been feeling all afternoon.

"I'm certainly thankful the war was over," she began. "But at the same time, I can't stop thinking about all the damage that has been done to people and families, to our country, and especially to all the men who have been wounded or who aren't coming home."

The room was silent in response and Sari, her eyes on the floor in front of her, was fearful she'd made a mistake by voicing her thoughts. She glanced up to see Claire wiping her eyes and nodding.

"I agree completely, Sari," Claire assented. "I've felt the same way all afternoon, thinking about Jesse, about Evan Dawson, about our neighbor Charles Anderson who died overseas a few months back. I'm glad the war is over, but I hurt."

"So you don't think it unpatriotic to be sad today?"

Daniel answered her with strength and gentleness, "No, Sari. I've felt all day as if the celebrations, the whistles and shouting, the toasts and laughter have been misguided. I'm relieved it's over, and I'm thankful, but happy? No."

Sari wiped her tears away and asked, "What happens now that the armistice is signed? Do all the armies just pack up and go home?"

"Actually," Daniel answered, "The armistice only means that the sides have agreed to stop the fighting. Now, the leaders of all the countries involved will meet and begin to draft a treaty and agree to terms. As I understand it from a radio broadcast I heard today at City Hall, the agreement to end the conflict was signed in a railroad car near Paris. The Germans have agreed to give up 2,500 heavy guns, 2,500 field guns, 25,000 machine guns, 1,700 airplanes, and all their submarines and move back behind the Rhine River as well." He paused then added, "Part of their capitulation is that they will free all their prisoners of war right away."

Sari let that information sink in a moment before she looked up. "Then, that means there's still hope that we will hear from Jesse! I wonder how long it will take for the prisoners to be released and processed?"

Claire's eyes welled up and she slowly shook her head. She envied her sister-in-law's ability to hold on to any hope when she herself had already let go. Without any optimism of her own, she responded quietly, "We'll continue to pray."

37
farm near Richecour, France
November, 1918

Jesse slipped out of the house as dark descended one late evening. He wished Daphne and Maxim 'Bon nuit' and received a kind reminder from his hosts to 'faites attention.' Being careful and watchful had become second nature on his nightly excursions. He walked without thinking for several minutes, enjoying the freedom and the soft air. There was just enough light from the quarter moon to encourage him to push himself on a longer walk than he'd taken before. As he picked his way down a familiar path through the woods, his thoughts began to center, as they often did, on the past few weeks. He wasn't discouraged. On the contrary, he was highly aware of how fortunate and blessed he'd been to be found by Maxim and Rayan. Certainly, he'd have died in the creek without their selfless intervention, and possibly no one would have ever known what happened to him. Not only were Daphne, Maxim and Rayan his rescuers, but Jesse was highly aware that they'd risked so much for him and sacrificed their own food and supplies to care for him. He knew he'd never be able to repay them.

He counted his blessings, praying with deep thankfulness for how God provided for him. Yet, now that he was recovering from his pneumonia and wounds, he couldn't help feeling edgy. He'd wrestled again and again with ideas of how to get past the German patrols and rejoin his own life. It haunted him that his family didn't know where he was.

Finally, when he'd reached the crest of a hill that just last week had looked insurmountable, Jesse stopped to rest and ended his prayer. The night felt familiar, and he recalled the night walk he'd taken across the prairie so long ago. *So much is different, so much had happened since that night, yet God still reigns*, Jesse thought. When his breath had returned to normal, and ignoring the rising ache in his calf, he headed back.

As he walked, he thought more about the home he'd left. He pictured the cabin at Dillon where he'd grown up, then Claire and Daniel's home in Encampment. Then his thoughts settled on the house that he'd called his own.

His leg had begun to hurt in earnest now, so he concentrated on picturing each room, each detail of his real home, letting his imagination wander through the rooms. Eventually, his thoughts took him to the few hours he'd spent there with Sari, and he tried picturing the changes she'd told him she'd made to each room.

"This is November tenth," his quiet voice cut into the darkness and he looked around, assuring himself that he was alone before continuing. "I've been a married man for over a year now. I wonder how Sari feels about that? I wonder if she misses me or thinks of me at all?"

Jesse's foot slipped on the rocky path, sending a sharp pain up his leg. He clamped down, then, on any thoughts besides watching his step. Later, when the small light Daphne always kept burning for him beside the back door came into view, he was relieved and ready to fall into sleep.

He slept later than usual the next morning. When he descended the stairs, Daphne was alone in the kitchen. She noticed his limp and raised her eyebrows with inquiry.

"I twisted my leg as I walked last night. It's sore, but I'm alright," he reassured her.

"Are you sure?" she answered. She retrieved a plate from the oven and sat it on the table. "Rayan and Maxim have gone to town. I made them breakfast early, but I saved this for you."

Jesse smiled and tried to thank her but she waved it off. "I've come to know you, Jesse, and I know that if you had the opportunity to be in my shoes, you'd be even more generous and giving than I."

"I'm sure that's not true," he smiled. "I'm sure, though, that you wouldn't ever be as grumpy as I've sometimes been, or as much trouble."

They laughed and talked together as Jesse ate his breakfast. He helped Daphne clean up the kitchen, telling her how Daniel had made washing dishes the tradition when he was growing up.

"I think I would like to know Daniel," she answered, "and I applaud this tradition. I've never once seen either my husband or my son wash or dry a dish." She said it lightheartedly and without rancor. "But, I've also never plowed a field or shoveled out a stall," she finished.

Jesse removed himself to the barn after breakfast, leaving Daphne at the table engrossed in patching a pair of pants. He closed the barn door behind him and began working on a repair project he and Maxim started the day before. It was a tedious task, but one that made the afternoon pass.

Light slanted in the high loft window, signaling the waning afternoon when Jesse heard the distinct thuds of horses out on the road, coming fast into the yard. As they drew near, the voices, calling loud and excited joined the sound.

"Maman! Jesse! Come out! C'est fini! C'est fini!"

When Jesse was sure that it was Rayan and Maxim and not a German patrol, he left the barn to join the family. The torrent of French that passed between Daphne and her son and husband mostly eluded Jesse, but he was able to pick out phrases and words enough to begin to understand that the war was over.

It took a while for the family to stop hugging each other and Jesse and regain composure. Jesse helped tend and feed the horses while Daphne finished dinner. They ate in jubilation, and Jesse and Daphne happily listened again and again as the men described how the German patrols pulled out of Richecour within hours of the news, how the church bells in town rang all afternoon, and how the radio continued to extoll General Pershing's American offensive as the final blow to an already weakened German army. At the end of the meal, Daphne served apples and sharp cheese as a dessert treat and they made plans.

It was decided that Maxim and Jesse would go in the morning to town. There, they were sure, Jesse could get back in touch with his unit and be restored to the American army.

Rayan, in the broken English he'd begun learning with Jesse's help, remembered the uniform and papers he'd buried when they'd found their wounded soldier. "I will go and undig them for you right away," he told the group.

"May I come?" Jesse asked.

"Mais, oui!"

Soon, armed with a shovel, Rayan led Jesse through the woods north of the house. At the base of a large oak, Rayan shoved aside a small pile of rocks and began digging. Jesse, though thankful that they'd taken the precaution of hiding his uniform and satchel, was nervous about what shape they'd be in after being buried in the loamy ground. The hole Rayan uncovered was lined with gravel, and the package itself was wrapped in what looked like a thick layer of oilcloth. He handed Jesse the package, then quickly filled in the hole before the two returned to the house.

On the porch, Rayan removed the dirty outer wrapping, revealing a clean, inner layer of oil cloth. Then he led Jesse inside, to the kitchen table. It was a solemn procession as Maxim and Daphne joined them.

Proudly, Rayan unwrapped the parcel. First, he handed Jesse his dog tag identification. Jesse smiled and looped the chain around his neck. Next, Rayan offered Jesse his neatly cleaned and folded uniform. This wasn't what Jesse expected. He stared at the clothes in his hand for a moment then looked at Daphne. "I washed and dried them as best I could. The pants are still stained I'm afraid, I couldn't get all the blood out, but I patched the holes."

Jesse was touched. "When did you do all this?"

"Right away. We were afraid the patrols would come looking for you, but I knew that you would need a proper uniform—whether you lived or died."

Jesse nodded, unable to speak. Rayan next handed him the satchel filled with his orders and the now unnecessary communications. At the bottom, Jesse found his sidearm. Rayan said something to his mother in French. She nodded and then translated, "Rayan apologizes that he can't return your saddle and tack. The German patrol stripped the horse of it all."

Jesse, with solemnity matching Rayan's, shook his hand and thanked him for his care. On impulse, he retrieved the revolver and handed it to Rayan. "I'd like you to have this, as a thank you," Jesse told him.

Jesse was too excited to sleep well that night. He was awake and up as the sky was just beginning to hint at a pink and orange sunrise.

He got up as silently as possible, trying not to disturb the family below, but his concern was unwarranted, as the whole house came to life quickly as the sun rose. Jesse dressed in his uniform, noting that it fit much looser than the last time he'd worn it. He stripped his bed and folded the bedding neatly at the foot. He folded the shirt and pants he'd been wearing as well. He picked up his satchel, then lingered at the top of the stairs, thanking God for the safety of this room, and the healing he'd been given. Then, he left the attic.

Daphne had prepared a hearty breakfast, but no one ate much. The mood was somber. Maxim had already saddled the horses, so when the meal was over, it was only a few minutes before the four stood together on the front porch, the horses stamping nearby.

"I feel as if you are a son," Daphne told him, fighting tears. "I will think of you often, and say prayers to God for your safety and for your smooth and quick return home." She kissed him on both cheeks and he tugged her into a quick hug.

"I will write to you when I can," Jesse answered thickly. "I owe you my life. Your generosity and kindness saved me and have made me a different and better person. Thank you. I will never forget you. I will keep you in my prayers as well, as you and all of France rebuild from the destruction of the war."

After a flurry of hugs and handshakes, Jesse and Maxim rode away from the farm.

It was a quiet ride into Richecour. They dismounted at the depot, and with Maxim's help, Jesse learned that the trains were running. There were a few moments of panic at the ticket window for Jesse, when he realized that he had no money for the ticket, but Maxim shrugged and smiled, and produced coins enough from his pocket to pay the fare to Paris.

Jesse held out his hand to the man when the train was ready to depart an hour later, but Maxim ignored it and kissed him on both cheeks. Then abruptly he turned and walked away. Jesse, along with a blizzard of emotions, boarded the train.

38

Encampment, Wyoming
mid - December, 1918

The end of the war should have brought us all a measure of peace and happiness, Sari thought as she got ready for work. *But instead of relief, more and more worries just seem to pile on. There's been no news about Jesse, it's been bitterly cold, though dry, this winter, and the Spanish flu is marching its deadly way across the country. It seems more and more difficult to find things to be thankful for.*

Even as she thought it, Sari knew those words weren't exactly true. *I'm just tired,* she told herself.

Walking downstairs, dressed and nearly ready to leave, she stopped to note the growing pile of unmailed letters to Jesse in a basket on her desk. Each evening, she continued to write to him. Sometimes she wrote chatty and upbeat letters that chronicled her days and her hopes for their future. Other times she chronicled her fears and anxiety. She told herself that continuing to write them was futile, but she just couldn't stop because that would be proof that she'd accepted his death, something she just wasn't ready to do.

Slowly, as troops began coming home and the push for austerity eased, business began to pick up at the Copper Pot Hotel and Restaurant. Lilith and Chetley Wills rehired several of the staff members they'd let go, and life became more normal. By mid-December, Sari was convinced that her job was once again secure and that she could stop worrying about Mr. Bagley's threats of foreclosure. Royce had heard nothing from Cheyenne. The issue of her debt still weighed on her of course, and she resolved that after the new year began, she'd sit down and discuss the whole situation with Daniel and see if he could help her contact the bank and get the paperwork she needed. *Maybe,* she told herself, *just maybe I've saved enough to pay it off early.*

Sari continued to spend a few hours several times a week with Meredith and Dawson, who seemed content with their new life together. Baby Esther was thriving and had begun to coo and giggle as Sari cuddled her. Watching the child warmed Sari and helped her cope with her worries.

Claire mentioned once right after Thanksgiving that perhaps they should have some sort of memorial service to remember Jesse, but Sari put her off, still clinging to waning hope that he could still return. "Until we receive official word, I just can't let go," she told Claire.

It was fairly dark on Thursday, December nineteenth, when Sari finally left work. Though she was tired from her long day, she was happy to be heading to Claire and Daniel's for supper. She and Claire were planning their Christmas celebration. Gregory and Michael had challenged her to a checker tournament. As she walked the quiet street, Sari watched as a full moon rose above the Snowy Range to the east, and she thanked God for His consistent presence.

There was an undercurrent of tension in the house that marred conversations and dampened the meal. Greg and Mike exchanged snipes and Daniel's reprimand was perhaps a little more sharp than necessary. Claire looked drawn, tense.

Nothing was said until after the dishes were done and the boys were sent to their rooms. Sari stared at the remains of the tea in her cup as she sat in the parlor with Claire and Daniel, wondering what was going on, when Daniel spoke.

"Sari, have you been following the national reports about the Spanish flu?"

She looked up and answered, "Yes, a bit. It all seems contradictory. Some articles are saying that the worst is over, but others tell of new cases in new cities."

Claire joined the conversation, "I got a letter today from my brother on the east coast. He says that the newspapers still are not covering the seriousness of the flu, and that many, many people are dying each day."

Sari could feel their concern, though the outbreak still didn't seem like much of a threat to them. "I'm sorry, Claire. I'm sure you are very worried about him."

"I'm not just worried about him, I'm concerned for us—for Gregory and Michael, for all of us. Marcus' letter says that usually flu is most dangerous to small children and older people, but that this time, there are many teens and young adults who are dying."

"It's highly contagious and has a fast progression, too, according to Marcus. Seemingly healthy people sometimes die within hours of coming down with symptoms," added Daniel. "The worst of it for me though, is that there have been outbreaks closer and closer to us."

"I see," responded Sari, though she still felt that they were safe, so remote from the trouble.

Claire's next announcement took Sari by surprise. "We've decided to take the boys and go up to Dillon. We are going to leave the day after Christmas." Claire looked at Daniel for confirmation and support.

"Sari, we'd like you to come with us. Maybe we are being too wary, but we'd prefer to err for caution rather than take the risk. If you want, I'll go with you to talk with Chetley. You've been a faithful employee for a long time, I'm sure he'll understand and grant you a leave."

"If he doesn't, you could just quit," added Claire.

Sari didn't know how to respond. Just when tensions were easing at work, she couldn't ask for time off. Mr. Bagley and Mr. Wills wouldn't stand for it. She'd lose the house and the livery to foreclosure certainly, and she couldn't let that happen. She knew she couldn't agree, and regretted that she'd never confided in her sister- and brother-in-law before now. She considered spewing out the whole story right then, but the worried eyes that watched her didn't need anything else added.

Finally, she responded, "I appreciate your wanting to take me, too. I just don't think I can get away right now. Dawson has a lot of work lined up for the livery, and he needs me to be here and help with billing. There's also Meredith. She's come to rely on my help while the baby is so small. And, I'm really not sure that Mr. Wills would consent to my absence." She paused and tried to read Claire's reaction before she continued. "I'll promise to keep informed about the flu. If people here begin to get sick, could I come up then?"

Daniel nodded. "You would be welcome, of course, But, there are two issues with that. First, though it's been bitter cold, it has been a dry winter and the snowfall in the high country is quite light. We feel certain we can make it up to the cabin. All it will take is one or two good snowfalls and the trip will become treacherous or impossible. The second danger is waiting too long and then bringing the infection with you."

"I hadn't thought of either of those," Sari responded slowly.

"I know there is a lot to consider, Sari, and you don't have to make a decision right now, but promise you'll consider it."

"I will. If I let you know by Christmas Eve, will that be enough time?"

Daniel nodded. Sari finished her tea, which was cold and unappetizing as she swallowed, and then prepared to leave for home.

Before she entered her house, Sari looked up at the moon, now shining nearly overhead. The silvery-grey sphere cast cold light around her and she shivered.

On the other side of the globe, Jesse shivered at nearly the same time. He wasn't cold, though. He was enraged. Standing behind bars and a locked door, he concentrated on unclenching his fists and taking deep breaths. A corporal from the adjutant general's office stood on the other side of the bars.

"Corporal, I've gone over this so many times with you that I can't count them anymore. I did not willingly leave my post. I am not a deserter. If you could just contact General VanMeter, he's the one who sent me out that day. Or contact Lieutenant Jones of the Fifth Army Calvary Corps. They will confirm my report to you and vouch for me, I'm sure of it."

The corporal seemed bored. "As I've explained, General VanMeter is busy with patrols at the German border, making sure that the armistice holds. The Fifth Army Cavalry Division is on its way to Cherbourg to begin transport home. Neither is available right now to bother with a coward."

Jesse's temper snapped and he grabbed and shook the bars that separated them. The corporal stepped back. Through clenched teeth, Jesse told him, "Corporal

Barstow, be assured that I will remember you. Be also assured that when this does get straightened out, I will do all I can to expose your lack of humanity and the fact that you are not following protocol. I have yet to be seen by a medic even though my cough is getting worse each day. You have not yet contacted the French family who harbored me to corroborate my story. You have not notified my assigned unit. Don't even get me started on my family. Have they been advised that I'm alive? I have been languishing here for over a month now, incarcerated and unjustly labeled a deserter when only a few simple steps would prove you wrong. I outrank you, Corporal, and I will see that your ineptitude is brought to light."

The Corporal looked shaken but didn't respond. He merely turned and exited through the door at the end of the narrow hall. Once again Jesse was alone. The cell he was in was damp and poorly lit. He paced up and down the tiny room for a while to expend some of his pent-up anger, but the pain in his calf grew into a menacing throb. He sat down on his bunk, his head in his hands.

A voice from the next cell broke the silence. "Hey Sarge, you alright over there?"

Jesse grunted in reply, still too angry to answer civilly.

"If I were that corporal, I'd be scared thoughtless with the steel in your voice. You sure sounded like you were coming right through these bars at him." The disembodied voice chuckled with admiration.

Jesse had never seen the man in the cell beside his because a solid wall divided them, though they'd talked quite a bit. He was a corporal named Christopher Duggan, and he'd quietly admitted that he had, in fact, deserted his post when the tension of the fox hole he'd lived in for several months became too much. He'd spirited himself away in the dead of the night and made a run for Paris. He'd spent two weeks living on the streets of Paris until the armistice was announced, then he'd turned himself in. He was expecting to face his court martial any day.

Knowing that the family was leaving for Dillon dampened Sari's Christmas spirit and threatened the hope she'd held on to. Instead of delighting in last minute Christmas surprises, Sari spent the evenings either helping Claire get ready or helping Meredith with Esther. In reality, Meredith was feeling well and was becoming a very able mother. Sari recognized this, but she relished having somewhere to go and something to do that brought her joy and comfort.

The restaurant was busy on Christmas Eve with last minute shoppers in town needing a noon-time meal. Predicting that customers for the dinner meal would be few, Sari and Lilith agreed that cold chicken and potato salad along with an array of pies would suffice for dinner. The menu was designed to allow Sari and most of the staff to take off early, but it heaped work on Sari earlier in the day.

Feeling frazzled and tired when her shift finally ended, Sari hurried home to clean up and change. Then, she rushed to Claire and Daniel's for what she hoped would be a restful and peaceful evening.

The house was anything but peaceful. Claire welcomed Sari with a hug, then quickly turned to bark at Gregory. "Greg, I've asked you twice now to carry out this pile of blankets. Please, do it now!"

Knowing she'd sounded harsh, Claire looked up somewhat sheepishly and tried to smile. "Sari, we've decided to leave for the mountains tomorrow right after breakfast. I truly wish you'd agree to come with us. I hate to think of you here in such peril."

Daniel came in from the bedroom then with his arms filled with coats and sweaters.

"What she means," he quipped with a grave smile, "Is that Claire decided we were leaving early."

"But Daniel, you agreed that with the clouds building to the west and with the news we just got from Cheyenne, it would be a good idea to set off sooner."

"I know, Dear, but I hadn't considered how much we still had to do to get ready." He nudged the back screen open and disappeared, leaving Sari wondering.

"What's happened to prompt this decision Claire?"

"I saw a Cheyenne paper this morning. Sari, the news is frightening. More than thirty people have died in Cheyenne of the Spanish flu since the first part of November."

"But Cheyenne is quite a ways away. Surely a place as remote as Encampment won't see many cases."

"Maybe, but one of the men who just died there worked for the Union Pacific. Up until he got sick, he was riding trains from Cheyenne to Evanston. That means he could have infected people very near to us. Oh Sari, I know I am probably being an alarmist, but my mother lived a very secluded and isolated life on the farm in South Dakota. She rarely went to town and had few visitors, yet she contracted and died of Yellow Fever during an epidemic. The Spanish flu is much more contagious and also more deadly." Claire met Sari's eyes with a pleading look. "Sari, we've lost Jesse. I simply can't take the chance of losing Daniel or the boys. Or you. Please come with us."

Finally, Sari understood her sister-in-law's panic. She pulled Claire into a tight hug and the two stood together, sharing strength and fear.

"Claire, I've talked with Royce. He knows where you will be, and he's promised that if things get bad here, he will load up his family and me and we will join you."

Claire wiped her eyes and smoothed her hair. "I know, and I'm glad there's a plan. I just can't help worrying."

Sari watched the effort Claire expended, then, to regain some semblance of a Christmas spirit. She and Sari set the table and finished dinner together. As the family prepared to sit down to a hearty meal of potato soup and toasted cheese on thick slices of home baked bread, Daniel stoked the fire in the parlor.

They ate together, allowing themselves to put away worries and enjoy the celebration of Jesus' birth. After dinner, all four pitched in to clean the kitchen and wash and dry the dishes. It wasn't long before they were all sitting by the fire in the glow of the Christmas tree lights in the parlor.

"Mama, I'm glad you agreed to let us open our presents tonight since we are leaving early," Greg announced. "I was worried you'd forgotten the gifts under the tree."

Claire laughed aloud, maybe for the first time in a week. "I see where your priorities are, young man," she scolded back.

"Here," Greg continued, "Mama you be the first to open one. It's from me."

Claire was touched at his gesture, and thrilled at the set of lace handkerchiefs the package contained. They took turns opening gifts. There was a new, warm scarf for Sari, a gardening book for Claire. Greg was thrilled with a travel-sized checker board and a deck of cards. "Thanks so much, Aunt Sari. I lost one of my checkers the other day, I can't find it anywhere. Now we'll have something to do up at the cabin."

"I know it's still early," said Sari after the wrappings and ribbons were cleaned up and the echoes of gratitude were quiet, "But it's been a long day and you have an early morning ahead, so I think I will head home."

"You're sure you don't want to join us? It's not too late." Sari knew Claire's invitation was heartfelt and genuine, and she would have loved to agree, but the fear of foreclosure kept her resolute.

Instead of answering with words, Sari hugged Claire, and whispered, "All will be well, you'll see."

A note on Sari's door when she got home brought a nice surprise. Bea's flowery script brought a welcome invitation, "Daniel told Royce that they'd decided to leave early. We hope you'll agree to come to our house tomorrow for Christmas dinner. Come when you get off work."

The work was light at the Copper Pot Christmas Day, and both the customers and the Wills were in jovial moods, so Sari's day went well. When she arrived for dinner across the street, she was greeted by smiles and warm, luscious smells that helped her shake off her loneliness and cares for a while. She'd decided to take the family a batch of cookies wrapped in a tablecloth on which she'd embroidered a flowered edge. The gift was a hit, even with Royce. They ate, then sat down to play several hands of gin rummy. The climax of the evening was an announcement by Harriet that she was expecting. "You

and Royce are going to be amazing parents," Sari told
them with her congratulations.

Buoyed by the fun evening and easy
companionship of her neighbors, Sari returned home
carrying a plate of leftovers and a new china tea cup from
Bea. She switched on the lamp and took off her coat. She
paused to admire the small tree she'd set up and
decorated in one corner of the parlor. A box of ornaments
from the attic along with a few candy canes made the little
tree festive. Underneath were two unopened gifts. Sari
knew it was silly, but she just couldn't let the season pass
without buying something for Jesse. Since she couldn't
mail anything to him with any hope that he'd receive it,
she'd wrapped the gifts she'd found at Parkison's in red
paper and placed them under the tree a week ago.

One box held a light green shirt Sari thought
would look good on her husband and the other, a more
narrow box, held a gramophone recording of the Dolley
Sisters singing "I'm Always Chasing Rainbows".

"Perhaps I am just chasing rainbows," she said
aloud to the little tree, "but who can blame me for wanting
to hold on as long as I can to the man who was willing to
marry me and give me this home?"

She stood there for a few minutes longer,
whispering prayers for Jesse and also for Claire and the
family on their trip up the mountain, then she began
preparing for bed.

There was no doubt that the absence of Claire,
Daniel, and the boys was difficult for Sari. For the first
week, she managed to ignore the gnawing solitude by
filling her thoughts and time with focusing on cooking at
the restaurant and visiting either Meredith or Bea and
Harriet. Her self-imposed mental oblivion carried her
through until New Year's Eve.

At the beginning of the holiday season, Lilith sat
down with Sari to plan a year's end celebration for the
restaurant. Lilith had envisioned an evening of candlelight
and special menu items to entice the people of
Encampment to celebrate at the Copper Pot. As the

Spanish flu threat crept closer and closer, however, and people's fear of crowds grew, the celebration was cancelled. When the restaurant closed early on the thirty-first, Sari found herself facing a long evening on her own.

Her loneliness pushed on her as she made herself a meal and tidied up the kitchen. Finally, sitting in the parlor alone except for the crackling fire and two unopened presents under the tree, Sari let down her guard and let her tears flow. She felt alone, not abandoned exactly, especially since she'd been urged to join her family in the mountains, but bereft of their support and the comfort of spending time with them. She'd felt this way before, and the familiar, hollow sadness tore at her.

She let herself have a thorough cry. Then, when all her tears were spent, Sari realized that while the feeling was familiar, the situation was wholly different. Before, she was a child at the mercy of others. Now, as an adult and because of Jesse's provision and kindness, she had control, or at least some control.

With that thought in mind, Sari dried her eyes and began making a plan.

39
Paris, France
late - December, 1918

Three days before Christmas, Corporal Duggan, the man in the cell next to Jesse, was court marshalled. After the hearing, he returned to his cell and happily related to Jesse what had transpired.

"Well, old man, it looks like I've lucked out. The General pronounced me guilty and took away one of my stripes. I'm demoted to private, and they are giving me a discharge for the good of the service. They are punishing me by sending me home."

Jesse took a wheezing breath and shook his head. Though he and Daphne had been certain that his pneumonia was gone, living for the past six weeks in the chilly dampness of his cell had brought back his cough and the ache in his chest. "So, when do you expect to be sent?"

The joy in Duggan's voice was unmistakable, "I leave right away! I'll be given orders and attached to an infantry company that ships out for England in a few days. It looks like I'll make it home within a month."

Jesse hung his head. He'd been asking to see or talk with someone, anyone who would listen to him and verify his story, but so far no one had even agreed to supply him with paper so that he could write a letter. He was sick, tired, and discouraged.

While he'd never seen the man whose disembodied voice had been the only saving grace of his time in the brig, the two had become fast friends.

After a few moments, Duggan spoke again, "Atley, if you tell me the names of your commander or others I could contact, maybe I could help you. When they let me out of here, I'll do everything I can to contact your CO."

With a glimmer of hope, Jesse coached Duggan on who to contact.

For two weeks after the new year arrived, Sari kept herself busy. She continued her habit of stopping in to see Meredith and the baby every few days after work. On other evenings, she stopped in at the hardware store to visit with Nathan. He looked good, Sari thought as she left one evening. He seemed comforted in spite of the recent passing of Miss Lillian.

At home, she cleaned and primped the rooms, rearranging furniture and adding small touches to make her home inviting and comfortable. She began a new embroidered tablecloth, this one for Claire, and worked on it as she listened to music in the evening. She also worked her way through the latest J.W. Jung Seed catalog, resolving to plant a larger garden this summer and put up her own produce.

News regarding the Spanish flu epidemic became more and more threatening as the days passed. Right after Christmas, news of the illness began to emerge from Rawlins, and in the first week of January, the Saratoga City Council met in an emergency meeting to discuss steps they could take to safeguard the city.

Royce supplied Harriet, Bea, and Sari with details he'd learned, "They are discussing quarantining anyone who wants to go into Saratoga. So many people are fleeing the threat in Rawlins and coming to Saratoga, that they are afraid the flu will take hold there."

"How long do they need to isolate newcomers?" asked Bea.

"At least three or four days. It sounds like that's how long the disease takes to present itself."

"Is Encampment thinking of any quarantines?" Harriet asked as she rubbed the small bump on her belly, clearly concerned.

"I haven't heard anyone bring it up at City Hall," her husband answered.

Three days later, Sari was frying chicken at the Copper Pot when Mr. Wills entered the kitchen. He stood silently and watched her work for a few moments before clearing his throat. Sari glanced up. His somber face made her feel cold inside.

"We've got a sick customer up in room eight. Doc Irwin just left. He's arranging to have the man moved up to Good Shepherd Hospital. He says it's the Spanish flu."

Sari felt like she'd been kicked in the stomach. She concentrated on removing the golden brown drumsticks from the pan and then slid the pan off the fire so she could concentrate on what she'd just been told.

"Lilith is notifying the other guests and telling them they need to check out right away." Wills paused and looked around the kitchen. "Finish what you are doing here and wrap that chicken up for me to take home. Get everything washed up and clean, take the garbage out like usual. I'll pay you for half of today, but then I won't need you again, we're closing down."

"Uh, how long do you think we'll be closed?" Sari asked.

"There's no telling, but when The Copper Pot does reopen, I'm not sure if I'll re-hire everyone. I might not need you again at all. I'll let you know if I do."

With that, he turned around and left.

When Sari left the Copper Pot an hour later, she stopped at Parkison's to pick up a few groceries and some more thread for her tablecloth project. The bell jangled happily as Sari entered the store. "Good afternoon, Mrs. Oliver," Sari called as she approached the counter. The clerk had her back to Sari and when she turned around it was clear she'd been crying.

"Oh hello, Dear," Mrs. Oliver answered. "You're here early."

"Mrs. Oliver, what is it? Are you alright?"

"Well, no. I've just heard the news that Mr. Suttles, you know, our other clerk? Well, he's got the Spanish flu and isn't doing very well."

"That's horrible news! He's such a nice man. When did he become ill?"

"Just last night, and he isn't the only one in Encampment to be sick. I've heard that Mrs. Carver has come down with it, and so have two of the Peryam children. I'm afraid our little town isn't safe any longer."

"That's true. A guest at the Copper Pot has become ill as well. Mr. Wills just closed the hotel and restaurant down."

"I know Mr. Parkison would never close us down, since people are going to need supplies, but let me assure you that I'm planning to stay home and stay out of contact with others as much as I can."

Sari considered the woman's words. "I agree. If you don't mind, I'd like to pick up several things so that I can do just that."

"Of course."

Within a few minutes Sari's order was placed and filled. Soon, laden with a box of supplies, she was on her way home.

Without someone to talk to, time barely moved for Jesse. His cough was worse, and he had a headache. Corporal Barstow stayed clear of Jesse. The local man who delivered Jesse's two meals a day spoke only French and was not inclined to attempt a discussion with him and his rudimentary command of the language, so beside hellos and thank yous, Jesse had no one to talk to and no way to break up the monotony of the day.

About mid-morning on the third day after Duggan left, loud voices carried down the hallway and within just a few seconds footsteps, solid and determined, grew nearer. A blur of Army green came into view and stopped in front of Jesse's cell.

Staff Sergeant Wiggins, his voice loud and imposing, slapped the bars and announced, "Hey Atley, we thought you were dead, Boy! So glad to see you came through this war."

Jesse stood up, astounded at the man's sudden appearance. Before he could respond, Wiggins continued, "Get that door open, Private. This man never should have been in this cell in the first place."

When the door was open and there was nothing between them, Wiggins offered Jesse his hand and shook it enthusiastically.

Jesse began asking questions, but Wiggins waved him off. "I'll have time to fill you in later, but we have a train to catch. There's a soldier out here that needs to talk to you a minute and then we have to dash to the station."

Side by side Jesse and Staff Sergeant Wiggins left the block of cells. In the outer office, a lieutenant Jesse had never seen before stood beside Corporal Barstow. Jesse and Wiggins saluted the officer.

"I'm Lieutenant Carson, Sergeant Atley, and it seems as if my office, and most especially Corporal Barstow here, have been responsible for your unjust incarceration, though I've heard of you only just this morning. I want to extend my sincere apologies to you for the mishandling of your file."

"Thank you, Sir," Jesse responded.

Then, Carson turned a stern eye to his corporal and waited. The man visibly squirmed and dropped his head, then quietly told Jesse, "Sergeant Atley, I do apologize that you've been here so long. Your case should have been handled more efficiently."

"Now Barstow, I know you can do better than that after what you put this man through." The officer's voice was hard and low.

Barstow swallowed and began again, "Yes, Sir. Sergeant Atley, I neglected to contact your unit when I should have, and I did not pursue the investigation in a timely manner. I apologize."

"You are dismissed, Corporal," the lieutenant told him and Barstow left the room.

"Atley, I assure you, Barstow won't be a corporal much longer. He will be reprimanded and steps have already been taken to make sure that he doesn't bungle anything else in my office."

Jesse was too surprised to feel jubilant or gloat that Barstow had been dealt with, but he did smile at the officer and thank him again.

"Beg your pardon, Sir, but if we aren't on the platform in fifteen minutes, we're going to miss our train to Cherbourg."

"Then you better hurry, Staff Sergeant," smiled Carson. "Good luck to you both."

They did make the train, though barely. The two arrived at the station just before the conductor called for boarding.

"This isn't a troop transport, Sarge," Jesse remarked as they climbed aboard.

"You figured that out, huh?" Wiggins teased. He led the way toward the front of the train, and picked two seats on the left side.

"Sit down. We've got some catching up to do."

Jesse sat down. The exertion of leaving the brig and getting to the station had worn him out and brought him to a coughing fit.

Wiggins motioned for the porter, who reappeared with a glass of water. When he could speak again, Jesse began, "Staff Sergeant Wiggins, thank you, for the water and the rescue. How did you find out I was there if my file was buried on that little weasel's messy desk?"

With a loud guffaw, Wiggins explained. "Well, apparently you made friends with one Christopher Duggan while you were in your prison. Duggan called the division yesterday, and I got the message. It took a bit, but I caught up with him and got his story about you. When I called the adjutant's office, I talked to Barstow and asked him about a Sergeant Atley. He said there wasn't anyone by that name, and we went 'round and 'round for a while. Turns out, that corporal, uh, private, had misspelled your name on top of everything else, and had it listed as Hatley."

Jesse stifled a cough, took another drink of water, then shook his head in pure disgust.

Wiggins continued, "The short version is, I ended up getting Lieutenant Carson on the telephone. I explained to him that you were missing, having been sent behind enemy lines on a sensitive mission. He put some pressure on Barstow. A couple hours later, they found your file plus the papers you'd turned in with sensitive battle plans you'd kept from the enemy. Then mountains began to move to make things right.

"They dispatched me this morning to come fetch you. Now, we are on our way to Cherbourg to join the division, and we'll be on our way home to New York within the week."

Jesse felt so relieved he couldn't find words. As the train began its slow trek out of the station, it finally occurred to him that the war was actually over.

40
Encampment, Wyoming
January, 1919

Once she got home and had her groceries put
away, Sari looked around her quiet home and wondered
what the next few days and weeks had in store. She didn't
feel panicky, but could readily admit to herself that she
was concerned about coming down with the flu. Her
contact so far had been far removed, both at the
restaurant and the store, she didn't think she was in
danger yet, but keeping herself safe was certainly on her
mind as the day progressed.

Dawson was busy with the horses when Sari
stopped in at the livery two days after the restaurant
closed down.

"Good morning," she called. A muffled howdy
returned to her as she took off her coat and sat down at
the desk. It had been over a week since she'd updated the
business' books. Smiling to herself, proud of all she'd
learned about bookkeeping and her home finances, she
opened the ledger and began rifling through the receipts
on her desks.

Dawson plopped down in a chair beside the desk a
few minutes later. They exchanged hellos and Dawson
assured Sari that both his wife and daughter were doing
well and feeling fine. "Esther has a little runny nose, but
Mere thinks she could be getting a tooth, so she's not
worried."

"She's just barely four months, isn't that too young
to get a tooth?"

"Meredith says she was pretty young herself, so it
probably runs in the family."

Sari spent the next hours at the desk with her
head in the livery's ledgers. Dawson was close by to
answer any questions she had, but he busied himself with
the horses and upkeep on the truck. *It's nice,* Sari
thought, *to be here in the daytime and not feel rushed and
tired when I'm working on livery business.*

She tapped her pencil on the desk absently as she
counted her blessings. The past months had been hard.

Bills were paid for the business and there had been enough to give salaries to both Sari and Dawson, but there'd been nothing left over. Times had been lean. Now that the war was over, she told herself, there was real hope that business would pick up enough that not only would the business survive, but maybe they could even grow a little. She had never discussed the future with Dawson, they had pointedly refused to even mention what they'd do if Jesse never came back. Now, she feared, they would have to face facts and have those talks and make plans. *I'll wait until Daniel comes back,* she decided. *I wouldn't want to make any decisions without his insight and advice.*

When she left the livery, her next stop was the post office. As she approached the center of town, it was clear that with the flu's arrival, life in Encampment had changed. The sidewalks were nearly deserted. When friends met at the post office, on the street, or in a shop, they stayed distant from one another. No one shook hands or accepted hugs. Conversations were cordial but brief, somehow laced with a kind of suspicion and fear of who might be carrying the deadly disease.

Sari collected her mail and continued on to Parkison's for eggs and flour.

A mourning bow hung at the front door. Inside, Ed Parkison, dressed in black, was at the counter talking with two ladies from church. Sari didn't know either woman well. Mr. Parkison greeted Sari and the women nodded, then the conversation resumed.

"Yes, it's a stunning loss," Parkison told the ladies. "Denver Suttles worked for me for many years. I will miss him immensely."

"Mr. Suttles was your best clerk without a doubt," added the lady wearing a blue felt hat. "The flu didn't take long to take him, though. He seemed very robust just last week when I shopped here."

"Hearing that William Parr succumbed last week to the flu was a terrible blow, and now we've added dear Mr. Suttles to the list. I wonder when it will end?" the shorter woman said as she dabbed at her eyes.

The other woman nodded then added, "Did you hear about Professor Sutton and his family? He died

Friday morning, and their baby died that same evening. Poor Mrs. Sutton died two days later, though I wonder if she died of the flu or a broken heart."

Parkison added, "Ella attended the burial for Mr. Parr on Tuesday. She said there were only two people there beside herself and Reverend Abraham."

This was all news to Sari, and she felt ill to know the deadly consequences Encampment had already experienced. She was frightened now, as she hadn't been before.

Ed Parkison noticed that she had paled during the conversation and assuring the ladies that their purchases would be delivered within a few hours, he turned to Sari and asked her, with a kind smile, how he could help her.

Sari handed the man her list and told him she needed to pick out some embroidery floss.

"I'll get this ready for you right away. Shall I have it delivered?"

Sari thought for a moment then replied, "Add some canned milk and three of those apples. please," she indicated a bin near the counter. "I'll take those with me, but the rest can be delivered if you don't mind."

Parkison smiled again and answered, "I don't mind at all, Mrs. Atley."

Sari picked out two new colors of floss for her tablecloth project, settled her account, and left the store. She was laden with worry as well as her package. She covered the few blocks between the store and Meredith's lost in concern.

Sari's apprehension grew as she approached the house. The curtains were drawn, which was unusual. Meredith loved to let the sun and light into her small home. It wasn't until Sari knocked at the door for the third time that she got a response and by then, Sari's heart was pounding. The door didn't open, but Meredith's muffled voice called from within, "Sari, you don't want to come in here. The baby is really sick. She's got a horrid cough and she's terribly fussy. I've been feeling really tired and achy, and last night I started to have a fever."

"Do you need help? Where's Dawson?"

"He's here. He's not feeling well either, but he's been taking care of me and walking the baby. It's the only way to make her stop crying."

"Do you need me to get the doctor?"

"No, he was here this morning. We just need to rest."

"I brought you some fruit and canned milk. I'll leave it for you here on the porch. Do you need anything else? I'd be happy to go back to the store and get you anything."

"No, I just went to the store the other day."

Sari hated not being able to offer more. "Meredith, I'm going to go home and make some noodle soup. I'll bring some for you for supper later, alright?"

"That would be wonderful, Sari. Thank you so much."

Having something constructive to do helped Sari endure the afternoon. As she chopped and cooked, she prayed for her friends and for Encampment.

While the soup was simmering, Sari baked a batch of cookies. As evening approached, she readied the meal, then carefully carried it to Dawson and Meredith. Fearfully, she knocked at the door. Dawson's voice came right away from the other side, "Is that you, Sari?"

"Yes, how is everyone doing, Dawson?"

"Meredith and the baby are both sleeping, finally. Mere's fever is high, but the baby's is much lower. Meredith's cough did seem a little better this afternoon."

"Your voice sounds pretty rough, how are you?"

"My chest hurts some, but I slept a while this afternoon. I think I'm alright."

"I've got soup and bread for you, and some cookies for dessert. The soup is still quite warm, but you can put it on to simmer for when Meredith wakes up."

"Thanks, Sari," answered Dawson.

"I'll check on you in the morning," Sari promised.

Sari felt better as she walked home. Surely her friends would be alright. She returned to her kitchen, thankful that she had stayed in town, certain that she'd been of use to her friends in a time of need.

41
Charbourg, France
January, 1919

In Charbourg, Jesse's first stop before joining his unit was the infirmary. He'd tried to disagree with Wiggins about going there, but his argument was met with a jovial, "They need to do something about that cough of yours, I like to got no sleep on the train for listening to you hack. They also need to document your injuries."

The doctor who examined him was impressed at the healing in Jesse's leg, but concerned about his lingering cough. "I'm making notes in your file for the ship-board doctor to keep an eye on you. It very well could be that your congestion is a result of your incarceration. I've seen several men who spent time in that brig in Paris who came out with worse symptoms than yours. But, since you were recovering from pneumonia when you arrived there, this could be a recurrence. I'm writing orders for you that forbid working. That means lots of rest and no standing watches or exerting yourself. Chances are, by the time you dock in New York, you'll be breathing fine with clear lungs thanks to the fresh, clean air. Try to spend some time walking up on deck. Sunshine and fresh air along with some light exercise will do your lungs and your leg good."

Two days later, on January 12, 1919, a spontaneous cheer broke out among the men standing at the rail of the steamship *Nansemond* as the ship cleared the harbor at Cherbourg, France on its way to New York. Standing next to Jesse at the rail were his platoon members, Griffin, Baird, and Rex. A few feet down from him, Jesse caught sight of Staff Sergeant Wiggins, who gave him a wave of triumph.

Jesse and his platoon had boarded the *Nansemond* the night before, and were assigned to berths on the third deck. Jesse had a small cabin to himself, while the other three shared a larger compartment one door down. When

he'd first entered his room, he was surprised to discover
that his wooden Army trunk sat safely at the foot of his
bed. Jesse had been afraid the trunk, which held his extra
uniform, plus the letters and small gifts Claire and Sari
had sent him, had been lost with his absence. Later, when
he mentioned it to Griffin, he was told that they had made
sure to carry it with them, thinking that they would send
it back to his family when they could.

Jesse looked around him. The ship was nearly five
hundred sixty feet long and eighty feet wide. Fitted to hold
nearly 27,000 men, it was a floating city. Built in Ireland
in the late 1800s, the ship had been operated by a
German company until it was seized by the Americans
and put into Allied service. As they crossed the Atlantic on
their way home, Jesse got to know it well as he roamed
the decks, following the medic's advice. He enjoyed being
reacquainted with the sea, but looked forward to going
home even more.

A twenty-one gun salute, banners, a brass band,
and a cheering crowd met the *Nansemond* when it docked
at Newport News, Virginia twelve days after she left
France. The doctor's prediction had come true and Jesse
felt much better. The dockside scene was jovial yet
bittersweet. Wives and families were there to meet several
of the companies onboard. Those men had been given
liberty to reunite with their loved ones and ordered to
report later for processing.

Most of the men, however, could only watch the
happy reunions as they were shuttled onto transports for
the next portion of their journeys home. Because he'd
been wounded in action, Jesse said good-bye to his
company and his platoon on the wharf and was taken to a
facility in nearby Richmond.

Armed with a casserole of eggs and sausage tucked into a market basket over one arm, Sari left the house with a light step. The sun was warm on her shoulders as she walked. The wind was calm and the sky a deep, rich blue. The peace and beauty of the morning brought renewed hope. Since it was on the way, Sari ducked into the post office to pick up her mail. The postmaster handed her two envelopes.

The top one was from the City of Encampment. *Probably my light and water bill,* Sari guessed as she moved it to the bottom. Then she froze. The return address listed on the next, thick envelope was the bank in Rawlins. Thinking that finally Mr. Bagley had sent her copies of her father's loan, she sat down on a small bench in the foyer of the post office, putting her market basket down beside her and carefully opened it.

She had to read it twice before the news of the letter sank in.

> *Dear Mrs. Atley,*
>
> *It has come to my attention that you are no longer employed at the Copper Pot. This letter will serve as notice to you that according to the terms of your loan, arrears longer than fifteen days will place your loan in default. We must receive payment of one hundred dollars plus a late fee of twenty-five dollars in addition to your regular payment of one hundred dollars for the current week in our office by February first in order to rectify this situation.*
>
> *If you are unable to fulfill this obligation, we will be forced to redeem the value of the full loan through foreclosure upon your home in Encampment, Wyoming.*
> *Sincerely,*
> *Edward R. Bagley, vice president*

Fighting panic and nausea, Sari swallowed hard and tried to breathe. *A hundred dollars a week? How could that be? My efforts at the Copper Pot weren't worth that much. They couldn't have paid such a huge amount.* Shaking, Sari flipped through the other papers in the envelope. They were the original loan documents complete with her father's bold signature. She didn't bother to try and read them as she sat at the post office. She did stare at her father's name and was assailed with memories of how small and abandoned she'd felt the day the bank had auctioned off her home and land. Overwhelmed with fear and doubts, Sari returned the letter and papers to their envelope and placed it carefully in her coat pocket.

I've got to talk with Royce, she decided. *I'll go straight to City Hall after I drop this food off with Meredith and show him this letter.*

The day had warmed in the time she was inside the post office, though the air still retained its winter bite. Sari didn't notice it now. She was mired in worry and kept her eyes low.

As she approached the Wiley family's porch, Sari could hear Esther crying. She knocked and stepped back off the porch to wait. No one responded, though Esther continued to cry. She waited a moment, then knocked again, harder. Still nothing. Sari put the casserole dish down on a bench on the porch and knocked once more as she called out, "Dawson, Meredith, are you awake?"

Beside the insistent cry of their infant, there was no sound from within. Sari felt frantic. She banged on the door and called again, then left the porch and ran around to the back. She pounded on the back door. The only response was crying. Sari tried the back door, it was locked. She returned to the front to check that door as well. Locked.

Near panic and uncertain what to do, Sari turned to see if anyone was on the street who might help her. Seeing no one, she made a quick decision. Turning, she hiked up her skirt and began to run. Royce's vehicle hadn't been parked in front of his house when she'd left hers, and she hoped he'd be at City Hall, two blocks away. Breathless, she entered City Hall and frantically looked around.

"May I help you?" the clerk asked warily at her abrupt appearance in the office.

"Yes," panted Sari, "I'm looking for Deputy Rogers. There's an emergency."

The clerk opened her mouth to ask what kind of an emergency when Royce emerged from the Mayor's office. With one look at him, Sari burst into tears, "Royce, it's Meredith and Dawson Wiley, they aren't answering the door, and the baby is crying."

Sari knew she wasn't making sense, so she stopped. Taking a breath she began again. "I've just been to the Wiley home. They've all three had the flu. I can hear the baby crying, but they won't answer the door, I'm afraid something dire has happened."

Royce nodded, "Let's go. Send someone for the doctor," he told the clerk. He gently guided Sari outside and to his car. He opened the door for her and then quickly got in and started the engine. "They live on MacFarlane right?"

"Yes," Sari responded, "Between 6th and 7th, the blue house."

"I think you should stay in the car," he told Sari as they drove up. "I'll go in."

Sari watched as Royce strode up the walk. He rapped on the door and waited. When there was no answer, he tried again, then tried the door. Then, in a quick motion, Royce shattered the glass of the door with his elbow.

Unable to stay sitting, Sari got out of the car and stood on the sidewalk as Royce disappeared inside. A car drove up and parked behind Royce's. An older gentleman in a grey suit got out and approached Sari. "I was on my way into town when the mayor flagged me down and sent me here. What's happened?"

Before Sari could answer, Royce reappeared in the doorway, "Doc, I need you in here."

The commotion on the street attracted attention. Neighbors stood on porches and watched, interested and caring but afraid to get too close. Sari stood rooted to the sidewalk near the street. Esther's wails were louder now with the door open, and Sari's heart felt shattered at the news she was afraid she was about to hear.

Finally, the man in grey appeared with the baby bundled in a blanket. Royce followed him down the steps and onto the sidewalk, holding a piece of paper and looking grave. Sari stepped forward, but was cautioned to stay away.

Royce spoke first, "Sari, do you know the doctor?" She shook her head no, concentrating on the bundle in the man's arms. "Dr. Harry Irwin, this is Sari Atley, Jesse's wife."

Irwin nodded and greeted her.

Royce continued, "Sari, I hate to tell you this, I know you were friends with Mrs. Wiley and that Dawson worked for you and Jesse. Both of them have succumbed."

He let his words sink in a moment then continued, "It seems as if Mrs. Wiley left a note for you." He looked at the doctor, who nodded, "It's probably safe to give it to her," he said as he calmly bounced the whimpering child in his arms.

Royce handed the page to Sari. The writing was scrawled, difficult to read.

Dear Sari, Dawson is gone. I am weak and can't pick up the baby any more. If I die, which I fully expect, please, Sari, please raise Esther as your own. She needs a Mama who loves her and I know you will.

Meredith

Sari stared at the words, understanding but not fully taking them in. Filled with sadness and something else akin to awe, Sari looked up from the note as tears freely flowed. "I'd be happy to take her," she whispered as she reached for Esther.

Irwin took a step back. "Wait, remember that the child has also had Spanish flu. You are risking infection if you take her now."

"I dropped off soup last night and spoke to Dawson through the door. He told me that the baby's fever had broken yesterday morning and that she was doing much better. She may not be contagious still, right?"

The doctor considered then nodded, "She probably isn't anymore, but her clothes and blankets still harbor the disease. I can't promise you aren't taking a risk."

401

"I understand," answered Sari, then she stepped forward and lifted Esther from his arms. "How long until we know for sure that she is no longer contagious, and how long before I begin to feel sick if I'm meant to?"

"Three days. I suggest we quarantine the both of you for three days. If you don't have symptoms and she is fever free, we can assume all is well."

"I'll take you home, Sari," Royce said softly. "Then I'll come back and help the doc deal with the, with this."

Irwin shook his head, and volunteered to take Sari and Esther home so that Royce could stay. As she was getting into the doctor's car, Sari asked him, "What about the baby's things, her diapers, clothes? Meredith was nursing her, I don't have any bottles, though I do have some canned milk."

"Because of the contagion, very little inside is salvageable for now. Once we remove the deceased, the house will need to sit empty for at least a week, allowing the contamination to die on its own. Then, the house and all its contents will need to be washed thoroughly before anything can safely be used. In the interim, I'll stop at Parkison's and put in an order for necessities for you, bottles and milk, diapers, some clothes, and blankets. I'll have them delivered to you as soon as possible. The child has exhausted herself from crying and is in danger of a relapse. Judging from how rank she smells and how papery her skin is, it's been too long since her last feeding. I advise you to bathe her and feed her right away."

Esther began whimpering again as Sari closed the front door a few minutes later. Laying the baby down on the settee, Sari removed her own coat and stood silently for a moment. So much had happened in so short a time, she couldn't grasp it all, and she knew she didn't have the luxury of even trying. Grief for her friends and concerns about Esther crowded out all other concerns.

Heeding the doctor's warning, Sari left Esther for a moment and hurried to the kitchen. She filled the sink with warm water and accumulated soap and towels. Ready now, she carried the child to the kitchen. Sari nearly gagged as she unwrapped the blanket surrounding Esther. "Oh my, Little One," Sari said aloud. "You do need a bath." She carefully undressed the baby then wrapped up her soiled clothes inside the blanket and put them outside on the back porch.

Sari had helped Meredith but had never given a child a bath before by herself. It wasn't easy for either of them. By the time Sari was satisfied that the baby was clean and rinsed, they were both tearful and wet.

At last, Sari wrapped Esther in a towel and stood, consoling her. Then, she pulled a dish towel from the kitchen drawer, folded it, and pinned it on Esther as a makeshift diaper. Wondering what to do about clothes for her, Sari thought for a moment, then took the baby upstairs. She rifled through Jesse's bureau, something she'd never done before, and felt triumphant when she pulled out a soft, white undershirt. She slipped it on the child. Laying Esther down for a moment, Sari shucked off her own, wet dress, and changed into another.

Back downstairs, Esther's cries diminished to pitiful whimpers. Knowing she was hungry, Sari warmed some milk on the stove, dipped a corner of another dish towel in the milk, and rubbed it gently on the baby's lips. Her response was immediate, and she began sucking. Sari tried it again, and the response was the same, but when Esther realized that she was only getting a drop or two of milk at a time, she became fussy and refused to try any more.

Sari was walking up and down, from the kitchen to the parlor, trying to sooth the child to sleep when there was a knock at the front door. "Yes, yes, who is it? I can't open the front door, we are quarantined."

"Yes, Ma'am. I know that. It's Jonah, Mrs. Atley, from Parkison's. I have a box here for you with things for the baby. I'm to tell you that Doctor Irwin says at first to only feed her two ounces at a time then wait for thirty minutes or so. You don't want to feed her too fast."

"Thank you, Jonah, I understand."

"Oh, and I nearly forgot, you are also supposed to put in one drop of the iron supplement he ordered into each two ounces. It will help her gain her strength."

Sari thanked him again, watching as he stepped off the porch and walked down the sidewalk. She put Esther down to retrieve the package. Soon, warm, dry and fed, Esther was sleeping soundly in the middle of Sari's bed.

For the rest of the evening, Sari concentrated on Esther, banishing sadness or worry. She attended to practical matters, forcing herself to stay calm. As she fed and rocked her charge, she thought about the extra bedroom upstairs, and decided to make it Esther's nursery. There was a small chest of drawers in that room which would work perfectly to hold the baby's cloths. There was a single bed in that room, too, that might be used when Esther was older, but for now Sari knew she would need a crib for her. She wondered how she could ever summon the strength to go back to the house where her friends died and retrieve Esther's belongings.

For the night at hand, she considered making a bed for the baby out of a drawer. Finally she decided to just bring Esther into bed with her. She decided someone warm and near might help Esther feel more secure, then wondered if she was trying to console the baby or herself. "After our quarantine, we will have plenty of time to fix up your nursery," she told the sleeping child.

Sari fed Esther for the third time, and quietly carried her upstairs. Surprisingly, they both slept well. Once, at about three fifteen, Esther came awake and began fussing and crying. Sari was pleased and surprised when four ounces of milk and a new diaper put her back to sleep, and that she was able to drop off herself.

43
Richmond, Virginia
mid – January, 1919

Berthed in a large barracks full of snoring soldiers when he arrived in Richmond, Jesse had trouble sleeping. The next morning, he was sent to the medical clinic. After waiting a short time, he was escorted to an examination room. There, a haggard, grey-faced doctor in a wrinkled lab coat gave Jesse a thorough medical check-up.

"I have some paperwork to do for you, Sergeant," the doctor told him as Jesse buttoned his shirt. "If you'll just wait in the waiting room, I'll be with you as soon as I can."

With that, Jesse found himself sitting on an uncomfortable wooden chair in an austere but busy receiving room. An hour later, he was shown to a tidy office and asked to sit down.

Within minutes the same, worn-looking doctor came in and sank into his chair behind the desk.

"Sergeant Atley, you seem to be a lucky man all in all," he began. "I've read through your file. It's a wonder you aren't deaf from that explosion, that you didn't lose your leg from infection after being shot and spending the night in a frigid, muddy creek, and it's a wonder you didn't succumb to pneumonia and sepsis. But here you are, quite healthy and hearty."

"Yes, Sir," Jesse agreed with a smile.

The doctor continued, "I don't know how your relationship with your Maker is, but I'll tell you one thing, He clearly has something in mind for you to accomplish since He went to such lengths to save you and restore you to health. I hope you recognize that and use the time He's given you to good advantage."

On the voyage across the Atlantic, Jesse had entertained similar thoughts. Now he responded to the doctor's admonition with a sincere nod of the head.

"Following the guidelines the Department of War has given me, I'm declaring that your leg injury, the reduced hearing in you left ear, and the lung issues you've experienced make you unfit for further service to your country. I've signed your honorable discharge papers as well as this other form that says you are eligible for a veteran pension. You'll need to take these documents and orders to the accounting office and they will register them and help you make plans to get back home."

Jesse expected the discharge. The medics in Cherbourg had already indicated to him what the Army was likely to do, so he wasn't surprised at the papers the doctor handed him. What did astonish him was how efficiently the clerks at the accounting office processed the paperwork. It was early afternoon on January twenty-fifth that Jesse, discharge in hand, walked away from the Army.

Fortified with a wallet full of back pay and the feeling of freedom, he arranged to have his foot locker sent ahead to the train station. He headed first to a dry goods store where he purchased a new pair of pants, two shirts, a pair of boots, and some under garments. Then, he checked himself into a modest hotel and took a long, hot bath.

At the same time Jesse was soaking, Sari was sending prayers of thanks heavenward. Esther was lying on the bed, gurgling and cooing as she kicked and squirmed. Her smiles reminded Sari of Meredith, and sadness at the passing of Meredith and Dawson muted the bright rays of sun that streamed into the house.

Sari combatted the sorrow by staying as busy as she could. She lined a wicker clothes basket with a soft blanket and put Esther in it on the floor of the kitchen while she cooked herself some breakfast. By the time Sari finished the dishes, Esther had nodded off for a morning nap.

Sari left her, warm and safe in the kitchen, and moved to her favorite chair in the parlor. Now, rested from the shocks of yesterday and in the safety and solitude of her home, Sari had time to think about all that had happened. She let herself feel the grief she'd postponed and considered the new responsibilities she'd acquired.

There's a lot here, Lord, Sari prayed. *Meredith was my good friend, and I'm so sad she's gone. Dawson is the reason the livery is still open. How am I supposed to raise their daughter and keep the livery open myself? If I can't run the livery, how am I supposed to live with no income and no job and also raise Esther all alone, especially if the bank takes away our home?*

Tears and heartache surrounded Sari like a blanket. She cried for Meredith and Dawson, their lives cut so unfairly short. She cried for Jesse, trying to absorb that he, too was gone. She cried for Baby Esther, who would never know her mother. And she allowed herself to sob and feel sorrow and fear for herself.

After a time, Sari stopped feeling sorry for herself and began to think rationally again. She got up and blew her nose. She decided to tackle each problem one by one. Armed with paper and pencil, she made a list.

First, Esther. Sari smiled. That was easy in comparison to the others. She certainly had doubts about her ability to be a mother all alone, but Claire, Daniel and the boys would eventually come back, and she knew without a doubt that they would support her and help her in any way they could.

Next, she retrieved the bank's letter from her coat and read it again. Carefully she studied the loan papers. Her father had borrowed thirty-five thousand dollars at fourteen percent interest. Nowhere in the papers was there any indication of what the bank received at auction for the land, the house and their personal effects. There was also no indication of how much the Wills had paid on Sari's behalf. Sari reread the terms, perplexed. That the loan was outstanding conflicted with her memories of celebrating that her parents were debt free. In addition, she'd always thought her father was a careful and practical man, and a loan this large and at such a steep rate of interest seemed out of character. Comforted by what Royce had shared with her about possibly crooked dealings by the bank, Sari tried to tell herself that with Royce's help, they could sort this out. Setting aside the letter, she turned to her other pressing concern.

Income. Of course, the whole point of their marriage was so that she could receive money from Jesse's life insurance if he didn't return. Before he left, Daniel discussed that policy with her. He told Sari that he expected, now that the war was over, that the government would begin processing those policies, even for men who were missing like Jesse. He volunteered to take her to Rawlins as soon as they could so that she could check on the life insurance and fill out the necessary paperwork to begin receiving widow's benefits. "I can't rely on any of that for now, though," Sari whispered, "And according to this letter from the bank, I have until February first to sort out my father's loan and pay them. *Just how am I going to support myself?*

With Dawson gone, Sari knew that either she'd need to hire someone right away to work for her at the livery, or she'd have to close the business down. Closing Jesse's business didn't feel right, and Sari saw that as her very last resort. The livery was her income and livelihood, and she needed to protect it. Certainly, Daniel or maybe Nathan would have an idea of whom she might hire, but until she could talk with him, Sari knew that she had no recourse but to temporarily shut down.

A single thought brought Sari suddenly to her feet. The horses! There were horses at the livery that needed food, water, care. Sari's heart began to race as she realized that it had probably been two or three days since Dawson became sick and the horses had been tended.

"I've got to let someone know!"

Her loud exclamation startled Esther, and she began crying. Sari, near tears herself, hurried to the kitchen to check on her. Sari was just coming out of the kitchen with Esther in her arms, when someone knocked at the front door.

Sari, relieved and also concerned, stood beside the closed front door and called out, "Hello! I'm under quarantine, so I can't open the door. Who is it?"

"Sari, it's Bea. I know what's happened. Royce told us all about Meredith and Dawson. I'm so sorry! Are you and Esther alright?"

"Yes, we are both healthy so far. I feel just fine. But Bea, I've got a terrible problem." She continued, telling Bea about her fear that no one was caring for the horses at the livery. "Someone needs to go there right away, Bea!"

"I'll tell Royce as soon as he comes home, he won't be gone long. But Sari, I came over to tell you that Royce is taking me and Harriet up into the mountains. Apparently, Royce and Daniel Haynes discussed our moving up to Dillon with them if things got bad here. And Spanish flu is hitting Encampment hard now. Edith Dunbar, the telephone operator is very sick and might not survive, and five or six of the Peryam family are very ill, too. Did you know Professor Sutton, who was the principal of Encampment School? Well he, his wife and baby daughter died within a day of each other, just like Dawson and Meredith. Do you remember Mrs. Carver from our aid society meetings?"

Sari answered hesitantly, "Yes, she's so sweet, is she ill?"

"She was sick but is getting better from what I hear, but her brother, Edward Stambaugh has been here visiting her, and he's died. Oh, and William Parr, who was one of the first residents in the area, has also died. Reverend Abraham has been conducting funerals every day or two. Sari," Bea's voice cracked as she continued, "Englehart's mortuary buried Dawson and Meredith this morning. It's so sad and frightening that Harri and Royce decided that we have to leave."

The list seemed to go on and on. Sari had trouble grasping that more people she knew, friends, were dying and she'd never see them again. She understood the decision Royce and Harriet were making, but the thought of them leaving, too, made her stomach hurt.

"Sari, we want you and the baby to come with us."

Bea had to repeat herself before Sari focused in on the invitation.

"It was Royce's idea, and we all agree, we can't leave you here. Please say you'll come."

Sari looked down at the child in her arms, sleeping once again, then put her back to the door and slid down. "But Bea, I'm under quarantine. I can't leave for at least two more days. I can't run the risk of taking the flu up to Claire and Daniel, or infecting you and Harriet. I couldn't take that chance."

"Royce has that all worked out. He just left to check on a few things and get supplies. Harri and I are packing heavy clothes, blankets, and food to take with us so we are ready to leave when we can."

"I don't know, Bea. I don't know if Esther is strong enough for the trip. I, I just don't know."

Bea answered softly. "Sari, you can't stay here alone. Please think about it. If something happened to you, I couldn't bear it. As soon as Royce gets home, I'll tell him about the horses. He'll take care of finding someone to look after them. Please, think about it."

Sari promised she'd consider it and then listened as her friend's footsteps retreated down the sidewalk.

Afterward, she sat for a long while with her back to the front door, thinking about the offer she'd just received. When the baby began to fuss, Sari pulled out of her reverie and headed to the kitchen to warm a bottle. Her thoughts swirled, unsure of what she should do. She debated with herself as she fed Esther and continued the contest as she put the baby down on the floor and watched her play and kick.

The sound of Royce's vehicle pulling up in front of his house across the street got Sari's attention and within minutes there was a solid knock on the door.

"Sari, it's Royce, please open the door. It's alright."

She hesitated but complied. Royce smiled reassuringly and asked to come in. "First, Bea told me you were concerned about the horses at the livery. I stopped in to check on them, and they are fine. Nathan Jameson from the hardware store was there. He told me that when he'd heard about Dawson's passing and you being quarantined, he stepped in to take up the slack."

Sari sighed, thankful once again for Nathan. Royce continued, "I think you need to come with us. The outbreak here is severe, more than anyone anticipated. Besides all that are sick and have passed on right here in town, there are more and more cases in the whole valley. I've just been told that eight men and one woman have died at a French Creek tie camp. Before they left, Daniel assured me that he'd prepare a cabin near them just in case this happened. We will stay sequestered from the others for a few days once we arrive, making extra sure we aren't carrying anything. My wife and sister-in-law, along with Claire, would probably never forgive me if I didn't insist you come with us." His shy smile pushed Sari's decision over the edge.

"You are convinced we won't spread the flu to you, Harriet, and Bea, or take the disease up to my family?"

"Sari, I'm sure. You and Esther are healthy with no symptoms. We will take all the precautions we can and stay away from them until we are all certain it's safe. I also talked again with Doctor Irwin. He agrees that this isn't rash."

Sari hesitated. In the end, it was the thought of being left all alone without friends or family that persuaded her to agree.

"Great," Royce told her when she gave him her decision. "But it's clear that there's a storm coming in, so we need to get going."

"We're leaving today?"

"Yes. As soon as we can. We've packed enough food for an army, including a case of canned milk. You need to gather what you need for the baby and clothes for yourself. I want to be pulling out of Encampment within the hour if we can."

Sari closed the door when Royce left a few minutes later, her heart pounding. Esther was still happy on the parlor floor, so Sari raced upstairs to pack.

While his wife was preparing to run for the mountains, Jesse lingered as he finished his bath, relishing his new freedom and the luxury of peace. Deciding he was hungry, a few minutes later he was out on the busy street, happily dressed in civilian clothes.

He ate a hearty meal and read the *Richmond Times-Dispatch*. He was interested to see a short article reporting that General Pershing was planning to stay in Europe until the last American was evacuated and that Pershing and President Wilson were both hoping that all Americans would be home within the next eight months. Other articles described the constant stream of troop transport ships arriving back in America each day. Jesse smiled to read that evangelist Billy Sunday was hosting a three-day revival in Richmond, calling the meetings a "Campaign

against Satan in Richmond." There were articles
chronicling the ratification of Prohibition in America.
Though he'd heard many conversations about the Spanish
flu epidemic, there was nothing in the paper about it at
all.

When he'd exhausted the news, Jesse paid for his
meal and headed towards the train station.

A train west was scheduled to leave in just a few
hours, so he checked himself out of the hotel, sent a
telegram both to Claire and to Sari telling them to watch
for him in three days, and bought himself a ticket home.

44

Dillon, Wyoming
mid – January, 1919

Snow was beginning to fall when Royce turned the
car off the main road. The twenty miles behind them had
taken six hours to cover. Harriet, sandwiched between
Royce and Sari, dozed with her head lopped to one side.
Bea was wedged into the back seat, barely visible among
the boxes and blankets they'd packed in. Royce glanced
sideways. Seeing that Sari was awake, he told her quietly,
"We're only about four miles from Dillon but this might be
the hardest part of the trip. That frozen creek under the
bridge we just crossed is Haggarty Creek."

"I've heard of it. It's named for Ed Haggarty, right?"

"Yes, we actually will cross the creek two more
times on our way up. I don't expect we'll have any trouble
with the crossings even though there are no more bridges,
everything is frozen solid. I'm certainly glad we stopped up
at the top of Battle Mountain to put the tire chains on,
though. That grade down the mountainside would have
been treacherous if we hadn't." He paused, then motioned
with his hand, "Do you see this road? That leads to the
cabin that Nathan Jameson and his wife lived in."

In the dim headlights Sari could just make out
where the road forked. The path leading to the right trailed
off into the trees and darkness. She remembered several
stories that Nathan had told her about his life in the
mountains. "I'd like to visit here some day in the light,"
she told Royce.

"It's beautiful up here when the snow's gone, but
not very inviting in the winter."

The road became increasingly rough and winding.
Sari listened as the engine labored up steep slopes and
around tight curves. Her arms ached from cradling Esther.
The night plodded on. Twice they were stopped at snow
drifts across the road and Royce had to shovel a path
through. The beam of the headlamps barely disturbed the
gripping darkness. Low clouds cut off all but temporary
glimpses of the moon and occasionally a star flashed
above them in quick defiance of the gloom. Sari felt as if

they were bumping through space. Finally, as the moon began its downward arc toward the horizon, the trail widened and flattened out. Royce's voice seemed overly loud, "We're almost there. Ladies, welcome to Dillon."

Sari watched as tall shadows began looming. The effect on her tired mind was menacing. After they passed the first set of buildings, Royce turned the car left onto a side street. Within a few seconds, he made a second turn to the right. He honked the horn twice and pulled the hand brake.

A light came on, and quickly afterwards Daniel's silhouette appeared in the door. Royce got out of the car but didn't approach the cabin. "Daniel, it's Royce. I have my wife, sister-in-law, and Sari with me. We want to take no chances of infecting your family, which cabin should we move into?"

"Let me get my coat," Daniel answered, disappearing inside. Moments later, he reappeared, carrying a lantern. "I'll keep my distance, Royce. Just follow me and I'll show you where to go and help you get the fire started."

A few minutes later, with lanterns lit and a fire dancing in the fireplace of the nearby cabin, Daniel called, "Good night" to the travelers and moved away. Only then did they pile out of the car and approach the cabin.

Sari was pleasantly surprised. There were two bedrooms plus a loft in addition to a large kitchen and dining area that served also as the parlor. Instead of looking as if the place had been abandoned for years, it was newly dusted and swept. Clearly, Claire had worked to prepare the cabin for them.

"Sari, why don't you and Esther take that room? Royce and I'll take the other. Bea, will you be alright in the loft?" asked Harriet.

"Of course," Bea answered with a grin. "It will be the warmest room in the place."

Sari put Esther down in the middle of the bed in the smaller of the two bedrooms and shook her arms, thankful to be able to move. Then she went to help Royce unload the car.

"I know we're all tired," he said as they carried in the first load, "But I'm afraid our food will freeze if we leave unpacking until the morning."

"Anyway," Bea added, "We're going to need our clothes and blankets right away."

It was snowing hard by the time the car was emptied. Sari stood watching the large, wet flakes catch shards of light from the window, sparkling as they fell.

Jesse sat alone towards the back of the train car. He noticed that people on the train and in the station seemed wary of their fellow travelers. Everyone stayed as far removed from one another as possible. He wondered aloud to the conductor about his observation. "It's because of the threat of the Spanish flu, Sir," the man answered. "The coast seems to be recovering, but the contagion has been moving west." Without anyone to talk with, the trip quickly became monotonous so Jesse helped himself to a dime novel someone left in the dining car, thankful to have something to help while away the hours. Watching the scenery pass by the train window was tedious at best. From Richmond north all the way to Chicago, trees hemmed in the tracks, obscuring all but fleeting glimpses of anything interesting. After Chicago, the view was wider, but Jesse soon became weary of the sameness of flat, winter farmland.

Somewhere near Ogallala, Nebraska, the monotony began to end. Even, tilled ground slowly gave way to gently rolling grasslands. Jesse felt happy as the train pulled out of Pine Bluffs, Wyoming and he began to see grey, greasewood sagebrush dotting the prairie. He smiled to himself as the train labored up the steep grade between Cheyenne and Laramie knowing he was getting ever closer to home. Familiar names began to greet him. Bosler, Medicine Bow. He stared as Elk Mountain, stately and imposing, dominated the horizon to the south.

Finally, Wolcott Junction chugged into view. Jesse grabbed his valise and stood at the door, ready.

He only had a short layover in Wolcott before the Saratoga-Encampment train pulled into the station. Jesse watched as they loaded his foot locker onto the baggage car, then he swung himself aboard.

Jesse purposely sat on the right side of the train so he'd have the best view. Slowly they gained speed. That he'd arrived just after a winter storm was clear—drifts of snow created an artful texture on the flat, sage covered floor of the Platte Valley. When at last he could see the Sierra Madre mountains, the sun echoed off the clean, snowbound summit of Bridger Peak like a lighthouse beacon.

Jesse blinked back the tears that came. He was home. *I was so sure when I left that I wouldn't return,* he thought. *So certain that my life would be spent as wages for war. Now here I am.*

Encampment, snuggled down in a shallow depression, wouldn't be visible until they had nearly arrived. He kept his eyes on the mountains above town as they crept closer. Not for the first time, Jesse let himself think of the future. *What now?* He asked himself. The doctor's words came back to him, and he wondered just what God's plan was for him. He thought about Sari, wife and near stranger when he left. Now though, because of their letters, he knew there was a connection. *Will it be enough to make an actual marriage work?* He wondered. He hoped so.

Once again Jesse was standing at the door when the conductor opened it. He alighted on the platform in Encampment before the train was completely stopped. He looked around, expecting any minute to see Claire and Daniel and the boys. Maybe even Sari would be there to welcome him. He knew he hadn't told them exactly when he'd arrive, but his wire had told them three days and there was only one passenger train each day into Encampment, so he'd expected someone to be there.

He looked around, then tamped down his disappointment.

A young man stood by the depot door, "Paper? It's the *Saratoga Sun.*"

"Is it today's?" Jesse asked with a smile as he reached into his pocket for a coin.

"Yes, Sir. January twenty ninth. It's got all the news about the storm and updates about the Spanish flu."

Jesse handed the boy a nickel and tucked the paper into his valise. He looked around and found a porter. He offered the man a quarter and asked that his valise and foot locker be stored for him. "I'll be back later this afternoon to pick them up," he told him, thinking he'd stop by the livery to see Dawson and drive the truck down after he'd been home.

Jesse set off. He'd decided that since it was early afternoon, he'd go see Claire first. After a brief reunion, he'd go to the Copper Pot to meet Sari. Surely, they'd planned a reunion dinner for him for this evening.

All the drapes were closed at Claire's and despite knocking several times, no one answered. Jesse was perplexed. He hustled down the street towards his own house. Both the front and back doors were locked.

Fighting rising concern, Jesse came off the porch at an uneven run and rounded the corner on his way to the livery. A sign posted on the livery door made him icy inside. "Due to the ravages of the Spanish flu, the livery is closed until further notice."

No! It wasn't a prayer, but yet it was. *No, please.*

He looked around, and for the first time noticed the emptiness of the streets of his home. The *Saratoga Sun*'s headline came back to him, "Spanish Flu Hits Hard in Encampment." Jesse stood in front of his livery, his mind rebelling against what his fears were telling him. He took a breath and made himself calm down. Rational thought returned and he set out for City Hall, intent on getting news and answers about his family there. He rounded the corner of 7th and Rankin and headed west. A car Jesse didn't recognize drove by, and he could see two women walking on the sidewalk ahead. The town began to appear a bit more normal.

Jesse was just across the street from City Hall when someone behind him called him, "Jesse? Jesse, is that you?"

Turning around, Jesse was elated to see Nathan Jameson. He turned around and took two quick steps towards his friend. "I can't tell you how good it is to see a familiar face!" Jesse extended his hand, but Nathan ignored it. Instead he pulled Jesse into a rough hug.

"Jesse, we thought you were killed in action."
Nathan's voice was husky, filled with emotion. He released
his hold on his friend and stepped back, "Sari got a
telegram saying you were missing. That was back in the
fall. When there was no new information, we feared the
worst."

"I was wounded behind German lines. A French
family hid me and cared for me. But right after the
armistice was signed I made it back to Paris. Sari and
Claire should have been notified."

"To my knowing, there's been no news of you since
that first telegram."

Jesse paled. "You mean no one, not Claire, not
Sari, knows I'm alive?"

Nathan nodded, his eyes showed deep regret. "Let's
don't stand here on the street. Come down to the store."

Nathan led the way, and Jesse sat heavily on the
same stool he'd occupied a few days before he'd left for the
war. Nathan poured them each a cup of coffee from the
pot on the wood burning stove, then took the stool beside
him.

"When I left Paris I was told that my family had
been notified. You're telling me that they weren't, and that
they've thought all this time that I was dead? That they
still do?"

"Yes, after no news for so long, we all became
resigned to it. All except Sari, that is. She refused to
accept that you were a casualty. The subject was a raw
one at times between her and Claire I'd guess. Claire
wanted to have a memorial service for you. She started
talking about it about the first part of December, but Sari
wouldn't agree."

Jesse sipped his coffee and let this news sink in.
Then, his thoughts turned to the empty houses and his
closed business.

"Nathan, where is everyone? I've been to Claire's
and to my house. They are locked up tight. The livery has
a sign that says it's closed until further notice. What's
going on?"

Nathan shook his head, "Your family is all fine, the
last I heard. Be easy about that." He watched as Jesse
exhaled and his shoulders relaxed a little before he

continued, "Many people died in Rawlins, then in Saratoga. Claire became worried and insisted that Daniel take her and the boys up to Dillon to wait out the epidemic. She told me she just couldn't stand losing anyone else after losing you. They left on Christmas Day. Sari stayed behind, but then the flu arrived here, and hit the town hard. We've lost about a dozen people to it, though there is hope it is slowing down now."

"Sari didn't go with them? Why not?"

"She wouldn't go. She didn't want to leave her job at the Copper Pot." Nathan shook his head, but Jesse instantly understood why Sari would make that choice. "Then she must be at work right now," Jesse began to stand but Nathan put a steady hand on his arm.

"Wait, there's more to tell. Claire and Daniel had been gone a couple of weeks. More and more people became ill, and finally businesses began to shut down. The Copper Pot is closed."

"Then why wasn't Sari at the house?"

"Sari has become friends with Sheriff Royce Rogers and his family."

"I'd heard about that in her letters, I've been really glad. They are really good people," Jesse added.

"Yes, well, Harriet, Royce's wife, is with child, and they decided four days ago to join Claire and Daniel in the hills. They took Sari with them."

Jesse sighed. "So they are all fine and out of harm's way?"

"Yes, I believe so. They were healthy when they left here."

Jesse's relief was evident, but then he asked, "But what about the livery? Why has Dawson closed it down?"

Nathan's look was grave, and Jesse sensed hard news was coming. "Dawson died, Jess." He explained softly, "I'm sorry, I know he was a good friend. He'd worked so hard to keep the livery going and provide service that you'd be proud of."

The news hit Jesse like a blow to the chest. He took a ragged breath.

"What irony, Nathan. I go to war and make it back alive, but Dawson stays here and doesn't."

Nathan nodded. After a moment he continued, "I've been going in to feed the horses every day. We got hit with a quick, ugly storm three days ago, so they haven't been exercised enough, but other than that, they're fine." Nathan realized that since Jesse had been out of touch for so long, he probably didn't know about Dawson's marriage or the child. He decided that perhaps news of that could wait.

Jesse sipped his coffee and tried to absorb all Nathan had told him. This was not the homecoming he'd anticipated.

"When are they coming down out of the mountains?" he asked after a time.

"As I said, Royce and his group left just four days ago. They rushed out of here as the storm was approaching. Royce indicated that they'd taken food enough for at least three weeks since they didn't know how long the flu would continue to be a danger here. This last storm dumped a lot of high country snow also, so getting back down might be a challenge."

Jesse finished his coffee, then sat the cup down on the table with a decisive thunk. "Nathan, I just can't wait any longer to see my family, or let them continue to think I'm dead. I'm thinking I'll be heading up there in the morning."

Nathan nodded. "I'm not surprised, but traveling alone through those hills this time of year isn't wise."

Jesse looked at the man with defiance, ready to argue, until Nathan finished his sentence, "so it seems I'll be going with you. What time do you want to leave?"

45
Dillon, Wyoming
mid – January, 1919

Snow and wind raged through the night and most of the first two days that Sari and her companions were in Dillon. Blizzard conditions whited out any possible view of their new surroundings. They had no contact with their neighbors, the storm kept them all inside. Sari really didn't mind. She and Esther were tired from the bouncing trip. The stress of their new relationship and missing Meredith also made them both weary.

When the sun cleared the peaks above and light touched the cabin windows on the third day, Sari peered outside. The sky was an effervescent blue accented by a few high, wind-curled clouds. Sunshine glistened off the fresh snow creating contrasts of dark shadows and bright, stark white. Sari stared at the ghost town around her, marveling at the tall structures on the streets below.

Harriet treated them to a hearty breakfast of eggs, biscuits with homemade raspberry jam, and thick slices of bacon. Afterwards, Bea and Sari happily washed dishes using melted snow they heated on the stove while Harriet gave Esther a bottle of warm milk.

"She's such a sweet baby," Harriet remarked. "I hope the one I'm carrying has her disposition."

"I hope he's naughty," teased Royce as he pulled on his boots. "Just like I was."

The bantering was interrupted by a strong knock on the door, "Hey, are you up?" came a call from outside.

Royce opened the door to find Daniel, Greg, and Michael outside, wearing thick hats and coats, and shod in snowshoes.

Daniel smiled, "How is everyone feeling? Everyone alright?"

Royce pulled on his coat and answered, "Yes, we are all healthy. How long do you think we need to stay away from you all to make sure we haven't brought unwanted pestilence with us?" His tone was jovial, but his words serious.

"Claire says that if everyone is feeling good, then we've waited long enough. She's about to go crazy in want of some feminine company and has sent me over with strict instructions to bring her friends right over!"

It wasn't long before Harriet, Bea, and Sari were bundled into their coats and boots, ready to go calling. Esther wasn't pleased when Sari wrapped her tightly in a blanket and covered her face as she left their warm house. It wasn't far to their neighbor's cabin, but the deep, powdery snow made walking a challenge. The sun continued to shine as it slid across the azure sky, but the thin air held on to very little warmth. By the time they'd reached Claire's doorstep all three women sported red noses and cheeks.

Claire opened the door as they arrived. She hugged Harriet and Bea and welcomed them inside. Sari was a bit behind and was last to enter the cabin. Claire stepped back as Sari entered and gave her sister-in-law a quizzical look. "What's in the bundle?"

Sari handed the wiggling parcel to Claire and said with a wink, "How about you unwrap it and find out."

The three newcomers laughed as they watched Claire's face when she discovered the annoyed child inside her wrapping. "What?" began Claire, then a confused "Who?" She paused to study the child as Sari removed her own coat and hung it on a peg beside the door.

"But Sari, why do you have Esther?"

The ladies became subdued as Sari explained. "Meredith and Dawson both passed away." Sari gave Claire a few details and ended by telling her sister-in-law, "There was a scribbled note from Meredith asking that I raise Esther as my own."

Claire wiped a tear from her cheek and looked up at Sari. "She couldn't have chosen a better mom for her daughter, Sari."

With their plans to leave in the morning made, Jesse left Nathan and walked the quiet Encampment streets back to his home. Using the key hidden under the porch, Jesse let himself in. He shut the door, then leaned back against it with closed eyes. He took a deep breath and whispered, "Thank you," to God for allowing him to come back home.

Only then did Jesse notice the envelope on the floor at his feet. He recognized the yellow and brown paper and knew it was his unopened telegram from Richmond. No doubt the delivery had arrived not long after she'd left for Dillon.

He took a slow stroll through the rooms, noting how the furniture had been rearranged, the new curtains in the kitchen, the doilies on the parlor tables. He nodded his approval at how Sari had made small and large changes , making the rooms prettier, and he relished how sparkling clean and shiny everything was. The smell of wood oil and Lysol brought a smile.

Sari's presence was especially evident in the large bedroom upstairs. A new, flowered bedspread with matching curtains had converted his austere and useful room into an inviting and comfortable refuge. He was surprised to find all his clothes still just as he left them in the tall bureau, but then remembered Nathan told him Sari had never given up hope of his return.

After his tour, Jesse lit the stove in the kitchen to take the chill from the house. He put on a pot of coffee. Waiting for it to begin perking, he sat in the kitchen, feeling and enjoying his surroundings. *Sari's done a great job with the house,* he mused. *She's made it a home that I still feel a part of.* Details jumped out at him. His dusty cowboy hat was still hanging on the hook by the back door where he'd left it, but now beside it hung a feminine straw sun hat with green grosgrain ribbons.

A few minutes later, armed with a cup of steaming coffee, Jesse moved into the parlor. He stared for a long time at the Christmas tree, still decorated but quickly losing its dry needles. He knelt down to inspect the two packages resting beneath, moved that both were adorned with labels naming him as the intended recipient. That Sari had held on to her hope that he'd return touched him deeply. He smiled, thinking how he would add the gifts he'd purchased for Sari in Charbourg and Richmond to the tree, imagining the fun of celebrating Christmas when they were finally back home together.

When he stood up, the gramophone beckoned him. Soon, Mozart's music replaced the silence. A basket full of papers beside his desk in the parlor caught his eye. When he stooped down for a closer look, he realized that the small hamper contained dozens and dozens of envelopes, each unopened and addressed to him. In awe, he picked up the one on top, turning it over several times. He stood up, then, and reached for the letter opener that lay on the blotter. He carefully slit the envelope open and withdrew a single piece of paper.

Sari's familiar script seemed hurried, almost reckless, and when he read her note, he understood.

> *Dearest Jesse,*
>   *I am so frightened. Sickness and death are all around us and I feel so alone with Claire and Daniel gone. Royce has just convinced me that we need to run to the mountains. I hesitate, what if there's news of you while I'm gone? Who will take care of the horses at the livery? Bigger questions loom: How will I run things now that Dawson is gone? How am I going to answer the foreclosure letter from the bank? So many questions and simply no answers. I just can't even think straight. I wish you were here. Your steady thinking and confidence would be enough to get us through. I'm praying that if God has chosen for me to face this alone, then He will give me some of your insight for the decisions I need to make. Royce will be here any minute. I need to pack.*
> *Yours, Sari*

Jesse could feel Sari's burden and see the tension in her hand writing. He didn't understand what she meant about foreclosure but his determination to see this woman was stronger than his curiosity. He wanted to reach into the basket again and keep reading, but he knew that there wasn't time for that now. Thoughts of her letters reminded him that he had all her other letters tucked safely in his foot locker, and that he needed to get the truck from the livery and retrieve the locker and his valise from the depot.

Royce and Daniel chopped wood for the cabins' fireplaces and then helped the boys build a snow fort while the ladies chatted and visited inside. The reunion was joyous despite the news from town and details about the ravages the flu had brought.

Greg came in after a while, stamping snow from his boots and wiping his nose on his sleeve. "It's cold out there. I need to warm up," he told them as he began shedding his coat and hat.

"Put your boots and wet clothes over by the fire, Son," Claire coached. "They'll dry faster."

He plopped down on the floor in front of the stove in his stockinged feet and leaned against the side of Sari's chair. "Do you think I could hold her?" Gregg asked Sari as he watched her rock Esther.

"She's just fallen asleep, but when she wakes up, yes of course you can. I'll bet you'll be able to make her giggle, too." Sari answered. Then she asked Claire, "Would it be alright if I put her down on your bed for now?"

"Yes, of course."

When Sari returned to the kitchen, Claire asked her, "Where did Esther sleep last night?"

"Actually, she's been sleeping with me. I will need to get her crib when we get home, but the poor thing has been through so much, I've thought she might benefit from feeling someone close to her."

"I'm sure that's true," responded Harriet, who was helping Bea put a jigsaw puzzle together. "Some people say that it isn't good to sleep with your children, but my ma did."

"Yes," added Bea, her attitude light, "But Ma also kept lambs and piglets in the house all the time also, so maybe she isn't the best one to use for advice."

This brought chuckles from each person in the room. The conversation drifted to other topics. Greg seemed to doze by the stove. Suddenly he sat up, "Mama, we still have a baby bed out in the lean-to. I saw it when we got the sleds out. Couldn't Esther have that for herself?"

Claire looked surprised, "Well, Greg, you are right. The crib both you and Michael used when you were babies is still here, we had no need for it in Encampment so we left it when we moved. That's a good idea."

Instantly, Greg was up and pulling on his boots. "I'll get it!"

It took him three trips, but before long he had the bed inside. With a little help from Sari, Claire, and a screwdriver, the bed was assembled and scrubbed. Sari stood back, admiring the finished product. "Claire, this is beautiful."

The crib had thick, turned wood posts made of dark oak. Thick slats of matching polished oak created the sides. "Was the mattress for it out in the lean-to?" Claire asked her son.

"Well, yes, but one end was frayed where there'd been a mouse nest in it, so I didn't think you'd want that."

"You're right about that," Claire chuckled. "We'll use a quilt as a mattress for now. No mouse nests for my niece."

"I'll ask Michael to help me carry this over to your cabin after a while, all right, Aunt Sari?"

Michael poked his head in the door a few minutes later to coax Greg to come back outside again. Greg solicited his help with the crib and with that errand complete, soon the brothers joined Daniel and Royce sledding and exploring. The afternoon slipped by, filled with laughter and easy banter. In the late afternoon, the men rejoined the ladies. Michael was excited to describe the snow fox they'd seen.

Dinner was a pot luck affair full of good conversation. Greg and Michael took charge of Esther, laying her on the floor by the hearth and taking turns making her chortle and laugh with their funny faces and noises.

Sari cherished the day and didn't want to do or say anything that might spoil the festive air, yet again and again her mind kept returning to the problems that loomed back in Encampment. Toward the end of the evening, she quietly said to Royce, "I've received a letter from the bank in Rawlins. They are threatening foreclosure now that I don't have a job. Would you be willing to look at it and give me your advice?"

Royce nodded, "Of course." After a pause he added, "I think it would be a good idea to include Daniel."

Sari didn't hesitate, "Yes, I think you are right, and Claire also."

At the end of dinner, Sari noticed Royce speaking quietly with his wife. A few minutes later, when they were all relaxing beside the warm fireplace, Harriet stood up. "This has been a wonderful day, but I am tired. Bea, I think it's time for you and I to go back to our cabin."

Bea, who was already nearly asleep, nodded.

Harriet continued, "Sari, how about Bea and I take Esther with us? I'll feed her and put her down for you."

Royce walked the women home, returning quickly. A few minutes later, Claire sent her boys to bed, leaving Royce, Sari, Daniel, and Claire together. Sari felt shy now, worried. "I wonder," she began, "if we four could move over to the kitchen table? I have something I need to discuss with you, if you don't mind."

It was evident to Sari that Royce had already said something to Claire and Daniel. They quickly assented. Claire made sure that she sat next to Sari, and the meeting began with Claire's hand supportively resting on Sari's.

Daniel and Claire listened intently as Sari briefly told them about her first meeting with Mr. Bagley when he came to Miss Milton's and about the arrangement they'd made for her to work off her father's debts indentured to the Wills. She added her memories of celebrating being debt free. A wide range of emotions, from sympathy and concern to anger and outrage played across her in-law's faces, but they listened to her story in silence, except for a few quiet questions from Daniel.

When she told them about Bagley's earlier threats against Jesse's home and business, Claire gasped. Finally, her telling complete, she pulled from her pocket the letter she'd just received.

Sari sat in tense silence as first Royce, then Daniel, and then Claire read the letter. When she'd finished, Claire looked up at Sari with tears in her eyes. Daniel quietly took the letter from his wife and perused it again as Claire reached over to hug Sari.

"I'm so sorry. I can't believe you've carried this all alone for so long."

"I really wasn't all alone. Jesse knew about it. I tried to not marry him because of my debts. I didn't want him involved, but he said it was alright, that he and I would face it together. We wrote to each other about it."

"Did he have any suggestions after Bagley threatened you the first time?" Daniel asked.

"Jesse'd gone missing right before that, so he never knew."

Royce spoke for the first time. "I've always thought Bagley's timing was based on the fact that Jesse was missing. Sari would appear to be an even easier target for them as a widow."

"I'll do anything it takes to pay off my father's debt and keep the house and livery safe. I feel so desperate right now, though. I no longer have a job, I have Esther to think about, and this letter says I have until February first to pay the loan. I have some money saved up. In fact, I have enough to get the loan current, but I don't know how I could continue payments of a hundred dollars a week."

She paused, fighting the tears that wanted to fall. "It's been most frustrating because I've asked Mr. Bagley repeatedly, in person and by letter, to provide me with information about the remaining balance on the loan. My father's house and land weren't huge, but the house was nice and he had a hundred and sixty acres, I think. I don't know what they got for all of it at the auction, and I don't know how much Mr. Wills has given the bank as payment for my work."

Royce added, "Daniel, you might not be aware that Bagley is Wills' brother-in-law. They are in this together, no doubt."

The conversation continued. Finally, Daniel looked squarely across the table. "Sari, I want you to stop worrying about this. I've no doubt that there are shady dealings here, and I just know that together we can get to the bottom of it with a good solution. When we can, you and I, and Royce, too," he glanced to see Royce nod decisively, "will go to Rawlins. We'll meet with the bank president. I know him and he's always seemed to me to be a fair and honest sort. We'll demand to see all the paperwork, including the auction receipts and your pay receipts. We'll get a subpoena from a judge if necessary. There's no way Bagley and Wills take away your home or livelihood."

Sari could feel the anger and resolve emanating from Daniel. It reminded her of her wedding day when Jesse had confronted Mr. Wills. She had no words for the gratitude she felt.

46
Encampment, Wyoming
mid – January, 1919

Nathan arrived at the livery just after sunrise. Jesse had the horses saddled and was ready to go.

"Those steady Belgians will walk through the snow as if it wasn't there," Nathan remarked as he tied his bedroll behind his saddle. "They are such beautiful beasts."

Jesse rubbed his horse's neck and nodded. "These draft horses are hard workers. They never complain, never balk. I've really missed them."

The men swung themselves up into the saddle and nudged their horses into a walk.

"I'd suggest we go up towards Cow Creek. We can follow the tram route most of the way. It'll be quicker than on the road, and the snow shouldn't be too deep on this side of the range," Nathan told Jesse.

"I've never been on that route, but I imagine you know it well."

"I do. I've used that route many times. I estimate it will take us about six hours if we don't run into trouble," Nathan concluded.

They were traveling light, each man rode one horse laden with a bedroll and extra coat and trailed a second horse behind to carry food and necessary supplies.

It was a quiet day in Dillon. The men and boys lazed inside until after lunch. In the afternoon, Greg convinced them to do a little more sledding. Claire and Sari sat together for several hours, both intent on needlework projects. Sari concentrated on the flower edging of her tablecloth, while Claire's crochet hook darted in and out of a shawl she had nearly completed. Bea and Harriet worked on the jigsaw puzzle for a while, then Bea picked up a book while Harriet went to take a short nap. Clouds wrestled with the wind, sometimes covering the sun and sometimes leaving the blue above in peace.

The group was happy to share caring for Esther. They kept her fed, changed, and rocked. Sari fed her about three o'clock then laid the sleeping child on Claire and Daniel's bed for a nap. Smiling, Sari stood by the fireplace. "She slept like a rock all night last night," she said. "Your crib must have magical powers."

"It doesn't hurt that we've all given her so much attention and worn her out," Claire added.

"My back is sore from bending over this tablecloth," Sari continued. "I think I'd enjoy a little walk outside."

Claire rubbed her own neck and nodded. "That sounds good. I'd like to join you."

Bea looked up from her book, "I'm at a good part in this story. I'll stay here and listen for Esther. You two go ahead."

The snow was considerably deeper than when they'd arrived, but powdery enough that they could easily kick their booted feet through it. Sari and Claire headed down the hill. They'd walked just over a block when Claire began reminiscing. "I loved living in Dillon, though you can already tell it wasn't an easy life." They turned a corner and headed north. "That tall building with the pounded tin siding ahead was the Dillon Hotel. Malachi Dillon, who founded this town, was a shrewd businessman. The hotel was nice, elegant enough for the married ladies that lived here and rowdy enough to satisfy the appetites of the miners and sheepherders."

They continued their walk with Claire identifying businesses and telling Sari anecdotes about the town and its inhabitants. They strolled all the way down the main street, enjoying the brisk air and freedom. Somewhere on the ridge above them to the north, they could hear the gleeful shouts of Greg and Michael, so at last they turned uphill and followed the noise.

"This is so stunning," Sari said as they climbed towards a small plateau above the ghost town. "What a view." The women stopped to enjoy the colorful vista with its contrast between the deep velvety green of the trees, the carefree blue sky, and the white, perfect snow.

Turning uphill again, they climbed a bit farther to join Daniel standing on a small, flat bench at the bottom of a knoll. His hair was tangled by the wind and exertion, his smile broad and relaxed. "Hello Ladies. Come to take a run on our hill?"

"I don't think so," answered Sari right away. "It looks a little steep." No sooner than the words were out of her mouth, Michael came zipping past them, whooping and hollering.

Daniel laughed. "Those boys have that path so slick now, I'm afraid to try it."

They watched as first Gregory, and then Royce took a turn. Gregory stopped his sled at about the same place Michael had at the bottom of the slope, but with his extra weight, Royce's momentum didn't allow him to stop until he face planted in a snow drift several feet farther down the slope. He came up chortling and spitting snow, and Sari laughed until her sides hurt.

"Mr. Royce, that was the best crash of the day!" Greg announced with glee.

"I'm getting a little cold," Claire began when the merriment faded. "How about we go to the cabin and I make some hot cocoa for us all?"

The boys readily agreed and the troop turned downhill and back toward the cabins. They hadn't walked far when Michael stopped to watch something down the draw behind them. "Papa are those elk down there?"

Daniel turned around to look where his son was pointing. "Elk aren't this high up this time of the year son. I think those are riders."

Sari, Claire and Royce stopped and six sets of eyes strained to see.

"They *are* riders," said Greg with excitement, and he began to wave.

One of the horsemen responded by removing his hat and flapping it side to side. Michael squinted, then said solemnly, "Mama, that sure looks like Uncle Jesse. It even looks like his hat."

His observation was met with stillness as they all studied the newcomers.

The riders began their assent from the base of the valley, kicking the horses into a gallop. "Oh, God," Daniel whispered, "I'm sure those are Jesse's Belgians, and that looks like Nathan Jameson."

Sari felt rooted to the mountain. She forgot to breathe as she watched the riders close the distance between them. Suddenly, Claire let out a yelp. She hiked up her skirts in one quick motion and began to run. She hadn't gotten far when one of the riders pulled up close to her, quickly slid off his mount, and swung her up into a tight hug.

Daniel and the boys reached him next. The hills echoed the mirth of the reunion. Somehow, Jesse lost his footing when his nephews piled on him. Claire barely escaped before they tumbled like puppies in a happy heap.

In the middle of the muddle, Nathan dismounted and joined the group. Royce was the first to shake his hand. Daniel peeled himself away from the pile and brushed himself off, then shook Nathan's hand. Claire, sobbing, hugged Nathan tightly before letting Daniel tuck her protectively under his arm.

Sari stood a short distance removed, watching with wide eyes as the scene unfolded in front of her. Her breath now came in short gasps. Three words repeated in her mind, *thank you God, thank you God.*

Jesse regained his feet finally and looked around, searching. Gently setting Greg aside, his eyes locked on Sari's and he grinned. They were several paces apart, and she met him half way.

The next hour was controlled bedlam in Dillon. Claire refused to be far from her brother and Jesse held tightly to Sari's hand, so the other three men and the boys pitched in to get the horses cared for, fed and sheltered. In the meantime, Harriet and Bea were summoned and the women and Jesse converged on the cabin. Harriet took charge of preparing a meal, and eventually sent Jesse, Claire and Sari with the task of bringing the kitchen table and extra chairs from 'her' cabin so they had enough room to feed the group. Sari noted as she held the door for Claire and Jesse, that her husband favored his left leg as he walked, and that his breathing seemed labored at times. She didn't mention it, knowing there would be plenty of time for the hard details. For now, the conversation was joyful and light hearted.

Before long, the noisy troop was seated, though perhaps a bit cramped, at the extended table at Claire and

Daniel's. When they were settled and finally quiet, Daniel's prayer was short, "Thank you, God for bringing Jesse back to us. Your grace and mercy are overwhelming. Amen." Eyes glistened with tears and joy as they began their meal.

Claire sat next to Jesse, on his right. When everyone's plate was filled, she touched his arm and said quietly, "I understand your refusal to answer questions since you arrived. It was just too crazy. But I wonder, will you tell us now what happened and how the Army lost you?"

Nodding, Jesse took a bite of mashed potatoes and began. He told the story truthfully, though Sari, sitting on his left, was sure that he glossed over the worst parts, downplaying the danger he faced and the severity of his injuries to spare them all. Plates were empty and he was just describing how meek and mild Corporal Barstow acted when the lieutenant demanded he apologize to Jesse, when Esther, who had been sleeping in the other room, began crying.

Sari scooted her chair out and started to get up when Harriet stopped her. "I'll get her, Sari, you sit still."

Jesse gave Harriet a fleeting, bewildered look, but Greg distracted him by prompting, "I'll bet that dumb corporal felt pretty bad, didn't he Uncle Jesse?"

Smiling, Jesse nodded. "He did, I'll bet, but not as bad as I would have made him feel if there hadn't been an officer around."

The group had listened intently while Jesse talked, but now there were questions. Patiently, Jesse provided the answers. A few minutes after she left, Harriet reappeared, carrying a fussy Esther. She handed the child and her bottle to Sari and told her, "She doesn't seem to want me."

As soon as she was in Sari's arms, Esther settled down and began to eat. Shyly, Sari looked up and met Jesse's puzzled look.

"You must have a special touch with babies if Harriet's own child wants you instead of its Mama," he quipped.

Sari took a breath. "Well," she began, "the truth is, Esther isn't Harriet and Royce's child, though they do have one on the way. She's, well, she's mine, um, ours."

Jesse let that sink in a moment, but couldn't seem to understand. "But, how?" Jesse's mind reeled to places he didn't want it to go. *If this was Sari's child, who was the father?* Betrayal and hurt played on his face.

Sari read his reaction and tried to quickly quell his conclusion. "No! No, I didn't give birth to her!"

Now Jesse's confusion was complete. He looked around the table for support as Sari continued, "In all the excitement of your coming home, there's so much we have to catch up on. Did you receive my letter telling you that Dawson married Meredith, the young woman I worked with at the Copper Pot?"

"No. I didn't know that, but Nathan has told me that Dawson was taken by the flu."

"Okay. Well, Dawson and Meredith were married last year. Esther here was born in September." Sari paused. She knew that she would tell Jesse the whole story of Esther's parentage, but didn't want to talk about it in front of everyone. She continued, "All three of them contracted influenza, but Esther miraculously survived. Meredith and Dawson both passed away. Before she died, Meredith left a note asking me to take Esther."

The table was quiet. Jesse glanced at Claire then back to Sari. "Wow," he said finally. He realized that he would need time to absorb the changes around him, but he also knew that this wasn't the time. "You mean I'm a dad?" His crooked, playful grin let Sari know that all was well.

"Yes," added Claire, "and we are going to expect you to learn to feed your daughter and change her, too!" Laughter reigned once again at the table, and all talk of war and flu were abandoned.

"I'll tell you what," Sari said after a few minutes. "I'll give you your first dad lesson right now, and you can take Esther for me while I help clean up the kitchen."

"It's a deal." Sari couldn't tell whether Jesse's voice held a tinge of fear or reverence. She placed the contented baby in Jesse's awkward arms and got them settled together, then she turned to help the others.

Jesse cradled Esther, feeling her warmth through the blanket that wrapped her. Soon, Jesse decided to move out of the way and relocated to sit by the fireplace.

The ladies bustled around, clearing the table and conversing as they washed and dried dishes, Jesse and Esther became an island of peace and quiet. At first, Jesse concentrated on the child. He thought he could see a bit of Dawson in the set of her eyes, and hoped that she had inherited her father's kind spirit. The weight of his responsibility to be a good father to his friend's daughter settled on his shoulders and he was surprised to realize that it was a burden he was content to carry.

He looked up when Claire perched on a stool beside him. "They ran me out. How are you doing?" she asked her brother. "I still can't quite believe you are here."

"Me neither, Claire," answered Jesse softly. "I had my doubts that I'd ever make it back." They chatted together quietly, a combination of reminiscing and catching up. A noise caught Jesse's attention and pulled his attention toward the kitchen. Sari's laugh rang through the room as she stood drying a dish shoulder to shoulder with Bea. Unnoticed, Jesse and Claire watched her as she talked and teased.

"She's very different," he observed. At first, he thought the change was only physical. Certainly, her hair, in a loose braid down her back, was a style he'd not seen her wear before. The dress she wore was pale pink with an attractive rounded neckline, not like the grey or brown high-collared frocks he'd seen her in before.

"Yes, she's grown up a lot." Claire answered.

He pondered his wife as she concentrated on her work and finally realized that her transformation was deeper than any hair style or clothing choice. *She isn't keeping her head low and her face turned away,* he realized with surprise. *She isn't the timid, ashamed, and fearful girl I met.* He spoke his thoughts to Claire, "She seems comfortable with herself."

"Indeed," Claire responded. "She's become much more self-assured."

"Yes, that's it." He didn't speak his next thoughts, *She's contented both with those around her and with herself. Her head is high, and even though her scarred cheek remains, it doesn't seem to matter much now. She's beautiful in her confidence.*

"Daniel and I have been so impressed with her. She's been managing the books and paperwork for your livery all by herself for months."

Jesse was surprised at this, and felt a rush of pride and admiration for Sari.

As if she'd heard his thoughts, Sari turned around, and caught Jesse staring at her. Instead of turning away as she might have done another time, she smiled at him, letting her blue eyes rest on his surprised brown ones.

Not long after the dishes were washed and dried, heads began to nod. Royce, Harriet, and Bea donned their coats and wished everyone a good night before they left for their cabin. With a yawn of her own, Claire pointed at Greg sleeping by the fire and said, "Nathan, I'm going to make up a bed on the floor out here for Greg. How about you sleep in Greg's bed and share a room with Michael? It's comfortable even though it's a narrow cot."

Michael added with a smile, "I'd love to have you share a room with me and the bunnies, Mr. Nathan."

Nathan was puzzled until Claire explained, "The boys refused to leave their rabbits behind, so they have a crate in the corner."

"That sounds fine for me, but I hate to turn the boy out onto the floor, Claire," Nathan answered.

Claire laughed, "He seems to be doing a fine job of it already. That child can sleep anywhere."

"I'm tired enough to lie down beside him myself," quipped Jesse. "I haven't ridden that far in a long time, and especially not on a wide-backed draft horse. I'm going to be sore tomorrow."

"Well, it's a good thing you have a thick feather mattress and a warm wife to cuddle, then, isn't it?" Daniel, teased.

Sari felt her face redden. In all the excitement, she hadn't considered their own sleeping arrangements.

"Daniel, behave yourself," Claire chided her man when she saw Sari's reaction. She turned to her brother, "Sari's been staying at the cabin next door, Jesse. We set up the boys' old crib for Esther. Do you think you'll sleep well over there?" Then she pulled Jesse into a long hug. As she stepped back, Jesse glimpsed his sister's tears. "Jess, I'd given up any expectation of ever hugging you again on this earth. I believed you were gone and I grieved my loss. But I want you to know that Sari never quit believing you'd return. She held on to her hope." Jesse responded with another hug.

Sari cuddled the sleeping baby against the night's chill as she and Jesse began the short walk next door. The quarter moon was overhead. Its crescent was bright against the cold, star-filled sky. Snow crunched underfoot and sparkled with tiny pinpoints of glistening moonlight. The couple hadn't been alone since Jesse's arrival. Sari's steps slowed. She had so much to convey yet found that no words would form.

On his journey home, Jesse's head overflowed with thoughts and ideas he wanted to share with Sari. He knew that there would be time for that in the days to come, but for now, restored to his life and among the mountains he loved, he, too, was mute.

They paused between the cabins and stood together then, in the profound silence of the still night and of their own souls.

Jesse searched the sky and took a deep breath, then turned toward Sari and met her eyes. They stood together, connecting and connected in the night's crisp, silvery radiance.

Finally, Sari whispered, "Welcome home, Jesse. I'm so thankful God has seen fit to restore you to us, to me."

"There were so many hours when longing for here, and you, were all that sustained me." He tenderly leaned forward and kissed Sari's forehead, relishing her warmth. He put his arms around her and they stood together until the bundle between them wiggled.

"Are your toes cold?" Jesse smiled, "Mine are."

Once inside, Sari led Jesse into the room they would share. She unwrapped Esther, laid her in her crib, then took off her own coat.

Jesse, who had removed his coat and hung it on a chair in the kitchen, stood just inside the bedroom door, watching Sari. Once again their eyes met, and he felt a sudden awkwardness. "I, well, if you have an extra blanket, I can sleep on the floor over here," he suggested.

Sari smiled shyly, "Jesse, we aren't strangers like we were before you left. We've shared too much, in letters and in life. You are my husband and I your wife. There's no reason for you not to sleep in our bed."

He studied her in the dim glow of the kerosene light. He let himself linger in the intensity of her blue eyes. Slowly, gently, he stepped forward and reached for her. "I have missed you, Sari, longed to be back with you."

Just as slowly, nearly reverently, she stepped into his embrace, and this time there was nothing, no one between them. It took a while before Sari had a voice, and when she spoke it was in a whisper, "Claire told you I always stayed hopeful. That isn't exactly true. She had Daniel and the boys to hold her together when her hope was smashed. My hope was as fragile and shattered as hers, but I knew that if I ever let go of you, I'd be completely and forever alone, and I was afraid. I held on to you and to the belief that you'd come back because I couldn't imagine a life for myself without you."

Jesse kissed her mouth then, a sweet and lingering promise that spoke more than all their words.

The bright sunshine reflected off the snow with a blinding glare the next afternoon. Greg and Michael were again sledding, their happy voices echoed through the streets of Dillon. There wasn't a cloud visible above their heads as Sari and Jesse walked, hand in hand, back up the hill toward the cabins. Jesse motioned to Sari to stop, and they stood, catching their breaths and resting from the exertion. "Between this thin air, my healing leg, and my weakened lungs, this is quite a climb," Jesse told her.

Sari nodded, "It's a hard climb for me as well. I notice that you are limping more today than you did yesterday. Are you alright?"

Claire had grilled Jesse at breakfast about his wounds and his health, and he'd given her lighthearted assurances that he was 'hale and hearty'. Sari was gratified when he answered her seriously, "The Army doctor I saw on the ship home told me that both the bullet and the infection afterwards did damage to the muscles and meat in the calf of my leg. He thought that the destruction would heal, but cautioned me that it would take time. He also said it would slow my progress if I tried to do too much too soon."

"That makes sense. Perhaps your long ride up here and the walk we've just done could count as overdoing?"

Jesse nodded, "I'd imagine so. It feels good to be out and moving, though, after being unable to do anything for so long."

"We'll have to work together to find a good balance of both so that you recover completely as soon as possible."

"Yes, Ma'am," he answered with a grin. "Thanks for going with me to check the horses," he told her as they neared the cabin. "I know it's a bit of a walk, but housing them at the old livery only made sense."

"It was a good idea, I think, to keep them there. And I was really glad to get outside for a while myself. Thank you for telling me about working at the livery when you were young and sharing your memories of living up here. It must have been quite an adventure for a young man."

The boys returned to the cabin a few minutes after Jesse and Sari came in, and soon afterwards Bea cajoled the group into playing charades. Sari declined the offer as she cuddled and played with Esther. Nathan took the seat next to Sari and claimed jovially to be 'too old for such foolishness'. He and Sari became the audience, laughing and cheering at the antics of the three competing teams, Royce, Harriet and Bea took on Jesse, Michael and Greg while Claire and Daniel formed the third group. When Esther became restive in her arms, Sari pulled the leather lace with its little key necklace from around her neck and dangled it for the child to reach for and play with.

After several rounds, it became clear that no one could beat Claire and Daniel at the pantomime game. In exaggerated defeat, Bea plopped down on the floor beside the fireplace and hung her head. "I can't believe you are so bad at this game, Harri and Royce," she lamented as the rest laughed.

"Did you play charades when you were a little girl, Mama?" Greg asked Claire.

"I don't think we ever did," came the reply. "Our father was a stern man, and he didn't have much patience for silliness and games."

"You were poor, weren't you?" Greg knew the answer, but loved to hear the stories.

"Yes, we were," Claire answered,

Jesse took it from there. "We were poor enough that I remember each winter our mother would put newspapers between the blankets on our beds to add some insulation so we wouldn't be as cold."

"I still got cold," Claire said quietly, "The house was so drafty."

"Aunt Sari, were you poor when you were a little girl, too?"

In the past, Sari dodged questions about her childhood because thinking about it made her recall what she'd lost. Today though, sitting among family and friends, the recollections were welcome, and she answered eagerly. "No, I don't think we were. I don't remember a great deal, I was only about your age when my, um, when I moved from there, but my memory is that we were very comfortable. I don't remember ever being cold or hungry."

"Did you live in a nice house?"

Sari smiled. "Yes. My parents homesteaded north west of Encampment. My father and mother had our house built before I was born. It was a two-story, white house with a red door and blue trimming around the windows."

"Was this out by the A Bar A Ranch, Sari?" Daniel clarified, surprised and pleased that Sari was sharing.

"I'm not sure where it was exactly, I was so young. I just know that out our front window was a perfect view of Elk Mountain. There was a little reservoir not far from the house, I don't think it was on our property, but sometimes we'd go there on picnics and catch fish." Sari stopped, happy in her memory.

She didn't notice the look that passed between Harriet and Bea, or that Bea reached over to grab her sister's hand.

Michael asked, "What was the inside of the house like? Did you have your own bedroom?"

Again, Sari smiled. "My mother liked wallpaper, and my father liked books. Downstairs, the parlor had pale blue and off white wallpaper and there were tall bookshelves for my father. My bedroom was upstairs, beside my parent's room."

Bea interrupted, her face pale, "And your room had white wallpaper with tiny pink roses and green vines."

Sari met her friend's gaze, stunned. "How did you know that?"

A solid lump formed in Bea's throat, "Because I've been there," was all she could say.

The room became very still. Harriet continued with a question, "Sari, was that house sold at auction?"

Confused, Sari nodded carefully, "Yes, right after my parents died the bank sold it." As she spoke, Esther got her hand tangled in Sari's necklace. Sari looked down and patiently unwrapped the leather lace from around the baby's hand.

Bea stared at the tiny brass key and took in a sharp breath. She closed her eyes for a moment, then stood up. She gave Harriet an odd look before hurrying to the kitchen. She grabbed her coat and rushed out the back door.

Clearly, something important was happening, but the group and least of all Sari, understood what.

"Where are you—" Sari began, but the door was already closed behind her friend. Sari looked at Harriet, "I don't understand, you've been to my parents' house?"

Harriet exhaled. "When we were young, my father and mother bought some land adjacent to ours. It came with a house and from your description, I think maybe it could be the same place." The stillness continued, and Harriet added, "That would have been probably in 1909."

Sari glanced at Daniel then Jesse, "Is it possible? Could their father really own the house I grew up in? We were neighbors? How wonderful!"

"But Sari," Harriet felt the weight of sadness and a kind of guilt, "The house isn't there anymore. It burned down."

Sari's smile faded. "What a shame," she said. "I would have liked to see it again."

Daniel had been taking in the conversation, thinking about what Harriet told them. "Harriet, do you have any idea what your father paid for it all?"

"I'm not sure, though somehow three thousand dollars sticks in my mind. I remember he was very pleased and surprised at how low the price was. I remember him saying that there weren't many people at the auction."

Sari understood Daniel's thinking. "If we could find that out, and if he had the sales receipt, then that might help us deal with the bank," she remarked and Daniel nodded in response.

Harriet didn't understand Sari's last comment completely but added, "Knowing Pa, he still has all the paperwork. He's a stickler for keeping documents safe."

Jesse was unaware of the latest developments regarding Sari's debt, but he understood the reference. He stepped around behind Sari's chair, putting his hands on her shoulders and said, "This is good news."

They heard the back door open and then close with a solid thud. Bea shucked her coat off and draped it across her arm. She walked across the room to stand in front of Sari.

Bea took a deep breath. "We went to the house, your house, after Pa bought it. Pa and our brother Harlan were there to ride fences and build a dam to get the new land ready for our sheep. Harri and I went along to cook for them. We had such fun exploring the house. It was the most beautiful place we'd ever seen. We hoped that maybe we could talk Ma and Pa into moving there. That afternoon, I was in the parlor downstairs, and I found a little secret compartment in one wall." Bea fidgeted with her coat, dropping it beside her on the floor, to reveal that she'd been concealing a small wooden box.

"This was inside the compartment. I can hear and feel that there is something inside it, but the box itself is so pretty and I've always had such fun imagining what could be inside, I never wanted to force it open." She raised her eyes to see that Sari was staring at what she held in her hands. In the moment, tears spilled over and made their way down Sari's cheeks. Bea continued, "Do you recognize it?"

Sari nodded, unable to speak. A memory surfaced of her mother with the box on her lap.

"I'll bet that your key will fit in the tiny lock on the side." Bea whispered.

Jesse quietly took Esther out of Sari's arms, freeing her hands. No one spoke. Sari accepted the box from Bea, who stayed, kneeling, in front of her friend. Sari laid the familiar chest in her lap. Her hand shook as she pulled her necklace from around her neck. She swiped at the tears on her cheek and had an achingly vivid memory of her mother's warm smile. Carefully, she fit the key in the lock. It turned easily. Sari lifted the lid.

Sari's mother's kind eyes and father's warm grin, in two daguerreotype photos, lay on the top. She carefully lifted each, rubbing a loving finger over their beloved faces. Beneath these was another photo of all three of them together. Sari stared at her own face, perfect and innocent, and new tears fell.

"Are those your parents?" asked Bea quietly.

Sari nodded, and after another look, she handed the photographs to Bea. Her attention turned back to the box on her lap. Lying on the top now was a soft white cloth with an ornate tatted edging. Another memory unfolded as she held the piece up and Sari explained, "My mother made this. It's the bonnet I wore when I was christened."

She held the cap up and Claire remarked, "That's beautiful, Sari."

"Once when she was showing me this, my mother told me that she looked forward to one day seeing my children wearing it." Another tear coursed down Sari's scarred cheek as she relived that moment. "I hadn't even thought about christening Esther."

"Is that another baby hat?" Greg had come to kneel next to Bea by Sari's chair and was peering into the box.

"I don't think so," Sari answered as she put the cap aside and reached in. "No. It's a hankie," she continued. "But something is wrapped in it." By now the whole group had migrated into a tight circle around Sari's chair. Everyone leaned in a little to see what treasure the hankie held.

"Oh." Sari caught her breath as she lifted up a necklace. The chain was delicately filigreed gold. Suspended beneath was a pendant about the size of a quarter. A sparkling blue stone was rimmed by a circle of green.

"This was my grandmother's. Jesse, I think I told you about this necklace in one of my letters. My great-grandmother carried this with her when she came to America from France."

"Are those jewels real?" Michael voiced what they were all wondering.

"Yes, I think so. The center stone is a sapphire and the smaller stones are emeralds."

"Oh Sari, put it on," encouraged Bea. "It will look so beautiful beside your fair skin."

Sari fiddled with the clasp for a moment then sat back, letting the group admire and comment on her prize.

"I have a note from my mother's Bible that promised this to me, and I've wondered so many times what happened to it." She stopped and looked up at Bea, "And to think, all this time you were keeping it safe for me."

Greg was becoming impatient with the gathering and interrupted the fashion show as he stood up. "All that's left in that box is some old papers. Necklaces and baby stuff aren't much of a treasure chest." With chuckles from the other bystanders, he left the circle.

Sari reached in once again to withdraw and unfold a sheaf of papers. Jesse leaned closer and together they discovered what would turn out to be the answer to all her questions and her prayers. "This is a Promissory Note," Sari said aloud after a moment. "Daniel, Royce, this is the same Promissory Note that Mr. Bagley gave me a copy of. Except," her voice raised slightly in pitch, "This one is marked in red across the bottom, 'Paid in Full.' It is dated not long before my parents died."

She looked at Jesse, "I knew I remembered celebrating that they'd paid off a loan. This proves it."

Royce asked if he could have a closer look at the documents. Sari handed him the papers.

Sari hastily returned the pictures and cap to the box and closed the lid. Holding it carefully in one hand, she stood up and clumsily hugged Bea with the other. "This is such an amazing gift. You have no idea how important these papers are," she told the girl.

"I'm sorry I have kept this all these years when it really belonged to you."

"You couldn't have known. No one did."

"And," added Harriet, "Remember, if you hadn't safeguarded this box all these years, it would have burned in the fire with everything else, and Sari wouldn't have it now."

"Can you tell me about the fire?" Sari asked.

The group drifted back to their seats around the cabin as Harriet and Bea took turns telling the story of how the house had burned. As they discussed the events, Daniel and Royce got up, moving to the table. A minute later, Jesse handed Esther back to Sari and joined them. As the others talked about the fire, Daniel and Royce filled Jesse in about the foreclosure letter Sari had received.

"What an exciting turn of events," Claire answered after a time, "I'm just amazed to hear of this connection, though I'm so sorry, Sari, that your childhood home is gone." She stepped over and gave her sister-in-law a hug. "I'm going to put the kettle on for tea or hot chocolate. Does anyone want something?"

A chorus of orders rang out. Sari looked around.

Royce was standing at the table, the papers from the box spread out before him. He, Daniel, and Jesse had their heads together over them.

"Sari, where is the letter and papers you just received from Mr. Bagley?" Daniel looked up and asked.

"I put them in my satchel the other night after I showed them to you."

Daniel's voice was serious, "We need to see those."

"Tell me where they are," Bea volunteered, "and I'll run get them."

When Bea left, Sari joined Claire in the kitchen to warm a bottle for the baby. When it was ready, Harriet volunteered to feed Esther, "I'll bet you'll want to hear the discussion with the men," she told Sari.

Sari joined the huddle at the table as Bea returned with a handful of documents. Royce laid the two copies of the Promissory Note side by side on the table. Daniel made a quiet whistle through his teeth, and Royce grunted, "Do you see what I see?"

"I sure do," answered Daniel. "The document Bagley sent Sari has been altered."

"What?" The men moved aside so that Sari had a better view. After a moment she exclaimed, "My father's copy lists the loan amount as five thousand dollars at four percent, but this other one reads thirty-five thousand dollars at fourteen percent. I don't think I understand."

Jesse leaned closer and studied the second document. "If you look closely, you can see how someone carefully added the number three here and the word thirty there to the original document. Then again, I think with a looking glass, we'll be able to see that the percentage rate was changed as well, from four to fourteen."

Royce looked up in triumph. "This is clear proof of fraud. We've got all the documentation we need right here to put Bagley, and probably Wills and anyone else who was working with them, away for a very long time."

"The most important thing," Sari offered, "Is that this proves I no longer have a debt to the bank. Jesse's home," she hesitated then corrected herself, "Our home and business are not in danger of being taken away."

"It also seems to me," Daniel added pensively, "That the bank in Rawlins owes you a substantial sum of money. At the very least, Sari, they owe you fair market value for your father's land and home, and certainly they owe you your wages for all the hours you worked at the Copper Pot."

47
Dillon, Wyoming
late – January, 1919

The current residents of Dillon, Wyoming weathered another snowstorm two days after Jesse and Nathan arrived. It came complete with raging winds and stinging ice in accompaniment with an added foot of snow. No one minded much as their quarantine in the mountains afforded everyone precious time to reconnect with Jesse. The close confines and isolation enabled the family to hear details of Jesse's war experiences and tell him their own.

For Sari and Jesse, the time became a kind of odd honeymoon. Their days were populated with the other inhabitants of Dillon and the demands of their newborn, but nights, after their cabin mates and Esther were sleeping peacefully, the couple snuggled into their shared bed to enjoy long, whispered conversations while they became accustomed to the warmth of the other's body and heart.

Three days after that storm passed, conversation at the breakfast table turned to a familiar subject. "I'm concerned that if we don't start clearing a road out of here soon, we won't get the vehicles down until after the spring runoff," Royce told the group.

Daniel agreed, "We might be too late already."

Greg spoke up then, "But what about the influenza? How do we know it's safe to go back now?"

The adults took him seriously, and it was Nathan who answered, "Greg, Jesse and I happened to meet Mayor Rankin on the street as we were leaving town on our way up here. He told us that there hadn't been a new case of the disease in a day. Based on that, and since we've been up here almost two weeks since then, I think we can consider it safe to go home."

"The road was difficult coming up here and the snow is deeper now. How are we going to make it down the road?" Harriet's voice was filled with concern.

Nathan cleared his throat quietly and began, "Going out down Haggarty Creek, the way you brought the cars in, isn't an option anymore after that last snow. I hiked down that way about a mile yesterday, and even with my snowshoes I got bogged down under the trees. We're going to have to go up past Rudefeha Mine and to the ridge at the top, then pass Bridger Peak and out. It isn't going to be easy."

"That grade just up from the mine is hard on horseback. Is it possible with a vehicle?" asked Claire.

"I'm not sure if any of you noticed, but there's a sleigh in the back corner of the old livery." Jesse spoke up. "Sari and I noticed it yesterday when we were tending the horses. It looks like it needs some repairs, but I think I can have it fit in just a couple of hours if I have the boys help me."

Claire looked worried, "Jesse, I'm not sure how the sleigh will help."

Jesse nodded, "The sleigh is actually a godsend. With the horses to help tow them, it will take hours and hours, maybe even a couple days to get the vehicles to the top. We can't have you ladies and Esther in the vehicles all that time, plus the added weight," he ducked his head and grinned when Claire slapped him on the arm in mock anger, "Sorry girls, but what I mean is that we men can take our time and work the cars out, using the horses to pull them if necessary. We can travel back and forth using the sleigh. Then, when the cars are on top, we can ferry everyone up there with the sleigh and go the rest of the way."

Nathan nodded in agreement and added, "I also saw a block and tackle hanging in the livery. Using that will allow the horses to pull the vehicles easier."

"Good idea. That will help a great deal," Jesse was thankful the men were warming to his plan.

"That's a good plan," agreed Royce, "but this is still January, and it won't be long before the next storm arrives, so we are going we need to hurry."

A few minutes later, after some serious conversation, a plan was set. Jesse left soon after breakfast with Greg and Michael to work on the sleigh while Royce, Daniel, and Nathan began accumulating supplies and tools and then set to work.

Three grueling days later, as the sun was setting behind Bridger Peak and the wind was swirling the first flakes of snow from a new storm, the troop cheered as they entered Encampment.

The sun wasn't up yet, but the eastern sky was a pink glow a week later when Royce knocked on Jesse and Sari's front door.

"Royce, it's good to see you. Hello, Bea, come on in." Jesse greeted his neighbor with a handshake. "We sure do appreciate you both for helping us with this."

"It's my pleasure, Jesse," answered Royce. "I'll get a lot of satisfaction seeing this case closed. It's weighed on me for too long."

As Sari came out of the kitchen, Jesse noted how pale his wife looked and smiled warmly at her. "Good morning," she greeted Bea and Royce. "Esther is still asleep, Bea. She often is a sleepy head, so you should have an hour or so of peace before her day starts."

Bea grinned, "I brought a book to keep me occupied. Don't you worry about us one bit, I'm looking forward to spending the day with Esther."

Sari hesitated, then turned to retrieve her coat. She felt shaky inside, anticipating the day ahead of her, but she reminded herself once again that the actions she was taking were not only for Jesse and their family, but also for her parents. She'd dressed carefully in preparation. She'd taken extra time with her makeup and hair, and chosen a demure blue dress with black velvet trim that fit her well. The small pillbox hat she'd added sat at a confident angle on her head. She knew that the tiny veil didn't cover much of her face, but served to draw attention away from her cheek. She was convinced she didn't need to be ashamed or worried about her appearance. She checked for the third time that she had all the papers she needed, then let Jesse usher her out the door.

They'd decided to travel in separate vehicles, so Jesse followed Royce's official car on the trip. It was a quiet drive from Encampment to Rawlins.

They parked side by side about a half block from the bank and met on the sidewalk. Royce smiled reassuringly at Sari and told her, "I have the bill of sale from the auction of your ranch. My father-in-law was happy to give it to me. Also, I asked a deputy friend of mine to manufacture some excuse to make sure that Henry Bagley was away from the bank this morning, so you won't be running into him. As we've discussed, I'll stay out here while you confront the bank president first to try to get a feel about whether he and Bagley were in on this together. I'll be close by for whatever you need from me."

Jesse nodded. They'd been over their plan several times. He offered Sari his hand as they turned toward the bank, "Wow, your hand is like ice. Don't worry, this is all going to be alright."

Sari took a deep breath and nodded. She whispered a prayer for strength and squared her shoulders. "I'm alright," she assured him. "I know I can do this."

When they entered the bank, Sari headed straight for the teller. "Good morning. My name is Sari Atley. I need to speak to your bank president, Mr. Parker, please."

The clerk, a middle aged man with a receding hairline, nodded. "Yes Ma'am. I'll let him know."

A short minute later, Sari and Jesse were escorted down a carpeted hall and into a large, richly paneled office. As they entered, Ezra Parker came around his large desk. Introductions were made, and he invited the couple to sit down. "Now, Mr. Atley, what can I do for you folks?"

"Your business right now is with my wife, Sir," was all Jesse said.

"Oh," the president faltered, "I just assumed, um. I'm sorry. Mrs. Atley, how can I help you?"

"Mr. Parker, you've been with this bank for many years, am I correct?"

"Yes, I have," he answered. It was clear he was unsure of where Sari was going with her query. "I've been with the bank for years, and I became the president in 1907."

Sari reached into the valise she'd placed beside her on the floor. "So, then, I am correct that you are the Ezra

Parker who signed the bottom of this document?" She handed him the Promissory Note she'd found in her mother's wooden box.

Parker took a long minute to look over the page. When he looked up, he smiled, "Yes, this is my signature. It was a transaction I did with Ralph Webber."

"Mr. Parker, my name is Sari Webber Atley, and the man who held this loan was my father."

"How nice to meet you after all these years! I admired your father. He was a man of integrity and compassion. I was sorry to hear of your parents' tragic accident." Parker glanced down at the Note in his hand then continued, "Mrs. Atley, this Promissory Note was paid off a very long time ago, I remember the transaction well in fact. What is the nature of your inquiry about it now?"

Sari's heart began to race. Her tone was a little sharper and louder when she answered, "You *remember* that this loan was paid off, yet you sold my home and land and took the profits within days of my parents' deaths, leaving me penniless. For the past two years you've forced me into indenture and are now threatening to foreclose on my husband's home and business? What kind of business are you running here?"

Parker looked as if he'd been slapped. All the color drained from his face and his eyes grew wide. He faltered as he fought to answer Sari, "Indentured? Foreclosure? Mrs. Atley, I, I—" He looked from Sari to Jesse then back. "I don't know what you are talking about," he said finally.

Sari reached again into her valise, and withdrew the papers she'd received from Mr. Bagley. "Are you going to tell me that you do not know about these?"

The office was silent for the next few minutes as Parker scrutinized the documents she'd handed him. He carefully compared the two Notes. When at last he looked up and met Sari's eyes there was regret and confusion there, but not fear or guilt. At that moment, Sari became confident that Mr. Parker had not been a part of the fraud she'd experienced.

"Mr. and Mrs. Atley, I am at a loss to explain this foreclosure letter, or this second Promissory Note. It did not come from me, or this bank. I see on this letter that the address posted for the bank is a post office box that I do not recognize. Would you mind starting at the beginning and helping me to understand all that has happened between you and Mr. Bagley, who signed this foreclosure letter?"

Parker alternated between anger and nausea as he listened to Sari's recounting. He interrupted her narrative infrequently with careful questions. When she'd finished, he sat with his eyes fixed on his desk. The silence stretched. Finally, with one more glance at the original note, Parker looked up.

"What you've been through is a nightmare of such monumental proportions that I can only say to you that I admire that you've endured. I cannot fathom how something this treacherous, this—this *evil*, happened in my bank without my being aware. Be assured that now that I am aware, we *will* get to the bottom of this and that the responsible parties will be held accountable."

"That is exactly what our goal is as well," Jesse spoke quietly for the first time. "And to that end, we invited Deputy Marshall Royce Rogers to accompany us to Rawlins today. He's waiting outside. If you will excuse me for a moment, I will bring him in."

"Certainly, Mr. Atley, please do. I've met Deputy Rogers before."

Sari sat quietly as Jesse left the room. She was emotionally drained from telling this man her story, but also encouraged at his response. Jesse had only been gone a moment when Parker asked her, "Your recollection is that the auction of your family ranch and home was not long after the accident, is that correct?"

"Yes. I believe it took place the day after the funeral."

"Do you have any idea of the date?"

"The date of the bill of sale for the ranch's auction is the twentieth of February, 1909."

Sari turned when she heard footsteps in the hallway. Mr. Parker rose to shake Royce's hand and invited the group to once again be seated. In a show of humility and cooperation, Parker brought his own chair out from behind his desk to join a tight circle in the middle of the room.

When they were all seated, Parker began, "Mrs. Atley and I were just discussing the timing of events—the accident and sale of the ranch. We've narrowed the time frame to sometime around the twentieth of February, 1909." He looked to Sari for confirmation and she nodded.

He continued, "This is significant because my wedding anniversary is February nineteenth of that same year. I left Rawlins on the twelfth, riding a train for Denver. My wife and I were married on the nineteenth. We enjoyed Denver for seven days after our wedding. We returned by train to Rawlins. I was gone for right at two weeks, having left our head cashier, Henry Bagley, in charge of the bank."

"With due respect, sir, be aware that I will work to confirm those dates beyond just your claims," Royce replied.

"I understand. I would expect nothing less, Deputy."

"Tell me about Henry Bagley," Royce continued. "How long had he been working at the bank by this time?"

The questioning continued with a staccato back and forth between Royce and Parker. Bagley had been with the bank only a year less than Parker. His current position at the bank was head clerk, not vice president as he'd claimed repeatedly to Sari. Yes, there had been occasional issues with short teller drawers or other questionable ledger entries through the years, but none that could be solidly attributed to Bagley. No, Parker and Bagley were not friends, they didn't socialize.

A few times Jesse added a comment or posed his own question as Sari listened. It didn't take long before Royce and Jesse also were convinced of Parker's innocence.

"What needs to be uncovered now is if Bagley had other partners in his underhanded dealings with Mrs. Atley, and just how involved Chetley Wills and his wife were in the scheme," Royce offered.

"Chetley Wills?" Parker asked.

"Yes, Wills is the man who received the benefit of Mrs. Atley's indenture," Royce answered.

"I'm sure you know him," Jesse added. "He has quite a substantial loan from this bank, taken to start his business. He explained to me that his willingness to employ my wife is how he paid his own mortgage to you."

"Wills? What sort of business does he run?"

Royce answered, "He owns a hotel and restaurant in Encampment called The Copper Pot."

Parker shook his head, "I am aware of all our mortgagees, and I can assure you that this bank does not have an outstanding loan for such an establishment in Encampment. Of course, I will check all my records to make certain I'm not mistaken."

Jesse was close to losing his temper, "Bagley and Wills are shysters. Evil men who don't deserve the air they breathe. Just how many other people have fallen victim to them?"

"Oh dear, we will need to considere that," Parker interjected. "Do you think there are more?" he asked Royce.

"Yes I do. I was getting to that. I have evidence that Mrs. Atley is not this vulture's only prey," replied Royce.

Parker was visibly shaken. "O Lord, how far is this debacle going to reach?"

"I think it prudent for us to conduct a thorough audit of the bank's mortgages as a beginning," Royce answered.

"The unanswered question in all this is why?" Sari said quietly.

Her question fell heavily into the room. It was a question Jesse, Royce, and Daniel had mulled over.

Then Parker spoke up, "Can you all indulge me a bit of speculation? It seems to me that the most likely scenario is this. With my absence from the bank, Henry took note of the death of the Webbers and saw an opportunity to profit. He acquired a copy of the original Note, altered it, and scheduled a hasty auction. All was said and done before I returned, and there was no reason for me to ask questions. He succeeded in selling the property and pocketing the proceeds."

"That doesn't explain why he would pursue me ten years later, convincing me that there was still an outstanding debt. He bullied me into working for the Wills and living in a lean-to, but for what? If Chetley Wills didn't have a mortgage on his business to the bank, then why did he need me?"

Jesse answered, "Maybe we'll never know."

"I hope you are wrong, Jess," Royce responded. "In my experience in law enforcement, I've come to understand that greed is a powerful motivator. Perhaps, Sari, the explanation is as simple as that. If there is something else, we will uncover it with a thorough audit of the bank's records and all of Bagley's dealings."

Royce stood up, "Mr. Parker, it's important that we secure all the bank's files right away so evidence can't be removed or destroyed."

Parker rose quickly, "Yes, of course. Most of our mortgage files are in cabinets in the file room. I'm sure there are documents of concern in Mr. Bagley's office as well."

"Let's start in his office first, though I'd appreciate it if you would secure the file room so that nothing can be removed until we have an opportunity for a thorough search."

Parker agreed and led them all out of his office. He stopped to lock a solid wooden door part-way down the hallway, telling Royce that he had the only key. Then, he led them across the lobby toward a smaller office near the teller's cage.

Just after they entered Bagley's office, Royce turned to Sari and Jesse. "With Mr. Parker's testimony, the doctored Promissory Note and the fraudulent foreclosure letter, I already have plenty of evidence to arrest Bagley and Wills right now. I'm going to take a minute here soon and call Marshal Helugs in Encampment to let him know to go pick Wills up. By the end of today, I promise you they both will be behind bars.

"The rest of what I need to do here at this point is police work. Gathering evidence and making a criminal case takes time. The two of you don't really need to stay while Mr. Parker and I comb through these files."

Jesse nodded.

Sari hesitated. She was relieved that the truth had come out. She tried to grasp that the debt that had weighed on her for so long was lifted and that both Bagley and Wills would be held accountable, but somehow she felt unsatisfied, like something was unfinished. Picturing the men in a cell did little to ease the burden of shame and guilt, work and worry she'd carried for so long. The events of the day, a day she'd looked forward to for a long time, seemed disappointingly anticlimactic. Suppressing a sigh, Sari smiled and nodded back at Jesse.

"Mrs. Atley, if I may?" Mr. Parker reached for Sari's hand. "I understand that there are no words or actions that could compensate you for what you have been through. You've been victimized and defrauded. I am so sorry. You have my word that I will do all I can to make this right, for you and anyone else who has been harmed in my bank's name."

"Thank you, Mr. Parker," Sari appreciated his earnest apology. Jesse was speaking quietly to Royce as Sari left the office and crossed the lobby. Craving air and sunlight, she stepped outside to the dusty sidewalk in front of the bank.

Sari took a deep breath, willing the tension away. As she flexed her shoulders, Henry Bagley rounded the corner with his head down, lost in thought. Only a few steps from the entrance, he glanced up and recognized Sari. His eyes rested for a moment on her. "Miss Webber, are you here to see me?" he asked with measured ease.

Silently, Sari held her gaze on him as she rejected all residual fear of the man before her, then with new confidence she answered, "Well. Mr. Bagley. I've come to straighten out my affairs with you and the bank."

He stepped closer and lowered his voice, "Let's adjourn to my office where there is more privacy for our business."

Her earlier, looming disappointment evaporated and she felt cheerful. "That's a wonderful idea," she answered with a knowing smile. She stepped aside, indicating that Bagley lead the way. He led her inside and across the lobby to the doorway to his office when he stopped. "What?" he faltered. "Mr. Parker, who are these men and what are you all doing in my office?"

Sari stepped beside the man. "I told you outside, Mr. Bagley, I came today to settle certain dealings you and I have. Actually, I've already had a very satisfying morning and as you can see, we are well on our way to success.

May I introduce you to my husband, Jesse Atley, and also to Deputy Marshall Royce Rogers?"

Bagley stood frozen.

"You see, Mr. Bagley, I have located the strong box I asked you about when we first met. I now am in possession of the *real* Promissory Note my father had with this bank. The real, paid-in-full Note, that is."

As understanding assailed him. Bagley's eyes darted from face to face. He stepped backwards, a gesture that spurned Royce into action. "You won't make it far if you choose to run, though it would give me a good excuse to chase you down. Should that happen, I can't promise you won't be hurt in the ensuing scuffle."

Sari allowed a quiet laugh to escape as it occurred to her she might enjoy that scene. She became serious again quickly, though. Turning to face Bagley, who was still rooted to his spot, she told him, "I will never understand how you sleep at night with all you've done to me and probably others. You stole my inheritance and security. You've bullied and manipulated me and used me for your own profit. I certainly hope the benefits you reaped as a result were dear enough to you that the memory of them will carry you through what you now face."

As she spoke, Royce approached. He grasped the man's arm and wrapped a small chain around Bagley's wrist, twisted the ends, and secured them together.

"Hey now, what is the meaning of this?" Bagley tried to withdraw his arm then winced.

"These are called 'come alongs'. They will ensure we get you safely to the city jail. I'd suggest you not fight against them, as the more you do, the tighter and more uncomfortable they will become. Mr. Henry Bagley, you are under arrest for fraud. I feel certain we will also be adding a mountain of other charges as well. Embezzlement, theft, false indenture—you know, charges like that. Be aware, sir, that since you've done these crimes in affiliation with a national bank, the charges are felonious."

The bank lobby was silent. Every eye watched Royce maneuver Henry Bagley through the room and out the door. It took several moments for the onlookers to return to their tasks. Sari and Jesse remained in the office doorway a little longer before they said goodbye to Mr. Parker and found themselves back outside.

48
Encampment, Wyoming
Tuesday, May 6, 1919

Sari stood before the mirror and finished smoothing her hair into a loose chignon. Her cheeks were lightly powdered. The scars on her right cheek were visible, but they rarely occupied her thoughts any more. She was concentrating instead on what the day ahead had to offer. She rehearsed a list of tasks she needed to complete before she, Jesse, and Esther were due at Claire's. When she was satisfied with her hair, Sari took a moment to smile at the woman reflected in the glass. "Happy birthday," she told herself softly before turning away.

A half block away, Jesse finished feeding the horses and headed towards the front of the livery when he heard a voice. "Jesse! Jesse Atley, are you here?"

"On my way," he called. Jesse broke into a grin as he saw who was standing in the door. "Wilber Toothaker! You are a sight for sore eyes! You've finally made it back home!"

The two men shook hands and exchanged greetings. "Yup, came in last week. I didn't let no one know I was a comin' in. I hitched a ride from Wolcott, and they dropped me off in front of the Bohn Hotel. I knew I was home when Miss Mary spotted me. She come runnin' out of the hotel and give me a hug, all crying and blubbering. It was as good a homecoming as a man could want."

As Jesse clapped his friend on the back, he had a fleeting memory of their last meeting. He'd stood a long time watching as the train pulled away from Rawlins carrying his friend off to war. He'd been resigned then that they might never meet again. They settled themselves on the bench in front of the livery, eager to catch up. An hour slipped by as they shared war stories and plans for the future. Both agreed that they were glad to be home.

"You hear anything from the Peryam boys?" Wilbur asked at length.

"Both of them are good. John was home not long ago. The Army sent him to vet school. He wasn't too thrilled with that prospect, but while he was in California at school he met a lady and married her. They had a few rough spots after he got sent to Europe, but it sounds like they've come through it alright."

"I'm glad to hear it," Wilbur replied. "Now that I'm home, I've got it in my mind to find a wife myself. I've got my eye out, for sure."

Jesse laughed. "I wish you luck. I wouldn't trade being married to Sari for anything in the world."

A few minutes later, Jesse watched his friend walk away. Smiling, he pulled his leather gloves on and went back to work. He glanced at his pocket watch. *Michael should be here any time,* Jesse thought as he finished tying down the load he needed to take out to Condict's ranch. Thinking about Michael made Jesse smile. The end of the war had brought new hope and increased business to the Encampment area. When it became clear that Jesse couldn't meet the demands at the livery on his own, he'd talked with Claire and Daniel over dinner about finding a hand to help. Mike spoke up without hesitation, "Uncle Jesse, I think you should hire me. I'm a good worker, I know the horses and how to care for them. I can drive the truck, and I've watched you at the forge so often I know that with just a little coaching, I could help there, too."

Claire began shaking her head, "Michael, you're too young, and what about school?"

"Just hear me out, please? I know school is important to you, Mama." He turned back to Jesse. "I could go in to the livery and feed the horses and help you get things loaded and ready for the day before school." He interrupted Claire's protest with a hand as he continued, "I did that often last year to help out Dawson and it didn't hurt my studies. If I work hard, I can get my school work done by noon and then come in and work the rest of the day. Uncle Jess, you'll get your money's worth, I swear. I'm getting pretty good driving the truck, and you know I'm a hard worker. You can count on me."

Jesse was impressed with his nephew's zeal. "You've thought about this, then? Not just right now?"

"I *have* thought about it, and for a long time. I started when I heard Dawson had passed away, thinking I could keep the livery and some of the deliveries going for Aunt Sari. I love working at the livery, I always have."

With a bit more discussion, even Claire gave her blessing to the arrangement. Now, several months later, Jesse couldn't imagine running the livery without Michael. It had been a good business decision.

"The evening is warm enough for us to sit out on the porch, don't you think?" Claire asked when Jesse, Sari, and Esther arrived that evening.

"Yes, it's been a beautiful day – a gift after the wind and snow we've had in the last few weeks," Sari answered. As she spoke, Jesse lifted the baby buggy up onto the porch, and Sari put a blanket behind Esther to help her sit up.

"She is growing and changing so fast," Daniel remarked.

"She sure is," Greg kneeled by the buggy's side and handed Esther a brightly colored rattle. "She crawls real fast when she's down on the floor."

Claire offered drinks to the group, telling them that supper would be in about half an hour. Sari disappeared into the house behind her to lend a hand.

"How was your outing with Bea the other day?" Claire asked as she poured lemonade into glasses.

"We had a wonderful time," came Sari's answer. "I'll admit, I had mixed feelings about going out there, but I'm glad I did."

"It wasn't too painful, then, to see the ruins of the house you grew up in?"

Sari pictured the charred remnants of her family's home. "It was a shock, certainly. Between the fire and years, there really is very little left of the house. But the joy of the day was sharing memories with Bea about what it used to look like. We took a walk and so many memories flooded back of games I used to play in the small stand of trees and the tiny creek nearby."

"You weren't sad?"

"A little, but it was a kindly brand of sadness, filled with good memories also."

When the ladies arrived back on the porch, Jesse and Daniel were discussing the news. "There's a lot of conflict remaining in Europe, even though the war has ended. We still don't have a treaty. Reports are it will take months to make an agreement and get it signed," Daniel's face was grave.

"There are a lot of parties to pacify," Jesse responded, "and that will take time. Something I read the other day does concern me, though. There's a lot of left-over hate, especially in Germany. Unless the diplomats get ahold of that and all the factions are brought to the table and satisfied, I'm worried that our Great War won't result in peace like we'd like."

"I don't want to think about Europe anymore. We've given them enough of our support and our men," Claire responded.

Daniel shrugged in agreement, "I suppose you'd rather talk instead about important matters, like how our days to drink a beer in America are numbered, or how the U.S. House has passed an amendment to grant women the right to vote. I read today that the representatives are considering voting again, to spur the Senate into action."

"It's certainly about time all women are allowed the vote," answered Claire, "The rest of the country needs to catch up with Wyoming. We were given the right in 1890."

"That's true," Sari sat down next to Jesse as she spoke, "but didn't that happen more to entice women to come here more than to make women equal?"

Jesse nodded, "Yes, and it makes me glad to hear that the whole country is taking it seriously now and for the right reasons."

Greg looked up from playing with Esther and remarked, "Homer and I were in Parkison's yesterday doing an errand for his mom. I overheard Mrs. Baker say that she was happy the Congress had voted to throw the Devil out of our country. What did she mean?"

At the mention of Mary Nell Baker, both Claire and Sari stiffened. Claire answered her son, "She was talking about an amendment to our Constitution that outlaws alcohol. It's called Prohibition, and—"

Daniel interrupted his wife with a good natured guffaw. "Now Claire, let's be precise. The Eighteenth Amendment makes selling, producing, or transporting alcohol illegal, not the actual consumption of it. If Jesse and I just *happen* to have a substantial stock pile of assorted libations tucked away somewhere, it won't be illegal for us to drink from that stock as we choose."

"Don't you dare let Mary Nell or the rest of her Anti-Saloon League friends know what you have up your sleeves," warned Claire.

Daniel nodded. With seriousness he looked at Greg. "Son, the prohibition law doesn't take effect until the beginning of next year, and even after it does, we won't be breaking the law by having some beer and wine in the root cellar. Even so, what is down in the cellar isn't to be discussed in any way now, or ever. Not with Homer, not with anyone. Do you understand?"

"Yes, Sir," Greg answered in all sincerity.

A moment later, a car pulled up in front of the house, and the group's attention was drawn to the last of Sari's birthday celebration guests. Bea, Royce, and Harriet, who was holding their month-old son, were happily welcomed.

Soon, the group was seated around Claire's elegant dining table, laughing and talking. Sari sat back, listening contently to the banter. She watched as Michael and Bea, sitting together at one end of the table talked quietly together, and she wondered if something more than a friendship might grow between them some day.

"When is Aunt Sari gonna get to open her presents?" Greg interrupted Sari's thought.

"How about now?" answered Claire. Sari enjoyed the attention of her friends and family as she opened the brightly wrapped boxes Greg quickly retrieved from the sideboard. The first was a wooden bird from Greg. "I whittled it myself, Aunt Sari. I know you like robins."

"It's beautiful," she answered, touched at the work and thoughtfulness of the gift. Next, she opened a larger box. It held a soft pink, crocheted shawl from Claire. Sari laughed, "You tricked me by telling me that this was for Ella."

Claire nodded, "That way I could work on it when we were together without ruining the surprise."

"I love it, Claire. Thank you!"

The last package was from Royce, Bea, and Harriet. "Oh my," Sari said as the contents were revealed.

"This is the cookbook I've been admiring at Parkison's. Thank you!"

Royce nodded gravely, "and we expect to be used as your test subjects on any new recipes you try."

"I will keep that in mind," Sari teased back. She took a moment to thumb through the pages. When she looked up she told them, "Thank you all so much."

Greg looked puzzled, "Uncle Jesse, didn't you give Aunt Sari anything for her birthday?"

Jesse smiled innocently. "As a matter of fact, I did. I gave it to her this morning."

"What was it?"

Claire started to shush her curious son, but Sari broke in with her answer, "Jesse's gift to me is a promise to take Esther and me on a camping trip into the mountains in July. I've talked over and over about going back up there to see Dillon without snow."

When there was a lull in the conversation at the table a minute later, Sari cleared her throat and reached beneath her chair. "I have a present to give tonight as well."

When she held everyone's attention she continued. "Bea, I know that this little box, which you rescued from the fire, has always been important to you. I'd like you to have it back."

She handed the wooden chest across the table to a surprised Bea, who rubbed her hand lovingly over the smooth top. "It will be much more useful, though, if you also have the key." With that, Sari pulled the key from under her bodice and handed it to her friend as well.

Bea started to argue, but Sari cut her off, "I really want you to have it. Please."

Nodding, Bea smiled then. She turned the key, opening it for the first time herself. "I love it, Sari. Thank you so much."

A few minutes later, Claire invited her guests to adjourn to the parlor. Within minutes, Esther sat playing on the floor beside Harriet's son with Greg nearby. The rest sat comfortably, enjoying the cool evening breeze as it puffed through the windows.

Jesse caught Sari's attention when he asked, "I thought Nathan would be here tonight, Claire."

"Oh I invited him last week," came her light answer. "But he left on Monday to go to Cheyenne for a visit with his sister. He sends his birthday greetings to Sari and asked me to tell everyone hello. He was sorry to miss the celebration but he had already made his plans for a visit."

"Speaking of Cheyenne, I got some information from the District Court there this afternoon," Royce began. "I've been anxious to share it with you all. You already know that Bagley and Wills were charged in not only your case Sari, but also with the foreclosure on Floyd Cramer's land and that of two others. Now, a new set of charges have been filed against both Henry Bagley and Chetley Wills. This time, the indictment also lists Lilith Wills and one other person as co-conspirators."

"What?" Sari didn't hide her surprise. "Have they found evidence that Lilith had something to do with their crimes?"

Royce met Sari's eyes, "Yes, and you'll be shocked to hear her part. It turns out, Lilith's maiden name is Milton. She and Lauralee Milton are sisters, Henry Bagley is their half brother." He paused to let the fact settle on the table. Sari drew in a sharp breath but didn't speak, so Royce continued.

"We've found three other women, two are in their twenties but one is only sixteen, who were orphaned in Wyoming then hastily sent to Kansas to reside at an orphanage for girls."

Sari breathed out, "You mean Miss Milton's Home for Girls?"

"Yes. All three cases are quite similar to your own. A child orphaned tragically, a quick and unscrupulous sale of the family's holdings, and then quickly shuttling the girls off to Lilith's sister's orphanage. In the case of the two older victims, they were also indentured like you."

The table was quiet. Sari let Royce's announcement echo through her mind for a moment. "But why?" Sari asked. "I'm back to the same question I asked in the bank when we first met with Mr. Parker. Why? I understand the land grabs, that was pure theft and greed. But why send them, us, to the same orphanage and then con us into working?"

Royce's answer sent a chill through the group, "Well, Kansas investigators answered part of that question when they audited Miss Milton's books. She received a substantial stipend from the state of Wyoming for housing you and the other three. You were not quite the charity case she'd led you to believe. She's made a great deal of money through the years from housing girls from our state. Apparently, additionally, she got a generous cut of the money Bagley and Wills received from the land sales."

While Royce was talking, Jesse reached over to hold Sari's hand. He spoke now, "Okay, now I can follow their demented thinking. They all made money by selling the land and then sending Sari and the others out of state, but what did they gain from indenturing them later?"

"Again, it seems as if greed is the answer," Royce responded. "Like Sari, the other two were sent to work for businesses owned by Chetley and Lilith. They convinced all three of you that you were paying off your debts, when in fact you were working as free labor for them. Their avarice was unbounded, and Wills has continued to claim there was nothing wrong with his system because each young woman was taken care of, protected, and given an opportunity they might not have had otherwise."

Harriet had been quiet through Royce's telling, but now she prompted her husband, "Royce, this is supposed to be a celebration. Tell Sari the best part."

Royce gave his wife an unfettered grin then looked across the table at Sari. "The district judge in this case has ruled that any and all holdings that Lauralee Milton, Chetley and Lilith Wills, and Henry Bagley enjoyed as a result of their long-term and fraudulent enterprises will be compiled and liquidated. Apparently this is a large and wealthy accumulation that includes all bank accounts, all land and business ventures they owned as a result of their thievery—even the house Milton owned and ran as an orphanage." He paused for a moment then continued triumphantly. "When all holdings are dealt with, the judge has ruled that the money will be divided equitably between the four women who were their victims."

There was a moment of silence as the friends took in what Royce had said. Finally, it was Michael who spoke, "You mean, that Aunt Sari is going to be rich?"

The diners processed Royce's news with excited and loud conversation. Laughter and congratulations abounded. Sari smiled and listened but didn't join in. She had trouble grasping that such a happy ending might include her.

Claire stood after a time and announced, "I've got birthday cake to help us celebrate this good news and our dear Sari's birthday. Harriet, will you help me serve?"

Harriet nodded and joined Claire in the kitchen.

Daniel stood as well. "I have a bottle of wine downstairs. I think we need a toast." As he left the now quieter room, Sari asked Royce, "Are you sure the others are being cared for? What about the girl who was still at Miss Milton's?"

"Yes, I have made inquiries. All the orphaned girls who were living at Miss Milton's have been placed with families or in other group homes. The one who was a direct victim of Bagley and Wills, I think her name is Kathryn, has been taken in by the pastor and his wife in Baggs. They had asked to adopt her when her parents died, but Bagley thwarted it. She arrived back in Wyoming just a few weeks ago. Of the older two, one is married and living in Medicine Bow. The other is attending the Normal School in Greeley studying to become a teacher. I can get their addresses for you in case you'd like to contact them."

"I think I'd like that very much," Sari answered.

"They all owe you a debt of gratitude for your courage and persistence in finding the truth, Sari, I hope you realize that."

Soon, after they'd sung "For She's a Jolly Good Fellow" to Sari, cake was served, and glasses distributed, Daniel stood. He looked around the room, making eye contact one by one with those seated around it. "Claire, Darling, thank you for such a fine meal and for being the mortar that holds my life together. Greg and Michael, I am a better man because you are my sons, and I'm proud of you and who you are becoming. Royce and Harriet and of course baby Mathias, thank you for your friendship and your concern and help. You have been an ever present help in trouble and in joy. Bea, you've been a sweet friend to our Sari and a good school chum for Mike. We are glad you moved to town to join our circle."

Daniel turned to look at his brother-in-law. "Jesse, you are the man I always try to be. Thank you for coming home from war mostly in one piece, and thank you for bringing Sari into our lives. Esther," Daniel lowered his voice when he realized the baby was sleeping comfortably as she sat on Jesse's lap, "Esther, we promise we will all do our best to raise you and love you, I can't wait to see who you are going to grow up to be." He raised his glass a little higher as he continued. "And Sari, happy birthday. We are so blessed and thankful that in His wisdom and through such hardship and trouble, God gifted us with you."

Claire dabbed a tear on her cheek then echoed the others as they clinked glasses and called "To Sari."

Photos, People, Interesting Additions,
Notes and Acknowledgements

W.T. and Alice Peryam

Photos courtesy of Andy Peryam

donna coulson

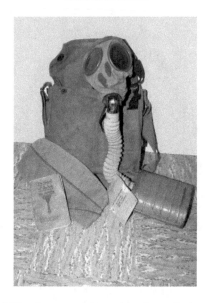

World War I gas mask and ruck sack, hat, and
The Gospel of John for Soldiers.

Photo by donna coulson, artifacts belonged to Ben Smith, Karl
Coulson's grandfather

Tie Hack near Hog Park, early 1900s

Photo courtesy of the Grand Encampment Museum from the
Lora Webb Nichols collection

First Bohn Hotel in the background. Ella Parkison driving friends in a buggy.

courtesy of the Grand Encampment Museum from the Lora Webb Nichols collection

Headstone of Denver Suttles, one of Encampment's Spanish flu casualties.

Photo by donna coulson

Winter on Main Street of Dillon, Wyoming.

Cabin in Dillon, Wyoming. Possibly belonging to George and
Julia Ferris.

Both photos courtesy of the Grand Encampment Museum from
the Lora Webb Nichols collection

Freeman Avenue looking at the New Bohn Hotel, 1908. The town was celebrating the day the S&E Rail Road made its inaugural run into Encampment. Note the ore buckets suspended above the street.

Good Shepherd Hospital, Encampment.

Both photos courtesy of the Grand Encampment Museum from the Lora Webb Nichols collection

Changing Skies Characters

One of the fun things about writing historical fiction is the ability to meld real events and people within my imaginary story. It's also dangerous. Before I put words in the mouths of real people and in order to be faithful, accurate, and fair to those historical lives, I look at pictures, listen to those who knew them, and read biographies, newspapers, letters and other historical documents to try to get a sense of who those people really were. While I invent their conversations, I make an attempt to represent them well. You'll find inside my imaginary story great anecdotes about people, included to help us know them better. For example, Alice Peryam really was offered ten thousand dollars for her son Ben, Lena Fulkerson often dried her long hair over her clothes line, and Ella Parkison was famous for her jelly roll.

Here is a list of the real, historical people you've met in *Changing Skies* (in order of their appearance):

Tom Fisher	Carpenter and cabinet maker
George Willis Emerson	Businessman and author, reputed founder of Encampment and investor in the Rudefeha mine.
Barney McCaffrey	Partner with George Emerson
Ed and Ella Parkison, Hoyt and Mildred	Owner of the first mercantile in Encampment Hoyt and Mildred are their children
W.T and Alice Peryam	Local rancher and his wife. WT served in the Wyoming legislature from 1907 to 1915
John, Tom, Crever, and Ben Peryam	Sons of local ranchers W.T. and Alice Peryam
Joe Peryam	Nephew of WT. He was a member of Buffalo Bill's Wild West Show
Colonel Parks	Commander, Fort D.A. Russel in Cheyenne
Bert and Lora Oldham	Local ranchers. Lora was a renowned photographer.
Mary Bohn	Owner and operator of the Bohn Hotel

Bill Condict	Rancher
Jim Rankin	Businessman, livery owner, sometimes mayor and councilman of Encampment
South Paw Cunningham	Stage coach driver
Mr. Sterrett	Foreman at the Big Creek Ranch
B.L.Miner	Attorney
Ed Smizer	Store owner
Jack and Lena Fulkerson	Jack, also called, G-String Jack, was a well-known horseman and freighter.
Newton Baker	Secretary of War from 1916 to 1921 His remarks by radio at the draft lottery are verbatim.
Enoch Crowder	Provost Marshal General and Judge Advocate General of the United States Army from 1911 to 1923.
George Earle Chamberlain	US senator from Oregon, served from 1909 to 1921
George Helugs	Encampment city Marshall
Ed Haggarty	Prospector who found copper in the Sierra Madre mountains and began the Rudefeha mine.
A.J Rosander	Proprietor of the Royal Bodega Saloon and also owner of a brick kiln and brick making operation
Wilbur Toothaker	Encampment area resident from the Beaver Creek Ranch who fought in WW1
George Ferris	Civil War veteran, delegate to the Wyoming Constitutional Convention, state legislator, and partner in the Rudefeha mine
Julia Ferris	George Ferris' wife
Mrs. Anderson	Cook at the Big Creek Tie Camp
Pastor Emmett Abraham	Pastor in Encampment
Denver Suttles	Clerk at Parkison's mercantile
C.H. Sanger	President, Encampment State Bank
F. H. Healey	Cashier, Encampment State Bank
Mr. Armitage	Teacher at the school in Encampment
Ellen Sproat	President of the Encampment Ladies Aid Society
Mrs. Rankin	Vice president of the Ladies Aid Society, wife of the mayo

Captain John Hedley Captain Jimmy Makepeace	British aviators. The story of Hedley falling out of the plane and Makepeace catching him is true.
Mrs. Young	Director of Cottage House, a home for 'betrayed, misled or unfortunate' women in Denver
Lieutenant General Sir Charles Kavanagh	Officer the British Cavalry Corps
Commander Henry Rawlinson	General who commanded the Fourth Army of the British Expeditionary Force at the battles of the Somme (1916) and Amiens
Dr. Perdue	A well liked doctor in Encampment who opened and operated the Good Shepherd hospital. In 1905, he was shot and killed by his wife.
Dorothy Peryam	Midwife and daughter of W.T and Alice
Douglas Preston	Wyoming Attorney General from 1012 to 1919. Also served at the Wyoming Constitutional Convention, in the State Senate, and House of Representatives
Charles Anderson	Encampment resident and casualty in World War I
Doctor Harry Irwin	Doctor in Encampment. * We can document that Dr. Irwin was practicing in Encampment, and had an office in the E & H Building in 1905, but there is a lack of documentation about doctors after that. I've taken the liberty of extending Dr. Irwin's tenure in Encampment.
Edith Dunbar, Professor Sutton, his wife and baby daughter, plus Edward Stambaugh and William Parr	The telephone operator, the principal of Encampment School, one of the first residents in the area – all residents of Encampment who died in the Spanish flu epidemic

The Grand Encampment

When copper was discovered in the Sierra Madres Mountains by Ed Haggarty on July 25, 1897, the Boom began with a bang. George Willis Emerson and a group of associates believed that The Grand Encampment would become a large and prosperous town as a result of the area's mining. In late summer of 1897, Emerson hired surveyor Tom Sun survey and stake out the town. Each block was numbered. Streets running (somewhat) north/south were avenues named for Emerson's associates. Cross streets ran basically east/west and were numbered. The exception was that the intended main street of the town, the street on which City Hall was to be built and which lay between 5th and 6th Streets, was named Emerson Boulevard.

Immediately the town began growing. Businesses opened and homes were built. Though many of those buildings survive today, many more were lost to several devastating fires. Businesses moved and changed owners. To my knowledge, no map exists for Encampment specifically showing the town in the 1917 to 1919 era. Using interviews, newspapers, photographs by Lora Nichols, fire insurance maps, and the wonderful archives at the Grand Encampment Museum, I have pieced together the layout of the town and the setting of *Changing Skies*. One disclaimer must be made however: local residents of Encampment, both historically and in the present, pay absolutely no attention to the names of the streets in their dear home. For the book, I have described the characters movements using street names, but in reality, the people who lived there and then would not have done so.

On the following pages is a list of the names and locations for many of the buildings and businesses that existed in Encampment in 1917-1919. I've arranged them by Block.

Building	Location
Good Shepherd Hospital with16 bedrooms on two floors	Just off Emerson on the far east end of Encampment
Frank Lordier Druggist	? had at least two locations
Saratoga and Encampment RR Depot	North east of Encampment near present day rodeo grounds
White Dog Saloon, Building later was IOOF Hall	?
Creamery	Corner of 3rd and Barnett Block 2
Rosander House, home of A.J. Rosander, built in 1900	515 Freeman Block 5
Croat Home	Freeman next to Rosander Home Block 5
Garage	Freeman Ave between 6th and Emerson across the street from Bohn Hotel Block 6
Baker's Café, owed by George and Grace Baker	Freeman Ave between 6th and Emerson next to the Garage Block 6
Plummer Store	Freeman Ave between 6th and Emerson next to Baker Cafe Block 6
Economy Drug	Freeman Ave between 6th and Emerson Next to Plummer Store Block 6
Second Parkison Store, built in 1910	6TH across from the E and H Building Block 6
Harness Shop	next to the Electric Company on McCaffrey Block 11
Emerson Encampment Electric Company	Corner of Emerson and McCaffrey Block 11
New Bohn Hotel, built in 1900. A laundry was behind the hotel.	Freeman between 6th and Emerson Block 11
Davis and Ashley	next door to the New Bohn on Freeman Block 11
Hardware Store	corner of Freeman and Emerson next door to Davis and Ashley Block 11

J.H. Schmidt Harness Shop	McCaffrey between Emerson and 5th next to Englehart's Block 12
Engleharts Hardware and Mortuary	McCaffrey between Emerson and 5th Block 12
Chidester home and land	McCaffrey between 4th and 5th Block 13
Bakery	McCaffrey between 3rd and 4th Block 14
First Bohn Hotel, then became Encampment Mercantile built in 1899	McCaffrey between 3rd and 4th Block 19
Carver House, owned by Zacharia and Ada Stambaugh, built in 1900.	314 Lomax Block 19
Tin Plate Café built in 1898. Became the first Bohn Hotel in 1898. One of oldest buildings in town.	315 McCaffrey Block 19
Kinsella Hotel, a two story building with balcony all across the front.	Emerson between McCaffrey and Lomax Block 22
4C's Grocery	Emerson between McCaffrey and Lomax just east of the Kinsella Hotel Block 22
Butcher Shop next to 4C	Emerson between McCaffrey and Lomax next door to 4C's Block 22
The Wyoming built in 1906	McCaffrey between 6th and Emerson Block 22
Palace Bakery and Ice Cream built in 1906	McCaffrey between 6th and Emerson next to The Wyoming Block 22
Parkison's General Merchandise first store location, built in 1900, burned down in 1912.	McCaffrey between 6th and Emerson next to Palace Bakery Block 22
Royal Bodega Saloon owned by Mr. A.J. Rosander	Winchell between Emerson and 5th Block 24
Plummer Saloon	Winchell between 6th and Emerson Block 25
Town Hall. Built as the firehouse and town hall in 1902. Opera House was added in 1903.	622 Rankin Block 26

Willis House. Intended to be a brothel owned by Lydia Propps Willis. It was unfinished until 1931.	621 Winchell Block 26
Englehart Lumber yard and mill	corner of 6th and Heizer Block 27
Spencer Home	corner of Lomax and Emerson Block 27
School	corner of 5th and Lomax Block 29
Bashore Home	corner of 4th and Lomax
Garrotte Home	Corner of 3rd and Lomax. The rest of Block 30 was a pasture.
Fisher House, built in 1904	1004 Rankin Block 53
Rankin's Livery	Corner of 6th and Rankin across the street from the Town Hall Block 53
Clemens House, built in 1903	Winchell and Seventh Block 53
Kuntzman's Insurance and real estate business built in 1900. The stage stop was between Kuntsman's and the Post Office before the PO moved to the E and H building 1907-1913 There was also a Café in that building.	On Freeman south of the E & H building Block 54
E & H Building: North American Bank Post Office Ed Smizer's store Frank Sherrod's Barber Shop Billiard parlor	corner of Freeman and 6th street Block 54
Blacksmith	between 7th and 6th on Rankin Block 54
Hardware store, then became Kil's Garage	across the alley west of the E and H building on 6th Block 54
Parkison House. Built for Ed and Ella Parkison. by Henry Ball, who also built the Virginian in Medicine Bow	111 East Sixth Block 56
Nelson Home	corner of 6th and Lomax Block 57
Lambert House	Heizer between 6th and 7th Block 57

Ed Anderson Home	Heizer between 7th and 8th Block 57
Ruby Home	corner of 7th and Lomax (north) Block 57
Herring Home	7th Street between Hsizer and Barnett Block 58
Eberhardt House owned by George and Josephine Eberhardt in 1902. George was a business partner with Ed Parkison and also mayor and City Councilman in Encampment.	818 Winchell Block 88
Kyner Houses, built in 1901	801, 802 and 804 Winchell Block 88
Henry House. Built in 1901.	803 Winchell Block 88
Kalling Home	8th Street between Macfarlane and Winchell Block 88
George and Grace Baker home	Rankin between 7th and 8th
Provost House built in 1902	414 W Eighth Block 90
Masonic Hall. Originally this building housed the *Grand Encampment Herald*, built in 1897. It became the Masonic Hall in 1913. Upstairs was the telephone office.	820 Freeman Block 90
Kuntzman House, owned by George and Nan Kuntzman, first home to have an indoor bathroom, built in 1901	816 Freeman Block 90
Hull House built in 1902.	822 McCaffrey Block 91
Presbyterian Church	McCaffrey between 8th and 9th Block 91
Austin Home	corner of 7th and Lomax (south)Block 93
Wilcox House, owned by J.F. and Emma (Baggot) Wilcox owned this home built in 1902. There was a large barn on this block as well.	807 Lomax Block 93
Homes on this block: Hammer, Benson, Clements, Bingham, Dettiger	Heizer between 7th and 8th
Dunbar Home	8th Street between Lomax and Heizer
Wombaker Rooming House	McCaffrey between 8th and 9th Block 102

Old Wyoming Rooming House	McCaffrey between 8th and 9th next to Wombaker's Block 102
Tillou Houses, built in 1903.	922 and 924 McCaffrey Block 103
Fulkerson House owned by G-String Jack and Lena Fulkerson.	McCaffrey between 8th and 9th Block 103
Department of Agriculture Forest Service office built in 1912	Ninth between Winchell and Freeman Block 104
Couzens Store Groceries and Hardware	Ninth between Winchell and Freeman Block 104
Drury House.	906 Rankin Block 105
Fowler M.E. Church	Rankin between 8th and 9th Block 105

Acknowledgements and Bibliography

Many hands have added their support and help in the writing and publishing of *Changing Skies*. I'd like to convey my most sincere thanks to:

Mary Jane Parkison Cozzens who has been such a wealth of information about her grandparents and her own life in Encampment. I treasure her encouragement and support.

Andy and Susan Peryam for generously sharing information and pictures about W.T. and Alice Peryam and their family.

Tim Nicklas, Director of the Grand Encampment Museum, for his patient help with research at the museum and quick responses to email questions.

Nancy Anderson for the afternoon I spent with her talking about Encampment and Lora Webb Nichols and for giving me access to those great photos.

Dauna Wessel for taking me on a tour of the Fowler Church and around town.

Judy Stepp for her friendship and for help with mapping Encampment.

Dr. Jarrett Knight for being my willing and highly able editor.

David Steege for his kind and insightful final editing of this manuscript.

Shauna at Huckleberry Hearts, LLC, for the great text-break graphic design. Used with permission ©
www.Huckleberry-Hearts.com

and to Karl Coulson for my life of love and adventures, and for his unfailing love and support.

As I have with the other two novels in this series, when general historical questions arise – like abortion in 1918, the history of the baby shower, or when the candy corn was invented, I use Wikipedia and similar online searches. For other, more in-depth or more local information, I rely of a variety of sources. Local newspapers not only tell the news, but provide insights into fashions and trends, medical practices and medicine, local businesses, and society. The newspapers I read and gleaned information from for *Changing Skies* include: *The Encampment Record*, *The Encampment Echo*, *Platte Valley Lyre*, *Battle Miner*, *Saratoga Sun*, *The Encampment Valley Roundup*, and *The Grand Encampment Herald*. Another wealth of information is the archives of unpublished documents at the Grand Encampment Museum including diaries, letters, and photographs.

More specific sources I used include:

Mayor and council members: Encampment Town Council Minutes 1901 – 1919

Wilbur C. Toothaker WWI diary, GEM archives.

Handcuffs used in the 1910s: Q13 Fox News online. "Flashback: History of criminal restraints including 'Thumb Cuffs' invented by Seattle police officer" https://q13fox.com/2015/03/27/flashback-history-of-criminal-restraints-including-thumb-cuffs-invented-by-seattle-police-officer/

Orphanages in Wyoming: Wyoming State Archives

Colorado Cottage Home: *Life in Colorado before WW1* "The Colorado Cottage Home" by Sherilyn Brandenstein, pages 329-236 https://www.historycolorado.org/sites/default/files/media/document/2018/ColoradoMagazine_v53n3_Summer1976.pdf

Syphilis: *Journal of Military and Veterans' Health.* "Syphilis – Its early history and Treatment until Penicillin and the Debate on its Origins". https://jmvh.org/article/syphilis-its-early-history-and-treatment-until-penicillin-and-the-debate-on-its-origins/

Trench cake recipe: I Love Old Recipes.com. http://iloveoldrecipes.com/recipe/world-war-i-cake/

Make up: Glamour Daze:A vintage Fashion and Beauty Archive. "1900's makeup: 1900-1919. https://galmourdaze.com/history-of-makeup/1900-1919

*Regarding the Spanish flu epidemic:
Saratoga Sun Jan 2, 1919 and *Saratoga Sun* January 23, 1919

Wyoming State Tribune, November 14, 1918 for information about the Spanish flu epidemic in Cheyenne.

History. com "Spanish Flu"
https://www.history.com/topics/1918-flu-pandemic

Centers for Disease Control and Prevention. "1918 Pandemic". https://www.cdc.gov/features/1918-flu-pandemic/index.html "The pandemic was so severe that from 1917 to 1918, life expectancy in the United States fell by about 12 years, to 36.6 years for men and 42.2 years for women."

Smithsonian Magazine online. "How the Horrific 1918 Flu Spread Across America".
https://www.smithsonianmag.com/history/journal-plague-year-180965222/

*horse remedies:
Keystone Equine online Blog, "Old-time Equine Remedies"
https://keystoneequine.net/old-time-equine-remedies/

The Chronicle of the Horse
https://www.chronofhorse.com/forum/forum/discussion-forums/horse-care/113971-looking-for-old-horsemen-s-remedies-treatments

*World War I:
The draft: National Archives.
https://www.archives.gov/research/military/ww1/draft-registration

Draft Lottery: Gjenvick-Gjønvik Archives. "The World War One Draft - Reporting of the First Draft Lottery – 1917"
https://www.gjenvick.com/Military/WorldWarOne/TheDraft/SelectiveServiceSystem/1917-07-20-Draft-DrawingTheFirstNumber.html

Soldier life insurance: US. Department of Veterans Affairs. "United States Government Life Insurance" https://www.benefits.va.gov/INSURANCE/usgli.asp

Battle of Amiens: History.com. https://www.history.com/topics/world-war-i/amiens-battle-of

Battle of Amiens: Warfare History Network. "Battle of Amiens". https://warfarehistorynetwork.com/daily/miltary-history/battle-of-amiens.

Mihiel Offensive: World War I .com. "The Story of the American Expeditionary Forces Doughboy Center: The St., Mihiel Offensive" http://www.worldwar1.com/dbc/stmihiel.htm

The end of war in Encampment: "Looking Back My True Memories from 1908-1996 as told by "Real Cowboy" John Rodney Barney" GEM archives

Life Magazine, Oct 4, 1917, jolly cook on cover flipping pancakes.

Troop transport ship Nasemond: "Moving the U.S. Troops Home After WWI". http://swansongrp.com/troopships_returning.html

donna coulson is a novelist and blogger who loves God, her ever-patient husband Karl, snorkeling, Wyoming's mountains, and telling stories. For more, find her at www.donnacoulson.com, or on Facebook.

Other books by donna coulson:

Mountain Time

Peaks and Valleys

The Archer's Perspective